FRIENDS INDEED

FRIENDS INDEED

Rose Doyle

Hodder & Stoughton

First published in 2001
by Hodder & Stoughton
A division of Hodder Headline

British Library Cataloguing in Publication Data
A CIP catalogue record for this title
is available from the British Library

Hardback ISBN 0 340 77132 1
Trade paperback ISBN 0 340 77133 X

Typeset by Hewer Text Ltd, Edinburgh
Printed and bound in Great Britain by
Clays Ltd, St Ives Plc

Hodder & Stoughton
A division of Hodder Headline
338 Euston Road
London NW1 3BH

For my friends.

ACKNOWLEDGEMENTS

I first heard about the Wrens of the Curragh when Kevin Myers wrote about them in *An Irishman's Diary* in *The Irish Times* of 24th July, 1996. Like countless women in history, they had been overlooked, and forgotten. I've incorporated many of their stories, along with factual detail, into *Friends Indeed* and hope this will, in their case, go some way towards putting things to rights.

Starting was easy. Getting an agent like Darley Anderson made finishing it easy too. Thanks, Darley, for the kick start. Then there was the masterly job of editing by Sue Fletcher, who ironed it out, gave it a name and sent it into the world all polished up. Thank you, Sue.

None of it could have been written without the generous and good humoured help of a lot of people. My thanks to Kevin Myers, unwittingly inspirational but that's life, and a very special thanks to John Bannigan who, learned beyond words, shored up my ignorance about things medical. Dr Maria Luddy, Director of the Women's History Project and an historian who knows all about the Wrens, gave unstintingly of her time and knowledge. Comdt. Victor Laing of the Military Archives in Cathal Brugha Barracks pointed me in the right direction and Comdt. Rory Hynes, Librarian at the Defence Forces Training Centre on The Curragh, helped bring the conditions under which the Wrens lived to life. My thanks too to Col. Des Travers and to the Kildare Historical Society. I'm indebted to Mairead Dunlevy of the National Museum at Collins Barracks for the tour of the costumes, to Ian Lumley for the tour of his Henrietta Street home and to Liam McNulty for the tour of Na Piobairi Uilleann's premises on Henrietta Street. Dr Con Costello's history of the Curragh camp, *A Most Delightful Station*, was indispensable. So were the writings of James Greenaway, journalist with the Pall Mall Gazette who, in 1867, wrote in riveting detail of his time spent with the Wrens – as did an outraged Charles Dickens the same year. For books and incidental detail, thanks to Brendan O Ciobhain, Bernadette Madden, Lorraine Dunne, Bernie Doolin, Eamonn Russell, Kate Bateman, Brendan Keenan and the ever obliging staff of the Gilbert Library in Pearse Street. And, for the ending, great thanks to Elgy Gillespie, in San Francisco.

Part One

CHAPTER ONE

Allie

August, 1867. Dublin

The smells were the first thing. The heavy, fetid stench of animal sweat and fear and excrement, the evil smelling miasma from the river Liffey.

The stink that was Dublin.

They were what made me feel, at last, that I was home.

'Close up that window,' my father said.

His eyes, bloodshot and weary and watchful, were open again. He'd been asleep since leaving the North Wall, tired as I was after the journey from Paris.

'There's a herd of cattle ahead of us,' he said, 'you'd no business unlatching it.'

'I need air. The carriage is stifling,' I said.

'You don't need what passes for air in this part of the town.'

His short, hairy fingers were clamped to his knees as he leaned forward. He smelled in need of a wash and of the wine he'd been drinking.

My poor father was not made for travelling; he'd slept on the train journeys between Paris and London and been ill without stop on the boat crossings.

'Close it up like I tell you, there's my good girl.'

But though the air through the window reeked it was at least air. I'd taken a discreet sniff and balanced the closeness of my father's stale odours against the reek from the cattle ahead and decided that as long as we kept moving, and had the window open, I could put up with both.

'I'd rather we kept it unlatched, Dada,' I said and he straightened in his seat. I knew what he would say next.

'I spent a lot of money on you in that Paris convent. I hope, Alicia, that it wasn't wasted. I don't see any great improvement in your manners.'

He studied the hands on his trouser-clad knees. He wore breeches usually; the suit of dark green trousers and coat had been meant to impress the nuns though he could have saved himself the discomfort. The Emperor Napoleon III in all his medals would not have impressed the sisters who'd taught me deportment and the French language.

'The waste of money was in bringing me home,' I leaned over and touched one of his hands, 'though I'm glad to be with you, Dada. You know that.'

His hand, holding mine briefly, was hot. 'I know that, girl.' He paused. 'Your mother will be pleased to have you home,'

'No, she won't.'

I looked away from the longing in his bloodshot eyes, gazed instead at the seabirds circling and cawing like drunken street traders above the Custom House. I wished I was one of them, high over the city and on the wing elsewhere. Back to Paris maybe, where the waters of the river Seine were limpid and flowing and never muddy like those of the Liffey. I hadn't expected, when I'd been sent to Paris to become a lady. that I would feel so free and love to travel so much. *C'est la vie.*

And now I was home and I couldn't say, as my father wanted me to, that I would be glad to see my mother. I'd never been dishonest and two years in France hadn't changed me that much.

My poor, poor father. He expected such a great deal from me, and from the fine education he'd paid dearly for.

A bellowing and the roars of the drovers made the herd of cattle seem very near. The weather, even at that early hour, was warmer than I ever remembered in August. According to my father it had been a summer of uncommonly hot, festering days and the city had the look of it. The streets were straw-filled and dirty and the people so dusty it appeared as if an ashy brown was the fashion colour of the summer.

Carlisle Bridge, when we got to it, was thick with a bustling dawn traffic of working women on their way to service, with horse-drawn omnibuses, hay carts, delivery lads on bikes and barking dogs. I don't care for animals and there were a ferocious number of them in Dublin that morning.

We'd slowed to a near halt when, ignoring my father's protests, I leaned my head out of the window. 'Westmoreland Street is packed tight with the cattle herd,' I said, 'we'll be the rest of the day getting through them.'

'We will not, by God.' My father's anger was sudden, aroused as much by my behaviour as by the animals' delaying us. 'I'm paying that slouch of a driver good money to get us home before eight o'clock.'

His colour had risen and he thumped so hard on the carriage ceiling I thought the cane would go right through it. It didn't, but the carriage didn't move either. Muttering an oath he took my place at the window. 'Keep going, you scoundrel,' he roared, 'I want to get to Haddington Road before nightfall.'

The carriage jolted forward and he sat back, his face a mottled purple. He'd always had a temper but this new shortness worried me. I put it down to the amounts of wine he'd drunk in Paris and on the boat.

Ahead of us the drovers bellowed and the cattle thundered into the opening between the Parliament buildings and Trinity College. They were headed for the marts and would be in front of us for a bit yet. The carriage bounded after them.

'Your mother'll be waiting,' my father said and I looked away from him again. My mother would be doing no such thing, and he knew it.

My mother would very likely be in her bed still or, if not, at her morning-long toilette. My father was as full of wishful thinking about my mother's behaviour as he was of an unfortunate adoration of her beauty. And she was indeed beautiful; everyone said so.

She was half mad too, though not many people outside of myself, and my father when he was honest, could see this. Her disenchantment with my father was something else which was obvious to all but him.

When it came to me, Alicia Eleanor Buckley, her only child, she wasn't so much disenchanted as uninterested. She wasn't a woman had taken naturally to motherhood.

'You'll be anxious too to see your new home,' pride mixed with hope in my father's voice.

'Yes,' I said, 'I am.' This was a lie and we both knew it.

I'd been happy enough living over the cattleman's public house my father had owned near the Broadstone. Things could be rough in the pub but our rooms were comfortable and the people around were my friends, and my father's friends. But when the railway station coming to the Broadstone had made the pub a valuable property my father had put in new glass windows, done away with the boarded-up shutters and got in gas lighting. This had made it worth even more money. While I was away my father had sold it and written to me that we, as a family, had 'moved into respectable society'.

He now called himself a man of business and bought property. An old mansion in Henrietta Street, now a tenement, was one such purchase. He'd also bought a house for us to live in in the south suburbs.

We were almost at Trinity College when the carriage stopped.

'By the Lord Jesus Christ I'll have that driver's guts.' My father hauled himself out of his seat and put his head through the window again. 'Didn't I tell you to keep going?' he shouted to the driver. 'Didn't I tell you to make a way through them animals?'

The carriage shook.

'There's a couple of them's bolted,' the carman's voice had a note of panic in it, 'the rest of them's unsettled. It'd be better to wait 'til the drovers have got them under control . . .'

A bullock, careering back the way it had come, glanced off the side of the carriage and was set upon by a drover with a stick.

'Damn you to hell,' my father roared first at the drover and then at the carman, 'I'll be the one decides whether you stop or go. Drive on.' He shook a hairy fist and I worried that he might have a fit in front of my eyes. 'Drive on or by God I'll have your licence taken off you. There's plenty would be glad to take your place up on that seat . . .'

We'll never know what the man would have done because the stampede started then, with a savage drumming which made the ground seem about to burst open under us.

Within minutes College Green was a nightmare of mutilated and dying animals, of chaos and panic and the screaming agony of hurt and frightened people. The tormented squeals and bellows of crazed cattle soon drowned the human cries and the stench of fear surrounded the carriage as thickly as a wall. It was as if hell had been let loose.

My father managed to close the window and, trapped in the carriage, we braced ourselves against the battering by animal flesh, stiffened at the smack of bone against the wooden frame.

The carman had got down from his seat and could be heard, without much success, trying to calm the horse. The windows darkened with spurting blood. It seemed to go on forever.

'We'll be all right. We'll get out of this.'

My father's colour had drained. He was white as any sheet. I'm sure I was white myself. My heart felt as if it would burst from my chest and though I wanted to scream I couldn't make a sound.

It ended as suddenly as it had started. The nightmare silence which fell on the streets was broken only by whimpers and pitiful cries and the retreating hooves of the cattle, their occasional bellows becoming fainter and fainter.

'We didn't travel this far to be beat at the last fence . . .' My father reached to touch me but was thrown against the back of his seat when the carriage horse gave a screaming whinny and reared. 'No need to be afraid,' he said, 'we'll be out of here in no time. No time at all.'

'I'm not afraid.' I held myself tight in my corner and stared through the window. 'The drovers are herding the cattle up Dame Street,' I tried to assure him, and myself, 'the worst is over, I think . . . the worst . . .'

There were terrible sights through that window. I saw people lying about the place in broken, unnatural positions, limbs and bodies askew, blood oozing from many of them and others looking as if they might be dead they were so still. I saw an overturned omnibus, fallen on one of the horses which had been pulling it. The other horse, also dead, appeared to have strangled itself in an attempt to be free of its harness. Some of the injured nearby had clearly been passengers.

Even as I watched the police arrived, about a dozen of them at a hard run, and with them two doctors who went immediately to help the wounded.

'The worst is over,' I said again.

It was what I wanted to believe and was all I could find in myself to say. The cost had still to be reckoned, the dead and dying accounted for, the injured if possible made well. The pain would go on, both of loss and ruined bodies.

The worst was only beginning.

The driver appeared at the window. He was an older man, about my father's age, which was something over fifty, with a bald head and whiskers. He'd lost his hat and the deep folds of his face were awash with perspiration.

'They're saying it was a young heifer started it,' he rubbed his eyes with a shaking hand. 'The story has it that she broke ranks with the herd and went headfirst into the pair of horses pulling the omnibus . . .'

When my father would have cut him short the man caught and held my eye. His own were full of tears.

'That's the thing of it, that's how life is. It can turn on you any minute. There's two young people stretched out there in the street who got up this morning without a thought of death between them.'

'That's enough caterwauling out of you.' My father's hands

shook every bit as much as the carriage driver's. 'Get back on your perch and get us out of here. There's nothing to be done but clear the space for the police and doctors to do their work.'

'Maybe we can be of help,' I said but my father would have none of it.

'Are you mad, girl?' He was shouting again as, wordlessly, the carman left the door and went back up on his seat. 'This is none of our doing or affair. We're best out of here. Your mother is waiting . . .'

I looked at him then, a hard look, and he stopped shouting. He wanted no more truths from me about my mother. Since the truth was that he lived in fear as well as in awe of her he knew as I did that she wouldn't be waiting. I was tired of the pretence.

'Stop the foolishness, Alicia,' he used a more sober tone, 'I don't want you endangering your life. We'll go on home.'

'It's you who have endangered my life, bringing me back to live in this city.' Anger made me irrational. 'I'll rot here, if I'm not killed first.'

'In the name of God be silent! What happened just now was an accident. It could have happened anywhere, even in your glorious Paris. Your taste for drama will be your undoing, I've always said so. I'm doing what's best—'

'What's best for you, Dada. What happened here is a bad omen. I feel it. You gave me freedom and now you've taken it back. I could have stayed and been a teacher of English in Paris . . .'

The carriage jolted and moved forward slowly.

'And ended in the gutter, like many a young woman before you.' My father, now we were on our way again, settled weighty and worried into his seat. 'I sent you to learn manners and because you were too headstrong and this is what my money gets me. You're nineteen years and should be thinking of marriage, like other young women your age.'

I could have told him that what I'd seen of marriage growing up had done nothing to enamour me of the state. I kept silent because I'd seen enough of his efforts to please my mother to know he wasn't to blame for their misery.

Instead I asked a question I half dreaded the answer to. 'Is Sarah Rooney married?'

'Not married, no,' he was irritable, 'but a woman none-theless.' He shifted in his seat, his weight seeming a greater burden to him than usual.

'What do you mean?'

'I mean nothing, nothing at all.' My father plucked at his moustache distractedly.

I let the subject of Sarah Rooney go. I would see her soon enough.

Sooner than I thought.

The carriage inched its way past the gates of Trinity College. I was full of bad humour and irritability, staring through the blood-splattered window, when I noticed her. She was easy to spot, a good head taller than the people penned in with her behind the college gates.

Seeing her changed everything: my mood, the prospects for my life ahead. It didn't matter, in those minutes, that she hadn't replied to my last two letters. Sarah Rooney was the friend of my youth, the sister I'd never had, the one person who would make my life bearable now I was home.

It was Sarah, in our shared childhood, who'd shown me that to really live life you had to be fearless. Sarah, penniless and living in the tenements, had confirmed in me my belief that money and respectability were cloaks to drape over hollow lives. It was thanks to Sarah too that I'd learned never to expect loving arms, or caring, from my mother.

She hadn't known she was teaching me these things. All she'd done was be my friend.

'Sarah's over there, Dada, in the crowd the police have locked behind the gates.' I pointed. 'We can't leave her there. We'll have to stop and take her with us in the carriage.'

'Sarah Rooney's no longer the child you knew,' he was curt, 'she's in service in the Haddington Road house now, along with her mother. She should be there at this hour, earning the money I pay her to keep the place in order.'

'What's wrong with you?' I stared at him. 'You'd leave her there because you pay her a wage? Does that make her a different person?' I peered again through the window. 'Bess is inside the gates too.' I grabbed the carriage cane and stabbed at the ceiling. The horse stopped. 'They're in a terrible crush behind there, Dada, with the police shouting at them. You'll have to get them out of it. The police will listen to you.'

'Things have changed and it's best they make their own way. Allie. They're born to it, people like that.' He stared balefully through the window. Being notoriously short-sighted, it was unlikely he saw either Sarah or her mother. 'Shouting or sweet talk, it's all the same to the likes of the Rooneys. They'll be let out of there soon enough and, by the Lord God, if either of them looks for full money for this day they'll be barking up the wrong tree. A fool and his money are not so easily parted.' He reached for the cane but I held it fast. 'Stop this foolishness, Allie.'

He shrugged. With his great, sloping shoulders it was an oddly helpless gesture. 'Things have changed,' he said again.

'It's you who've changed, Dada.' I kept my eyes on Sarah and her mother. 'Bess Rooney has always worked for us and Sarah is still my friend, even if I haven't seen her for a while. Some things don't change.'

'You'll see soon enough that they do.'

My father was muttering and sighing, close to exhaustion. He wasn't as young as he'd used to be and he needed to sleep off the wine.

'It's like this, Allie.' He put his hand over mine. I didn't turn from the window. 'Bess still does the cooking, it's true, and as a kindness, and for the sake of old times, I've given work to Sarah. But your mother has engaged a housekeeper to take charge of things.' He sighed. 'It's a big house.'

Three servants. That must please my mother. My father, reading my thoughts, said, 'Your mother has a position in society now. You've a position now too.'

I'd had a position before and liked it. It was my mother who'd hated her position as a publican's wife, thought herself better than her neighbours and her husband. I could see how she might find it hard to live with my father's rough and ready manners. But his heart was kinder than many beating behind a more polished exterior. Or had been, when he was a publican.

It was because things were not as before that I'd wanted to stay in Paris. The last thing in the world I desired was to be a French-speaking addition to my mother's dinner parties until a husband was found for me.

The carriage shifted as the standing horse grew restless. On impulse, and in a sudden fury of determination, I pushed open the door, gathered my skirts and jumped down into the street.

'We can't leave Sarah and Bess,' I kept going, 'not with the police bullying them like that.'

I stopped when I heard the gunshots and saw why the police had herded people behind the gates. The dead animals were being gathered into carts. The wounded ones were being executed.

'Now will you get back in here? Their kind are more than able to walk. Are you gone stone mad or what?' My father was out of the carriage, angry and shouting again. Fearful for me too, but I couldn't help that.

'I am no madder, Dada, than I ever was. I won't leave Sarah and Bess while we've got a carriage.'

When he started to come after me I picked up my skirts and ran for the gates. My dress had a Paris bustle so my movements were easier than if I'd been wearing the crinolines still in fashion in Dublin. I called to Sarah and Bess as I went, forcing my voice above the noise of the police and crowd and dying animals.

'Sarah, Sarah Rooney!' I called, 'can you hear me, Sarah? It's Allie. I have a carriage. Shout out my name if you can hear me.'

I'm not much more than five feet tall and when I stood in front of the college gates I couldn't see a thing over the crowd behind. I turned for my father but he'd stopped following me and was back with the carriage. When I faced the gates again a policeman was blocking my way. He was was about my own age, or might even have been younger. His chest buttons were at a level with my eyes.

'Move on out of here, miss, get back to your carriage. Better for you to be on your way.'

'I'm here to relieve you of two of your charges.' I was shyly anxious, looking up at him with wide eyes. My French deportment lessons had taken many forms. 'I'd be much obliged if you would call to a Miss Sarah Rooney and her mother for me.' I laid a hand delicately on the low square of my dress bodice, as if the task I'd set myself was suddenly too much. 'There's a place for them in our carriage.' I kept my eyes on his and smiled, tremulous and stricken. 'This is a terrible thing to have happened . . .' I lowered my eyes and caught a tearful breath and fiddled with a lock of my hair.

'Tell me the names again,' he said, 'I'll get them out of there for you.'

He had a countryman's accent and a countryman's way of doing things. Within minutes Sarah and Bess Rooney were on my side of the gate.

'The Dublin Metropolitan Police is always glad to be of service.' Their rescuer smiled pinkly, full of a boyish need for praise.

'You do the force credit and I'm grateful to you.'

I gave him my hand and another, happier, smile. I'm nothing if not kind and I was grateful to him. He touched my fingers, gently, and bowed and went away.

Sarah and I looked at one another awkwardly. She was the one who spoke first.

'You always did have a way of getting what you want,' she said as she looked me up and down, 'only now you've got manners as well. You look very well,' she put her head to one side, 'like a doll.'

In my rose-pink silk dress with its darker velvet stripe I was overdressed for the occasion, it's true. But I couldn't help my height.

'Is that all you have to say to me?' I said. 'I may not have grown as tall as you have but I'm—'

'Thank God for that,' she laughed, and was suddenly the Sarah I knew, 'they'd have had to put me into the circus if I'd grown any more.'

We hugged each other then, tightly and for a long time before separating to laugh and look at one another and hug again. Sarah was wearing a bleached-out blue cotton dress.

'You didn't answer my last two letters,' I said.

'No,' she said, 'I didn't.' I waited but she didn't explain why.

Bess, who'd wisely remained silent through the ceremony of our greeting, spoke at last. 'Dear God Allie what a terrible situation for us to be meeting in you're a good girl to stop and pick us up like this . . .'

She spoke fast, without pauses and in a rasping voice that was the result of a doctor damaging a nerve in her neck when she was a girl in the Liberties. Forever afraid her voice would go before she got the words out, she stopped only when she needed to take a breath.

'We're lucky we weren't all killed and we might have been only that it wasn't our time to go and the good Lord spared us.' She took a breath then and held out her arms, bony like the rest of her and nearly as long as her daughter's. 'You're not too grown and changed to come to Bess I hope.'

I went to her for a hug as warm as Sarah's had been; I'd spent more time in Bess's angular arms as a child than I'd ever spent in my mother's. Or my father's, though he did his best in other ways.

'We'd better go,' Bess stood back, 'your father's waiting for us with a face like a fighting dog on him he'll be ravenous and wanting his breakfast.'

My father growled as we climbed into the carriage.

'That was a terrible thing to happen Leonard those animals bolting like that,' Bess said as we moved off.

'It was, Mrs Rooney, it was.'

My father's frown said he did not want her calling him Leonard but Bess, if she noticed, paid no heed.

'It's the omnibuses Leonard dangerous things I always said did you hear about the catastrophe at the Portobello Bridge?'

My father gave a discouraging grunt but Bess got on with her tale anyway. She seemed older to me, worn-looking but still gentle. Her dress was a dull brown with a black stripe.

'There were eight passengers on the omnibus when it happened and the driver stopped on the incline on the Rathmines side of the bridge to let a man and his son get off . . .' she took a breath, 'Holy Mother of God but what happened then was terrible one of the horses backed and dragged the other with him and without warning the omnibus horses passengers and driver all went into the lock chamber and ten feet of water . . .' she stopped. 'To make matters worse the lock-keeper opened the sluices of the upper instead of the lower gates.'

She gave a mighty sigh; she'd always had a fine sense of timing.

'The six dead bodies had to be got out through the roof . . .'

'That's enough about disasters,' my father said. 'I want a bit of peace and silence for the rest of the journey.'

'And you deserve it,' Bess was placatory, 'after your journey but I'll nevertheless remind you all that it's always been my contention that animals and machinery don't go together and I'm being proved right.'

'What other news of Dublin then?' I asked Sarah.

'Dublin is as you see it.' Sarah observed the passing street. 'People manage their lives as best they can. As they always did.'

'Is that all you have to tell me?' I was impatient. 'The same could be said of any city. No wonder you didn't write if that's all you have to say. Tell me what there is that's new.'

'The smallpox was big in the town last year, This year it's the cholera the people are worried about—'

'Cholera is known to the people of Paris too,' I cut her short. It was as if she didn't want to talk openly to me. If she was inhibited by my father then I was having none of it. 'So are smallpox and diphtheria and typhoid.'

'You're such an expert on the cities of the world I wonder

you don't know more of your own.' Sarah shrugged. 'I'm sure you'll find out soon enough that living in the city is no longer fashionable in Dublin. Those that can are moving out beyond the canals. You'll be safe enough from disease in Haddington Road.' She turned to my father. 'I'm surprised, Mr Buckley, that you haven't assured Allie how safe she'll be from the gases and vapours given out by animal filth in the city centre.'

'She said nothing about being worried.' My father was stiff.

'That's because I'm not.' I spoke hurriedly. 'Tell me, Sarah, how things are in Henrietta Street.' The old mansion my father had bought was the same tenement building in which the Rooneys had lived for years.

'You'll have to visit and see for yourself,' said Sarah. My father said nothing.

'Your new home is very grand, Allie.' Bess looked sideways at my father. 'Things will be different for you now.'

'So my father keeps telling me.' I was short. 'He says too that my mother has engaged a housekeeper. What sort of woman is she?'

'Low-sized your mother took her on just a week ago.'

That was as much as I could get out of her about the housekeeper.

There was very little said about anything else either for the rest of the journey, and nothing at all by my father. But I was glad to be with Sarah again, and with Bess, and put his bad temper down to exhaustion after our journey.

I should have paid more attention. I might then have been more alert, better prepared for what was to come.

I might have been, but it's unlikely; I was never what you could call farsighted.

CHAPTER TWO

Allie

There was a barrier to be got round before I saw my mother. It came in the shape of a woman called Mary Connor and I'd never in my life come across so small an adult. She could have been one of the oldest too except that Mary Connor's age, as with everything else about her, was shrouded in mystery. With her humped back she was the closest thing imaginable to a witch: Not a benign one either.

She was the housekeeper my father had spoken about and she opened the door when we arrived, her withered face full of reproach.

'Mrs Buckley was worried. You were expected a good hour ago.' She spoke only to my father. Her voice was high and thin, like a child's.

'An animal stampede delayed us.' My father, when she didn't step aside, squeezed hurriedly past her and into the hallway. 'Is Mrs Buckley inside?'

'She is.'

Still the woman didn't move, not even to blink a pair of eyes so pale they were almost colourless.

I stayed where I was on the doorstep, waiting for her to let me come in. A full half-minute passed while we eyed one another, neither of us prepared to move.

I thought then that the immediate animosity I felt was what decided the future of our relationship, but I was wrong. Mary

Connor had a hostility towards the world in general and towards me, as my mother's daughter, in particular.

She had a high, bony forehead and her mouth was a narrow opening in a web of puckered skin. Her tiny body was neatly dressed in darkest grey and she appeared to have no hair at all under the tight, white-frilled black skullcap covering her head.

My father brought the impasse to an end. 'Come inside. Allie, don't be shy of your new home.' His joviality boomed through the house with false *bonhomie*. 'Don't be shy with Mary either. Your mother's very pleased with the housekeeping she does for us.' He beamed his contrived smile on the small woman. 'Tell Mrs Buckley we've arrived, Mary.'

'She knows. She heard the door knocker.' Mary Connor stayed where she was. 'She's waiting in the drawing room.'

'I'd be obliged if you'd go ahead of us anyway.' My father's smile became manic and she moved at last.

Her back was rigid as a marionette's as she went down the hall and, without knocking, through the second door she came to.

I left the safety and light of the granite step for a hallway so cold and heavy with drapes I might have left winter outside.

The house was a fine one, large as my father had said, with an arch at the end of the hallway leading on to an elegant staircase and to steps down to the kitchen and cellar. But the only daylight came from a high, rear window and all of the doors were closed. I felt as if I'd entered a prison. There wasn't even the comfort of having Sarah and Bess Rooney about since they'd gone, with the driver and my trunks, to the back entrance of the house.

'Pay no heed to Mary Connor.' My father rubbed his hands together but couldn't quite manage to keep the smile on his face. 'She's a bit contrary but she suits your mother . . .' He fell silent as the housekeeper reappeared.

'Mrs Buckley's waiting,' she said with the barest movement of her mouth.

'Grand, that's grand.' My father put a hand on my back. 'Go and meet your mother. I'll help that fool of a driver with your trunks.' With a speed I had not known him capable of he disappeared down the steps at the back of the hallway.

My mother barely raised her head from the book on her lap as I came into the room.

Albert, her grey, long-haired cat, looked up just as reluctantly from where he lay against my mother's feet as they rested on a footstool. She was wearing gold-embroidered morning slippers. Albert had got fat.

'Hello, Mother.' I stood in front of her.

Mary Connor remained inside the closed door, very silent and very still, a sort of ghostly slave to my mother.

'You haven't grown a great deal,' my mother observed, extending a hand that was white as the cuff of lace on her yellow silk morning dress, 'but then I didn't expect that you would. You've always inclined to your father's build.'

I took and briefly held her fingers; we were neither of us keen to prolong the contact. My mother studied me then, silently, her black eyes chilling my heart in the way they had been able to do since I was a child. The cat watched us.

'You appear to have spent your father's money on at least one gown which is in good taste,' my mother said. 'I hope the contents of your trunks display a similar discernment. Mary will unpack for you presently. I'll help her myself.'

I said nothing. I didn't want Mary Connor unpacking my clothes. I didn't want her anywhere near my belongings, or anywhere near my person either. My mother, who had a great interest in fashion and jewellery and ornamentation of every kind, was of course entitled to see what I had brought from Paris.

'I hope your new home compares with what you've grown used to in Paris.' My mother made a languid gesture at the room.

I looked around. It was very much to her taste. The deep buttoned settee was upholstered in a ruby velvet which matched the curtains, there were antimacassars on balloon-backed chairs, a six-light crystal gasolier and, over the mantel, an ornate, gilded mirror. All of this, I'd no doubt, reflected the best that Dublin had to offer in furniture and decorating.

'It's very nice, Mother, very elegant.' I hesitated. 'I'd like Sarah to help me unpack.' I went on looking around the room, avoiding my mother's eyes. She sighed, as if my response was no more than she'd expected. In the silence Mary Connor cleared her throat.

'Sarah Rooney is preparing the breakfast with her mother.' My mother's feet uncrossed themselves on the footstool, 'and Mary, in any event, is better suited to arrange your wardrobe.'

The cat, with a malevolent look my way, rubbed himself against her feet as my mother gave a longer sigh.

'I must say, Alicia, that I'd hoped you would have acquired maturity and grace. Your father, of course, doesn't set a good example. It wasn't the socially correct thing to take the Rooneys with you into the carriage.' She fondled the cat's ears, smiling. 'Sadly, one cannot make a silk purse out of a sow's ear.'

She had always known how to diminish me but I was older now, and wiser. Or so I thought. I walked to the mirror and removed the ribboned diadem I'd worn travelling.

'In Paris,' I said, 'coiffures are softened this season with a sprinkling of powder. Women are wearing their hair off their foreheads with curls on the temples.'

My mother's dark hair was unpowdered and dressed in a heavy chignon. Her voice, when next she spoke, had hardened. 'I won't have Sarah Rooney handling your French wardrobe.'

'And I won't have Mary Connor doing it for me.' It was as if I'd never been away; we were disagreeing as we'd always done. 'I don't know Mary Connor. Sarah is my friend and knows how I like things. Sarah and Bess were always—'

'Bess Rooney was a servant who didn't know her place. Sarah was a precocious child.' With a delicate yawn my mother stood next to me at the mirror. 'These things were of no consequence when we lived among them and their kind.' Frowning, she smoothed a strand of hair into the chignon before, carefully and coldly, studying my reflection.

I saw myself as she did and notions of my worth and beauty learned in Paris vanished. My mother was taller and more beautiful than I would ever be; beside hers my reflection was that of a pale girl with a small face. I'd a couple of good points and those I'd got from her anyway: my eyes were large and dark and my hair, freed from the diadem, was a pale, flaxen colour.

'Such a pity . . .' My mother didn't say what the pity was, she didn't need to. Everything about me was a pity as far as she was concerned. 'I want you to listen carefully to what I have to say, Alicia.'

She walked to the window and stood looking at the barren and untended rear garden. She had no interest in the outdoors or in growing things.

'Your father, I hope, will have explained to you that the social position of this family has changed.' She didn't turn around and spoke as if she'd rehearsed. 'Every employer has a right to establish rules for her household. That is why I've engaged Mary as more than a housekeeper. Because your father insists on giving work to the Rooneys I've allotted Mary the task of helping them to rid themselves of their former habits, low way of thinking and familiar way of speaking to their mistress and master.'

She straightened the edges of the curtain but didn't turn. 'You will have to marry, Alicia, and must be prepared. There's a lot Mary can teach you.'

'I don't doubt it,' I said. My mother would ignore my irony, I knew, just as I would ignore *her* talk of marrying me off.

'Even the wisest and best of us have something to learn.' Mary Connor's voice was close behind me. She'd moved from the door without me hearing a sound. 'The happiness of society arises from each of us keeping to our station, and being contented with it.'

I turned and stared at her and she met my gaze, her skinny neck extending like a voracious chicken's as she looked up at me. I wanted to ask her what she knew of happiness, or contentment for that matter, but perhaps fortunately my father came through the door just then.

'Your trunks are gone upstairs, Allie.' He looked from me to my mother, the appeasing smile back on his face. Mary Connor, without a word, sidled round him and out of the room. I knew she'd gone to inspect my trunks.

'I want Sarah to help me unpack.' Even to my own ears I sounded childish and petulant.

My father, with an instinct born of experience, picked up the mood between my mother and me.

'Go on up and see your room, Allie,' he coaxed, 'it's as fine as anything you'll have seen in Paris.'

The bedroom I'd been given was high and narrow with a window overlooking the front garden and the road. Mary Connor had opened the largest of my trunks. She didn't turn when I came in.

'You don't need to trouble yourself with my unpacking,' I said.

Even then she didn't immediately turn round. When she did, finally, her face was alight with spite. 'You cannot do it yourself and Sarah Rooney has other duties,' she said. 'Best to get things sorted out now. I run an orderly household.'

'I'd like to be alone in my room for a while.' I held the door open.

I thought she wouldn't go but she did, gliding silently past me, not even the bunch of keys hanging from her waist making a sound.

The new bedroom was nothing like my old one over the pub in Broadstone. It held none of my belongings from that room either. Not even my beloved picture of the Bazaar at Suez, whose candlelit shadows and dark faces had terrified my childish imagination.

I longed for it now, and almost wept.

My new bed was narrow and covered with a lace counterpane. There was a wardrobe, large and with a mirror fitted inside the door, as well as a washstand, chest of drawers and a chair which in France would have been called a *chauffeuse* and put in front of a fire. It was low and uncomfortable-looking but must have been fashionable in Dublin or my mother wouldn't have bought it.

I was hungry and tired and in no mood to do further battle with either Mary Connor or my mother. I slid open the sash window and let the warm air gust gently about me. The view was good and the scene lively enough.

The Beggar's Bush Barracks stood almost directly opposite, with soldiers in red and blue uniforms coming and going between granite gateposts. Carriages and a milk cart with churns rattled over the crushed stone surface of the road between, avoiding places where deep holes were filled with loose metal. Servant women with baskets walked in the direction of Baggot Street, the skirts of their faded dresses turning up swirls of dust as they went.

I would have turned away and lain on the bed awhile if Sarah had not come running round the side of the house just then. She was unrolling her sleeves as she went, the shortness of the skirts swinging about her ankles marking her out as a servant. I called to her as she started to cross the road but she didn't hear me and kept going until she reached the barracks' gates. She stopped and spoke briefly to a sentry before slipping inside.

I was trying to follow her disappearing figure across the barrack square when my mother and Mary Connor came into the room behind me. Albert slithering into the room after them. He jumped on to my bed and lay watching me while my mother plucked a green satin dress from the top of a trunk and held it against her.

'What a pity your figure is so childlike,' she shook a regretful head, 'I might have had my dressmaker copy a couple of them if your gowns were more . . . womanly.' She dropped the dress on the floor. 'Let's see, Mary, what other delights my daughter has brought with her from France.'

With sly speed Mary Connor's sparrow hands buried themselves in the trunk. She didn't say a word and a fury, born of exhaustion and misery and fear for the future, took a sudden hold of me.

I grabbed the lid of the trunk and held it poised to drop. 'If you don't remove your hands they'll be severed at the wrists.' I was shrill and knew I was close to hysteria.

The housekeeper looked up at me and there was no fear in her, nor apology. But she was wise enough to take her hands out of my clothes.

'I'll come back another time,' she said.

'Stay where you are, Mary.' My mother's lips were white. 'Alicia will apologise.'

'I'll do no such thing.'

My mother, shaking, stepped closer to me. I was shaking too. I hadn't wanted things to go this far. I wanted to say I was sorry, that my mother and the housekeeper could have the trunks and everything in them, that I was really too tired to care. But I didn't, because I did care. Not about the trunks, or what was in them, but about being in the power of my mother and her housekeeper.

'I can't compel you and your father, I know, will not compel you.' My mother picked up the cat. She seemed calmer and I relaxed a little.

I should have known better. I should have remembered the unpredictability of her temper. But I forgot because I'd been away from her and living with normal people. I'd forgotten how lunatic she could be and so I stood, frozen and immobile, as she did what I should have foreseen she would do.

In a sudden frenzy of abandon she threw the cat from her and began to hurl boots, dresses, shawls about the room, tearing a bonnet apart when she came to it. She threw a jewel box so hard it crashed against the wall and burst open and spewed the contents as far as my feet.

'You will not,' she stopped, panting, 'display to that low and wretched Sarah Rooney what this family's money had bought for you.'

'In the name of God Almighty what's going on here?' My father, in the doorway, smelled of whiskey, a drink he said steadied his nerves. He turned on me.

'Couldn't you have kept the peace for one hour at least? Couldn't you have let things be?'

I said nothing because anything I said would have been

wrong. I'd always been the source of trouble between my parents.

Mary Connor, standing on the *chauffeuse*, closed the window.

'Come away, Harriet.' There was resignation in the slump of my father's round shoulders. 'Come away and lie down.'

'That's where your money went, Leonard.' My mother kicked at a pile of clothing. 'Into silks and feathers for the strumpet we spawned. You thought you were buying yourself a lady when you sent her to Paris but you've wasted your money. Our money. She's not a lady and nothing will ever make her one, in the same way that nothing will ever make a gentleman of you. You're coarse and insignificant and I am damned, damned, damned to be forever by your side.'

She closed her eyes. The chignon had come loose and there were lines to the side of her mouth which had not been there before.

'I rue, every day, the hour that my father made me marry you.'

'I know that, Harriet,' my father said quietly, 'I know that.'

This seemed to please my mother who opened her eyes and went to the mirror. There, with the utmost concentration, she gathered her hair into place.

My father, in the same quiet tone, said, 'The table is laid for the breakfast. The child has only just arrived home and is tired.'

'Child?' My mother, critically examining her reflection, gave a short laugh. 'There's no child here. There's a brazen young woman who thinks she can do as she likes and defy her mother. I will not have it. Tell her, Leonard, that she must obey.'

I could take no more. 'Mary Connor may do what she likes with my clothes.'

I stepped over my strewn possessions and left the room. I knew what my father would say. He would tell me to obey. I would always be sacrificed to his need to please my mother.

Bess Rooney was in the kitchen wearing a large white cap and apron.

'Where did that Mary Connor come from? Where did my mother get her?'

I started to shake again and to pace touching things as I went: an oil lamp, a copper pot, silver laid out for cleaning, a jug of fresh milk. I stopped.

'Can I have some milk, Bess, please?' I sat edgily at the scrubbed, wooden table while she poured it for me. 'Was it Mary Connor decided you should wear that thing on your hair?'

'Drink the milk and be still and I'll answer your questions one at a time.' Bess shook her head. 'I don't know where your mother's housekeeper came from though it was nowhere good Cork maybe or Kerry.' Bess had an aversion to anywhere more than ten miles outside Dublin. 'and you're right it was her decided I should wear the cap.' She gave the snort that was her way of laughing. 'It's a small thing wearing a cap and not worth arguing over,' she sighed. 'Judging by the sounds I heard coming from upstairs you've not learned the wisdom of a bit of silence yet Allie Buckley.'

'Are you saying that nothing in life is worth arguing over?'

I sipped the milk. It was warm, not long milked from the cow.

'You'll have to decide that for yourself.'

Bess went to a cooking range that was twice the size of the one we'd had in the Broadstone. When she opened the oven the smells of the breakfast she'd prepared made me weak with hunger.

'Can I eat here, now?' I asked.

'You've no self-control none at all you're like a child still.' Bess shook her head and came to the table and cut me some bread which she buttered. She made bread better than any baker.

'That's all you'll get by the time you've changed your clothes the breakfast will be on the table.'

'Where's Sarah?'

'Outside.' She waved a vague hand. 'What happened upstairs?'

While I told her she didn't interrupt and she didn't once stop working; making butter balls, heating plates, boiling water. Bess was uneasy.

'I've wondered manys a time myself where the Connor woman came from,' she said, 'whether she was born or made but she's here and you might as well get used to her and keep out of her way.' She took a breath. 'Keep out of your mother's way as well.' She stood looking at me. 'You were scrawny when you left but you've grown up fast and you're nearly a woman. The air must be healthy enough in France.'

'I saw Sarah crossing the road,' I said. 'She went into the barracks.'

'You've no business here in the kitchen.' Bess turned away and filled the teapot with boiling water from the kettle on the range. 'You should be above stairs picking up your clothes and dressing yourself for the breakfast.' She put a tray on the table. 'I'll be serving it any minute now.'

'You won't be serving anything until Sarah gets back.' I was not going to be put off so easily. 'What's she doing in the barracks?'

'Holy Mother of God why can't you let it go I've enough to contend with . . .' Bess crossed herself and her lips moved and she began to pray. Bess prayed a lot. 'Sarah's gone for provisions.'

I knew she was lying.

'She's meeting a soldier, isn't she?' The idea made me feel ill. I'd lost Sarah to a soldier, that was why she hadn't answered my letters. 'She's got a soldier lover. That's it, Bess, isn't it?'

I got up from the table then sat down again. My legs were hollow. If it was true that my friend had a lover then she would have no time for me. I'd seen too often how women forsook women friends when they fell in love with a man, even the best of women.

'She's gone to see him . . .' I stared at Bess. Dublin without Sarah would be unimaginable. Sarah *was* Dublin, for me.

Sitting there, gazing at her mother, I remembered a summer's day ten years before when Sarah and I had gone walking across the city in search of Sandymount Strand. The idea had been Sarah's and we'd gone after school.

'Your mother won't miss you and mine won't worry,' she

assured me. We put our books in one bag and took turns carrying it, me trotting by her side, two of my steps matching every one of hers. But at nine years old we'd no idea of distances, nor of direction. By six o'clock we were lost, standing on a bridge close to where the river wound past the train sheds of a great railway station.

'There's no station like this in Sandymount.' I'd never before been so tired, nor so hungry. But I wasn't frightened, yet.

'How much money have you?' Sarah asked. I always had money.

'I've sixpence,' I said.

'We'll buy bread and milk and keep on looking.' Sarah squinted down the river. 'I can see the sea from here.'

'I can't.' I squinted too. 'I think we should get a horsecar at the station and go home. My father will pay.'

'If that's what you want,' Sarah sniffed but it was what she wanted too.

It was my idea to walk through the sheds. We went slowly, the adventure gone out of the day and the sheds, all around, looming dirty, mostly empty and dark.

The boys had been walking behind us for several minutes before Sarah turned to look at them. A mangy dog sloped at their heels.

'Are ye following us?' Her height always made Sarah brave.

'We are,' the boys surrounded us quickly. There wasn't another person in sight.

'What's in the bag?' demanded the boy who'd spoken, a fellow of about thirteen with a pale face and a nose that came down to his mouth.

'None of your business,' Sarah said.

'Books,' I said, hurriedly, 'school books.'

'They'd be worth money . . .' One of the other boys poked at the bag with a stick. You could tell he was the kind liked to torture cats.

'You'd better let us pass,' said Sarah, 'or my father'll have the police after the lot of you.'

The third boy laughed. 'Your father isn't here.' The cap over his eyes didn't hide their hard glitter. He terrified me, but having Sarah by my side gave me courage.

'Take the bag,' I handed it to him, 'and let us pass, please.'

'Say please again,' he sneered.

'You have no manners,' I said.

I was a small girl and he was a big boy and it was easy for him to knock me to the ground. I lay there on my back, stunned. I was struggling to sit when Sarah grabbed the bag, swung it at the boys and raced, like a loose horse, through the gap as they parted. The boys, as one and screaming curses, took after her.

I stood alone between the dark sheds, bereft and crying out for Sarah. She'd left me alone and that was all I could think about. When she returned, in minutes and with a man in uniform, I was not mollified.

'You left me,' I sobbed.

'I went for help,' she said. 'I saw this man in the distance.' She held up the bag. 'I have our books too.'

We were put in a horsecar and sent home and soundly punished by my father and by Sarah's mother. But it was days before I could forgive Sarah for deserting me.

'I went for help,' she protested, over and over.

'You left me,' I said, and turned my back on her.

The days which followed were the most miserable in my life till then. My mother's cruelties and moods were frivolities compared to what I saw as Sarah's betrayal.

'I'd never leave you.' Sarah stood crying in my path as I came out of school two days later. 'You're dearer to me than my own sister. It was fear for you gave me the courage to swing the books and run for the porter.'

'I wish I'd been the one to save you.' I hugged her, contrite and understanding.

'You tried, by giving them over the bag,' Sarah took my hand and, in the way of small girls, we pledged undying loyalty. 'I'll always be your friend,' she said, 'even when we're grown women, even 'til death do us part.'

'Me too,' I said, 'me too.'

Remembering, I wanted Sarah to come through the kitchen door and tell me again she would always be my friend. But there was only Bess, spreading her hands on the table and studying them as she said, 'Sarah doesn't tell me her business these days.'

Her hands were raw and sinewy, the knuckles like doorknobs. They moved across the table gathering breadcrumbs as she went on. 'You're not children any longer you and my Sarah nor even young girls.' She took a deep breath. 'You'll have to be strong Allie and put childish things behind you.' She put a hand over mine and I knew she wasn't going to tell me about Sarah. 'You must pray to the Lord Jesus and His Holy Mother to guide you through what's ahead.'

'I'd benefit more from earthly guidance.' I decided to get information of another kind from her. 'You've always known my mother's mind, Bess, and my father's too. I know they want me to marry, my mother has said so and my father has alluded to it . . .' I took a breath. 'Have they decided who it is I must marry?'

'It's not for me to say.'

'It's not for you to remain silent. I'm alone. There's no one else to tell me, to help me.' The sound of my father's voice, then of a closing door, came from upstairs. 'Tell me, Bess, if you have the courage.'

'Courage? Courage is what we use to get us through our daily lives and we use all we have of it for that.' She put a hand on my head. 'It takes courage to accept your lot and courage to live it and I would not be courageous if I told you who the man is your parents want you to marry.' She got up from the table. 'I would be foolish and I'm many things Allie Buckley but a fool is not one of them.'

'You *are* a fool, Bess Rooney, if you think that I'm going to marry a man I don't know. I've decided,' I stood too and faced her, 'that I will never marry. What I've seen of the state hasn't impressed me a great deal.'

'You were always full of big ideas Allie and whatever

education you got beyond in France doesn't seem to have improved you much,' Bess said.

'Miss Buckley's education is not yet complete, any more than is your own, Mrs Rooney.'

Mary Connor was by the range. I marvelled again at her stealth and wondered how long she'd been there.

Bess said nothing but I saw her agitation in the clenching and unclenching of her great knuckles.

'The family will breakfast as soon as Miss Buckley is refreshed.' The housekeeper looked around the kitchen. 'Where's your daughter?'

'I saw her follow the milk cart down the road,' I said.

This wasn't exactly a lie and it wasn't exactly the truth. Mary Connor gave me a sharp look.

'From my bedroom window,' I added.

'We're not in need of milk,' she said, 'I order exactly what the household requires.'

'I drink a great deal of it,' I lied wholeheartedly this time.

From where I was standing I could see the door in the back garden wall open and Sarah come through. She was carrying a pint measure as she came up the garden.

I grinned at Mary Connor. 'You weren't to know how much extra would be needed.'

Sarah came through the kitchen door. She was smiling as she put the milk into the cold safe on the wall. 'I caught up with the milkman,' she announced as she put a cap like the one Bess was wearing on her head, 'so now we can get on with the breakfast.'

We'd always had a finely tuned telepathy, Sarah Rooney and I.

CHAPTER THREE

Sarah

August, 1867

It's hard to keep a secret in Henrietta Street. With everyone outside it's near impossible. And the heat, this summer, has kept everyone outside.

In the evenings, and for a good part of the night, the women sit on the steps. They talk about the world and their neighbours. They take note of comings and goings. They miss nothing. The children play alongside them. Men with no money for the pubs sometimes sleep, for hours, in the doorways in the sun.

And why shouldn't they? It's a great deal more pleasant outside than it is for many of them in the rooms they live in.

Any other summer I'd have been glad to sit with them. But this summer I have wished, heartily and often, for wind and rain to drive them indoors. This summer I have a secret, a life of my own outside Henrietta Street. I will not share it with any of them. Not yet.

There are suspicions in the street that I have a man. But no one knows for sure and no one would dare to question me. They know the sharp edge of my tongue too well. My mother may even suspect I have a soldier.

My mother is right, as she usually is. But Private James Vance of Her Majesty's Royal Welsh Fusiliers will stay my secret for a while longer. I'm nowhere near ready to risk my happiness by exposing Jimmy Vance to my father's wrath, my grandmother's disapproval, my mother's anxiety, the gossip of neighbours. I'll keep him to myself for as long as I can, precious and hidden 'til I'm more sure of him. Then, if I should lose him, and I pray to God I won't, I'll at least have my memories of our time together intact and unsullied. Or, if all goes well and we grow old together, then I'll be able to talk to him about the things we said and did.

But if I have a secret then Allie's mother, Harriet Buckley, has one too. Has had one as long as I have, maybe even longer. And if it is what I think then her secret could have an effect on us all. Especially Allie. My innocent and good best friend only half knows what her mother is like. Now that she's back from France she'll unfortunately have the rest of her life to find out. Allie is going to need a friend – I was not the friend I should have been to her on her first night home. A meeting already arranged with Jimmy Vance was all I could think about.

I was on my way to meet him when Beezy Ryan stopped me on the steps. 'You never have the time to talk to anyone these days.' She was fanning herself and leaning against the railings, her red hair loose down her back. She watched me closely.

'You don't often have a lot of time yourself.' I smiled to hide my impatience. 'Things must be quiet in North King Street or you wouldn't be here.'

'Too quiet,' Beezy agreed, 'not even the divils of men want to be inside these evenings.'

Beezy ran a kip house in North King Street. Some of the women in Henrietta Street hated her because their men went there. Others because they said she was a whore of Babylon and should be cast out.

Some feared her. Beezy was nearly six feet tall, had a tongue like a razor and used it to say what she thought. Most liked her. She'd been reared by the nuns in a Magdalen and though she was hard and her life was hard she was fair.

I knew Beezy better than most. This was on account of my mother befriending her when she first arrived in the neighbourhood and had got herself into a spot of trouble. That was nine years before. But I'd a clear memory of Beezy sitting in our room while I made her a cup of hot, sweet tea and my mother bathed a wound to her forehead. Beezy was seventeen at the time and had run away from the nuns. With her wild red hair and great eyes I thought her the most beautiful woman I'd ever seen. She'd been selling herself in Henrietta Street when three of the neighbour women attacked her.

'If you won't go back to the nuns child,' my mother dabbed and Beezy winced, 'then you'd best find yourself some cleaning work it's safer.'

'My mother was a whore,' Beezy was harsh, 'and I'm a whore too. It's an honourable calling.'

'There's plenty would disagree with you,' my mother sighed. 'But you'd best take your business elsewhere. Henrietta Street won't tolerate you.'

Beezy took herself elsewhere, but not too far. Within four years she'd opened in North King Street, a madam in her own kip house. But she never forgot my mother and at Christmas, and certain other times of the year, would arrive in Henrietta Street with cheese and whiskey. One was to nourish, she said, the other to fortify. Beezy was a great believer in the benefits of whiskey. Ill-matched though they were, she and my mother would on these occasions open the bottle and sit talking for up to an hour. Beezy liked to gossip and my mother knew everything that went on. My mother, who prayed a lot, liked to question Beezy about the nuns.

I always liked Beezy myself. Both of us being tall gave us that much, at least, in common. I also knew her well enough to know I wouldn't get away from her on the steps that evening without making some excuse for my busyness.

'Allie Buckley is home from France,' I said. I let the implication that Allie had been occupying my time hang in the air — I put my guilt about not being with my friend on her first night home to the back of my mind.

'Is she indeed.' Beezy raised her eyebrows and eyed the low neck of my sprigged cotton dress, the way I'd caught and curled my hair. 'So you're off to see your old friend . . .' She laughed. 'You've gone to a lot of trouble for her.'

The other women on the steps pretended to ignore us. They did a bad job of it. 'And how is Leonard Buckley these days?' Beezy gave a different kind of laugh when she said this. It left no one in doubt about how, and how well, she knew Allie's father. 'Now there's a man's come up in the world.' Beezy looked round her audience then back at me. 'I'm told he wears two-piece suits and has taken on a housekeeper to smarten up yourself and your mother.'

'Leonard Buckley's not the one took on Mary Connor.' For old times' sake and the man he'd once been I felt I should defend Allie's father. 'She was Harriet Buckley's idea.'

'Oh?' Beezy, scenting trouble, and gossip, straightened. 'What sort is this Mary Connor?'

'She's an old woman, small and wizened.'

There wasn't much else I wanted to say about the Buckleys' housekeeper. It would have been normal to feel kindness, or even pity, for a woman her size and age. I felt nothing but dislike.

'And the daughter, Allie, is still your friend, even though her father's your landlord? She hasn't got too big for her Paris boots while she was away?'

Beezy lifted the hair from the back of her neck and coiled it languorously on top of her head. She wore rings on every finger. It was said she never took them off, no matter what she was doing.

'Allie's not the type to change,' I said, 'and she's not responsible for her father either. Leonard Buckley, in any event, is not the worst of them.'

'She can't help her father, that's true,' Beezy shrugged, 'nor the fact that he's one of a type the city's full of these days. Fat-bellied buffoons, the lot of them, buying up empty houses before they fall down and filling them with the poor . . .'

'He's better than most to his tenants.'

God alone knows why I went on defending Leonard Buckley. The signs were that he was becoming everything Beezy claimed he was. Maybe it was because he'd been decent enough in the past and my mother believed he would continue to be so for the future. I hoped she was right.

'Could be you know what you're talking about,' Beezy shrugged again, 'or maybe it's just that he's got good cause to behave himself where you Rooneys are concerned.'

Beezy knew everything, or thought she did. She knew that my father's withered leg, and the reason he couldn't get work, was the result of barrels falling on him in the Buckleys' public house. She also knew that it was because my father had no work, and in spite of his wife not wanting me near the place, that Leonard Buckley had taken me into service in their new house,

If she thought too that the barrel accident was the reason he'd kept my mother on as cook she was wrong. The Buckleys kept my mother because there wasn't a cook in Dublin could match her.

Beezy began fanning herself again. 'So, what does Miss Allie Buckley have to say about France?' she asked.

The women on the steps had grown quiet, openly listening now. Beezy had a way of attracting, and keeping, an audience.

'She only arrived home this morning,' I said, 'I haven't had much of a chance to talk to her yet.'

'You might make hay while the sun shines then,' Beezy looked over my shoulder and waved a hand, 'and be off before Bess gets here and finds something for you to do.'

My mother was coming slowly up the hill. Her day in Haddington Road was longer than mine so her arrival home meant it was later than I'd thought. I'd allowed Beezy to delay me too long.

'Is your father at home?' my mother asked as I came up to her.

'No. But I've given Mary Ann and Nana their tea. Nana's gone to bed. She says she'll go to the markets in the morning.'

I hoped my mother wouldn't ask where I was going. I didn't want to lie to her.

'Your sister's too young to be spending her time indoors. She'd be better off outside.' My mother sagged a little as she looked up to our second-floor windows. 'Take her with you, Sarah, for the walk and the airing. She'll behave . . .'

'She won't. She'll drag out of me and torment me. I want to look at the shop windows on my own.'

My mother sighed. 'Go on then,' she said.

I knew she didn't believe me about the windows but was too filled with panic to care. I was late. Jimmy Vance might not wait for me. I ran all the way, fast as my skirts and decency would allow.

Even so, and taking what I thought the shortest route, by Rutland Square and the Rotunda Maternity Hospital, it took me twenty minutes to get to our meeting place in front of the New Mart in Sackville Street. There was the usual commotion and bustle of people about the store. There was sign of Jimmy.

I was breathless and too hot as I leaned against the side of a window to gather myself together. My hair had come down and there were three inches of dust circling the hem of my dress. In the glass of the window I looked like a wild-eyed tinker woman. I did what I could with my hair. There was nothing to be done about the hem.

There was still no sign of Jimmy Vance.

There were some soldiers about but he wasn't one of them. He wasn't the sort to be easily missed in a crowd. He was tall and carried his head high and had a naturally good-humoured expression that drew people to him. Either he hadn't arrived yet or something had happened to him and he wasn't coming at all.

Anxiety devoured me. We'd only made the arrangement that morning. I'd lied about going across to the barracks, saying I was going for milk.

Maybe I was being punished for the lie. Maybe I'd seen the last of him. Maybe my father had found out and gone storming the Beggar's Bush Barracks with his crutch and bottle of whiskey. It was the sort of thing he'd do. He was a supporter of the Fenian struggle and thought the British Army 'made up of nothing but the pickings of the gutter'. He was right too, as far as some of the soldiers were concerned. But they came from Irish gutters as well as English ones and this my father would never acknowledge.

Another thought came as I waited. Maybe Jimmy Vance not turning up was a punishment for putting him before my old friend Allie. For refusing her when she'd asked me to stay on to help her sort the clothes she'd brought from Paris. I paced the windows, seeing nothing of the fashions on display. Nowhere the reflection of a tall soldier either.

The panic died in me and an angry acceptance had begun to take its place when I saw him. He was watching me from the corner of Sackville Place, a grin on his face. I knew instantly that he'd seen my panic and had kept his distance to tease me. I stood where I was. I don't like to be made a fool of. No Rooney does.

He crossed the road and came quickly to me. 'You're angry,' he said as he took my arm, 'it was only play-acting, to tease you . . .' 'You made me look a fool.' I pulled my arm free. 'You can take yourself back to Beggar's Bush and play-act with your own kind there. Maybe they'll think you amusing.'

I turned on my heel, back the way I'd come. Jimmy Vance was a step ahead of me, blocking the way.

'I'm sorry, Sarah.' He looked it. He had taken off his cap and his hair stood on end. 'Please don't go. It was a feeble-minded thing to do.'

I said nothing, just stood staring at him as my anger faded. The way it always did with Jimmy. It had been a childish thing to do, typical of the simplicity I liked about him. He was a soldier who took his Queen's shilling and didn't interest himself in politics, or even religion. He was my own age but still a boy, as all men were, even when they were a lot older. He hadn't intended to be cruel.

'It was cruel, but not meant to be,' he said.

He often read my thoughts. I allowed him take my arm again. 'I wouldn't hurt you for the world, you know that.' He grinned. He couldn't help himself. 'Am I not worth the wait?'

'You're worth a couple of minutes,' I said, 'no more.'

We walked in silence until we came to the Carlisle Bridge. Halfway across we stopped and stood looking at the boats and the distant opening of the river.

'You're still upset,' Jimmy said. He was gentle for a soldier.

'I thought you weren't coming. I thought all sorts of things . . .'

'I'd never let you down,' Jimmy said and we walked on, desultory as the evening itself.

It was half past eight and there were streaks of flame in the dusky sky when we got to the end of Grafton Street. Though it was still hot the days were shortening with the first warnings of the winter to come.

'I've to be back in the barracks by ten o'clock,' Jimmy said.

'We haven't long then,' I said.

It was always like this, getting ready to part almost as soon as we met. I took his hand, not caring if the whole of Dublin saw us. Our fingers held tight. I was shameless when I was with Jimmy Vance.

Tonight I was going to be reckless too.

We walked on up Grafton Street, past the fine homes and quality stores. The street musicians were everywhere playing but making sure to keep two steps ahead of the police. Outside Pigott's music shop we came upon the blind Zosimus playing 'Eanach Dhuin' on the whistle. Jimmy drifted towards him but I was not in the mood to listen to a tune which tells the story of a tragic drowning.

'It's too sad,' I said, 'let's keep going.'

'He plays well,' Jimmy was coaxing, 'and it's a fine air . . .' He held me beside him while we listened.

Zosimus played beautifully. But the sad loneliness of the music filled me with an irrational fear for myself and Jimmy Vance.

I was wishing he would stop playing when the police arrived. Zosimus protested, full of dignity, shouting at them that even Homer was allowed to 'sing the praises of his country on the public highways'. The police took him away anyway.

I felt another kind of guilt then, as if my wish for him to stop playing had brought the police. But I felt glad too. I'd had enough of 'Eanach Dhuin' and all that it signified. Our walk up Grafton Street was not as aimless as it appeared. We'd a destination in mind.

We planned to be alone, Jimmy and me, to find ourselves a

private corner in St Stephen's Green, be together among the bushes and sheltering trees. In the months since we'd met we'd done nothing more than snatch kisses along the canal bank near Beggar's Bush. I wanted to kiss Jimmy properly, to feel his arms tightly about me. I felt nervous and talked a lot as we walked.

I told him about Allie, how unhappy she was to be home.

'Not that I blame her. There's not much joy in that Haddington Road house. She has no friends there, except for me . . .' I paused, 'and I refused her tonight. I'll have to find a way to share myself between you and her.'

'But not yet.' Jimmy squeezed my hand. 'I'm not ready to share you yet.' He looked thoughtful. 'Do you think she would suit John Marsh? Or is she too grand for a common soldier?'

'She's too good for John Marsh,' I said, 'but it has nothing to do with him being a soldier.'

I was sorry as soon as I said this. John Marsh was Jimmy's best friend. I didn't like him but shouldn't have been so hasty. Jimmy's silence was full of offence.

I tried to make amends. 'It's just that Allie is fond of learning and books . . .'

'John has read a great deal,' he was stiff, 'and the fact that you're learned and I'm not doesn't come between us. Does it?'

'No,' I said, 'only I'm not so educated as all that.'

I'd gone to national school until I was twelve and had learned a good deal about reading and writing. But I was by no means the great scholar Jimmy thought I was.

'They're not likely to meet anyway,' I said, 'since my mother says Allie's parents have already chosen the man she's to marry.'

'I hope he's good enough for her,' Jimmy said.

I was wise enough myself to leave things there. John Marsh and Jimmy had grown up and joined the army together. They were like vinegar and milk, with John Marsh devious as Jimmy was straight. He was jealous too of me taking Jimmy from him. I saw it in his baleful eye each time we met.

The lamplighter was making his rounds when we got to the top of the street, creating pools of soft gold each time he lit a mantel. Children followed him as he went round St Stephen's Green park, boys and girls with thin rickety legs. He kept shooing them away. When they didn't go he brandished his pole.

Jimmy and me crossed the street to St Stephen's Green quickly, stepping together like soldiers. We knew it was a private park, for the use only of those living in the big houses all around. But the barriers about it were low, simple granite posts with chains between them. When we found an unlit spot opposite the Royal College of Surgeons it was a small matter to step over a chain.

It was quiet in the park and, with the trees and bushes all about, much darker than in the street. We were very alone, very quickly. I couldn't see Jimmy's face when his arm went round me.

'I want you to touch me as a man touches a woman,' I said. I was shaking. It was what I wanted. It was also what I didn't want.

'I am afraid of you, Sarah, and afraid for you.' Jimmy was almost whispering. 'I haven't known many women . . .'

'I know that. I wouldn't care for you if you were a Jack the Lad.'

In front of us, waiting, there was a shadowy seat for two. We sat there, holding hands, a life away from the street sounds of hooves on cobblestones and the ballads of the musicians. I looked up through the leaves, at a patch of inflamed sky.

'Red sky at night,' I began.

'Is the shepherd's delight,' Jimmy finished. His hand tightened about mine. 'I will think of you always in the sun, Sarah, with your black hair shining. I will never be able to think of you in the wind or rain or cold.'

The excitement in me died. Dread, like a leaded weight, lodged itself about my heart.

'You're going away then?' I said.

'I won't be staying in Dublin, you know that.' He kicked with his boot at the gravelly ground. 'The army will move me on. There's talk of a new regiment coming in, of others going home and of some of us being shipped out to . . . India.'

I'd have been a fool not to hear the hesitation and then the longing in his voice as he said the name of the sub-continent.

'That's where you want to go, isn't it? You want to go to India?' I kept my voice calm. I did well, considering.

'I've given it thought in the past,' Jimmy admitted, 'before I knew you.' He took both my hands in his and held them to his mouth as he spoke. 'Since knowing you it's like I've been thrown into the air and am spinning up there and don't know how to get down again.' His breath was warm on my fingers. 'I'd want to go to India, if it came down to it, but I wouldn't want to go without you.'

The dread eased a bit. 'I'd be sad if you went,' I said.

'Sad . . .' He repeated the word as if testing it. 'I'd feel more than sad without you, Sarah. I'd feel a part of my life was gone from me.'

'India is a long way from here.' I was imagining a hot, red sun, baked earth, silks and spices, mysterious, brown people. It was all I knew of India. I thought wildly that I would follow him there. But that would have made me a camp follower and so I said nothing.

Jimmy pulled me to him. 'I've not got word yet anyway about moving on. If it happens than I won't leave you behind.'

'You're just saying that to please me . . .'

'I'm saying it because I love you.'

'Kiss me then, because I love you too.' I held my face up to his, and closed my eyes as he kissed me on the mouth.

It was a kiss longer than any we'd shared before. When he opened his mouth I did too and felt his tongue moving against mine. It was what I'd wanted. Only I hadn't wanted to feel frightened.

I pulled away. 'We mustn't.' I couldn't stop the trembling.

'I won't hurt you.' Jimmy's hand caressed my neck. He was trembling too. 'There's nothing wrong in us loving and wanting one another.'

He put his mouth to mine again and this time I didn't draw away. He eased my dress from my shoulders and kissed the bared flesh and said my name, over and over. I felt half conscious, and more alive than I'd ever felt in my life before. I felt no shame. I wanted to laugh.

I wanted to weep.

'Jimmy,' I said and he lifted his head and began kissing me again on the mouth. I'll never know how our lovemaking would have gone because it ended there, cut short by a raucous, ear-splitting laugh from a woman in the trees just behind us. It might have been a rifle shot for the effect it had on us.

We stiffened at once and moved apart, listening. I wanted to run; it was all I could do to hold myself on the seat beside Jimmy. He put an arm about me and pulled my dress back over my shoulders.

The laugh came again, rougher and closer and followed by a crashing in the trees and drunken, bloody oaths from a man. I felt shame then, and disgust at myself. I felt hot tears on my face too, though I'd no sense of shedding them.

'We shouldn't have come here,' I said. 'This place is no more than a hideaway for whores and prostitutes. I should've known better.'

Jimmy, his arm about my waist, half carried me back the way we'd come. 'Don't cry, Sarah, please don't cry . . .' He had only his hands to wipe my tears but he used them, rubbing one cheek first and then the other. 'We'll find a place to be together. I'll find us a place.'

'Any fool would have known what this park was used for.' Shame made my cheeks burn and I turned my back to him while I tidied my hair and made myself ready for the street. 'Any fool but me.' I put my hands over my cheeks.

Jimmy turned me and held me against him. We stood there for a long time, at the edge of the shadows, passion gone but not wanting yet to step back into the light.

I remembered what he had said about India and was afraid again. 'Did you mean it when you said about finding us a place to be together?' I asked.

'I meant it,' Jimmy said.

CHAPTER FOUR

Sarah

My mother was tired. Tiredness made her irritable. When she was irritable it was best to keep out of her way.

'Did you scrub the front steps?' she demanded.

'I did.'

'And you polished the door brasses?'

'I did.'

'Empty the chamber pots then, and be quick.'

'Neither Allie nor her mother are out of their beds yet.'

'Empty them,' my mother said and I knew her irritability had as much to do with me as with her tiredness. I knew too that it was because of her suspicions about Jimmy Vance. If she'd had evidence she would have confronted me.

Allie was still asleep. Or she was at any rate lying with her eyes closed and not speaking to me. She was hurt about my having forsaken her the night before. Looking at her she didn't seem to me any bigger, or older, than the twelve-year-old girl who, during a summer every bit as hot as this one, had made me a present of her favourite bonnet of mixed yellow and cream straw. Her mother, not pleased, had flown into one of her rages and chopped Allie's hair to within an inch of her head.

I'd given Allie back the bonnet but she'd refused ever after to wear it. She'd gone the whole of the rest of that summer hatless, her cropped head a statement of brazen defiance against her mother.

I stood by the bed for a minute, the pot in my hand, willing Allie to open her eyes. I would remind her about the bonnet and we might laugh together about it. But she didn't move a muscle. I knew from old that when she was hurt she took her time about forgiving.

It wasn't, in any event, the best of times to make up with her. Not with Harriet Buckley writing a letter in the next room, being fussed over by Mary Connor. Leonard, who slept alone in the smallest bedroom of all, was long gone. His room I had cleaned and his pot I'd emptied.

I kept out of my mother's way for most of the rest of the morning.

I was trying to get iron mould out of a linen tablecloth with sorrel and salt when Mary Connor arrived in the kitchen. She wore the pale flush she often had when she'd been with Harriet Buckley. I'd swear she was half in love with Allie's mother. That old woman was strange enough for anything. She'd been the bane of our lives every livelong day since she'd arrived.

'The family will have luncheon at one o'clock,' she informed me as she stood over me and added unnecessary salt to the sorrel. 'Make sure you clean that cloth well. It'll be wanted two nights from now. Mrs Buckley is to give a dinner party.' She paused. 'It's to celebrate Miss Buckley's return and will be by way of an introduction to her new life.' She sniffed and looked up at my mother. 'It'll also be a test, Mrs Rooney, of your culinary skills. I hope you'll be up to the occasion.'

It was a foolish person questioned Bess Rooney's cooking. If Mary Connor wanted to provoke my mother she couldn't have gone a better way about it. My mother knew her value as a cook.

She stood over the housekeeper with her hands on her hips. 'My culinary skills as you call them are well tested,' she said. 'I've had no complaints about my dinners in the past and I don't expect there to be any this time either how many of them will there be at the table?'

'Seven. I'll draw up a menu.'

'I'll draw up the menu myself it's the way I work.'

'You forget your place, Mrs Rooney. It's your job to cook and clean and be directed by me . . .'

'I'll not be directed in matters relating to cooking and I'll not be directed at all if you interfere any more.'

My mother wiped her hands on her apron and turned to the range. I thought Mary Connor would combust. My mother didn't give her a chance to do anything before turning on her again.

'The range was slow to start today because it wasn't properly stoked this morning the luncheon could well be late as a result.'

Stoking the range was Mary Connor's job, done at daybreak. The old woman's lips peeled back from her teeth.

'A bad workman will always blame his tools,' she said. 'The range was stoked in the usual fashion. If the luncheon is late it'll be on account of your laziness and your daughter's.'

'Be very careful Mary Connor how far you go with that tongue of yours.' My mother was dismissive, not even looking up from what she was doing.

'It is you who should take care,' the housekeeper's voice was high and tinny, 'I *will* be obeyed. I *will* improve the standards of service in this house.'

'Maybe you should be concentrating on standards above stairs then and on your own myself and my daughter know our jobs well we've been doing them a long time now . . .' My mother stopped and frowned at the housekeeper. 'Stay out of the kitchen Mary Connor because I'm not one bit impressed with your knowledge of housekeeping even if the woman who employs you is.' She took a breath. 'You'd be wise to remember that I know this family and they know me and old knowledge is what counts in the long run so the less you and me have to do with one another the better.'

Mary Connor left the kitchen. She went quickly, her chest puffed out like a sparrow's, and without another word.

'She won't be gone long and she'll cause real trouble now you mark my words.' My mother was still angry, but resigned.

I'd all but got the stain out of the tablecloth. 'She's must be eighty years or more,' I said, 'she can't live forever.'

'That's a fact,' said my mother, 'but if that's a curse you're putting on her may the Lord God forgive you.'

My mother was right about Mary Connor. We'd only just got a luncheon of clear soup and fish pie ready when she reappeared in the kitchen.

'The family has gathered in the dining room,' she sniffed about the range, 'they're expecting to eat in five minutes. Put your cap back on.' This last was to me.

I replaced the cap on my head. It was starched and flat, like no maid's cap I'd ever seen. Probably a design of Mary Connor's own. It made me look like a class of nun. I hated Allie seeing me with it on.

She hadn't come to the kitchen all morning anyway.

Mary Connor sniffed. 'Straighten it up, miss, it's crooked.'

She would have said more but for a bell ringing just then in the panel over the door.

My mother, who was seasoning the soup, said, 'That's the dining room Sarah see what it is they want.'

'It'll be Mrs Buckley.' Mary Connor slithered to the door. 'You can be getting the soup on to the tray while I go to her.'

'When you're up there, Sarah,' my mother went on as if the housekeeper hadn't spoken, 'ask Leonard if he'd like to try a glass of the Madeira port was delivered this morning before he eats.'

'You'll attend to your duties here, missy.' Mary Connor, voice shrill, spun to face me. 'I'll answer the bell.'

The accident happened so quickly neither myself nor my mother could afterwards say clearly how it occurred. In all likelihood it had to do with the midget-sized heels on the housekeeper's shoes. They were so small that when she spun my way one must have caught in a groove between the floor flags. Whatever the cause she stumbled, clutched at the table, missed her hold and pitched forward, shooting her two arms out in front to break her fall. She broke her fall all right, but in doing so did harm to an ankle.

As she lay on the floor, face down and one of her short legs crookedly beneath her, my mother and I could only stare. The shock of it was paralysing. Mary Connor, because of her size, looked pitiful, like a broken doll, fragile and pathetic.

The service bell went on shrilling.

My mother was the first to recollect herself. She dropped to her knees beside the fallen woman.

'Are you all right, Mary?' She put a hand on her shoulder. 'Can you shift yourself is the leg broken?'

'Miss Connor to you . . .'

Her face more corrugated than ever with the pain, the housekeeper shook off my mother's hand. Pulling herself into a sitting position she leaned against the table and held her ankle with both hands. She looked up at my mother's worried face and I saw, in a quick flash there was no mistaking, the light of opportunity blaze in her pale eyes.

'You'll not get rid of me so easily, Bess Rooney,' mixed with the pain there was a malevolent glee, 'you'll not be long in this house now that you've been the cause of injuring me.' She closed her eyes and leaned back. 'The bell . . .' It was still ringing.

'Answer it, Sarah,' my mother was brusque, 'and tell Leonard Buckley what's happened here.'

'Give a true account, mind.' Mary Connor groaned but did not open her eyes. 'Honesty is the best policy, no matter if you are in the wrong.'

'I'll tell what I saw happen,' I said.

The dining room was one of my favourites in the house. It had a long front window and walls filled with framed engravings and coloured prints. A crystal chandelier with wax lights hung over the table at which Allie and her father were sitting. Allie was plucking at the embroidered tablecloth. Leonard was drinking from the whiskey bottle in front of him.

So much for my mother's offer of Madeira port.

Harriet Buckley was standing by the fireplace, cold fury on her face and her hand pulling on the bell rope. 'Why has no one answered my call before now?' she complained as she dropped the rope. 'It's fully five minutes since—'

'Mary Connor has fallen in the kitchen.' I cut across her, directing what I had to say at Leonard Buckley.

'How badly hurt is she?' he said.

'She's in pain and holding her ankle. She twisted it under her when she fell. I don't know any more than that. My mother is with her. She'll be better able to tell you what the damage is.'

'She's not able to walk then?' Harriet Buckley's voice had risen. 'She wasn't fit to come here to tell me herself?'

'She's in pain . . .'

'She cannot be so badly hurt as all that.' Allie's mother clasped and unclasped her hands. 'I need her services—'

'From the sound of it your housekeeper wants medical attention.' Allie pushed back her chair and stood. 'Maybe a doctor should look at her ankle.'

Her mother glared before, without a word, walking to the window and standing with her back to us. Her ill humour filled the room with a sourness.

'Get a doctor then.' Her voice was flat.

'What doctor will come at this hour of the day?' Leonard Buckley was petulant. 'They're all in their hospitals or dispensaries. The woman is old and frail and should never have been engaged in the first place. It'll be throwing good money after bad, keeping her on.' He downed what was left in his whiskey glass. 'A man has a right to eat in his own home without carry-on like this forever getting in the way.' He lumbered to his feet. 'I'd best see to the old crone . . .'

He left the room unsteadily, clearly the worse for wear. He'd never have spoken in such a way about Mary Connor if he hadn't been filled with whiskey.

Allie, without a word or look right or left, followed him.

I was about to go after them when Harriet Buckley, her voice low and hissing, called to me. 'Stay where you are, Sarah Rooney, there's something I want you to do.'

I turned, slowly. Harriet Buckley's face wore an expression of supreme distaste as she looked at me. She spoke again as soon as the door closed behind Allie.

'With Miss Connor incapacitated I unfortunately must place my trust in you, Sarah.' She took a deep, dragging breath. 'I want your word that you will speak to no one, not to your mother, not to Alicia, not to anyone, about the task I am about to entrust you with. Do I have it?' Her black eyes were on mine as if she would force an oath from me.

'I'm not a secretive person,' I lied.

'Oh, but you are, Sarah, you are a very secretive person when you want to be.' Harriet Buckley smiled her chilly half smile. 'Perhaps I should speak more plainly . . .'

'Please do.'

My interruption was sarcastic and cheap. I made it to cover a sudden, frightening fear that she knew about Jimmy.

I should have resisted the urge. It merely added fuel to the spite Harriet Buckley was full of. She moved silently to the table and began drumming her fingertips on its surface. They made the sound rain did in a gutter.

'You will regret that,' she said, softly, 'don't think my husband's wish to keep you here means you are safe.' Her smile widened. She looked quite happy. 'Don't think either that your own secret is safe. You should be more cautious, Sarah, about the company you keep and about where you keep it. The loss of your virtue is of no concern to me but would greatly agitate your mother were I to talk to her.' She paused. 'Leonard too. He would worry about your leading Alicia astray.' She walked to the fireplace and ran a finger over the gilding of the carriage clock there. 'This needs dusting,' she said, 'you really will have to keep your mind on your work, Sarah.'

She put the clock down and with a sigh turned to look at her profile in the overmantel mirror. It was a habit she had. From that angle she was quite beautiful. The tightness about her mouth and closeness of her eyes were only apparent when she was full face.

'Maybe it's the commandant of Beggar's Bush Barracks I

should be talking to or maybe,' she clicked her fingers as if remembering something, 'it's your father I should talk to. Cristy Rooney would be *most* unhappy to hear his daughter was parading the town with a soldier.' She turned to me. 'Don't you agree?'

So she knew. Maybe she'd seen me with Jimmy. Passed us in a carriage perhaps and kept the information to herself, waiting the chance to use it. Or maybe it was the spying Mary Connor who'd seen us. Whichever, Allie's mother knew about Jimmy. I took some hope from the fact that she didn't know Jimmy's name. She would have used it if she did.

'You're blackmailing me,' I said.

'Yes, I am.' She looked delighted. 'I don't like your lower-class, smart-tongued way of putting things but it seems that at last we understand one another. Since you will not give me your loyalty I must extract it somehow.' She glanced at the clock and became brisk. 'Go to my room. On the chiffonier you'll find a sealed envelope. Take it to the last house on the west side of Merrion Square. Wait for a reply. On no account return without one.' She waved a dismissive hand and turned again to the mirror. 'Go quickly.'

The envelope was cream-coloured and thin, only one sheet of paper inside. I sat with it on the bed, tracing the shapes of the exotic birds on the counterpane, gathering myself together. I thought about Allie's mother.

There was a fever in her, a desperation driving her to take risks. I'd no doubt she had a lover. I'd suspected her for a long time. It wasn't so hard to see in her the same terrible need to be with someone I was so often consumed with myself. But terrible as her betrayal was I wasn't shocked.

Nothing Allie's mother did would ever shock me. She was a woman lived only for herself. She always had and always would. I'd often thought her not quite sane. She was a wretched and cruel mother too. All through our schooldays together Allie had dreaded going home. She'd spent as much time in Henrietta Street as she had with her own family in the Broadstone. As a child I'd hated Harriet Buckley with a child's hatred for the way she treated my friend. Harriet had, in turn, hated me for bringing the pleasures of friendship to her daughter's life. She still hated me.

Sitting in her bedroom I felt a terrible sadness. A feeling of waste. Harriet Buckley's abandon to the self was everywhere: in the dressing table strewn with potions and hair brushes, in the gowns thrown across chairs, the crinoline hoops on the floor. My feelings were partly for Allie's father. He was a greedy man but kind enough in his own way. But mostly they were for Allie. She'd never known a mother's care and love. Now she was home betrayal was going to be added to that indifference.

I'd no doubt Harriet Buckley's adultery would be found out. Dublin was too small a city for secrets to remain secrets very long. Only they wouldn't be told by me. Harriet Buckley hadn't needed to use blackmail. I would have kept her secret for Allie's sake in any event.

As I left I opened the window to rid the room of its heavy, musky smell. Harriet disliked fresh air.

From the top of the stairs I saw Mary Connor below me in the hallway. Holding on to the wall with one hand and with a stick in the other she was making her way slowly towards the closed dining-room door. One of her feet was tightly bound in muslin bandages. Even handicapped she moved silent as a cat.

As I watched Allie and Leonard Buckley came along behind her. The old woman refused Allie's offer of help and when she reached the dining-room door, which was held open by Leonard, she passed inside with a grim nod to her employer.

My mother appeared then, with a soup tureen on a tray. She followed them all into the dining room. No one closed the door and, as I was trying to slip past, Allie saw me. She made frantic signals with her eyes. I couldn't ignore her and went inside. It was as well I did. My mother was in the dock. Mary Connor had put her there.

'She can deny all she likes but the truth is that I fell when Mrs

Rooney knocked against me.' The housekeeper was leaning on the stick, pain pinching her face.

'That's not how it happened.' My mother was still holding the tray. 'You spun too quick on your heel no one was next or near you at the time.'

'I am telling you, Mrs Buckley,' Mary Connor ignored her, 'that my fall was no accident. I'd had reason to take issue with Mrs Rooney only minutes before . . .'

'You're a liar,' I said from the door, 'my mother didn't touch you.'

I could feel Harriet Buckley's eyes on me, the frenzy in her that I hadn't yet left the house.

'I didn't expect either you or your mother would be truthful,' Mary Connor's voice had the rasp of a boot on a grate, 'but the Lord God will be the judge of both of you.' She paused. 'God and Mrs Buckley.'

'I've never known either Sarah or Bess to lie.' Allie stood stiffly. 'You must be mistaken.'

'You've never *known* them to lie.' Mary Connor shook a pained, reproachful head. 'That is the difficulty with liars, they don't reveal themselves.'

'I want to more of this talk.' Leonard Buckley, who had poured himself another whiskey, thumped the table with a fist. 'Bess, serve up that soup.' He slumped to the table, muttering. 'I want peace. Peace is all I want. I'll not tolerate squabbling women in my house.'

You poor fool, I thought, as if you had a choice with a wife like yours.

My mother put the tray and tureen down on the long sideboard. There was silence while she took the lid off and began ladling the cold, clear soup into bowls.

'It might be as well to have a doctor look at the ankle.' Allie was the first to speak. 'Miss Connor is not young and her bone is brittle. She may need a splint of some kind.'

'The ankle is sprained, not broken.' My mother put the bowl of soup in front of Leonard. 'With God's help it will fix itself in a few days.'

Leonard crossed himself, tucked a napkin into his collar and began to eat. My mother watched him for a minute before filling a second bowl and putting it in front of his wife.

'I'll bandage the ankle again tomorrow,' she said.

'I'll look after it myself,' Mary Connor limped to a chair and sat down.

'You'd best go to your room and rest.' Harriet Buckley picked up her spoon. 'I won't be needing you this afternoon.'

The old woman stared at her. 'I have a stick,' she said, 'I can walk well enough.'

Harriet Buckley, eating her soup, ignored her.

Mary Connor, after a full three minutes during which my mother served Allie her soup and another uneasy silence stretched, limped from the room.

I should have felt sorry for her. I might have too if it hadn't been for the look she gave me as she went through the door. It was full of a deranged resentment and promised vengeance to come. I'd no doubt she knew full well I was to deliver Harriet Buckley's letter. That she felt I was usurping her position.

It was for this I would be punished.

The house to which I delivered Harriet Buckley's letter was one of the grander homes in Merrion Square. It was hugely tall, with long windows. There was an air of cold wealth about it. My grandmother was forever saying how much finer such houses had been when Dublin had its own government. When the gentry and such had lived in them. They seemed to me stately enough still, occupied as they were by doctors and lawyers and the city's new rich.

It was three or four minutes before a maidservant opened the door, and then only wide enough for me to see the side of a wizened face.

'What is it you want?' she said.

I held out the letter. 'I'm to wait for a reply,' I said.

The woman looked at the envelope. She made no attempt to take it from me.

'Who is awaiting the reply?'

'Mrs Leonard Buckley.'

She opened the door. 'You may step inside.'

I stood into a hallway as big as the dining room in Haddington Road and stared at her. She gestured me to a polished wooden seat along a wall.

'Why is it you who are delivering this letter?' she demanded as, still staring, I sat down. I couldn't help it. 'Answer me.' She held out her hand for the envelope.

'Mary Connor has sprained her ankle,' I said at last.

'How bad is she?'

'Not so bad,' I said.

'Good. Don't leave that seat 'til I return.'

She walked with the same gliding motion as Mary Connor. She had the same parchment skin, ancient features, slate-coloured eyes. Apart from the fact that she was of more or less normal height she could have been her twin.

She was certainly her sister.

I waited on the seat in the hallway for fully five minutes. Even if I'd wanted to I'd have thought twice about venturing on to a timber floor so polished it was like glass. I spent the time studying a tapestry on the wall opposite. I was mesmerised by its green, woodland nymphs and the naked women they were chasing after.

I was unaware a woman had come into the hallway until she spoke to me. 'What is your business?' She wore an expression of surprised irritation on a face that was handsome, though certainly not young. Her black hair was turning grey and smoothly braided low on her neck. She was fashionable; her black dress had a bustle, a rare enough sight in Dublin where the crinoline was still popular.

'I'm awaiting a reply to a letter.' I stood, carefully, not trusting that glassy floor.

'Then you must remain here, I suppose.' Frowning, she looked a lot older. 'If you should come again please wait on the steps outside.'

I thought about leaving without the reply but thought again

and stayed where I was. Mary Connor's sister arrived almost immediately.

'To be given to Mrs Harriet Buckley *only*,' she said.

'Do you have any word for Mary Connor?'

'Why should I?'

'No reason.' Except, I thought, that she's your sister and is old and has damaged her ankle.

Merrion Square was busy, the day unpleasantly close when I stepped outside again. From the footpath I looked up at the long windows, scanning them for a face, a hand. A movement of any kind which might have given a clue as to who had written the letter in the envelope I was carrying.

There was nothing.

CHAPTER FIVE

Allie

There wasn't so much as a breeze the night of the dinner party celebrating my return. Even at eight o'clock, when the first of the guests arrived, the air in the streets was heavy and full of a dead heat.

Yet it might have been winter inside the house in Haddington Road. It was Mary Connor's way to keep windows and drapes tightly closed night and day. Doors too, except when of necessity they had to be opened. The result was a house so dark and cool it could have been a crypt. It was silent as a crypt too.

At seven o'clock, when Sarah lit the gaslights in the hall and the candles in the chandelier in the dining room, it became a glowing, golden crypt.

I was in my room when the first carriage drew up and halfway down the stairs when Sarah opened the door. My father, full of whiskey and jovial to the point of grovelling, appeared in the hallway to greet his guests.

I stayed where I was, in the shadows close to the wall, watching.

My father had asked me to 'practise my best manners' while my mother had reminded me that the occasion was for my benefit. Bess had refused to tell me if the man my parents wanted me to marry would be among the guests.

'Whether he is or not they are wasting their time,' I said, 'and mine.'

59

'Maybe they are,' Bess said, 'and maybe they aren't.'

My father, in the hallway, pumped the hand of a man his own height, age and girth, but with a much more whiskery face. He wore a long, loose jacket fastened with one button. I suppose it was all he could get to fit him.

'Maurice, my good man, come in, come in. We don't stand on ceremony here.' My father turned to the man's female companion. 'Jane too. You look resplendent, my dear.'

The short, plump girl of about my own age who curtsied in an old-fashioned way was anything but resplendent. She was sullen and pallid in a too-tight, too-heavy dress of quilted satin. An unseasonal Paisley shawl clutched about her shoulders didn't help matters.

'Thank you, Mr Buckley.' She peered about as if expecting ghouls to appear from the shadows. 'I'm delighted to be here.' She didn't look it.

'Alicia will be with us shortly,' my father boomed and beamed at her. 'She needs friends her own age now she's home and is impatient to meet you.'

This nonsense made me look at Sarah, standing composed and remote inside the door. Her eyes flickered towards the stairs and I knew that she knew I was there.

'Come along, come along . . .' My father led the way to the drawing room and my mother. 'Terrible weather we're having, terrible. The mood in the town is sulky, sulky and broody. Very broody indeed. We need a fall of rain to dampen things down. A heavy fall of rain would do the trick.' To Sarah he said, 'Tell Alicia our guests have arrived.'

It was a performance worthy of his calling as a publican but for a dinner party host it was, as the French say, *de trop*. Everyone had been very fond of my father the publican. So had I.

'Who are those people?' I hissed to Sarah as the drawing-room door closed behind them.

'You'll find out soon enough,' she grinned, 'the father's a doctor. He's been here before. His name's Maurice McDermott.

His resplendent daughter is called Jane—' A knocking on the front door interrupted her.

The woman who came in was followed by a much younger man, her son by the look of him. Both were tallish and black-haired, the woman turning grey. She looked about the hallway, ignoring Sarah's attempts to speak to her as she took her wrap while the man smiled and held on to a silver-topped cane.

'Don't trouble yourself,' his charm made up for his mother's lack, 'but you might go ahead and announce that Mrs Edith and Mr Ned Mulvey have arrived.'

I don't remember moving, or even taking a breath, but Ned Mulvey somehow knew I was on the stairs. He trailed behind Sarah and his mother and as he passed where I was looked directly up at me and raised silent, friendly eyebrows. Before going through the door he looked up again, this time giving a mocking salute. I felt a lot better about the dinner ahead.

I'd dressed carefully. This was partly a childish arrogance on my part: I wanted to outshine my mother with my Paris style and I wanted to appear travelled. The dress I wore was of blue silk with six flounces and a pointed bodice of a paler blue silk, opening in the front and showing a chemisette of tulle. I'd piled my hair high and allowed curls to tumble to the front.

The drawing room smelled of the roses my mother had insisted be put in vases everywhere. She herself, wearing a cream-coloured dress I thought too young for her, was languid in a chair.

My father was holding forth about a port he'd had delivered that day.

'Alicia,' he said, looking relieved when I came in, 'our guests are waiting to meet you.'

Sarah had been right about all of them.

The fat man was a Dr Maurice McDermott and up close he resembled a frog with whiskers. His mouth was full and wet and his eyes bulged. When he took my hand I stiffened but instead of his moist lips I felt only the shivery, hairy touch of his beard. I wondered if he had a wife and, if so, whether she too had something of the amphibian about her.

His daughter Jane widened her eye and stared when we were introduced and Mrs Edith Mulvey hoped, with a wintry smile, that I would not find Dublin boring after the French capital.

Her son, assured and sleeker than he'd appeared from the stairs, bowed and smiled and said he was delighted to meet me. He was at least thirty-five years old and, if he was the man my parents had chosen for me, I couldn't, for the life of me, see why he didn't already have a wife.

Then I looked again at his formidable mother and saw a very good reason.

In the dining room my own mother sat at one end of the oval table, my father at the other. The chandelier candles, twenty or more of them, threw a pool of light over the table and created shadows everywhere else.

Bess had prepared a banquet: cured salmon and prawn paste to begin with, beef olives with any amount of vegetables to follow. The wine jelly dessert, as events turned out, didn't make it to the table.

Sarah served with Mary Connor in hobbling attendance on a walking stick.

'You were sorry to leave Paris, Miss Buckley?' Ned Mulvey wore an evening suit with a green satin waistcoat and necktie. With his long face he would have made a good bird of prey at a fancy dress ball. He spoke from the other end of the table where he sat next to Jane McDermott.

His mother, with her starched face, sat opposite me. The hairy doctor sat beside me.

'I was,' I admitted. 'I grew to like it very much.'

'It would be difficult not to.' He looked at me thoughtfully. 'Its citizens are a sophisticated lot. Have the French nuns sent us home a worldly young woman?'

'Alicia was protected from the looseness of French society by the nuns,' my mother was sharp, 'she learned deportment and how to conduct herself.'

'Indeed she did,' Dr McDermott agreed, 'the nuns are to be congratulated.' He beamed, and blotted his lips delicately. 'They say that the Frenchman is a frog-eater and that horse flesh too is eaten for dinner . . .' He stopped when his daughter made a mew of protest. 'I forget myself. We medical men can be too robust by times.'

'You haven't been to Paris?' I said.

'To my shame I have not,' he was mournful, 'but I fully intend making a visit.'

'When?' His daughter was eating great amounts of Bess's bread. She kept her head down as she spoke. 'When will we go to Paris?'

'When the time is right,' her father replied vaguely.

'I would love to go to Paris.' Jane McDermott, her expression forlorn, looked up and into my eyes. 'Tell me what it's like there, please do.'

'It's much bigger than Dublin,' I thought for a moment, 'and the life there is different. In the evenings the boulevards from the Madeleine to the Bastille are crowded with promenaders. The restaurants are filled with people taking wine or coffee and reading their papers and there are seats under the trees. You find kiosks everywhere selling cigars and tobacco.'

I'd seen all of this while part of a procession of girls chaperoned by a nun.

'Maybe, when we go there, you could be a guide to my father and me.' Jane McDermott's round face was pretty when she smiled.

'All in the future, my dear,' Maurice McDermott said, 'we've only just met Miss Buckley.' He turned to me. 'How are you finding Dublin?'

'Hot,' I said, 'and smelly.'

Bess, who was leaving the room, frowned at me from the door.

'I suppose the city is both of those things, at the moment.' The doctor sighed. 'As long as animals are driven through the city the air will be malodorous. There will also be a subsequent danger to the health of the population.'

Ned Mulvey laughed. 'It's hot everywhere in the month of

August. It's hot in London, where I've lived for the past year, and it's hot in the French capital. By God, but it can smell too in Paris.'

'It's true that Paris smells,' I agreed, 'but not so much as Dublin.'

'I found the French people themselves had an overpowering smell about them,' my father said. My mother put a hand to her chest and shuddered.

Sarah collected our plates. As she left the room, Mary Connor clucking at her heels, my mother leaned towards Mrs Mulvey.

'Is it true Sir William Wilde has resumed giving parties at his home in Merrion Square?'

'He continues to entertain,' Edith Mulvey said, 'on Saturday afternoons there can be up to a hundred guests, all the worse for drink when they leave.'

'The man is shameless,' said my mother.

'The real shame is that a man who did what he did is allowed to continue the practice of medicine.' Dr McDermott looked severe.

Sarah and Bess had begun to serve the second course but the only appetite I had was for gossip. 'What did he do?' I asked.

'He disgraced the profession of medicine and should have been struck off.' Dr McDermott looked even more severe. 'It's a sign of the depraved times we live in that there was only myself and a few others prepared to speak against him.'

'But Sir William Wilde is known even in Paris as an inventor of medical instruments,' I protested, 'what has he done that was so terrible?'

'Nothing you need concern yourself with.' My mother was curt.

'It's easily enough explained.' Ned Mulvey played idly with his drinking glass. 'Sir William and Lady Wilde were brought to court by a Mary Travers on foot of a letter written by Lady Wilde. The jury found for Mary Travers and she was awarded a farthing in damages.'

This explained nothing, as far as I was concerned.

'What was the letter about?' I asked.

'It told of an unseemly relationship between Miss Travers and William Wilde,' Ned Mulvey sipped his wine, 'an adulterous relationship.'

My father, wine now gone down on top of the whiskey, gave a bellow and thumped the table with his fist. 'They were adulterers! The both of them should have been stoned in the streets. It was all over the town that Wilde had assaulted the Travers woman. The wonder of it is that he got away with his life and that not one of this city's great doctors stood to be counted against him.' He stopped and mopped his brow as Bess put his dinner in front of him.

'I may not be recognised as one of the great doctors,' Maurice McDermott sniffed, 'but I spoke against him to anyone who would listen. There was criticism of him too in the *Dublin Medical Press*. None of it made any difference. Wilde is a man who cultivates power, and uses it to effect.'

'Your stand against him is well known, Maurice,' my mother said, 'and both Leonard and I applaud you for it.'

'Wilde's wife is a Fenian.' Edith Mulvey's voice was low but everyone, her son included, turned to listen to her. 'She writes poems and tracts under the name Speranza, all in favour of the Fenian cause. She would be better occupied spending the time with her two small sons.'

'The Wildes are notorious. I've heard talk about them before but I didn't know they had children . . .' Jane McDermott leaned forward, so gaping and agog I wanted to shake her. She had no *savoir faire* at all.

'They've two small boys called William and Oscar,' Edith Mulvey snorted, 'who will, I'm sure, be no better than their parents when they're men. Example is all in the matter of raising children.'

She gave her son a sharp look which he ignored. His eyes were on mine and smiling. I smiled too and for a minute we were conspirators against parents and their ways.

'They are neighbours of yours?' Jane McDermott's mouth still gaped.

'Unfortunately, yes. But not friends.' Mrs Mulvey looked down the table at my father. 'You've bought yourself a fine house, Mr Buckley.' Her change of subject was adroit. My father was guaranteed to leap at a conversation about property.

'I got value for my money,' he said, 'the barracks being at this end of the road got me the place for half the price I'd have paid closer to Baggot Street.'

'The closeness of the barracks I would have thought rather unfortunate,' she said.

'Talking of the barracks,' Dr McDermott shook his head, 'there are more troops on the way, according to the papers, to deal with the Fenians and their bombing.'

'More troops!' My mother gave a groan. 'Be thankful, Edith, that it's only raucous neighbours you have. On this road we are forced to live with the sort of woman who follows soldiers. They're in the street every time one goes outside . . .' she sighed, '. . . and not only in the street. They're everywhere.'

Sarah, laying dessert bowls on the sideboard, almost dropped one. I tried to catch her eye as she straightened up but she was frowning and preoccupied.

'The *Freeman's Journal* said today that the government are withdrawing troops, sending them God knows where,' said Dr McDermott, 'it said they would be replacing them with twice the number. The Fenian leader James Stephens has been arrested in London and they've dispatched a troopship to Dublin this morning with the 71st Highland Light Infantry on board.'

'I'm all for them withdrawing troops from respectable neighbourhoods such as this,' my mother said. 'We've enough crime and its like to contend with without vulgar soldiery too.'

Dr McDermott nodded. 'Crime is on the increase every-where.' He turned to me. 'Even in Paris, they say. But,' he looked round the table, 'medical science may have found a solution. Research shows that crime, disease, even poverty, are the result of inherited tendencies. The population of this city, for instance, has more inherited diseases than could ever be transmitted by animals or otherwise. Eliminate these tendencies and you eliminate the ills in society.'

He speared a potato and ate, giving the rest of us time to digest what he'd said. I'd read about the ideas he'd put forward and knew they weren't so well founded as he seemed to think.

'You believe then that criminals inherit whatever it is makes them commit crimes?' I asked, 'and that diseases are inherited too? That the poor are poor because they're defective?'

'I do,' he answered enthusiastically. 'In time it is hoped to be able to eliminate such aberrations when they occur in the brain and to produce a hereditary pure people. Defectives would be locked up, not allowed to reproduce their own kind.'

'They should begin with the social slummers of the tenement buildings,' Edith Mulvey said. 'They're everywhere in this city and should be got rid of for social and sanitary reasons. They make it impossible for respectable people to live decent lives.' She signalled for water and Mary Connor, appearing from the shadows, filled her glass quite deftly while leaning on the stick.

My father, at the end of the table, looked greatly sobered. He was sitting upright, his hands flat on the table in front of him. Sarah was behind me, at the sideboard, her back to the table. She was standing very still.

All of this I saw very quickly and for what it was: the quiet before a storm. I started the thunder rolling myself.

'Got . . . rid . . . of . . .' I repeated Edith Mulvey's words slowly. 'Do you mean to send the people of the tenements to the countryside?'

She chewed on her food absently before answering. 'I doubt they would be made welcome in the countryside, though the air would no doubt do them good.' She raised her brows at Maurice McDermott. 'Does the medical profession not have a solution?'

'Sterilisation is the obvious answer since it would limit numbers.' He gave a small cough. 'It's the method agreed by most sane people.'

'I'm sane and I don't agree,' I said, 'and nor do a great many other sane people. What you're talking about is simply a theory being put about by a mad Italian and a few followers.'

'You have become too French in your thinking, Miss Buckley,' Dr McDermott wagged a reproving finger, 'and you have been protected from the horrors of life by loving parents.' This earned him a gracious smile from my mother. 'Dr Cesare Lombroso is not mad, though the French like to think so because they didn't come up with the idea themselves.' He laughed and his daughter laughed. The rest of the table smiled.

It was at that point Sarah whirled from the sideboard, her skirts making a sound like a sudden wind. She stepped into the light, behind Dr McDermott's chair.

'I am poor. I live in a tenement. Are you saying that society would be better off if myself and people like me were stopped from having children?' The doctor did not turn. 'Would you have my younger sister made barren? And my mother, who cooked for you tonight? They are poor too.'

Mary Connor made a clucking sound but Sarah waved her away. 'You're right that we inherit poverty. All belonging to me, seed, breed and generation, were born to poverty. But it was society made them poor, not their breeding and not their seed. The poor are kept poor and in their place and always have been. Now it seems that even their right to life is to be taken from them.'

God knows when she would have stopped if Mary Connor hadn't stood in front of her. I was standing myself by then, ready to support Sarah. Mary Connor tapped the floor, twice, with her walking stick.

'Sarah has forgotten her place,' she said, 'she will apologise and resume her duties.'

Sarah waved a dismissive hand at the housekeeper, knowing she'd gone too far, that there was no point now in holding her tongue. She was finished in Haddington Road and Mary Connor, realising she'd no more control over her, looked incandescent with rage. Had Sarah not been so close to Maurice McDermott's back I think she would have struck her with the stick.

'I want to know,' Sarah demanded, 'if Dr McDermott thinks I should be denied the right to have children because I'm poor.'

'You will leave the room, Sarah.' My mother's fingers drummed on the table, always a bad sign. 'Leave at once.'

'It wasn't my intention to cause offence in your home,' Dr McDermott spread his hands in a helpless gesture. 'But perhaps your maidservant should at least refrain from having children until she knows her place.' He still didn't turn to face Sarah.

'You are free to discuss anything you like at my dinner table,' my mother said, 'it is Sarah who has forgotten her place.'

'Sarah has a right to be offended. But I'm sure she'll accept that Dr McDermott didn't have her in mind when he gave his views.' My father was dignified, and sad: a peacemaker who knew he wasn't going to make anyone happy.

My mother's fingers beat faster on the table. 'Leave the room, Sarah, and send Bess to finish serving the meal.' She turned to her guests. 'She will not attend at table again in this house. None of you will ever again be faced with such rudeness, I promise you.'

'Dr McDermott has not answered my question,' Sarah said and I wondered how my mother could have forgotten how stubborn she was. 'He cannot even look one of those he would condemn in the face.'

'Come Sarah,' Mary Connor's hand gripped Sarah's arm, tightly, 'you can gather yourself together in the kitchen.'

Sarah looked down at her. 'He would have you made barren too, Mary Connor, if you were a younger woman.'

'Leave!' My mother stood. 'You are no longer in service here.' She was breathing hard. My father, at the other end of the table, got to his feet as well.

'There's no value in upsetting the whole dinner table on account of a misunderstanding,' he said, walking slowly to stand beside Sarah. 'The doctor was not talking about you, Sarah, nor about your mother or family. I want you now, for the sake of all the years I have known you and your family, to go to your mother in the kitchen.'

My mother joined her hands and appeared to be praying. Her knuckles were white and Sarah, looking at her, hesitated.

'Get out!' My mother's voice cracked, and I saw a flicker of triumph cross Sarah's face. We were in the eye of the storm. 'You are a trollop and I should never have allowed you inside my door.'

'Sticks and stones may break my bones, Harriet Buckley, but names will never hurt me,' Sarah was harsh, 'and you can never, at any rate, call me deceiving, or a betrayer. I'm going, but remember that I take a secret with me. Treat my mother well, and treat her fair, and that secret will stay with me.'

'Vixen!'

Mary Connor, either by design or because her stick slipped, pushed against Sarah who, instinctively moving backwards, collided with the sideboard. The wine jelly, in its bowl where she'd left it close to the edge, slid gently off the polished surface and crashed to the floor. It oozed slowly, spreading until it formed an almost perfect dark red circle.

The door opened and Bess stood there.

'The price of the crockery will come out of what pay you have coming to you, miss.' Mary Connor, her skirts splattered with jelly, made a clicking sound with her teeth. 'Your mother will clean up after you.'

Nobody moved, or spoke, as Sarah walked past her mother and through the door into the hallway. She tore the white cap from her head and threw it behind her as she went.

'Was there an accident?' Bess spoke to my father. She made no attempt to go after Sarah.

'Your daughter has left my employ,' my mother said as she sat down, 'and the dessert is ruined. We will have some sweetmeats with chocolate in its place.'

Bess looked at the pool of wine jelly. 'I'll see what I can do,' she said. Mary Connor hobbled out of the room after her.

'I've never cared for sweetmeats,' I said, 'so you will please excuse me.' I sidestepped the jelly and was in the hallway when my father, halfheartedly, called to me to come back.

Sarah had gone a good distance, almost to the corner with Northumberland Road, before I caught up with her. It was fully dark now, the gaslights all lit up and the people of the night in the streets. I saw two women I felt sure were prostitutes – their hair was long down their backs and they clung, giggling, to one another as they went along. A man, young and clean-shaven, said something to me as I hurried along and I know he thought me one of their profession. I called to Sarah but she didn't turn until I was just a couple of feet behind her.

'You should have stayed with your guests.' The walk had not improved her temper.

'What will you do?' I said, 'you're finished with my mother, that's for sure.'

'I know that poor eejit of a man was just making himself big, talking like that,' she said, 'but I couldn't keep quiet.'

'No, you couldn't. I'd have done the same thing myself.'

'I know you would,' she sighed and we began walking together, side by side, two of my steps to one of hers in the way we'd always had.

'It's nonsense, what he was saying, you know that,' I said.

'What little you know, Allie Buckley.' She was pitying. 'The poor are not human to such people. It could well happen.'

'Dr McDermott is a buffoon, you said so yourself,' I reminded her impatiently, 'and the Mulvey woman is evil and cold. I don't know why my parents have such people to their house.'

'The buffoon is the man they want you to marry,' Sarah said. I said nothing for a while. We walked more slowly, Sarah letting me take in what she'd revealed. The night air was clammy but I felt cold.

'The thought occurred to me but was so ridiculous I put it away,' I said at last. It was true. When the gauche Jane had asked about Paris I'd for a wild moment thought she saw me in the role of stepmother. I'd been right. No wonder she'd stared at me the evening long.

'So you attacked him on my account as much as on your own?'

'I suppose I did.'

'He's old and ugly as sin,' I said.

'He's rich,' said Sarah, 'and he's a widower. He wants a stepmother for his daughter.'

'Bess told you this?'

'She did. He's your mother's choice.'

'But my father went along with it. He would marry me off to that . . .' I couldn't find a word.

'Hairy toad,' Sarah supplied and though it wasn't so very funny we giggled, and then laughed, holding on to one another until tears ran down our cheeks and we had to lean over the wall of Mount Street bridge to gather ourselves together. The tears were joyless by then, a lament for the carefree days of our girlhoods, when nothing had been expected of us and we'd had all the time in the world to be together.

'It's not so funny as all that,' I said at last. Midges, millions of them, circled and massed above the murky canal waters. 'I thought my parents had Ned Mulvey in mind. He's handsome enough, at least, even if he's oldish and has that woman for a mother.'

'You're as well off without either one of them,' Sarah was sharp, 'you should marry for love, nothing less.'

'Is that what you intend doing?' I said.

'Nothing less.' Sarah, shrugging her shoulders and waving a hand, was too airy by half. I knew her. She was hiding something.

'You have a beau, haven't you?' I said. 'Is he someone in the Beggar's Bush Barracks?'

'He might be.' Sarah threw a stone into the canal. The ripples spread out and out but the midges went on massing and circling, undisturbed. I was hurt by her secrecy but said nothing. I did allow myself a sniff, however.

'I'll talk to you again,' Sarah said.

'When?' I demanded.

'Not with your father around, that's for certain,' Sarah said and I heard him then, his heavy footsteps pounding the road even before I turned. 'He'll collapse with his heart. You'd best go back to the house with him.'

'You've a lot of secrets,' I said quickly. 'What secret did you threaten my mother with?'

'Alicia, come home now, come back to the house with me.' My father's panting was like a steam engine, loud and puffing when he was still five feet away.

'I did what I could for you, Sarah, but you're on your own now.' When he stopped beside us the gasping breaths were full of whiskey and port. 'You were always pig-headed and look where it's got you.' To me he said, 'Come on home now, don't have me begging you.'

'I'm coming,' I said, 'but shouldn't Sarah come with us to wait for Bess at the house?'

'No. She can go on home for herself. It's early, not ten o'clock yet. I'll get a carriage for Bess when she's ready to go.'

'I wouldn't go back there anyway,' Sarah said.

'We have things to talk about,' I said, 'when will I see you?'

'I don't know,' she said.

I could see that she was tired, that her anger had exhausted her and, now it was gone, that she was beginning to face the ruinous reality of being without work.

'I have a present for you,' I said, 'I only this evening unpacked it. I've something for Bess too, and for Mary Ann. Presents for all of the Rooneys . . .'

I was aware of a pleading in my voice, but I was filled with a desperate fear that I might lose her. Even if she never told me her secrets I needed to be with her; I had no one else.

'Will I see you tomorrow?'

'Alicia,' my father urged me as he took my arm, 'come.'

'I don't know,' Sarah said again. She moved away.

'I'll come to Henrietta Street,' I called after her. She was running.

'You will not go to Henrietta Street,' my father said, 'Sarah is no longer a fitting companion for you. She has other friends now, at any rate.'

I looked at him. I had never seen him so weary, so unbearably pitiful.

'What happened tonight is for the good of everyone,' he said but I knew he didn't believe it. 'I've done all that I can to keep the peace. You and I will just have to go along with your mother and her plans from now on, Alicia. It's the only way.' He shook his head. 'You visiting Henrietta Street will not be part of her plans.'

Sarah, in the distance, was gone too far to hear.

CHAPTER SIX

Allie

It was two full days before I managed to get to Henrietta Street. During that time Mary Connor was a persistent guard dog, on my heels every time I turned round. My mother was an efficient warden too, piling me with sewing jobs which would have been Sarah's to do if she'd been there. They would help keep me occupied, she said. By the morning of the third day I'd had enough.

Close to midday my mother came into my bedroom; I'd gone there hoping she would leave me alone.

'Dr McDermott, you'll be pleased to hear, has been most understanding about your lapse of manners.' She paced as I sewed. When I didn't reply she sighed deeply. 'He's a good and kind man, Alicia, with a fine medical practice and an elegant home in Marlborough Road. He's got independent means, of course, and wouldn't practise medicine at all but for his devotion to his patients.' She paused. 'He's a lonely man too since his wife died.'

Still I said nothing, easy enough to do since I hadn't a desire in the world to talk about Dr Maurice McDermott. My mother gave an irritable tsk of her tongue and lifted the hem of the dress I was sewing. I was replacing the ribbons and lace which had been removed when it was washed.

'You'll be careful, won't you Alicia? You know how I dislike large or ugly stitching.'

I knew. 'I'll be careful,' I said. I would be slow too. She'd be lucky if I finished the dress in a week.

'Mary will be engaging a girl to take Sarah's place imme- diately,' my mother stood over me, 'she assures me there are countless numbers wanting to go into service. Sarah was difficult, impossible to train and a lazy worker. Mary will be able to run the household more efficiently with a smarter, more amenable girl.' She moved away, her impatience with me filling the room. 'Bess will need to smarten up too.' I looked up at her then. She was by my dressing table, uncorking my precious vial of attar of roses. The girls in the convent had given it to me when I left.

'Bess has always worked hard.'

I was immediately sorry I'd spoken; my mother was playing one of her games and I shouldn't have entered into it. There was a small smile about her mouth as she inhaled the perfume, deep and long, before answering.

'It'll be up to Mary to decide who works here from now on.' She slowly recorked the vial. 'It really has nothing to do with me whether Bess stays or goes.'

'The Rooneys would not survive without Bess's pay,' I said.

'True,' she agreed. She held up the vial. 'This scent is not at all suitable for a girl your age. I'll keep it for myself and buy you something more fitting.'

'It was a present . . .'

'A most inappropriate one.' She left with my perfume.

I dropped her dress as it was, ribbons and lace trailing. She could get the new girl, whoever she might be, to do her sewing for her. I was going to Henrietta Street to see Sarah.

Earlier that morning I'd been talking to Bess. I'd asked about Sarah. Bess was cross.

'Sarah's grand not a bother on her, it's Mary Ann I'm worried about. She's got a fever and a cough and I want to get home early and that Connor woman's laying more work on me than I can manage.'

We were in the scullery where Bess was scouring a copper pot; I'd never seen her use wood ash with such vigour.

'Is there something I can do?' I said.

'You can stop fighting your parents and accept what's in store for you and put childhood things behind you.' She took a breath. 'You and Sarah are women now and must live the lives of women and stop imagining you can be girls together again.'

'What do you mean?'

'That there are things expected of you now.'

'There are things I expect of myself,' I said, 'and marriage is not one of them.'

'What things?'

I didn't know what I wanted from my life, not yet. But I wasn't going to tell Bess that. 'Sarah is free to live her life as she chooses. I want to be free too,' I said.

'Sarah is not free.' Bess gave a sharp sigh. 'And you should be glad you have the chance of a life that promises comfort and ease.'

'I don't want comfort and ease. I want to feel alive. I want to feel of use.'

Bess put the pot away from her and sighed again. 'You'll learn,' she said.

That was when I decided I would go to Henrietta Street. My mother taking the vial merely copper-fastened the decision.

Getting away was made easy when, after lunch, my mother announced she was off to the milliner's in Baggot Street. Mary Connor, at around the same time, set to work on my mother's gloves, perfuming them for the winter.

I took a carriage and, when we got to Henrietta Street, asked the driver to wait at the end of the hill. It was only a couple of minutes' walk from there to the Rooney house and I wanted to get the feel of the place into my bones again.

It was more than two years since I'd been there and everything about the street filled me with nostalgia: the mansions which had seemed to me, as a child, like stone mountains with windows, the scrubbed steps with women sitting on them, the gaping doors, the screams of children playing a skipping game, the music made by an old man on a melodeon, the snarling of a cat, the curses of men.

It was the same, but it was different too. The houses looked more battered than I remembered, the children thinner and more knock-kneed, the women watchful and less friendly.

Halfway up the hill I realised they had always been like that, and that it was I who had changed.

My father's tenement was the last building before the few, still fine houses at the end of the street where the King's Inns were. Barristers and solicitors had offices and chambers in them.

The women on the steps bid me the time of day and followed me with their eyes as I passed into my father's house. Once inside it took me a full minute to adjust to the gloom before I could begin to climb the stairs. They were scrubbed white all the way to the Rooneys' door but the dark, red-painted walls were cracked and flaking and there was a stench I didn't want to put a name on.

The door was open. I gave a single, sharp knock and walked in.

Sarah was there, by a small range set into the wall where the huge old fireplace had been. She was filling a kettle from a bucket of drinking water.

'I came to see Mary Ann,' I said as she looked up, 'and to see you too.'

'Oh, Allie,' she said, and straightened. She was not her usual self. Her face was strained and under her eyes there were semi-circles of blue. All in two days. 'Mary Ann's not well at all,' she said, 'she's got worse since this morning.'

'I brought her a doll,' I said, 'from Paris.' It was all I could think to say.

'A French doll. She'll like that.' Sarah took my arm. 'I'm glad you're here. I'll make tea. I was making it anyway. Mary Ann's asleep. We'll go in to her in a while.' She nodded at an open door. 'She sleeps most of the time.'

'I've got something for you too, and perfume for Bess and your grandmother. I've a scarf for your father.'

I was embarrassed giving the presents to her, I had so much and she had so little and I didn't want her to think me above myself. I'd always needed to be careful with Sarah, who was very protective of her dignity. Once, when I'd given her a straw hat, she'd given it back to me after my mother became angry. Even though I'd refused to wear it she wouldn't take it back again.

But she loved the shawl. It was gossamer-fine, made of a filmy wool in a mauve colour that was all the rage in Paris and with purple tassels made of silk. Sarah draped it about herself in all sorts of ways before striking an elegant pose with it on one shoulder.

'I'll keep it 'til the day I die,' she said, 'and when I'm gone you may have it.'

'What if I die first?'

'Then I'll put it away and never wear it again,' she said.

I sat into an easy chair that was stuffed with horsehair and not a bit comfortable. The room was clean as it had always been but different in the way the street outside had been different. There was a bleakness about it that seemed new to me, a meagre look about the table, four chairs, stool, food cupboard and shelves that made up the furnishings.

But the goldfinch was a happy sight, sitting in his cage on the window ledge, chirping away. The Rooneys had always had a goldfinch; Bess said it was 'to add a bit of cheer'. One had fallen from the ledge once, into the street below. The cage had been smashed to bits but the bird had survived. I reminded Sarah.

'Poor Augustus,' she grinned, more like her old self, 'he was never the same after. That fellow's name is Nero. God knows why my father names them after the Roman emperors. Delusions of grandeur maybe.' She poked at the range to liven up the fire. When the kettle began to hum she put cups on the table. I walked around the room, telling her about my mother and Mary Connor, trying to feel at home in the way I'd used to.

The Rooneys' three rooms had been two very grand ones until they'd been divided up by my father. The room to the front was their parlour and kitchen, though I noticed there was a bed behind a curtain in a corner that hadn't been there before. The other had been made into two bedrooms. Under my feet the scrubbed timber floor was covered in part by worn rugs. The windowpanes were polished and shining.

'Where's Martha?' I said, 'And your father?'

'My grandmother went to the market early so she'll be hawking fruit in the town. My father should be here soon.'

Which meant Cristy Rooney was in the pub and would be home for his tea. No change there.

I stood by the range as Sarah poured and milked our tea. The range was the only heating and I remembered standing in the same spot as a child and shivering and thinking it was warmer in the street below, where at least you could face into the wind and be done with it. In that great room the draughts came from everywhere; viciously and sneakily from round the windows and door, roaring from the fireplace opening.

But that day it was warm, oppressively so for a child with a fever and cough.

'How did you get here?' Sarah put a cup of tea in front of me.

'I took a carriage. I have it waiting for me at the end of the hill.'

'Sarah . . .' Mary Ann's call was low and hoarse.

Both of us went to her.

There was one big, iron bed in the sick room. It was the same bed in which Sarah, her grandmother Martha and Mary Ann had always slept. The curtains were closed tight but an oil lamp burning on a shelf over Mary Ann's head made it easy to see her feverishly hot face. Her breathing came in shallow gasps and her eyes stayed closed when Sarah put a hand on her forehead.

'What is it, a croí, do you want something?' she asked.

'I'm burning, oh, Sarah, I'm burning.' Mary Ann's lips barely moved.

The few words exhausted her. There was hardly anything of her to be seen in the bed; she was a wraith with pale hair spread over the pillow. She'd always looked angelic but now her otherworldliness was frightening.

Sarah lifted her sister's head and spooned water between her parched lips. 'Allie's here,' she said, 'and she's brought you a doll from Paris.'

'A doll . . . let me see it then.' Mary Ann opened her eyes. Another thing about Mary Ann was that she'd always been a child to get her priorities right. She smiled and reached for the doll and immediately began to cough.

I thought her body would be torn asunder, it was so racking, so consuming of her small energies. Sarah held her and I could do nothing but watch and hold on to the useless, smiling doll.

'It's pneumonia and it'll have to take its course,' Sarah said. 'Nana spent this morning and last night putting hot mustard poultices on her chest. It did some good then but she's getting worse, I can feel it . . .' Her voice filled with panic as Mary Ann convulsed again in her arms. After a minute or so she gave a last, sighing cough and lay back on the pillows.

'I'll make another poultice and I need more camphorated oil,' Sarah said. 'Will you go to the apothecary, Allie? You remember him, in Capel Street?'

'Wouldn't it be better to get the doctor?'

'My mother and Nana have more faith in the apothecary than in ten doctors. They say he has the purest medicine of all. He makes up his own cures, right there in the shop.'

'But doctors are learning all the time, finding new cures. In Paris—'

'This is Dublin,' Sarah said, 'and there's no use you talking all the time about Paris. You saw the other night what passes for a doctor in this town. It's different with the apothecaries. The people are all the same to them. The apothecaries believe everyone deserves a chance to live. Will you go to Capel Street or do I have to go myself?'

I put the doll on the pillow before I left, close to Mary Ann's face so that she could see it when she opened her eyes. Its painted, porcelain face looked obscene next to that of the sick child.

The carriage got me to Capel Street in minutes. The apothecary was the same Bernard Wilmoth I could remember the people always going to, a slight, dark-faced, infinitely sympathetic man. He stood behind his three-foot-long maho-gany counter and I joined the queue of women with their demands for skin and stomach bottles, tablets for the kidneys, foot pastes. He had time for them all and when he couldn't find what he wanted on the narrow shelves behind him he got it from an unseen helper through a hatch in the end wall.

Though he did indeed seem to have a cure for everything I wasn't persuaded he would have one for Mary Ann. His cures were for the general ills of mankind; a good doctor would come to the little girl's bedside and examine and do what was best for her in particular.

Bernard Wilmoth gave me the measure of camphorated oil without question.

Sarah's grandmother Martha and her father were there when I got back to the rooms. Martha took the oil from me and put her hard, bony hand on my shoulder. 'You're a good child,' she smiled, 'though I suppose you think yourself a woman now.' It was from her grandmother that Sarah got her inches. Towering over me, her white hair in a long plait, she made me feel the child she still thought I was.

'I'm nearly twenty,' I said. 'the same age as Sarah.'

'Yes, indeed you are.' She took her hand away. 'I thought myself a woman and was married at that age. I'm hoping Sarah will have more sense.'

She said nothing about my parents' lack of sense in wanting to marry *me* off. Sarah pretended not to hear but her lips tightened and I knew she was angry, on her own account.

Martha went to Mary Ann and I sat for a minute at the table with Cristy Rooney.

'Cut me a piece of bread, there's a good girl.' He shook open the newspaper and I cut a couple of slices of Bess's soda bread.

If the world had been coming to an end Bess would still have baked bread. And if the world had been coming to an end Cristy Rooney would have read the paper and pretended it wasn't happening, just as he was now avoiding the reality of his sick daughter.

He had fine, curly hair and a wasted body with an empty trouser leg where once there had been a limb. He'd lost his courage, along with his leg, in the hour he'd lain half dead under fallen barrels in my father's public house. I was the one had found him and Sarah and Bess always said I saved his life. Cristy Rooney himself always said I'd have done him a bigger favour by leaving him to die. Drinking and reading the papers and shouting for a free Ireland had been his main occupations since then.

But he'd also become a tyrant to his family, tyranny being the refuge of the enfeebled and powerless. I knew well how quickly he could become full of a bitter fury so I put jam on his bread and listened while he read aloud what the paper had to say. The goldfinch, as if on purpose, sang the whole time.

'The Orange loyalists are up to their tricks again,' he said, 'raising no less than two flags on the steeple of the church in Clones last night. Says here one of them was orange and the other blue with William III on horseback in the centre. Not that it did them much good, they're floating there still but without a bit of notice being taken of them.'

'Neither the mustard poultice nor the oil is doing much good,' Martha reported as she came from the bedroom. 'Fill the kettle again, Sarah. We'll keep trying.'

'There'll be civil war and bloodshed before it's all over,' Cristy Rooney said, 'and even when it's over it won't be over, not by a long shot. All of the armies in the world won't make things right when the will of a people is put down and divided.'

'Let me get the doctor,' I urged, 'it can't do any harm and I've got the carriage outside.' I expected an argument. I got none.

'He might do some good,' said Martha and I knew then that Mary Ann's life was in danger. 'Go with her, Sarah, to the dispensary in Eccles Street. Get Dr Morgan. He's old but he's the best of them.'

'He could hardly get up the stairs when he came to Mrs Tarpey.'

Sarah's objection was for the sake of it. She was every bit as frightened as I was as she threw on the Paris shawl and we went down the stairs together. The women on the steps fell sympathetically silent as we went past them. Everyone knew everything in Henrietta Street.

The driver began muttering as he held open the carriage door for us. 'There's an unhealthy amount of sickness about,' he said as we climbed in, 'the Asiatic cholera, hundreds dead from that. My own nephew dead from the typhus. You'd wonder what plan God had for us all.'

'It's not religion we want from you but speed with the horses.' Sarah pulled the door shut with a snap.

We made Eccles Street in less than ten minutes and found the dispensary, not far from the new Mater Misericordiae hospital, in another two. It was after five o'clock by now and its shutters were closed up for the day. We stood side by side on the step as Sarah lifted a dull, unpolished brass knocker and let it drop, twice. We heard the sound resounding in the house behind. Then we heard a silence.

'God in Heaven, please don't let him be gone,' Sarah prayed with a passion that God didn't seem to hear. The silence stretched.

I lifted the knocker again, high. When it hit the door this time the sound echoed even in the street. Inside, someone began running down the stairs.

'Thank God,' said Sarah.

A young man in shirtsleeves and a waistcoat opened the door to us. He had bright red hair and a pale, plain, freckled face.

'The dispensary's closed,' he said. 'It opens at nine in the morning.'

'I want Dr Morgan,' Sarah said, 'my sister's sick. She needs a doctor. We've done all we can with her. She's ten years old.'

'In what way is she sick?'

'I'll tell all that to Dr Morgan.'

'I'm a doctor too. Tell me.' The way he said it there was no arguing with him.

'My grandmother says it's pneumonia. It began, without warning and with a fever, two days ago. Then a chill took over her body, rattling every bone, and then a cough. She's weak in her head and dizzy. She's too tired even to lift her head up.'

'Your grandmother could be right. I'll get my bag.'

'Dr Morgan is the one usually comes to Henrietta Street. We've got a carriage . . .'

'You'll need more than a carriage to coax Dr Morgan to Henrietta Street. He died two weeks ago. Of typhus.'

CHAPTER SEVEN

Allie

———◄━◆━►———

Dr Daniel Casey, sitting opposite myself and Sarah in the horse cab, folded his arms and looked out the window.

The driver had made no attempt to small-talk *him* about health matters, or anything else, as we climbed in. Daniel Casey wasn't the kind of man people were easily familiar with. He was remote and very serious.

'The patient is ten years old, you say?' he frowned fiercely as we moved off. I don't think he even knew he was doing it. He had sandy eyebrows and the green-grey eyes of a lot of red-haired people. They were his best feature.

'She will be eleven next month, with God's help.' Sarah tightened the Paris shawl about her shoulders.

'It's the help of man she needs now.' The doctor said this in a way that made me certain he was an atheist. I put the question to him.

'Do you believe there's a God who might help?' I said.

He unfolded his arms before answering. 'It's said that you only need scratch a man who practises medicine to find an atheist.' He half smiled. 'In my case this is true.'

I didn't ask him why; I didn't want to hear about nightmare suffering and the wonders of medical science. I had another question for him. 'What about women who practise medicine? Do they find it equally hard to believe in God?'

'I don't know. But the miracle of a woman being allowed to become a physician probably helps them have some faith.'

'There are still so few women in medicine then?'

'Hardly any at all,' he turned to Sarah. 'How was your sister when you left her?'

'Feverish. Full of a great lassitude. More and more racked by coughing.'

'Is there blood?'

'Blood?' Sarah straightened. 'There's no blood . . . that I've seen.'

'When she coughs does she bring up phlegm, or pus in which there's blood?'

'I haven't seen any blood,' Sarah repeated, 'but she complains of pain when she coughs.'

He didn't speak again until we reached Henrietta Street. Then he spoke only to excuse himself and rush ahead of us up the stairs. He had his jacket off and was bending over Mary Ann with a stethoscope to her chest when we arrived.

'He's young for a doctor.' Martha, filling the bedroom doorway with her large, bony frame and heavy skirts, made certain Dr Casey could hear her. She was annoyed at the older doctor for dying. 'Dr Morgan had no need for instruments. Like any good physician he could read a sick person with his hands.'

'He couldn't heal himself,' Bess said from the bedside, 'so be quiet and let this man do what he has to do.'

She stood as if praying while Daniel Casey gently examined Mary Ann. When he was finished he stroked the child's arm and told her she was brave and that he would come again tomorrow. She smiled, trusting him, her eyes like hot coals in her face.

'There's tea made,' Martha Rooney was gracious enough as he came out of the room, 'you'll have a cup?'

'I'll wash my hands if I may,' he said and Bess showed him the basin ready filled. The rooms had never seemed so clammy. It was as if the combined heat of the past months had slowly baked its way through the thick walls.

Cristy Rooney put his paper down when the doctor sat to the

88

table. 'You're young for a doctor,' he commented, echoing his mother.

'I'm fully qualified,' Daniel Casey took the tea Bess handed him,' and your daughter has pneumonia right enough. She'll need to be nursed, night and day, in just the way you've been doing. There will be a crisis on the ninth day.'

'We didn't need you to tell us she'd pneumonia or that she needs nursing,' Martha said, 'and the ninth-day crisis is well known to the people around here.'

'Yes. I'm sure it is. I'm sorry not to have better news for you.' He gulped the tea, then asked for a second cup. 'There are many things medical science has no cure for. This disease is one of them. Nature has its own way of dealing with it. I'll come every day. I live in rooms over the dispensary so you'll know where to get me if you need me at any time.'

'There are six days until the ninth day then we'll know.' Bess crossed herself. 'We must pray to God and His Blessed Mother that she'll be spared to us.' She took a breath. 'Prayer is all we have now.'

'Yes,' said Dr Casey, 'prayer will help.' His face, as he said this, was perfectly sincere. 'Children are resilient and make remarkable recoveries.'

'What's the point of the tube then, the stethoscope? Why did you put the child through that kind of thing for no reason?' Cristy Rooney looked angry. It was the only emotion he felt able to show.

'The stethoscope is a powerful assistant to diagnosing disease,' Dr Casey spoke as if in a classroom, 'it's an aid too in the detection of foreign bodies in the air passages. There's every chance she'll get well.'

'There's a fifty-fifty chance,' Cristy Rooney said.

Dusk was falling and the room filling with shadows as Martha lit a candle and put it on the table. She put another on a shelf. The shadows lengthened and the bird, which had been giving the odd warble until then, fell silent.

Dr Casey unrolled his sleeves and buttoned his shirt cuffs.

The candles highlighted the fine, dark red stubble on his chin and cheeks and made him look tired. He looked a lot less young too.

'Thank you for coming,' Bess said, 'my daughter and her friend will go to the end of the street with you.' She turned to me. 'You'd best go on home Allie they'll be wondering where you are I'll be at the house in the morning.' She stopped. 'Maybe you'd explain our situation to your father for me?'

'There's no need for you to come tomorrow . . .'

She patted my hand. 'There's every need so go on home now.' She stood. 'I'm going back in to Mary Ann.'

'I'll sit with you,' her husband said as he picked up his newspaper, 'for a while.'

Going down the stairs, with the doctor ahead of me and Sarah, I saw the quick, black shape of first one rat, then another, darting along the hallway to the back of the house. It was a relief to get out of there and into the noisy, gaslit street. We left Sarah on the footpath, both the doctor and myself promising to return next day, and walked towards Granby Row to get me a horse cab. Dr Casey said he preferred to walk back to his rooms over the dispensary.

'What will happen on the ninth day?' I asked.

'There will be a crisis during which the temperature shoots up.' He looked about, as if expecting a horse cab to appear from a doorway. 'The patient either dies, or miraculously gets better.'

I thought about Cristy Rooney's remark. 'So it's sure she has a fifty-fifty chance, if she lives that long . . .' I hesitated. 'Is there anything I can do?'

'There is little either of us can do, Miss Buckley.'

He didn't speak again until we got to Granby Row. There were a lot of people about but no cabs to be had and, because I found his silence unsettling, I said I would walk on alone to Rutland Square where I was sure to get one. When he insisted on coming with me I was irritated, and not one bit grateful. I couldn't stop him but I could do something about the silence; I began asking questions.

'You're not a Dublin man?' His accent told me this much.
'I'm from Galway.'

'Why did you choose to practise medicine?'

'My father was a general practitioner.'

It was like getting teeth from a hen but I persisted. 'Was? He doesn't practise any more?'

'He died of typhus. As Dr Morgan did.'

'Oh. I'm sorry. I didn't mean to . . . upset you. Or to pry.'

'It's all right. He died when I was a small boy.' His smile, when he looked down at me, made his face less plain. 'Contagious diseases are what you might call an occupational hazard for physicians.'

A silence, much worse than the first, stretched. It was that awkward time of evening when the horse cabs were all engaged taking people to the theatre and such and there still wasn't one to be seen. I embarked on a less personal line of questioning.

'What's your view of Sir William Wilde? Is he as scandalous as they say he is?'

'I have no view on Sir William Wilde's private life,' he said stiffly, 'he's a fine doctor and has made a special study of diseases of the ear.'

Pompous as well as overly serious, I thought. 'He hasn't been cast out by his peers then, on account of the scandal surrounding the court case he was involved in?'

'Certainly not.' He was curt. 'Do you think he should be?'

Touché, I thought, pleased I'd sparked a response. 'I don't know enough about the case to form a judgement. I've been away for two years. In Paris.'

'I studied medicine in Paris. At the Hôpital la Charité. I spent five years there.'

'Oh. I see.'

I felt flattened, and envious. He'd been in Paris far longer than I had. I wondered if he'd lived the life of reckless abandon student doctors were infamously known for there.

'What were you doing in Paris?' he asked.

'I was in a convent, learning deportment. I didn't really see that much of the city.'

'I spent my time there at the hospital,' he admitted. 'I was a conscientious student. I owe my education to a patron, a friend of my father's. I worried about letting him down and missed out on the life of the city.'

I might have known. 'You could become part of Dublin city life instead,' I said. It was then, just as he was beginning to talk, that a horse cab came alongside. Dr Casey helped me up and had closed the door before I sat down.

'Good night, Miss Buckley.' He strode away.

He didn't look back, once. He didn't give me a chance to even say good night or to thank him. He certainly hadn't been polished up much during his time in Paris; his manners were pure west of Ireland.

The days of Mary Ann's sickness lost their beginnings and endings and blurred into one long day as the week went on. I left Haddington Road early each morning and came back in the evening and in between sat with Mary Ann and read to her or sponged her small body to keep it cool. She got thinner. It was impossible to believe anyone could be so thin and live.

Sarah hardly left the rooms in that time and Martha Rooney went out only to sell what she could in the mornings. Sarah's father came and went and read his newspaper and looked at his daughter and went out again. Bess worked and sat with Mary Ann when she came home. Dr Daniel Casey came every day. Nobody talked about the ninth-day crisis. It was enough to be waiting for it.

My parents didn't try to stop me going to Henrietta Street. My father came once to visit Mary Ann but my mother said she felt too distressed to visit. Her distress didn't prevent her buying new gowns for herself, nor from telling me I'd fallen back into the ways and manners of Henrietta Street. On the seventh day of Mary Ann's illness she had Mary Connor purchase a basket of fruit for the sick child. Mary Ann couldn't eat any of it, of course, but Bess said it was the gesture that counted. I thought myself that my mother might have made a more useful gesture while she was at it. Money or bed linen would have served some purpose.

I was alone a lot with Sarah. Poor Mary Ann, whose terrible lethargy kept her asleep most of the time, was barely aware of us or our conversations. We talked a lot.

'I sometimes think Mary Ann getting sick like this is God's way of punishing me,' Sarah said one day.

'Punishing you for what?' I said.

'For my selfishness. For putting myself before everything. For my impurity. For offering myself to a man. For being without shame.'

We were by the window, the day dulled by a mist but still hot enough. I was standing, looking into the street below. Sarah was sitting on the sill, saying all of this as if reciting one of the litanies we'd been taught in national school.

'Who is the man?' I asked.

'He's a soldier. A corporal. His name is Jimmy Vance and he's stationed in Beggar's Bush Barracks. I met him early in the summer, one day in Baggot Street when I was shopping for provisions for your mother. He carried my basket for me.' She stopped, remembering. I waited a long time for her to go on. 'He made me laugh and he was so handsome in his uniform,' she said at last and looked up at me. 'How many women would you say have fallen in love with soldiers in uniform since the beginning of time?'

'Do you mean since they wore chain mail and plate armour?'

'Oh, Allie, please say you understand what I'm trying to tell you . . .' She was close to tears.

I made allowances for her weepy state, given how upset she was about Mary Ann. Tears, in my view, were for the great sadnesses in life and loving a soldier didn't seem to me something to cry about.

'You're telling me you love this Jimmy Vance,' I said as I pulled over the stool and sat facing her, 'and that you've given yourself to him, is that it?'

She didn't answer immediately, tracing the letter J with her finger on the window, thinking I don't know what thoughts. Now that she was confirming what I'd suspected I wasn't sure I wanted to know. Once it was spoken between us I would have to openly acknowledge another's right to her affections and loyalty. But it was too late to go back. She'd opened the gate herself and I would have to accept whatever came through.

'I haven't given myself to him in the sense that you mean,' she said at last, 'but I want to and do love him. He's—'

'Does he love you?' I drew the line at listening to the wonders of her soldier's personality and beauty.

'He says he does.'

'Has he asked you to marry him?'

'Not yet.'

'Do you think he will?'

'I know he will. He says he won't go to India without me.'

It was a minute before I could bring myself to go on with my questioning. For those sixty seconds I hated Jimmy Vance.

'You would go to India with him?'

'I would go to the planet Mars with him.'

'You might have to, when your father finds out.'

'Do you think I haven't thought of that?' She rubbed furiously at the letter she'd outlined in the window. 'He's the reason I keep Jimmy a secret.'

'Your grandmother won't be any easier,' I said, 'and your mother will wear holes in her knees, praying for you. But she won't oppose you.'

'I've thought of all that and I know my mother won't go against me. But her life will be made a misery by my father and grandmother. My father will rant night and day about me disgracing the family. My grandmother will be as bad but with her it'll be because she doesn't want me to marry anyone. Not in this country anyway. She wants me to go to America and find a life and a husband there. She says there's nothing in Ireland for someone like me and that there won't be for years to come.'

'Are you sure your Jimmy Vance is so very secret from them

all?' I said. 'I suspected that you had a man, after all. Your mother knows something is up and so does my father, I'm sure of it.'

'I know, I know all that . . .' Sarah looked at her hands in her lap. She'd made fists of them. 'There are suspicions all around me here in the street too. But suspicions are one thing and knowing's another.' Her voice hardened. 'Your mother knows. So does that malign midget Mary Connor.'

Her sudden anger was full of bitterness. Sarah Rooney had never been a bitter person. There was something here I didn't know about.

'If my mother knows why is she keeping your secret?' Loyalty and understanding were hardly the reasons.

'It would be better if you never knew what I'm going to tell you,' Sarah spoke slowly, 'but better still that you find out from me than . . . others.' Sarah told me then of her suspicions about my mother. About how she was certain she was betraying my father with another man.

'How do you know? Have you seen her with someone?'

'I know because I've seen her filled with the same fever as myself. And because she had me deliver a love letter for her.'

'Did you read it then?'

'I didn't need to.'

'Did you deliver it into the hand of a man who said he was my mother's lover?'

'No. I delivered it to a house and got a reply in minutes. The maid servant there was the living image of Mary Connor.'

'Which proves nothing. Certainly it doesn't prove that my mother has a lover.'

'I'm sure as anyone could be. She threatened to tell my father I was keeping company with a soldier if I told anyone about the letter.'

'That doesn't prove her letter was to a lover,' I spoke sharply, 'nor that she's an adulteress.'

The idea revolted and frightened me, mostly for my father's sake. I got off the stool and walked to the basin of water and began to rinse and wring the cloth I was using to sponge Mary Ann.

'The letter could have been about any number of things. She's most likely spending my father's money without telling him.'

I heard the pleading in my voice; I didn't want to know what Sarah was telling me. I didn't want to hear proof, if there was any, that my mother was betraying my unhappy, besotted father. He would have nothing to live for if it were true.

Sarah came and stood beside me. 'You're right. I could be wrong.' She put her hand on my shoulder, 'I'm sorry to have upset you.' When I didn't turn from the basin she went on, coaxing a little. 'Jimmy has a friend, another private. His name is John Marsh. Maybe, some afternoon, we could all go to a tea house together . . .'

I turned, shaking my head, saying no, just as Mary Ann called from the bedroom. There was something I had to say and I did, quickly.

'Do you really believe God is punishing you? Don't you think the one suffering here is Mary Ann? Your selfishness is in thinking her pain is your pain. If God is doing anything by making Mary Ann sick he's showing us there is no justice.'

'Is that the kind of God you believe in now?'

'I don't know what sort of God I believe in any more,' I said. She looked so worried I smiled and said, 'That's the God's honest truth.' She smiled too.

The change in Mary Ann came slowly. The illness exhausted her more and more but the terrible tiredness stopped her being fretful. By the seventh day she was more emaciated than ever but strangely calm. The flush had gone from her face and she was pale as the pillow. Except for her lips. Her lips were grey.

That was the day, in the late afternoon, that I asked Dr Daniel Casey how we would know when the crisis had arrived. I whispered the question, standing close to him by the side of Mary Ann's bed. He smelled of carbolic soap.

'We'll know,' he said.

I didn't ask him again.

By the ninth day Mary Ann had become the same grey as her

lips all over. The priest came and administered Extreme Unction and the rooms were filled with the smell of the oils and incense. Death seemed very close.

'I've seen worse cases turn around and get well,' Martha said.

She was scrubbing the floorboards; she'd scrubbed them three times already that week. Bess, who that day, and for the first time, hadn't gone to Haddington Road, knelt by her daughter's bed with her rosary beads. Mary Ann's father sat at the table with a single bottle of stout, sipping. It never seemed to empty.

Sarah lit the oil lamp and candles and the smell of paraffin and wax was added to that of the sacred oils. Mary Ann's breathing became so shallow it was at times hard to detect.

Daniel Casey listened to her lungs and then cleared the room of everyone but himself and her mother. 'Her temperature is rising and she needs to be able to breathe. You're not doing her any good,' he said, 'nor yourselves either.'

I was by the window. The goldfinch was singing and in the street below some men were playing a tossing game when Bess's voice called, 'She's going from us.'

I went to the door of the bedroom with Sarah. Martha, behind us, stopped scrubbing. Mary Ann's breathing pattern had changed. Deep breaths were followed by shallow ones as she fought for life.

'Prayers are all we have now,' said Bess and everyone prayed, silently and together. The doctor, helplessly watching his patient, was expressionless. He could very well have been praying too: it would have been hard not to, even for an atheist. After a while Mary Ann, exhausted, stopped breathing and didn't start again.

'We can pray for her immortal soul now,' Bess said.

Mary Ann was laid out in her first communion dress and veil on the bed in which she had died. Bess made a chapel of her child's hands and entwined her fingers with white rosary beads. The neighbours came and draped white sheets over the walls of the room and hung black bows across them and dipped a quill in holy water and sprinkled Mary Ann's dead body. Then everyone prayed, the rooms and landing filled with men, women and children. Most people wept too.

When the prayers were over, and the adults were drinking tea, four of Mary Ann's small friends came to Bess. The biggest of them, a boy of about twelve with a box in his hand, was pushed forward by the girls.

'We made a collection,' he said, 'it's in there. It's for you to buy her a wreath of flowers.'

'Thank you, Joseph.' Bess took the box.

'We saw Mary Ann,' one of the small girls said, 'there's a new star in the sky. It's her. She's up there already.'

'I know she is,' said Bess, 'I know she is.'

After a while the men, and some of the women, left for the pub with Cristy Rooney. Only Bess and Martha and a couple of keening women stayed on in the room where Mary Ann lay dead.

I sat at the table with Sarah and Dr Daniel Casey.

'I should have been able to do something for her.' He put his head in his hands. 'There should be a cure for pneumonia. It shouldn't be able to take a young life like that.'

'You did all you could, all that you knew how.' Sarah's voice was flat. 'No one expected you to save her from that disease. We're grateful to you for being here.'

He was stubbornly miserable. 'It is up to those of us privileged to be physicians to conquer disease . . .'

There was a pomposity in this I couldn't abide. I cut him short. 'You're only a doctor,' I said, 'you're not God Almighty. Anguishing like this won't do you, or anyone else, any good.'

'Forgive me.' He flushed. 'I shouldn't have troubled you with my conscience.' He stood. 'It's time I was going . . .' He spoke stiffly and I wished I'd kept my too-sharp tongue to myself. I'd offended him. 'You should get some sleep, all of you,' he said. 'Sleep is essential for life and health. Studies show that physical and mental disturbances occur after even a few days of sleeplessness.' He stopped, aware of Sarah and me staring at him. 'Forgive me again. I can only offer a lack of sleep as an excuse for my insensitivity.'

'There'll be no sleep here tonight,' Sarah said. 'Mary Ann is sleeping enough for all of us.'

I left with Dr Casey. My parents would have to be told of Mary Ann's death and my father asked to pay for her funeral.

Lack of sleep seemed to have the effect of making the doctor more talkative. He discussed the mist, circling us like damp silk, the approach of autumn, the fact that Victor Hugo was reported to have asked for £20,000 for his new novel.

'It's to be called *Ninety-three* and will come out in ten volumes. There are fears that the French government will stop it being published and sold in France.'

'They will bury Mary Ann in Glasnevin cemetery,' I said, 'in the grave with her brother. He died when he was a year old. From diphtheria.'

'I didn't know . . .'

'How could you? I hardly remember myself. When Mary Ann came along she replaced him, in a way.'

'I see, and now she is dead too.' He hesitated. 'I wouldn't like you to think me insensitive, Miss Buckley.' He stopped again, clearing his throat and searching for words. 'It's in my manner, rather than the reality of how I am. An unfortunate character-istic.'

'Maybe it's that you're too sensitive,' I said.

'No. It's not that. It's that I'm a rationalist.' He seemed proud of this.

'Does that mean you can't be sensitive? Don't rationalists have feelings?'

'Yes, of course they do. But as a rationalist I believe reason is the only source of truth and so can't be governed by my feelings.'

'You'll do well as a doctor then,' I said.

He missed the irony in this and said, with some passion, that he hoped he would since doctoring was to be his life's work. I was tired and saved from hearing more by the almost immediate arrival of a horse cab. He put me into it and this time stood in the road watching until we spun round a bend and into Rutland Square.

My father paid for Mary Ann's funeral. I didn't have to ask him. He left Haddington Road as soon as I got home the evening of her death and went straight to Henrietta Street. My mother didn't go with him, saying her fear of death would make a visit too upsetting for both herself and the Rooneys. It was the first I'd heard of my mother having a fear of death.

Though the month of September was more than half over the day of Mary Ann's funeral was bright and sunny. My father and I went to the church and graveside but my mother stayed outside the cemetery in Glasnevin in the elegant hired carriage.

Daniel Casey arrived in a fluster as the priest finished the graveside prayers and was shaking the holy water. He stood beside my father and myself as the gravediggers threw the first shovels full of earth on to the coffin. Cristy Rooney helped them. Sarah, her mother and grandmother all threw down some earth too.

While the grave slowly filled I introduced Dr Casey to my father.

'Your daughter has a skill and patience with the sick,' he said. He'd never said this to me and I was glad to hear it now. The news didn't greatly impress my father, however.

'I'd prefer if she applied her skill and patience elsewhere,' he said.

Sarah joined us then, in such bad temper that my father had the wisdom to say nothing more. Her grief had taken the form of a great fury at the ill-health and poverty which took so many children's lives. The grave was all but filled in when she said, with the bitterness I'd seen growing in her, 'Doctors don't need sterilisation to do away with the poor. Poverty and sickness will do it for them. It kills children and the women who bear too many of them. It kills the men who father the children when they can't get work and become diseased . . .' She stopped and I put my arm through hers.

'I'm sorry I couldn't do more for your sister,' Daniel Casey said stiffly, 'and I am not in favour of harming the poor.'

'I didn't mean to criticise you,' Sarah assured him quickly, 'I'd another doctor in mind.' She glared at my father who kept his gaze on the grave and his mouth shut. 'I was thinking of remarks made by a Dr Maurice McDermott, who is a friend of Mr Buckley's.'

'I've met Dr McDermott and don't share his views on many subjects.' Daniel Casey shrugged. 'He's not a notably good physician either.'

'He's a fine doctor,' my father contradicted him, 'and well thought of. I wouldn't be considering him as a husband for my daughter otherwise.'

'Forgive me.' Dr Casey's embarrassment was profound, his face an immediate and unbecoming pink. 'I'd no idea . . . I wouldn't have given my views . . .' He turned to me. 'I wouldn't have been so insensitive as to insult your fiancé.'

He was gone before I could assure him that he'd done nothing of the sort. I felt as if a net was closing in around me, as if my life and choices were being relentlessly taken from me. I turned on my father. I might have been less harsh if I hadn't been so distressed about Mary Ann.

'You may be considering Dr McDermott as a husband for me, Father, but I'm doing nothing of the sort myself,' I said. 'I will marry whom I like and when I like and not at all if it doesn't suit me.

'Enough is enough, Alicia.' He kept his voice low for the sake of Sarah and those around. 'You've gone too far with having your own way. Your gallivanting days are over. We will go now.' He held out his arm. I didn't take it. 'You've done all that you can here and in Henrietta Street. I want you to leave here now and come home with your mother and me in the carriage.' He nodded to Sarah. 'Alicia will be busy for the next while. Good day to you.'

Rather than cause a row I walked ahead of him to the carriage. Before getting inside I looked back at Sarah. She was standing by the grave with her head bowed and didn't see me as I lifted my hand in farewell. I climbed into the carriage and sat opposite my mother and felt the full weight of her oppressive discontent.

I would feel it a lot more in the weeks to come.

CHAPTER EIGHT

Sarah

My anger at a world which gave no chance to the poor, at a disease which took the innocent, at myself because I could do nothing, lasted for nearly a week after Mary Ann's death. Then it turned to sorrow, and I wept.

I wept for the times I could have been kinder to my sister, for the times she had been unhappy, for the pain she had endured while dying.

I wept most of all for the life she would never have.

When I wasn't weeping I saw her in every group of playing children in the streets and turned, full of momentary and stupid forgetfulness, whenever I heard the cry of a young girl. She was of course never with them or one of them. She never would be again.

My father went to the pubs and my mother worked to keep him there. That, at least, was how it seemed: she worked and he drank and very little was said by either of them. My grandmother worked too, selling fruit in the streets. But her face was like flint and people avoided her. She came home most days with the basket still less than half empty.

I made love with Jimmy Vance. It seemed more than ever the right thing to do: with death so quick to take life there was no time to be wasted. I wanted to feel alive and I wanted Jimmy Vance.

There was something else at work in me too but it would be a long time before I could admit it to myself.

'I didn't know what had happened to you,' Jimmy said when we met. Mary Ann had been dead a week. 'I thought maybe you were ill, or that you'd got work in some forbidden, distant part of the town.'

He held me tight against him as we walked along. When I'd arrived to meet him, at the lower end of the canal to start our stroll along the towpath, he'd looked so glad to see me I'd almost wept with the pleasure of it.

I was close to tears a lot of the time and wasn't proud of the fact. Tears were for the idle, my mother said, and she was right. If I'd had work to do I wouldn't have had half so much time for them.

'Did it never occur to you that I might have tired of you?' I managed to joke.

'No. Any more than it occurred to me that your sister might be dying. I'm sorry, Sarah, for you and for your family.' There was nothing I could say to this so he said, for the both of us, 'It's hard to accept that the young can be taken.'

We moved slowly along and he listened while I spoke of Mary Ann. I told him the sort of person she'd been, how full of fun. I described the pure gold colour of her hair, and her sweet singing voice. I told him the story of how, one day, she'd rolled under a carriage and come out the other side without a scratch.

'Everyone said she'd a charmed life,' I said, 'but they were wrong. She had the bad luck to be born poor and of the labouring classes.'

'She could be lucky and a member of the labouring classes too,' Jimmy said. 'It's not unknown.'

'It's rare enough to be almost unknown,' I said, 'though I'll grant you that bad luck doesn't only follow the poor. My friend Allie, for all her father's money, has the meanest of existences.'

'What's happened to her now?'

The way he said this I'd the feeling, and not for the first time, that he didn't care for Allie. Since he'd never met her it had to be something I'd said about her. Either that or he was jealous on account of my friendship with her, as she was of mine with him. All of that would end, I felt sure, once they met.

'She's being kept like a prisoner in the Haddington Road house by her parents and that dwarf of a housekeeper, Mary Connor. Her mother and father have chosen a husband for her, a doctor with a face like a bulldog and a daughter my age.' I pictured him and shivered, despite the heat. 'The poor man can't help how he looks though he could do with improving his character. It badly needs it. But he's rich, so it's unlikely he'll change.'

'Will your friend marry him?'

'No. Not if she lives to be a hundred. But her parents will persist and she will persist in saying no and . . .' I stopped and we looked together into the waters of the canal. 'I don't know what will happen, what will become of her. Any more than she does herself.'

The canal didn't have answers, no matter how long I looked. It didn't have the cleanest or most beautiful of waters either. But it was still and quiet and we had the towpath to ourselves.

'I worry about her,' I said. 'I've seen so little of her since she came home and nothing at all of her this last week.'

'She'll be all right. Women like your friend have a way of rising, like the phoenix, from setbacks,' Jimmy said.

'You dislike her,' I said, 'and without even meeting her. Why?'

'I neither like nor dislike her. Judging from all you've said about her, though, she seems to me someone who was a spoilt child and is now a spoilt woman.'

'She's nothing of the sort.' I shook my head.

'You talk a lot about her, Sarah.' He looked embarrassed.

I knew then that I was right and that the real reason he'd taken against Allie had to do with jealousy. He worried that she would occupy too much of my time and that he would see less of me.

'She'll never come between us,' I said. He went on staring into the water and I squeezed his hand. 'But she will always be my friend. In a strange way she's a part of me, the closest I have to a sister now Mary Ann is dead.'

He didn't answer for a while. The reeds around us were high as our waists and burned brown with the sun. They framed our reflections in the water, the blue sky above like a curtain behind us. I thought how nice it would have been for a photographer to make a picture of what would in minutes be a memory.

'I will like her because you do,' Jimmy said at last. He pulled me close again. 'You stayed away too long. You should have come to me sooner.'

'You said you would find a place for us to be alone,' I reminded him. 'Did you keep your promise?'

'I did.' He hesitated. 'It's not a palace but it's far enough from here, and from your home, for us not to be seen together . . .'

'Can we go there now?'

Jimmy had found a boarding house by Kingsbridge railway station where rooms could be rented for the day, or for an afternoon or night if couples could be together that long. It was not a palace, as he'd said, but for a house which made its money from illicit love it had a surprising air of decency about it.

Maybe it mirrored the attitude of the woman who took Jimmy's money and gave us the key to our room. She was round and pleasant, in a dark green dress with a lace collar. She said she hoped we would like the room and made what we were about to do seem the most natural thing in the world. Which of course it was, if nature was the only law to be obeyed.

Jimmy stood in the middle of the room, looking around. He had his hands in his pockets and looked carelessly handsome and devil-may-care. I knew he was as nervous as I was.

'Is it all right?' he said and I looked slowly around, nodding.

The brass bedstead had a dark blue cover and the walls were another, paler, blue. There was a wardrobe, two easy chairs and a standing mirror. Over the bed hung a picture of a bird.

It was perfect.

I went to the window and gazed across to where the river Liffey was making its way lazily out of the town. The room looked out on the railway station too. I'm sure it was because I was about to become a woman that I all at once and clearly recalled an incident from my girlhood with Allie.

We could have been no more than nine or ten years old. A misguided search for Sandymount Strand had ended at the back of the very same station. We'd been set upon there by boys and for days afterwards Allie had accused me of deserting her when all I'd done was run for help. How she could have believed I would leave her I don't know, unless it had to do with her mother's cruelty making her uncertain about affection in others. Even about how much I cared for her. In any event, our friendship had been made stronger by our understanding of that day. That and the fact too that my father owed her his life, whatever its quality. Only months after our excitement in the train sheds Allie, hearing a sound, had gone fearlessly down to the cellar in her father's pub. Finding my poor father pinned under fallen barrels she'd held the door to stop any more from tumbling on to him. Then she'd screamed like a tinker until help came. This deed, she said later, made her and me 'equal in the matter of helping one another'. I would always be grateful to her. My father's feelings were another matter.

Jimmy, coming to stand behind me, put thoughts of the past out of my head. The railway station, that day, was full of the bustle of men and women coming and going, of carriages and omnibuses lined up outside and a great many soldiers.

'Where are they sending the soldiers?' I asked.

I hadn't asked him again about India. I didn't care where the soldiers by the station were being sent. The question was to fill the silence. Because I didn't know what else to say, now we were alone.

'They're on their way to the Curragh,' Jimmy put a hand on my shoulder, 'they're no concern of ours.' With his other hand he closed the curtains. They were a dark saffron colour and the late September sun, shining through them, made the room golden. 'I love you, Sarah.' He turned me to face him and I traced the outline of his mouth with my finger.

'I'm afraid,' I said.

'Don't be,' he kissed me on the forehead. 'Not of me.'

He was trembling, a little, when he pulled me against him and put his face in my hair. He pulled the pins out with his teeth and as it fell loose spread it across my shoulders. 'Your black curls were the first thing I noticed about you,' he said, 'and after that your face.'

'I noticed you because you were the tallest of the soldiers in the street,' I said, 'and I gave you my basket because I was tired.'

All true. It was only as we walked, and he talked in his gentle way, that I'd taken account of other things about him.

'I want to see your hair against your skin,' Jimmy said.

I stood very still as he unbuttoned my dress, slowly because his fingers were awkward and the buttons small. I wanted to help him, but didn't. There was an exquisite joy in the waiting. When my dress lay on the floor about my feet we took the rest of my clothes off together, everything until we came to my stockings. I sat on one of the easy chairs and Jimmy unbuttoned my boots and then peeled off my stockings myself.

When I was naked he laid me on the bed. He looked at me all the time as he took off his uniform and boots. He stood naked himself, and smiling, before he came and lay beside me on the bed.

'Oh, God,' I whispered though I didn't want God anywhere near me, or even in my thoughts. I closed my eyes and covered myself with my hands.

'Please don't be afraid,' Jimmy said again. 'Look at me, Sarah.'

I opened my eyes and saw how close his were, how burning. He kissed me and his hands moved over my back, down to my waist. He turned me so that I lay again on my back.

'I'm not afraid now,' I said.

He opened my legs and put his fingers there and I gave a small cry, an instinctive protest.

'It will be good,' Jimmy whispered into my neck. His breath was hot.

I made no more protests after that. I heard sounds and words

I knew came from me but made no sense and others, distant and urgent, coming from Jimmy. When he climbed on top of me I was ready for him and held him to me in a frenzy of fear that he might stop. I cried out and he covered my mouth with his and moved himself between my legs, at last.

He came into me slowly and my body, with a will and rhythm of its own, did all it could to make things fine and wonderful for him. My back arched and my legs opened wider and he began to move in me. Thoughts that had nothing to do with that room and Jimmy flashed across my mind, my whole life until then going through my head in moving pictures. Jimmy moved faster inside me and I called his name and rose with him and felt a great swell inside me as stars exploded in a dark red sky.

When I opened my eyes and turned to look at him Jimmy was lying on his back staring at the ceiling. He seemed as far away from me as he'd seemed close a minute before.

I said his name, 'Jimmy?' and he turned to me and smiled and touched my face. Then he lay quietly beside me again.

'It will never be as it was between us,' I said, 'are you sorry?'

'Not sorry for what has happened.' He sat up, leaning on his elbow, and looked down at me. I was all at once conscious of my nakedness and pulled the bed cover about myself. 'Sorry that I must go back to Beggar's Bush Barracks and leave you. Sorry that we can't be together all of the time.'

'That'll come,' I said. 'For today we have this room.'

'We have,' he laughed and gathered me up, bed cover and all, and lifted me off the bed and began to dance. He was a good dancer. We made our own music and danced about the room until we fell, dizzy and breathless and ready to make love again, on to the bed.

'I'm alive, and so glad of it,' I said as we lay, warm and close, afterwards. I felt no shame, and no guilt. Not then.

Jimmy grinned. 'I'm glad you're alive too,' he said.

He touched me gently all over. He made me feel, for those hours, as if I was precious and wonderful.

We would spend other afternoons in that boarding-house

room, would even come to think of it as our own place. But none would be so perfect or wonderful as that first time.

The golden glow had gone and the room become dark before we left. We didn't notice.

I went looking for work. I knocked on the doors of the big houses in Mountjoy Square and Gardiner Street, and further away too. Without references no one was willing to take me on. There were plenty of girls and women with good references willing and able to go into service. My mother, and her work for the Buckleys in Haddington Road, was supporting myself, my father and, for the most part, my grandmother too.

I decided to pawn the shawl Allie had given me. I'd nothing else of value and it would only be for a week, until I got work. I was certain another few days would turn up something. I went to the pawnshop on a Monday, the usual day for putting things into hock. The way it went was that women pawned what they had on Monday, reclaimed them on Saturday, enjoyed them on Sunday and put them back in again on Monday.

The line of waiting women that morning was long. You'd have thought they were moving home there were so many framed photographs and mirrors, bed linen and curtains being carried between them.

Beezy Ryan was there, leaning against the wall, the smoke from a cigarette circling her head. She was the only woman I knew smoked her tobacco in a cigarette. She said a soldier home from the Crimea had shown her how. The other women used pipes. Beezy was not someone I'd have expected to see in the queue for the pawnshop. She was wearing a green satin dress that would have suited the evening better. She beckoned me to join her as I came along.

'That's a lovely thing.' She fingered the shawl. 'Pity you have to do without it.'

'It's only for the week.' I moved out of the way of the cigarette smoke. There was a lot of space around Beezy where the other women had moved away too. Some of them didn't want to appear to be in the company of a whore but others, like myself, weren't fond of the smoke and smell of the tobacco. 'Allie Buckley brought it to me from Paris.' I opened out the shawl so she could see the colours.

'That was nice of her.' Beezy shrugged, indifferent to the shawl immediately I mentioned Allie's name. She'd never liked Allie much, thinking her above herself. I folded the shawl.

'I've never seen you at the pawn before,' I said, 'business in North King Street must still be slow.'

Beezy laughed. 'You're the only one to say what the rest of them here are thinking,' she said, 'they'd prefer to whisper and watch and hope for my downfall.' She pulled on the cigarette and blew smoke into the air and looked up and down the line of women. A few returned her stare but most ignored her. Going into battle with Beezy wasn't a good idea.

'They're hoping, some of this lot, that I'm finished, that I can't pay the rent. There's good, Catholic Christians among them that would would rather see my girls in the workhouse than earning an honest penny in a kip house.' She spoke loudly and her voice carried. She seemed to me sober but it was often hard to tell with Beezy. Drunk or sober she was much the same person.

'That's not an answer to my question,' I said. Beezy laughed again.

'I'm here on an errand of mercy.' She held up a ticket, the rings on her fingers flashing all colours. 'I've a new girl up at the house. Mary Adams is her name and the poor creature was left in a bad way by the brute she married. She'll be all right now though, now she's with me.' She shook her head, resignedly. 'I'm here to get her wedding ring. She pawned it to get away from him and now she wants it back.' She sighed. 'The vagaries of womankind never cease to amaze me, but if it'll give her peace she might as well have it.'

We spoke of Mary Ann, but not for long since neither one of us could be trusted to keep going without tears. Beezy had always been kind to my sister, as she was kind to all the children of the neighbourhood. She'd given Mary Ann a white fur muff on her Holy Communion day and Mary Ann had treasured it always.

It was after I told Beezy about how she'd treasured the muff that we fell silent, inching through the door of the pawnshop as our turn arrived.

Alfie Toole, the pawnbroker, dealt with business quickly and the crowd of women had thinned a lot as we came close to the counter. Alfie was fair and my mother never went to anyone else. It was said that the rooms over the pawn were stuffed to the rafters with unclaimed goods, the floors ready to collapse under the weight. Alfie himself never seemed worried by the prospect. He was always good-humoured and gave a fair price. Maybe the story about the overfilled rooms was a story, nothing more.

'You lost your position with the Buckleys,' Beezy said as the woman ahead of us began to haggle with Alfie, 'your mother was telling me. I was sorry to hear it. It's the devil's own work, or it could be God's curse, but it's a fact anyhow that troubles never come singly.' She raised her pencilled eyebrows. 'Of course, if you kept your mouth shut it might never have happened.'

'Maybe you could give me a few lessons, Beezy, on how to be discreet,' I said.

'You'd be a bad pupil,' she said and shrugged, 'you're too fond of your own opinions.' She didn't seem to be enjoying the cigarette much, squinting at me through the smoke and coughing every so often. 'Maybe I've something to give you would be more useful . . .' Beezy fell silent.

Alfie, examining the shoes the woman ahead of us had given him, wasn't prepared to give her the price she wanted. Beezy was thoughtful as we waited.

'What is it you might give me?' I was curious, nothing more. Beezy was generous but there was often a price attached to anything she gave away.

'Work,' she said as Alfie and the woman arrived at an agreement, 'I'll give you work, as many days a week as you can manage. I'll pay you better than the Buckleys did but I'll expect you to look after the place and not be bothering me.' She gave a short laugh. 'Myself and the girls can't be expected to do everything.'

I stared at her. 'I'm not so desperate as to go working in a kip house.' Because I was shocked I didn't stop to think of the insult this would be to Beezy. 'I'll find something . . .'

'You might, and you might not.' Beezy, fingering the shawl again, was cool. 'Could be you'll have this in the pawn a lot longer than a week. All for the sake of being too proud to wash and clean in a kip house.'

I was silent while Beezy did her business with Alfie, ashamed of my response. I wished I'd chosen my words with more care.

Beezy wasn't like some of the other madams around. Her girls came to her of their own free will and it was well known that she looked after them well. Unlike other madams too Beezy Ryan didn't recruit from the ranks of the unfortunate or from country girls new to the city.

Not that any of this made much difference when it came to the question of me working for her. My parents would never accept it. My mother would pray her way into an early grave and my father would lay siege to North King Street, even if I went in there as a missionary.

'I'm sorry, Beezy, and I'm grateful to you.' I touched her arm as she examined the ring Alfie handed her. Beezy trusted no one and was checking the name on the inside of the gold band. 'But you know yourself how things are around here – if I go to work for you I'm finished as far as getting work anywhere else goes. And my father . . .'

'Your father . . .' Beezy was dismissive. Oddly, though men were her business, she didn't like them much. 'Cristy Rooney had a bit of bad luck with his leg but he's been making the world and your mother suffer ever since and I don't agree with that. As for the work – well, a bird in the hand is worth two in the bush.' She gave a loud laugh and, when I didn't laugh at the bawdy meaning, turned to the women behind us. 'That's right, isn't it girls? A bird in the hand's worth two in the bush . . .' She laughed again. This time some of the women laughed with her.

I turned to Alfie with my shawl.

'Nice bit of crafting in this,' he said when he held it to the light. 'Very nice.' Alfie always recognised quality.

'It's a lovely thing, right enough,' Beezy said, 'and its owner wouldn't have to pawn it if she wasn't too proud to take work when it's offered her.'

I did a deal with Alfie and he began writing me a ticket.

'You know what you're saying isn't true,' I said to Beezy, 'you know full well that my parents wouldn't stand for me working for you.'

'Are you telling me you do everything your parents want you to?' Beezy gave me a hard look and I turned away, took my money from Alfie and started toward the door. She followed.

'It's time you started looking out for yourself, Sarah, and money's what counts, when all's said and done. I'm offering you good money. I need someone I can trust to keep the house in order for me and you need the work. We'd suit each other well.' She gazed along the line of women still in the street as we came out into the sunshine. 'I don't see a procession of people coming up to you with work.'

'Let me think about it for a few days,' I said. Maybe a way could be found, an agreement made with my parents and grandmother.

I would have to find agreement in myself too. Though I liked Beezy some of her girls wouldn't be the easiest in the world to get along with. Drink and fighting over men were in the nature of their world. As well as this I was neither as brave nor as shameless as Beezy about how I earned my living.

Work and prayer were what occupied my mother in the weeks following Mary Ann's death. Her lips were in perpetual, muttering motion. She prayed for my father that he might come off the batter and for my grandmother that she might learn to peacefully accept my sister's death. She prayed for Mary Ann's soul too. These last prayers I thought unnecessary.

'Is Allie getting out of the house at all?' I asked her the day after I met Beezy.

'No.' My mother looked worried but at least she stopped praying. She was sitting in a chair by the window and put her rosary beads down when I sat opposite her. 'The poor child spends entire days in her room Mary Connor brings her her food there so I don't see her even at meal times the few minutes I saw her this last week she was very morose and gone into herself.' She sighed. 'I had to cook three dinners for that Dr McDermott and his daughter and he's visited the house in the afternoons too,' she took a breath, 'Leonard Buckley's away in Belfast God knows why he'd want to go there the mother comes and goes about her own business.' She shook her head. 'There were a few days last week when Allie's door was locked but it's not any more so I suppose she's resigned to her fate.'

'That's hard to believe.'

'You haven't seen her she's very down in herself not the friend you knew at all.' My mother picked up her beads. 'The girl Mary Connor engaged in your place is so slow I spend my time finishing what she starts.' She sniffed and said, without looking at me, 'Allie needs taking out of herself.'

'I'll go over to see her,' I said. A plan had been growing in my head while my mother spoke. 'There's someone I might take with me to see her—'

My mother cut me short. 'Do what you can Sarah do what you can.' She got up to peer out of the window. 'The evening's are getting dark quicker and quicker the winter'll be here before we know it.' She turned to me. 'Organise your own life while you're at it.'

'I'll do that too,' I said.

My plan had to do with getting Allie to meet with Dr Daniel Casey. There were several reasons for this. The first was practical. If Allie was as worn and morose as my mother said she was then a doctor should see her. Dr Casey might be a good person to tell her how to get out of herself. Also: though Allie might have been blind to the fact it was clear to me that Daniel

Casey liked her. He listened when she spoke. He had asked after her every time he came to see Mary Ann.

For a while I'd thought his interest had to do with Allie's very good way with Mary Ann. She'd endless and gentle patience with my sister, applying poultices and sponging her with a feathery touch. She'd known before anyone else did when her temperature began to rise. She claimed her skill was due to the nursing methods taught by one of the French nuns. But it was clear to me, and to Dr Casey, that much of what she did came naturally.

Nursing skills apart, I could see that Daniel Casey liked Allie. It was in his face every time he looked at her. He was no oil painting, God knows, and although she was not much enamoured of doctors on account of the odious Dr McDermott, he would be someone for Allie to talk to – about his time in Paris if nothing else.

She would be safe with him. He was a good and gentle man. He was close to her in age. She might even grow to like him and, since her parents were set on a doctor for her, they might approve her keeping company with him. They could hardly disapprove. Or so I thought.

I went to the dispensary in Eccles Street that very day. Dr Casey was there, even paler than when I'd last seen him, working as if he thought his energy alone would cure ill-health and disease. I explained about Allie, telling him of her parents' plan to marry her to Dr McDermott. I told him how, for more than three weeks, she'd been a prisoner and unable to stir out of her parents' house. He listened carefully and quietly. At one point he went to the window and stood with his back to me.

'Her father mentioned McDermott at your sister's funeral,' he said. 'I thought Allie was in agreement with the arrangement.'

I roundly disabused him of this notion and said I thought Allie needed company and taking out of herself. He agreed immediately then, saying he would help in any way he could. I told him my plan and he thought it a good one. I think he would have agreed to anything which ensured he would meet Allie again.

I went home and wrote her a letter.

My dear Allie, *I began,*

You cannot allow yourself be made a prisoner in your own home. You cannot allow yourself be lost to a morose sadness either. You're not friendless, as you well know. You're not without resources of character and courage either. Use both, as you've done so often done in the past, and get yourself out of that house to meet me in St Mary's Church at two o'clock in the afternoon this day week. I will wait however long it takes you to get there. Until the church closes if necessary. But I will expect you at two o'clock. I have things to tell you that I cannot tell anyone else. Come for my sake if not for your own.

The last line was in the nature of a bait. Allie had always hated me to have secrets from her.

I sealed the envelope with sealing wax. I didn't trust my mother not to read it, and didn't want her alarmed. I gave it to her when she left for Haddington Road the next day.

Not for a minute did I doubt that Allie would come to the church to meet me. Or that Dr Daniel Casey would come along on the same day, to 'accidentally' meet us in the street afterwards. That meeting was as far as I was prepared to take my match-making activities. I knew Allie well: she would run hard and fast from Daniel Casey if she sensed in him a need for more than friendship. Even to win her friendship he would have to be subtle.

CHAPTER NINE

Sarah

Allie, for all my confidence in her, didn't come to meet me that Thursday. It took her another full week to break free from the prison her parents had made for her in the Haddington Road house. When we did at last meet she'd become a pale, brown-clad shadow of her former self.

The week that led up to our meeting was not an easy one for her. I heard all about it from my mother. The final straw, she said had been yet another dinner with Dr Maurice McDermott. Allie had been rude and sullen throughout the meal. The next morning she'd thrown a grand-scale temper tantrum.

'I gave thanks to God and His Blessed Mother when I heard the roars of rage coming from her room,' my mother admitted, 'the poor child had been more dead than alive until then and not even able to leave the house with her walking boots locked up in Mary Connor's bedroom.' She took a breath. 'She told Leonard and her mother that she was going to take herself into the November streets in her petticoats and bare feet if they didn't stop treating her like a dog.'

'She got the boots back then?'

'She did and Leonard seems inclined to give her a bit of her own way she gave me a letter for you.' My mother handed me a creamy-coloured envelope. 'Don't go pushing her too far to do things Sarah she's in a delicate state.'

My dear friend, *Allie's letter began,*

I've taken steps to change the situation in this house and will definitely be meeting you on Thursday of *this* week.

I must say, Sarah, that you took long enough to write to me. I've been very low in myself and you're the only real friend I have in this cold and darkening city. It's hard for me to understand why I had to wait WEEKS for some word from you. I suppose you're very taken up with your soldier friend. I would never have left *you* so alone for so long.

Still, you've written now and your letter helped me gather myself together. I've a great deal to tell you — and to hear from you too, I hope.

She didn't sound low to me. She sounded bad-tempered and lively enough.

It was cold and windy when I set out to meet her. I didn't have the money for an omnibus. I'd got two days' cleaning during the week but had taken the Paris shawl out of the pawn with one day's money and given my mother the rest. I'd said nothing yet to my mother, or to my father, about Beezy Ryan's offer.

St Mary's Church in Haddington Road was said to be the richest parish in the city of Dublin. It certainly had the appearance of wealth about it, down to there being a carpet on the stone steps leading to the door.

I slipped into a pew just inside to wait for Allie. I'd never known her to be on time for anything in her life. From there I would have a clear view of everyone who came and went. I had fine views too of the wintry sun pouring through the saintly, stained glass windows and of the vaulted, and very grand, ceilings. The dark wood pews, shining the whole way up to the altar, gave off a suffocating smell of polish. I wondered how at home God felt there.

St Mary's parishioners were altogether different to the people who prayed in the pro-Cathedral alongside my mother. Some of those in the pro-Cathedral were lucky to have the clothes they knelt in.

Here they seemed to dress to impress God.

There was the woman in green who came bustling up the aisle wearing a short, loose paletot of velvet edged all round with fur. She sat while she prayed, her back rigid as a board. Another woman, who was older and knelt, wore a round-shaped bonnet with black, blue and gold tinted feathers. She frowned at my grey wool cape and uncovered head.

When I smiled, to reassure her I wasn't the Devil, she hurried out of the church with her head averted.

'Why've you got that lunatic expression on your face?' Allie slipped into the pew on the other side of me.

'That's a smile.' I stared at her. I couldn't help it.

'A smile?' She looked at me in her turn. 'It's more like the expression of a cat watching a bird in a cage.' She turned to gaze about the church and shivered. 'It's cold in here. Do you have any money?' She had the grace to look embarrassed when she asked this.

'I've got no real work yet.' I shook my head, still staring at her.

She looked as unwell as anyone could look and still be walking around. Her face was chalky white and her eyes had circles under them as dark as their own brown colour. She was wafer-thin, wrapped in a brown cloak which seemed too heavy for her frame and was so disagreeable-looking it might have been borrowed from Mary Connor.

'I'm sorry, Sarah, I should never have asked you for money,' she slumped against the back of the pew. 'I thought we might go to a tea house, somewhere warm. I've no money, none at all. My father won't allow me to have any.'

'What's happened to you, Allie . . .' I took her in my arms then and she began to cry, weakly, as if she hadn't the energy to sob wholeheartedly. She was no weight at all in my arms.

'I've been filled with a terrible despair about myself, about my life. Everything seemed to me to be over, as if anything good which might happen to me had already happened. All I could see and think about was that my life had been taken from me by my parents and given into the control of Mary Connor and that wretched McDermott man.'

She sat up straight and moved away from me. She brushed the tears from her face with small, hard gestures.

'I've allowed myself to wallow in this mood for weeks now. I've been feeling friendless, though I knew I had you. I've allowed myself be crushed under the weight of my parents' determination that I should marry. I could have borne it all if I hadn't felt so useless, that I had no function on earth and never would have.'

She took a deep breath, then sat on her hands and began to rock back and forth. 'Then your letter arrived.' She turned to me. 'I read what you wrote, three, maybe four times and my courage began to come back to me. I saw that my return from Paris and Mary Ann's death and the idea of marriage to that man had driven me to a kind of madness. I could see that I'd lost myself but just as clearly saw that I would have to find myself again.'

She took her hands from under her and hugged herself to keep warm. 'If I have to leave my parents' house and make my own way in the world I will do it, rather than marry and have my liberty taken from me by that man. Or any other.'

'Have you told your parents as much?'

'There's no telling them anything. You know that.' She was sharp, definitely coming back to her old self. 'Still, it's true that it's an ill wind doesn't blow some good.' Her face, smiling at me, was now less wasted-looking. 'The weeks alone in that house gave me time to reflect and I've decided to put my life to some good use. Solitude and idleness don't suit me and the idea of marriage appeals not at all. I'm on earth for a reason, I know it. There's a calling for me and I'm going to pursue it.'

'What calling? What is it you want to do?' I spoke slowly, hoping to calm her down. I'd heard Allie like this before, lit up and on fire with an idea.

It was in exactly such a mood that she'd once taken stout from her father's public house and given it to boys guarding cattle for the drovers. The boys, who were poor and had empty stomachs, had become spifflicated. The whole thing had ended in a near stampede. Allie had been eight years old at the time.

Now, nearly twelve years later, she stared with a great, silent ferocity at the bright, glass saints in the windows. She'd always been dissatisfied, never content to accept what life threw up. I put the question again. She raised her eyebrows at me.

'You think this is a whim, a caprice brought on by my time alone, don't you?' she said.

'I don't know what it is.' I was beginning to feel the cold in the church myself and wanted to go.

Her face, watching me, was trying not to be too hopeful. She needed me to believe in her. She had no one else.

'I don't think it's a whim,' I amended, 'and I'll support you, whatever you do. But I'd like to know what this calling is.'

'I've decided to become a doctor.'

'A doctor . . .'

I'd been wrong. It was a whim, a fancy. She'd been too alone for too long. If she'd announced herself recruited for active service with the Fenians I'd have been less surprised.

'There are no women doctors, Allie. You won't be allowed to study.'

'There are women doctors in America. I've heard there are some in England too. It's true that they're few, very, very few, and that the universities don't want women students. It's for all of these reasons,' she leaned forward, 'that I've decided to begin by becoming a nurse.'

'A nurse . . .'

'Can you do anything but repeat what I say?' she snapped. 'I'm going to care for the sick, in one role or the other.'

Two women turned at her raised voice, so stiffly I thought they would topple from their seats. I leaned closer to Allie and spoke in a whisper.

'Nurses do little more than scrub floors and wash bed linen and in between times act as servants to the doctor. Is that what you call a calling? Of course,' my whisper became a hiss, 'you could improve the quality of their dying by speaking French to the mortally ill.'

'You said you'd support me.' Allie didn't even try to whisper. The women made loud, reproving noises and bustled in their seats. 'I'm sorry I told you. I won't speak of it again. I know my parents will oppose me, that I will have a hard time convincing my father it's what's best for me. I didn't think I would have to convince *you*.'

'A doctor seems impossible and a nurse's job hard and dangerous and menial,' I said. 'You could do so many things, Allie, with your education and your father's money behind you.'

'I could marry, as he wants me to,' Allie said.

We were silent for a while after that, which must have pleased the praying ladies. I was silent because I'd just realised that I believed, in my deep heart and along with her parents and everyone else, that Allie was destined for a good marriage and the life of a lady.

I was shocked at myself, and ashamed.

'I'm sorry,' I said, 'you must do what is best for you yourself with your life.'

'I will.' Allie changed the subject. 'What news have you?'

I talked to her about Jimmy, about how he wanted to meet my family and how I couldn't risk it. I told her we saw each other as often as we could. I didn't tell her about the afternoons in the boarding-house room by Kingsbridge Station.

'Is there anything else?' she probed. 'You said you'd things to tell me.'

I told her about Beezy's offer of work and warned her not to tell my mother. None of it satisfied her. She went on probing; she'd always known when I was keeping a secret from her.

I stood. The days were short; it would be getting dark, Daniel Casey would be waiting. By now I was half hoping he might not be: Allie was likely to hurl questions at him about nursing and make demands on him that he help her, which wasn't at all what I had in mind when I arranged to bring them together.

'You've been too much in that house,' I said, 'you need a walk, even a short one.'

She followed me from the church willingly enough but stopped when we got to the porch. 'There's something I want you to do for me.' She pulled a small, embroidered bag from under her cloak. 'Will you take these to the pawnshop?' When I hesitated she closed my fingers around the bag. 'Please, Sarah, please do it for me. All that's in there are a pendant and a pearl choker I'll never wear again. Get what you can . . .'

'Alfie may not give me their true value,' I warned her as I put the bag into my skirt pocket. 'He doesn't have much call to deal in jewellery.'

'When you've got no money even a little is welcome.' Allie said this as if she understood poverty. Which of course she didn't.

It was almost three o'clock when we left the church. I'd arranged to meet Daniel Casey on the hour at Mount Street Bridge. If we took the short cut by the canal we could still be there on time.

The day had become damp as well as cold and the people in the streets were hurried and ill-humoured. It was as if, after the long, hot summer, they were still finding it difficult to adjust to the grey and dark of winter. I was myself. But it is indeed an ill wind: the misery in the streets made it easy to persuade Allie along the canal towpath for our walk.

She regretted it almost at once. 'The water's too still,' she shivered, 'and there's something dead in there.'

'If it's dead it can't hurt us,' I tried to keep her moving. The canal had its bad days and this was one of them.

'It's moving,' Allie said.

The dead thing was a pig carcass. Dead pigs in that stretch of canal weren't unusual. Like others before him this lad had no doubt escaped from the nearby cottages at Powers Court. The people who lived there reared and sold pigs. The movement Allie had seen was the mass of flies and other parasites attaching to it. I felt sick.

'Oh, Holy God.' I walked quickly, my hand over my mouth, very afraid I was going to vomit. Allie had to run to keep up with me.

'It's dead,' she reassured me, holding my arm, 'it can't hurt you.'

I didn't find this at all funny. I was so intent on keeping my eyes off the pig that I all but fell into the water when I collided with a man with a stick.

'Jesus Christ Almighty!' He roared and waved the blackthorn as we untangled ourselves. 'Isn't it enough that I've lost my pig! Do you want me to drown with him?'

'We're in a hurry and didn't see you.' Allie looked at him doe-eyed. She could be a peacemaker when she had to. 'What happened to your poor pig? How did it come to be in the canal?'

'He got free.' The man nodded with such vigour he nearly fell over. His eyes were full of tears and his thin red hair long enough to plait. His belly, from the smell of him, was full of beer.

'You'll know, I suppose, that the pig is an animal can't swim.' He moved closer to Allie. So did I. 'It's on account of the large toenails on the two short legs he has to the front. He paddles so fast with those legs that he cuts his own throat.'

Allie gave a small scream and the man roared with laughter, doubling up and holding his sides. We tried to move on but he hopped in front of us, blocking our way with the hawthorn.

'That was the biggest pig I ever reared.' He glared at Allie. 'I could've sold him to you, or the likes of you. You need fattening and from the looks of you you've got money . . .'

'I'm sorry about your pig,' Allie said, 'but you'll have to let us pass.'

'My family'll starve now the pig's drowned.' The man didn't budge. 'The price of that pig would be nothing to—'

'Unless you want to end up in the water with your pig you'll get out of here, fast.' Dr Daniel Casey's voice was just loud enough to be dangerous. 'By the time I reach a count of three I want to see your heels along the path.' He grabbed the hawthorn from out of the man's hands. 'Go on, get out of here.'

For a minute, as he glowered and muttered mutinously, I thought the man would fight for his dignity and the stick. But as soon as Dr Casey made a move towards him he swore, turned and disappeared at speed along the way we'd just come. He didn't so much as glance at his pig in passing.

'Thank you, Dr Casey,' Allie said, looking at him in a dazed fashion, 'it was lucky for us you were nearby. Remarkable too.' I ignored the look she gave me.

'Are you all right?' Daniel Casey took her arm. 'Do you feel faint? A hot drink is what you need. We're not far from a tea house.' He was leaning over her as he spoke, walking her towards the steps to the road. Every bit of him was absorbed in his concern for her.

If I'd fallen into the water with the pig I doubt he'd have noticed. He was showing his hand too clearly and too soon. Allie, given her independence of mind and present resistance to doctors, would need to be wooed with more cunning.

But there was nothing I could do about his lack of guile. I'd brought them together and what happened from now on was in God's hands.

Or so I thought then. If I'd known what God had in mind I'd have moved heaven and earth to keep them apart.

Allie, at the bottom of the steps, freed her arm and reassured Dr Casey. 'There's nothing at all the matter with me,' she shook the cloak's hood from her head and I saw Daniel Casey stare at how frail she'd become, 'except that I'm curious to know how you came to be by the canal. Do you have a patient nearby?'

He was not a good liar. 'I was on the bridge. I saw what was happening . . .'

'I asked Dr Casey to meet us,' I took him out of his misery, 'I was worried about your health and since you know Dr Casey I thought . . .'

'That the canal bank would be a good place for a medical examination?' Allie gave me a hard look which I returned with an open-eyed one of my own.

'A good place for a meeting of friends,' I said, 'and you haven't been too surrounded by those in recent times.'

That quietened her. I went ahead of the two of them up the steps and on to the bridge. Dusk was falling fast. The sharp, icy air was full of the smell of burning wood and coal.

'The tea house is at the hospital end of Baggot Street,' I began.

'There are also five victuallers, three wine and spirit merchants, four apothecaries, a ladies' outfitting warehouse,' Allie counted on her fingers, 'I've heard enough about Baggot Street from my mother and Mary Connor to last me a lifetime. I'd like to visit the new Shelbourne Hotel – couldn't we take our tea there?'

With more fun than I'd have thought he had in him the doctor crooked his arms and invited us to take one each. 'The Shelbourne it'll be then,' he said.

We walked quickly, through Merrion Square and into Merrion Row. Our breaths went ahead of us in small clouds as we talked. Only once did Allie's incarceration come up, and then it was she herself who mentioned it.

'My parents are fully intent on my marrying Dr Maurice McDermott,' she told Dr Casey, 'it seems that as a widower, most especially a widower who is also a doctor, he's in need of a wife. Have you got a wife, Dr Casey?'

'I'm not married,' he said.

Allie, for once, didn't pursue things further. We spoke instead about the great demands on the dispensary's services and about my own search for work. Dr Casey was more scandalised by my saying I might work for Beezy Ryan than I'd expected him to be. I changed to the subject of insurrection.

'Archbishop Cullen has denounced the Fenians.' I was worried how this would affect the movement of soldiers. If the Fenians pulled back the extra soldiers in Ireland would be brought home to England. Jimmy might be included in their number.

'Archbishop Cullen believes there's no hell hot enough, nor eternity long enough, for those who engage with the Fenian cause.' Dr Casey's tone was dry.

'Are the Fenians likely to listen to him?' Allie asked the question I wanted to ask myself.

'Not at all,' said Dr Casey, 'any more than they're likely to gain freedom for Ireland.'

'Why is that?'

'Because they're neither organised enough nor clear in their plans enough about what they should be doing,' he paused, 'more's the pity.'

'You're a supporter then?'

'I support the freedom and independence of all small nations.'

'Liberty, equality and fraternity too?' Allie was quite spirited.

'Those things too.' He smiled and I began to feel pleased with myself for having brought them together.

The situation didn't last long. We were outside the Shelbourne, admiring the bronze, female figures holding up their torch-shaped lamps, when Allie said, 'Do you think people should be free too, Dr Casey, to make choices about how to live their lives?'

'My name's Daniel,' he smiled, as he did every time he reminded her of this. He was an infinitely patient man. 'And the answer is yes. Free choice is the right of everyone, so long as it doesn't endanger the greater right to safety and security for all.'

'So you agree women are reasonable beings, able to develop their powers freely?'

'Of course . . .'

'Yet we're not allowed to vote,' Allie said, 'and nor do we have the same rights as men to places in universities.'

'I believe all men and women are born equal and that the differences between them have to do with education. I don't agree with restrictive legislation against women, nor with refusing them an education.' Daniel Casey paused. 'But I'm equally an admirer of the great duties women fulfil in the home.' He sounded inflated, in the way all men do when they hold out views, good or bad.

'So you wouldn't be for holding back women?' Allie, like a dog with a bone, was unaware that she stood in the way of people coming and going from the hotel. 'You would want them to have knowledge and to help themselves in any way they could?'

'Within reason. I don't agree with women abandoning their children.'

'Nor do I,' Allie was impatient, 'and since we're so much in agreement, Dr . . . Daniel, there's something I would like to ask of you.'

The way she smiled at him transformed the terrible thinness into a delicate beauty. Daniel Casey cleared his throat. 'If I can help I will,' he said.

'I'd like to work as a nurse attendant in the dispensary,' Allie began quickly, 'I'm not asking to be paid. All I want in return is for you to pass on some of your medical knowledge to me. You said yourself, to my father at Mary Ann's grave, that I cared well for her. I've had some training too in the convent in Paris.'

She looked disbelieving when Daniel Casey shook his head. 'You mean well, Allie, I know that,' he said, 'but I couldn't take it on myself to expose you to contagion and to all that goes on in a dispensary. You'd be at terrible risk . . .' He paused. 'Every day . . .' He paused again. 'I wouldn't like that.'

'You're at risk yourself. Is it only men who—'

'I'm a doctor.'

'Does that make you immune? You need help. I am not asking you to take responsibility for me. The choice is mine, not yours.'

'You don't know enough about dispensary work to make such a decision.' He spoke patiently, as if to a child. 'It's not as it was in the convent. Or even as it was with Mary Ann. There are the worst of diseases and injuries in a dispensary, and suffering,' he paused, 'and too often too little which can be done.'

'I've thought about all that,' Allie said, 'but I'll prove to you I can be useful. Will you allow me work there for a day, or two, as an . . . experiment?'

'You want me to allow my patients to be the subjects of your experiment?'

'The word was unfortunate. I would like to help.'

'Help yourself first,' he said with a shake of his head, 'you don't look well or strong to me.' He stopped and for a minute I thought he would produce his stethoscope there in the street. 'Eat. Sleep. Take walks. Get strong. Maybe in a month we can talk about this again.'

'Maybe? You think I'll have forgotten this in a month, don't you?'

Allie turned and walked quickly ahead of us through the doors. They were held open by a man in a maroon coat and as much gold braid as Archbishop Cullen on a Sunday.

'I won't forget,' Allie said as we stood in the reception hallway.

I'd never been in a place like the Shelbourne Hotel before and was woefully ill-dressed. Baleful glares and sidelong glances let me know it too. But I wasn't inclined to worry about the opinions of people I didn't know, and most likely never would. The three of us went on in and sat at a linen-covered table in the tea rooms. A man in a large, evening-dress necktie played Moore's melodies on the pianoforte. All about us there were gilded mirrors and painted ceilings and brocade, tasselled curtains. I felt at peace and would have been happy to sit there for a very long time. I would have sat there forever if Jimmy Vance had been with me.

Our tea came in an ornamented silver teapot. Allie poured it into delicate china cups. I followed by milking them. I was about to taste my own when a voice I recognised, but couldn't at once place, spoke above our heads.

'How nice to meet you again, Miss Buckley.' The owner of the voice sank, uninvited, into the fourth chair at the table. 'I wouldn't have expected to meet you here – though it's said that if you spend enough time in the Shelbourne Hotel you will meet the whole of Dublin. I'm delighted to find it's even half true.' Smiling and very sure of his welcome Mr Ned Mulvey signalled the waiter for a fourth cup. 'You don't mind if I join you?' he said.

'You're most welcome.'

The warmth in Allie's voice surprised me. So did the way she was smiling, coquettishly and with her head to one side. The flush to her cheeks greatly minimised their gauntness.

'You've been out of town, my father says.'

'I've been back to London, and to Belfast with your father,' Ned Mulvey said as he placed a pair of cream-coloured gloves on the table. He was wearing a black coat with a cutaway front over a cream waistcoat.

'My good and very old friend Sarah Rooney you've already met.' As Allie made the introductions he acknowledged me with a nod of his head. 'And this is Dr Daniel Casey.'

'Dr Casey.' Ned Mulvey extended a hand. Daniel Casey took and held it briefly. 'Are you also an old friend of Miss Buckley's?' Ned Mulvey asked.

'Oh, I'm not particularly old, nor even as old as I look.' Dr Casey deliberately misunderstood him. 'Though it's true that dispensary work does age physicians ahead of their time.'

'I'm sure it does,' said Ned Mulvey.

The table fell silent as Allie poured a fourth cup of tea. When I didn't offer to milk it Allie did that too. There was something about Ned Mulvey I should have told her. But, because it was only a suspicion and I'd not proof, I'd kept it to myself. I was now sorely regretting my discretion.

Ned Mulvey raised inquiring brows at Daniel Casey as Allie handed him the cup. 'You are lucky to be enjoying Miss Rooney's company, Dr Casey. She was anything but enamoured of physicians the last time I met her.'

'Then I'm indeed lucky,' said Daniel Casey.

It was clear Ned Mulvey thought Dr Casey and myself a couple.

'I was not enamoured of the ideas held by a *particular* physician, Mr Mulvey.' I hesitated. 'It wasn't clear to me whether you shared Dr McDermott's views.'

Ned Mulvey gave a short laugh. 'As it happens, I don't share Dr McDermott's views.' He smiled at Allie. 'I was lost in admiration of your spirited defence of your friend's rights, Miss Buckley.'

'They're not just Sarah's rights,' Allie pointed out.

'True. You spoke for all women of the labouring classes.' He leaned forward, still smiling, his hands resting on the silver top of a black cane. 'Your father tells me that, notwithstanding your ideological differences, you've been entertaining Dr McDermott.'

'My mother has been entertaining Dr McDermott,' Allie snapped. 'I've been enduring his company.'

Ned Mulvey's laugh was loud. 'Dr McDermott is a lucky man to have the company, whatever the circumstances, of two women as beautiful as yourself and your mother.' He sipped his tea, very elegantly, and looked over the rim of his cup at Allie.

'Perhaps you will call some afternoon?' Allie said. Her quick glance at Daniel Casey gave her away. Her coquettish behaviour with Ned Mulvey was a revenge for the doctor's refusal to allow her to nurse in the dispensary. 'I don't have a great deal to occupy me at the moment,' she went on, 'and would welcome the company.'

'I'd be delighted,' Ned Mulvey said. 'I'm in Dublin for the next while.'

'I may not be in Dublin all that long myself,' Allie said, 'I plan to make contact with the Society for the Emigration of Middle-Class Women. They send women to the southern hemisphere, you know, to find work and begin new lives.'

This too was for Dr Casey's benefit. She was telling him that she would go away if she couldn't do what she wanted to do in Dublin.

'And what will you do in the southern hemisphere?' Ned Mulvey was amused.

'I will teach French,' Allie said airily.

'The society you speak of didn't have a lot of success,' Daniel Casey was dry, 'to the best of my knowledge it's been defunct for a good while now.' He stood. 'I must leave to call on a patient. Maybe you would allow me take you home in my cab first, Allie? It's dark evening outside.'

Ned Mulvey got up too. 'Unless your patient is nearby it

would be more convenient for me to take Miss Buckley home. I'm going in her direction,' he said. 'Miss Rooney will in any event be needing a cab to Henrietta Street.'

I didn't like the way he said this. He made it seem as if I was fit company for Daniel Casey while Allie was not. Dr Casey, wrong-footed and awkward, stood frowning.

'Will you travel with me, Miss Buckley?' Ned Mulvey asked.

'Thank you,' Allie said, 'and please call me Allie.'

'I will call you Alicia,' said Ned Mulvey.

The two men stood waiting while the waitress made out the bill for the tea. Daniel Casey looked young, unformed, unsure and very plain. Ned Mulvey looked a man of the world, assured and handsome. Dr Casey, on the other hand, looked like a man to be trusted. Ned Mulvey did not and I wished, more than ever, that I'd told Allie my suspicions about him. It was unlikely she would agree with me but I should have told her anyway. I would tell her the next time we were alone together.

I wasn't to know that the next time we met I would be engulfed by worries of my own. Allie's problems would seem as nothing by comparison.

And so my matchmaking came to a wretched end. I shared a carriage home with a silent Dr Casey and Allie left in another with Ned Mulvey.

CHAPTER TEN

Sarah

The army, near the end of November, sent Jimmy Vance away from me. One day he was there, the centre of my life, just a walk across the city when I wanted to be with him. The next day he was gone. It was as simple and as brutal as that.

They didn't send him a great distance, only as far as the Curragh of Kildare. He might as well have been sent to India. I'd no way of getting to Kildare and, even if I had, Jimmy was in training and wouldn't have been allowed see me.

His wasn't the only regiment sent to the great camp on the midland plains. All the newspapers had the story of how the army had dispatched several, overnight, as reinforcement troops to deal with the 'dangerous and revolutionary activities' of the Fenians.

When I went to Beggar's Bush Barracks looking for him it was a sentry told me Jimmy's regiment was one of those sent off. That my fears of the months past were being borne out gave me no satisfaction at all.

Jimmy left me no word, no note or letter of any kind. But he did leave something precious in the small silver locket he gave the sentry for me. His mother had given it to him leaving home. He'd carried it in his pocket, always.

I saw the locket as his way of saying he would be back for me. That he'd been given no time to say goodbye, or to write. It helped, no doubt about it, but the blow of parting was a hard one.

I didn't even have Allie's company to console me. I hadn't seen her since the day in the Shelbourne Hotel. The fault this time was mine.

I'd got a couple of weeks' sewing work in a house in Gardiner Row. I was there most days until after dark. We wrote to one another, my mother delivering the letters. From them I knew that she was getting strong again. She'd taken to walking a great deal and was, she wrote, 'reading all I can lay hold of about education and medicine and disease. The money you got for me in the pawn has gone to good use in the bookshops.'

When the sickness began I put it down to loneliness. It was easier than facing what I knew in my heart was the real cause. But when nausea left me prostrate in the bed one morning I knew there was no point my denying the truth any longer.

'What ails you?' My grandmother, dressed for the early markets, stood over me with a candle. 'I heard groans. Are you not well?'

I'd tried to keep my moaning quiet. But my grandmother, always afraid disaster would strike without her knowing, slept with one ear open. She still kept to the bed she'd shared with Mary Ann.

I couldn't lie myself where my sister had died so my bed now was in a corner of the big room behind curtains.

'It's my time of the month,' I said. It was the first lie which came to mind. It was also what I wanted to be true.

'You'd be better off getting out of the bed then,' my grandmother said, 'lying there won't do you a bit of good. I'll make you a cup of sweet tea.'

When she left I swung my legs on to the floor and sat on the side of the bed. This made me feel worse so I lay back against the pillows. I wanted to die, both because of the way I felt and because I knew what was happening to me.

My grandmother was crusty enough when she came back. 'It'll pass, we've all had to put up with it in our time. Drink the tea and get out of the bed and clean the fireplace for your mother.'

The nausea rose inside me again when I took the cup from her. I lay back quickly, leaning against the wall as I sipped. My grandmother stood for a minute watching me. I told myself, as I thanked her and put a reassuring smile on my face, that the look on *her* face wasn't suspicion.

'You don't usually get it so bad,' my grandmother said.

'No,' I said. 'But I'm feeling better now.'

She left me alone at last. I lay wondering what on God's earth I was going to do about the child I was surely carrying.

I waited until my mother had left for work before getting up. My father wouldn't rise much before midday so I didn't worry about him. I slowly dressed and had more tea and decided on the first thing to be done.

The nausea was less, or maybe I was getting used to it, by the time I turned into North King Street. At Beezy Ryan's kip house the window drapes were closed tight. The front-door knocker, shaped like a lion's paw, echoed like the knell of doom when I dropped it.

It was fully five minutes before a thin woman with long, white-gold hair opened the door. In the murky light of the hallway she looked to me beautiful. I asked for Beezy.

'She's in her bed,' the woman looked me up and down, 'she needs her sleep. It's not yet eight o'clock. Come back another time.'

'I'll wait.' I pushed past her into the hallway.

I'd never been inside Beezy's house before and was surprised at the style. It wasn't elegant in the way of the Shelbourne Hotel, or even like the Buckleys' house. But it had style nonetheless.

The walls were wine-coloured and bordered with gold. Along one side there was a wine-coloured chaise stacked with gold cushions. Bright rugs covered the floor and a heavy, green velvet curtain half concealed an arch near the stairs. The silence, deep as any grave, was a surprise to me too.

And it was warm in Beezy Ryan's house, as if fires had been burning in the rooms until the small hours of the morning.

'You've seen enough now so get out of here!' The woman

who'd opened the door stood blocking my way. Her beauty was twisted by the fury on her face. 'Get out or by God I'll put you out and you won't like that . . .'

'Leave her be, Mary.' Beezy's voice came before her as she stepped from behind the velvet curtain. She stood looking at me, dressed in a red kimono with a black embroidered dragon circling her neck.

'You must need the job badly to be calling this early, Sarah,' she said slowly, 'or is there some other reason you're here?'

The woman called Mary folded her arms. She didn't try to stop me when I walked toward Beezy.

'I want to talk to you on your own,' I said.

'We'll go into the parlour,' Beezy gave a short laugh, 'it's where I carry out most of my interviews.' She cocked her head to one side. 'I've seen you looking better, Sarah. Are you not well?'

A crash from upstairs, followed by a string of curses and then silence, saved me from answering. No one in the hallway said anything. Maybe such sounds were so everyday no one heard them but me. I felt the palms of my hands damp. I rubbed them along the sides of my cloak.

But at least the nausea was gone. I was shaking though, both with worry and fear about my state and what I was going to do.

'Put the kettle on, Mary,' Beezy said, 'and make tea when it boils.'

'I'm going back to my bed.' The other woman was surly. 'She's no business here at this hour of the morning.'

'I've already had tea,' I said.

'Put the kettle on, Mary.' Beezy repeated this in a way that brought a chill into the air. She didn't look at the woman, just turned away, beckoning me to follow her, and opened the first door we came to. 'Wait in here,' she said.

Beezy liked dragons, no doubt about it. The walls were covered in dragon wallpaper, and a second chaise longue, this one bright red, was piled with dragon cushions. The easy chairs, though, were pink with flowers. A deck of cards lay spread on a

table alongside a near-empty whiskey bottle. Gas lamps spluttered weakly on either side of the mirror over the mantelpiece.
The curtains were closed.

All of this I saw while Beezy, in the hallway, spoke in a low,
hard voice to the woman called Mary. There was a short silence
and then Beezy followed me into the room.

'That's the Mary Adams I told you about,' Beezy said, 'she
has her good days and her bad days but all of her mornings are
contrary.' She sighed and shook her head. 'Of late, anyway.' She
sat at the table and began shuffling the cards. 'Now tell me
what's wrong with you.'

'I'm with child.' I hesitated. 'I think.'

Beezy spread the cards for a game of patience. 'When did you
last bleed?'

'I'm not sure. I've never been very regular.'

'You must have some idea.' Beezy didn't look at me.

'It could be two months ago.'

'What else?'

'I'm sick in the mornings. I feel tired most of the time.'

'Are you showing?'

Beezy looked at me at last. With the bad light and closed
curtains it was hard to see her face clearly. Her voice held
curiosity, nothing more. It was said that Beezy 'helped' her girls
when they fell pregnant. It was likely she thought I'd come to her
for the same kind of assistance.

'Is there a swelling of your belly?' she asked.

'No.' My clothes weren't any tighter.

'Tell me about the father.' Beezy, frowning, went back to the
cards. 'Where is he and what can you expect from him? Will he
stand by you?'

'He'll stand by me all right, once he knows.'

She played the cards while I told her about the Curragh and
how Jimmy and I had spoken of marriage. At the end of it I said,
'Does it seem to you, Beezy, that I'm with child?'

'You know well enough yourself that you're with child,
Sarah,' she sighed, 'and I knew it too as soon as I saw you in the

hallway.' She swept the cards together then and, with a bigger sigh still, stacked them.

So that was it, then. I was carrying Jimmy Vance's child. Beezy was never wrong about such things. It was known that she could tell just by looking at a woman whether or not she was in the family way. Could tell too how far gone she was by laying her hands on the swelling.

I sat on a chair at the other side of the table and tried not to weep. It was too late for that.

'It would be better for you, Sarah, to face the truth of things from the beginning.' Beezy began unplaiting her hair, her rings flashing with the speed of her fingers. 'If your soldier is gone to the Curragh then you might as well forget him. I don't care that he promised you marriage, that he was kindness itself, whatever it was made you dote on him. He's a soldier and an Englishman and he's had his way with you and if they hadn't sent him to the Curragh he'd have flown anyway. The army won't be kind to you either. It doesn't like its soldiers marrying.' She began on the second plait. 'Married men are harder to move around and once they've children they're less keen to fight in wars.'

'You're right about the army, and it's a problem I'll have to face another day,' I said, 'but you're wrong about Jimmy.'

She didn't, and couldn't, know how it was between us.

'I'm not a fool,' I went on. 'It doesn't matter that he's a soldier. Nor that he's English. He is what he is as I am what I am and we love one another.'

'You'll be left lonely and alone by any man,' Beezy said with a shake of her head, 'but a soldier's the quickest of all to be on his way. How will you tell him?'

'I'll write to him. Today. Then I'll follow him to the Curragh. He'd want me to . . .'

I stopped when Beezy shook her head. 'I never thought this would happen to you, Sarah Rooney. Of all the girls in Henrietta Street I thought you would be the one to escape.' She shook her unplaited hair. It fanned across her shoulders like a bush. 'Poor Sarah.'

I might have wept then if the door hadn't been opened by Mary Adams. She brought with her a tray on which there was a cup, teapot, milk and sugar. She put the lot on the table and filled the cup with tea.

When she handed it to me without milk or sugar I took it and thanked her.

'First things first.' Beezy got glasses from a cabinet and opened the bottle of whiskey. 'It's too early for me to have tea.' She half filled one of the glasses with whiskey. 'You'll need a glass of this too, my girl, to help straighten your thinking if we're to plan what you'll do with yourself.'

With the whiskey in her hand she went to the window and pulled open the curtains. The morning had brightened enough to light up the room. Everything was changed, utterly. The dragons on the wallpaper were torn and unhappy-looking, the pink easy chairs had more stains than flowers, the table was filthy.

Only Mary Adams, moving about the room like an aimless shadow in her calico night robe, was still beautiful.

I'd never before seen Beezy without rouge and eye kohl and it was a shock to me to see how girlish she looked still. Her skin was clear and a scattering of freckles made her look even younger. Her eyes, without the pencilled brows above them, had a wide-eyed look that could have been mistaken for innocence.

She finished the whiskey in two gulps and poured herself another. 'You can go back to bed now, Mary,' she said.

'I'll stay,' said Mary Adams.

'You'll go to bed.' Beezy put the glass down on the table. 'There's a lot I want you to do later in the day. We've a Friday night ahead of us. Go now.' She stared down the other woman who, for a minute, looked mutinous. Then she shrugged and turned away.

'I'll go to my room,' she muttered 'I'll leave my door open. That way I'll hear if you want me for anything.'

'I won't want you, Mary. Sarah is a friend.'

Mary Adams, on her way out of the room, gave me a look both hostile and poisonous. I shivered.

'She's jealous. Pay no heed to her,' Beezy said. 'She's the woman whose ring I retrieved in the pawn. The unfortunate creature had a terrible time of it with a father who beat and abused her and a husband who did worse. I came on her in the street one night, more dead than alive. She works fine here and most of the time she's happy enough.'

She finished her whiskey, put the glass beside the other on the table and filled a good measure into each of them.

'Mary's like a guard dog around me but I'm hoping she'll get over it.' She held one of the glasses out to me. 'To the wages of sin,' she laughed, 'which aren't death at all in the case of a woman, but life.'

'I didn't think of it as sin.' I took the whiskey and sipped. My tongue and throat burned as it went down. I felt warmer inside too. 'I wasn't ashamed either. What we did was natural, and right.'

'Of course it was,' Beezy was impatient, 'but it was a sin nevertheless in the eyes of God and the Church. Do you think having a fondness for a man transforms what you did? It was fornication, Sarah, and you might as well give it its name and be done with it, now you're going to have to live with the consequences.'

She leaned forward, looking at me. 'Will you go to term with this child? Have you thought about doing away with it?'

'I have not!' I shouted at her. I took another drink of whiskey. This time all it did was bring a chilly moisture to my forehead. 'How could you ask me such a thing . . .'

'I ask because I know more about the world than you do,' Beezy replied harshly. 'I know what's ahead of you, how your child will drain and drag the life out of you and how you'll be made an old woman before you're thirty caring for him. And for what? He'll be no better off than you are, Sarah, because, when all's said and done, you won't be able to give him anything more than you got yourself. You'll be poor forever, Sarah, and your child will be poor.'

'It won't be like that. I'll be with Jimmy and we'll rear our child together. Maybe even in England, or India. He'll have his army pay.' I finished the whiskey and stared into the empty glass. 'My baby might be a girl.'

'Boy or girl it'll all be the same,' Beezy was gentler, 'and if your soldier doesn't stick by you you'll need to think on all that I've said.'

'He'll stick by me,' I told her.

'Whether he does or not you'll need work and money.' Beezy became brisk. 'Are you coming to work for me?' She looked around the tawdry room. 'You can see I need someone.'

'I don't know yet,' I said. 'I haven't said anything about it to my mother or father.'

'There's a lot you've to tell them then,' Beezy said, 'and I don't envy you. Your father and grandmother will have you on the streets as soon as they know your situation so you might as well get out before that happens. I've offered you honest work. You can live and rear your child in this house. There's a free room beside the kitchen, at the back. My girls would be kind to a child among them.'

They would too, I knew that. Beezy meant to be kind. I knew that too. She would also get hard and honest work out of me. But living in Beezy's house would mean my child growing up to be reviled by the poor and despised by the rich.

'I'll be a soldier's wife,' I said, 'and the army will look after my child.' It must have been the whiskey made me so sure.

I wrote to Jimmy Vance that day, telling him he was to be a father and that I would come to the Curragh camp as soon as he made arrangements. I went with the letter to the General Post Office in Sackville Street. The clerk assured me that it would be in Kildare the following day. The return post was just as speedy, he said.

I expected an answer from Jimmy by Wednesday, at the latest.

The sickness continued every morning. I got up very early and made sure the worst had passed before facing my mother and grandmother.

While I waited to hear from Jimmy Vance, Allie wrote to me that we should meet. Afraid I would betray my secret to her I wrote back that I was unwell and anyway was busy looking for work. When she didn't reply to this I knew she was hurt. There was nothing I could do about it, then.

There was no letter from Jimmy by Wednesday so I wrote again. Five days later, when I still had not heard from him, I began at last to face the fear, growing inside me along with our child, that Jimmy didn't want either of us.

I became truly deranged, going quite mad with a terrible, sad loneliness that caused me physical pain. It tore at my insides and left me unable to feel or think about anything but that Jimmy Vance had deserted me. This was the worst of all to bear, much harder than the knowledge that I was ruined.

On a dark morning, with the rain beating like knife blades against the window, I awoke full of desperate thoughts. As I made my way down the stairs to the privy in the yard there seemed to me only one solution in the world possible.

Beezy was businesslike when I told her what I wanted to know.

'Be careful with the amount,' was her only word of warning, 'about half a teaspoon in a cup of water is all you need. No more.' She looked away. 'I've seen what happens when women try to make sure by overdoing the dose. There's no good taking two lives . . .' She turned and held me against her for a fierce, brief moment. I promised to be very careful.

I crossed the town to an apothecary in Blessington Street. He sold me a bottle of ergot without question. I lied anyway and told him it was for one-sided headaches. He was an old man and said he found it good for such pain himself.

I waited that night until my mother, father and grandmother were well asleep before taking myself with the ergot and a cup of water down to the yard behind the house. A navy-blue sky was full of stars and the ground crackled with frost under my feet. So did the washing, hanging stiff on lines as I crossed to the privy.

I leaned against the outside wall, out of sight of the windows of the house, and measured a half-teaspoon into the cup. Then, very quickly, I drank the lot. The church bells of St Saviour's were ringing for midnight as I put the cup down and began to walk about the yard. I knew that I could burn in hell's fire for all eternity for what I was doing. That my dead child would be consigned to limbo and denied the joy of seeing the face of God.

I would devote my life to praying for forgiveness.

I knew too, from other women who had done what I was doing, that my baby would pass from me in blood and sickness. For this reason I needed to be near the privy and had to hope that the other tenants would use their chamber pots for the night. The bitter cold made the chances of this happening more than good. That and the fact that the people of the tenements valued their night's sleep. They needed it.

There was a deathly quiet after the bells stopped. A stillness too. The yard might have been a cemetery, the low-hanging, frozen sheets headstones in the moonlight. I knew it was the morbidity of my mind made me see things this way but the images persisted as I walked between the sheets and held my mother's heaviest shawl tight about me.

I knew very quickly that the ergot was doing its work. I became full of an anxiety, then a panic that made me want to scream. I stuffed my fist into my mouth and walked in wider circles and more quickly until a drowsiness came over me that not even the icy air could penetrate.

My heart was beating loudly in my ears when the cramps began in my stomach, slicing and hot as if a malignant, knife-wielding creature was at work inside me. I doubled over so as to hold myself together, to stop myself being torn asunder. Vomit rose and subsided in me and the pain went on, an unnatural thing. I wanted to stretch myself and just lie on the frozen stone and clay of the yard. I might have done it too had it not been for the sickness, which I was afraid would choke me.

I stumbled into the privy and it was as if I was being emptied of everything I'd ever held inside me. I couldn't imagine that my baby would cling on in my womb. I knelt with my back against the wall, exhausted.

Mary Ann came to me then, in the dark and the cold of the privy, as my head reeled and I thought I was facing death.

She put her hand on my forehead and stood away from me, her face very serious and worried. She looked lovely, the way she'd looked before the pneumonia, neat and with shining fair hair to her shoulders. Her blue eyes lit up the dark of the privy. 'I would have been an aunt to your baby if I'd been allowed to live,' she said. 'I'd have liked that. Imagine: me an aunt!'

She smiled and I smiled back at her, weeping.

'It's too late,' I said, 'look at what I've done.'

'You've done nothing yet,' Mary Ann said, 'your baby is still alive.'

'Are you sure?' I asked.

'You'll see,' said my dead sister.

I knelt on and the pain subsided. Mary Ann stayed with me, patiently talking of this and that, about our father before his accident, about our grandmother when she had a drop taken and how funny she could be, about the way our mother put up with both of them.

She said she was happy and that I shouldn't be sad about her. She put a finger to her lips when I would have asked to know more.

The pains came again and with them a swirling blackness and icy cold. I lost consciousness.

When I awoke Mary Ann was gone. I called to her, begging her to come back and wait with me. When she didn't answer I prayed that my baby would not leave me. That Mary Ann might be an aunt. That Jimmy might be a father. That I might be a mother. I sat slumped against the wall, every pore in my body clammily perspiring. I knew I had been touched by death.

But there was no blood and I knew too my baby was still inside me.

As the bells of St Saviour's rang for three o'clock I left the privy. The house in front of me had already started to move into the day, women getting up for work even at that hour. As I stood in the middle of the yard. I prayed one last prayer before I went inside.

'Dear Mother of God, forgive what I did here tonight and let mine and Jimmy Vance's child stay in me. Let me give her birth and life. Amen.'

I had no doubt but that I was carrying a girl.

I don't remember going back up the stairs, nor lying again on my bed, nor falling asleep. I don't have any memory either of my grandmother and mother getting up for their day's work and departing.

It was Allie who shook me awake. 'What's wrong with you, Sarah?'

Her face above me was a blurry frown framed by a fur-trimmed bonnet. She helped me out of bed and I stood swaying weakly.

'I came to see for myself what was wrong with you,' she said as she put an arm about my waist and helped me to a chair. 'You look like a ghost.'

She set about making tea. It was eleven o'clock and my father's snores came loudly from the bedroom. 'I've been asleep for nearly eight hours,' I said in wonder.

'How do you feel?' Allie was brisk.

'Weak,' I admitted, 'a bit dizzy . . . sick in my stomach. I'll be fine after the tea.'

'You might,' Allie said, 'and you might not.'

We said nothing else until she sat opposite me on the stool with the tea, a cup for each of us in her hands.

'Tell me what's the matter with you,' she said and I did, in a low voice while my father snored and the goldfinch sang. I left nothing out, except the details of the afternoons with Jimmy in the room by Kingsbridge Station. Allie said nothing when I told her about Mary Ann coming in the night. She was right not to. Some things are given to people to experience and should be accepted for that.

When I finished I felt better. The talking had helped clear

the space in my mind I needed to plan what I would do. I didn't want opinions or advice, even Allie's.

She read my thoughts. 'What will you do?' she asked.

A fruit cake she'd brought with her sat round and fat on the table. The top of it was bursting with red cherries. They had a bad effect on my uncertain stomach.

'I will have my baby,' I looked away from the cherries, 'and I will call her Mary Ann.'

Allie nodded, as if this were right and proper. 'Where will you have her?' She looked doubtfully at my bed in the corner.

'I don't know,' I said, 'yet.'

Allie had taken the fur-trimmed bonnet from her head and in the sunlight looked girlish and delicate, though a lot better than when last I'd seen her. I felt very much older than she was, and a woman. For a minute I was filled with desolation for the loss of my girlhood. But this passed and I felt glad to be facing motherhood.

I lifted the bonnet from the table. The fur was feather-soft. 'It's beautiful. I suppose everyone in Paris wears bonnets like this?'

'Not everyone and probably not at all this season.' Allie reached and put the bonnet on my head. 'Come to the mirror,' she said, 'you look lovely.'

I looked nice all right but anyone would have looked well in a bonnet like that one. We tried it every which way, the two of us taking turns, parading and laughing until we cried, holding on to one another, and my father came roaring from the bedroom. 'A man needs his sleep,' he yelled at us.

Allie nodded and said of course he did. We left, quickly, taking the stairs two at a time until we got to the street.

'Jimmy has not forsaken me.' I dried the last of my tears. 'It's just that he didn't get my letters.'

'Perhaps,' Allie said.

'You don't believe in him, do you?'

'I believe in your belief in him.'

'That's not the same thing.' I was annoyed. 'I'll write again only this time I'll go to Beggar's Bush Barracks and ask them to send the letter directly from there.'

'How does the army feel about its soldiers marrying?'

'Bad,' I sighed, admitting my worry. 'Jimmy's told me fierce stories about wrongs done to women who marry soldiers. The army doesn't want the worry of caring for women and children in its camps.'

'I can see how it would be contrary to the purpose of an army all right,' said Allie. Though it was nearing midday there was frost on the ground. I still felt weak and walked slowly, afraid I might fall. I was grateful for the support when Allie put an arm through mine.

'Jimmy says there are ways of dealing with the army,' I told her as we rounded the corner out of Henrietta Street. 'But he says too that they allow only four soldiers to marry in every company of sixty. He says that sometimes wives have to share the billets of the unmarried men with only a curtain around the bed to give privacy.'

'But that's barbaric!' Allie stopped and stared at me. 'It can't be true! He really said that?'

'He did.'

'Then he's not very encouraging . . .'

I remembered something else. 'He says too that the army opens soldiers' letters.'

'Do you think they read yours and didn't give it to him?'

'I don't know.' I unhooked my arm from hers and leaned against a railing. 'I must rest a minute.' My legs felt so weak I would have sat on the pavement if Allie hadn't been there. But she would have worried so I hung on instead to the railings.

She worried anyway. 'You're green about the face,' she was sharp, 'it's time you saw a doctor. What you did last night was dangerous, Sarah, and you know it. We're halfway to Eccles Street. We'll go to the dispensary . . .' She stopped when I all but fainted again.

There was no reasoning with her after that, no protesting that I didn't want to see a doctor yet, especially not Dr Daniel

Casey, with whom I would feel mortified. Not the Eccles Street dispensary either, where I would be sure to see someone I knew.

'You've no choice.' She took my arm again and slowly, but with the tenacity of a terrier, moved me forward.

'I'll have to take the work with Beezy Ryan.' I thought this would stop her. It almost did.

'Beezy Ryan?' She raised her eyebrows in what I supposed was a Parisian way. 'Your friend the madam?' She sniffed and tossed her head. I wondered if she intended going through life with the affectations she'd picked up in France. 'You think growing up in a kip house will prepare your child for a respectable life?'

'No, I don't. But the other choice is to give her for adoption in a Magdalen convent.' I paused. 'Anyway, Jimmy will stand by me and all of this worry will have been for nothing.'

As we came into Eccles Street we saw people waiting in the street outside the dispensary.

'We'll go straight on in,' said Allie, 'you can't be expected to wait outside in the cold. Anything might happen to you. I'll say I am a nurse, and working there.'

Which is what we did.

CHAPTER ELEVEN

Allie

My girlhood ended the day I found Sarah half conscious and corpse-coloured on her bed in Henrietta Street. She didn't have to tell me she was pregnant; some things are a given and my certainty that she was with child was one of those things. Also, she'd been spending a dangerous amount of time with her soldier. Too much time, certainly, to have any left over to spend with me.

Even though I knew I allowed her to tell me about her baby, and was glad when she did. It got rid of my fear that the fact of her becoming a mother would put a barrier between us.

Her need of me meant we were able to take the step from girl-to womanhood together. Or maybe the real truth was that I'd taken that step on my own already, during my weeks alone in the Haddington Road house. It could be that Sarah's dire news simply helped me recognise how far I'd travelled in that time.

I knew, because of the horrific thing she'd tried to do in the night, that she had to see a doctor.

The doing of this fell neatly into place when she became ill again in the street. Since we were already halfway there at the time she couldn't put up any useful argument against us going to Eccles Street to visit Dr Daniel Casey. I told the crowd outside the dispensary that I was a nurse and we went ahead of them into the waiting room.

The moans and low, gasping cries from the other side of the doctors' examining room sent Sarah into a panic.

'We'll come back another time.' She pulled at my sleeve. 'Today looks like a bad day.'

'It's the day you need to see a doctor,' I said. 'Sit down and I'll find out what's happening.'

There was nowhere for her to sit. The benches, along two walls and across the room, were filled with patients. Some looked ill or had injuries, others looked to be merely sheltering from the cold outside, most were waiting to have medicines dispensed to them.

The room itself had a scrubbed, rough wood floor and a stove against one wall to provide heating as well as pots of boiling water. Half of the space was taken up by the dispensing counter behind which there was a huge collection of bottles on shelves.

No one offered Sarah their seat. I frowned at a man paring his nails. He was wearing a worn, and torn, frock coat but looked to me in fairly robust health.

'I wonder, sir,' I stood over him, 'if my friend might have your place on that bench? She's not well.' He ignored me. 'Sir?'

I shook Sarah off when, hissing at me to be quiet, she pulled again at my sleeve.

'I'm not well myself.' The man didn't look up. He'd a reddish colour, which might have been a sign of apoplexy.

'Forgive me,' I said, 'I mistook you for a gentleman.'

'You did indeed.' He looked up then, a grin all over his face. 'I was never a gentleman and am not planning on being one now or in the future either.' He squinted at his companions on the bench, then around the room. 'If it's gentlemen you're looking for you won't find too many here.'

He clipped another nail, neatly, and held it up for me to admire. He was still grinning.

'You can keep your seat,' Sarah said, 'I'm not so badly off as all that.'

The moans from the inner room had subsided a little but there was no sign of Daniel Casey anywhere, nor of any other doctor either.

A boy arrived with medical supplies and out of nowhere a man appeared behind the dispensing counter to take them from him. I prayed for a similar, sudden entrance by Daniel Casey.

It didn't happen. A woman on the bench beside me touched my hand.

'That's a misfortunate woman called May O'Toole inside there and about to have her baby,' she nodded to the closed door and spoke in the loud whisper people use in churches. 'She was out walking when she should have been resting,' the whisper got even louder, 'her waters broke. The pains came on immediately and she shouted for help. What else was she to do?'

Since she seemed to expect an answer to this I nodded. 'It was the right thing to do,' I said.

Encouraged, she went on. 'They brought her in here and she was put immediately up on the bed. She's been in there for an hour or more now.' She shook her head. 'She's a neighbour of my own and I know for a fact she's only the seven months gone.' She closed her eyes. 'There's nothing to be done but pray for her.' Her lips moved in silent frenzy and a pair of rosary beads appeared between her fingers. She had the whitest hair of any woman I'd ever seen, yet she wasn't old.

'The sickness has passed. I feel grand now.' Sarah had been listening. 'We should go . . .'

'We will not go,' I said, 'we will wait to see Daniel.'

'There are people here need to see him worse than me.' Sarah, hissing in my ear, pointed to a man holding a bleeding head in his hands, at a small girl with a ferocious stone cut on her knee.

'Dr Casey's not here, if it's him ye're arguing about,' the white-haired woman said without opening her eyes.

'What doctor is here then?'

'Dr Connolly's here. He's not young but he's all the better for that. He'll be a while with the poor woman in there.' She opened her eyes and looked at Sarah. 'The sick will wait for him. They're used to taking their turn.' She stared. 'You're from Henrietta Street. I've seen you there. Your grandmother's Martha Rooney, am I right?'

'You are.'

'What ails you?' The woman went on staring.

'Nothing ails her,' I said, 'she's here because she's with me. I'm a nurse.' Let her run with *that* as a story to Martha Rooney.

Slowly, the woman turned from her scrutiny of Sarah. She looked at my clothes first, then my face.

'You'll not last,' she said, 'any more than any of the others that were here. It's a job for a man. Or a strong woman. You're neither.'

'You don't know *what* I am.'

'You're not serious, I know that. You wouldn't come here dressed like a chorus girl if you knew what you were about.'

I could have told her my morning dress of garnet-coloured cashmere was the warmest I had. That my fur-trimmed bonnet was also for warmth. That dressing as if for a funeral didn't advance the cause of life. What I said was, 'Does Dr Connolly have help with his patient?' I used a lofty tone.

The woman smiled. Now she'd opened them her eyes were like a pair of dark grey pebbles and missed nothing. 'He has a nurse attendant with him, a woman as old as himself who's trying to save her soul with good works.' She gave a short laugh. 'I wouldn't let her next or near me even if I was dying.'

She looked briefly Sarah's way before closing her eyes again. It was a relief to have that prying gaze turned off. 'Prayers are what May O'Toole needs. There's not a lot doctors or nurses can do for her at this stage.'

I went to the door of the examining room and knocked. Sarah followed me but I ignored her agitation as I listened to the pained sounds and gasps and pleading cries from the other side of the door. After a minute, when no one answered, I stepped inside. Sarah slipped in after me and I closed the door behind us.

We were in a much brighter room and to the back of the building. Against one wall stood a wood-framed screen. The others displayed charts with anatomical drawings and such as well as a watercolour picture of a doctor visiting a patient.

A stove burned in this room too, with a kettle on top, and a table held medical equipment, lint and muslin. A thin, disapproving woman was pouring hot water into a basin.

All of this I saw before the doctor, without looking up, said, 'Who are you and what do you want? Are you a relative? Have you come to help?'

He was old, in his late sixties I'd have said, and he was heavy and mostly bald. He wore no jacket and his shirtsleeves were rolled up.

As he spoke he mopped the brow of the woman thrashing and groaning on a bed between the two windows. She wore a shift but no drawers. She still had her boots on, her foot showing through a hole worn in the sole of one.

I moved on into the room. Sarah stayed where she was.

'I'm a nurse,' I said. 'I'll help if you tell me what to do.'

'Maybe there *is* a God . . .' Muttering, the doctor looked at me. He shook his head. 'Though if there is He works in mysterious ways.'

He straightened and moved away from his patient. 'Take off your bonnet and gloves,' he said, 'and stand at the head of the bed and do what I ask of you. Don't do anything I don't tell you to.' To the woman washing her hands he said, 'You can go into the other room, Bridget, you'll be of more use in there. Talk to the patients, see if there's any of them can come back tomorrow.' He peered over his glasses at Sarah. 'Go with her. You've no business here unless you're a relative.'

I gave my bonnet and gloves to Sarah and stood where he'd asked me to. I didn't look up when the door closed behind Sarah and the other woman. To save my life I couldn't have taken my eyes from the woman on the bed.

Her sandy-coloured hair was a damp tangle on the pillow, her face plum-coloured and perspiring. Her arms and shoulders and chest were covered in freckles, as were her exposed legs.

She fastened a pair of terrified eyes on mine when I stood beside her. 'Glory be to God but I'm frightened. I've got four children at home.' She held my hand. 'All of them born in my own place, in my own bed . . .' she spoke fast, 'I never had a bit of trouble before. Nor a man doctor before either. Always the handywoman, always Ma Brophy. She brings home all the babies where I live.' She gasped and her grip tightened on my hand and she cried out, 'Oh sweet Mother of God why have you given me this pain . . . oh, sweet Jesus why . . . what did I do to you oh, God, what did I do wrong . . .'

I held on, mopping her brow as the doctor had done. Her back arched and she began a new and dreadful moaning.

'Calm her down.' The doctor, at the other end of the bed, was terse. 'Tell her to bear down and push.'

His head went between her legs and I looked away, taking deep breaths, trying to call up something, in all that I'd read in recent weeks, about childbirth. Little of what I remembered bore any relation to what was happening to the woman on the bed.

'Pretend I'm Ma Brophy,' I said as I wiped her forehead and held her hand, fast, 'bear down the way she told you with the others. You can do it. You did it for them. Four times, you said.'

'I'm trying, I'm trying . . .' She relaxed a little as the pain passed. I went on mopping her brow. 'Push when the pain comes again,' I said.

'I will, I will.' Fat tears rolled down her face. She caught them with her tongue when they went into her mouth. 'I knew all along things weren't right. I've been afraid all the time for this baby.' She gave a loud wail. 'It's going to die, I'm going to die . . . my children will be without a mother . . .' She threw her head from side to side. 'Oh, Mary Mother of God let my baby live . . .'

'Keep trying to calm her down,' the doctor said, washing his hands, 'the head's engaged. The next lot of contractions will do it.' His bald pate shone and he looked tired. And very worried.

'Tell me your name,' I said to the woman.

'I'm May O'Toole.' She'd grown pale and was trembling all over. 'I was sick from the first day and I've been feeling strange all of the time. All the time sick . . .' Heavy, silent tears continued to make channels down her face. 'I know what I have to do.' She looked at me. The trembling stopped. 'I know I have to bring this baby into the world but the only way I know to do it is the way Ma Brophy told me.'

'Tell me what to do,' I said.

'You must hold me down, when the pains come you must—' She took a quick, gasping breath.' Oh, Mother of God they're starting again. Hold on to me, hard, keep telling me tell me when to push.'

I looked at the doctor and he nodded.

'Now,' I said, 'push now, May, hard, I'm holding you. Now . . . and again.'

May O'Toole pushed. She half sat and I held her, talking to her. Her pain was terrible. She was a woman used to pain and hard times and yet she could hardly bear this agony. She was all but fainting when I heard the doctor's muttering.

'Too fast . . . this is too fast . . .'

He was listening with a stethoscope on May's bloated belly and I wished, for the first and only time in my life, that I hadn't read so much. I wouldn't have known otherwise that he'd found the baby's heartbeat and that it was beating too quickly.

May O'Toole lay against me limp and whimpering, exhausted by pain, her face clammy and cold.

'We've got to get her baby out,' Dr Connolly was brusque, 'let go of her and bring me the forceps. Quickly.'

As I handed him the forceps I saw the baby's head myself. It filled me with awe for the job that women have to do, for the great service they give the world.

It also decided me never to have a baby myself.

Dr Connolly applied the forceps and I went back to holding May O'Toole. Her contractions had eased but she was trying feebly to push nevertheless, and she was praying. The doctor, so as to get leverage, put his foot on the end of the bed and pulled with both hands. His face was purple with effort.

May O'Toole clung to me. The whole thing seemed to me so brutish, that there must be another way. There was no science to it. It was barbaric.

The baby came into the world quite gently in the end. One minute Dr Connolly was like a lunatic taking a cork out of a bottle, the next he was holding May O'Toole's blood-covered, newborn baby boy, delivering a slap to his buttocks.

The baby didn't cry. The doctor clamped and cut the umbilical cord and it fell away, limp.

'The airways will have to be cleared.' He laid the baby on the table and picked up a rubber bulb with a suction end. 'I'd be obliged, my dear,' he said this to me gently, 'if you would do this for the little fellow. I'll guide you. Hurry up now, hurry, hurry . . .'

I did everything he said, using the apparatus to suck mucus and fluids from the baby's mouth, listening all the while for the tiny chest to draw in, hoping the legs would kick, that somehow life would begin.

Nothing happened.

Dr Connolly took the baby and I stood again beside a silent May O'Toole while he splashed cold water on its back. But there was no life in the small body and there never would be. The silent room held all the answer we needed.

'Give me my baby.' May O'Toole held out her arms.

'There's no point, May.' Dr Connolly was gentle. 'He's gone. You know that.'

May O'Toole didn't ask again. She lay down and was very still and silent while he went behind the screen with the body. She looked up when he reappeared with it wrapped in a cotton sheet. 'His father will make his coffin today,' she said, 'he'll come to take him away in it when it's ready.' She rubbed a hand over her eyes. 'Someone'll have to go and tell him.' She made a small, grunting sound. 'I don't feel so good.'

Dr Connolly positioned the screen around her bed. 'The boy

will get your husband,' he said gently, 'you'll be at home in your own bed in a few hours and the handywoman'll look after you there.'

I'd cleaned the table of the baby's blood and was looking at the sad shape his body made in his cotton shroud when Dr Connolly reappeared from behind the screen.

'You did well,' his eyes were bloodshot, 'you were a good help to Mrs O'Toole. It wasn't an easy one.' He put the stethoscope on the table and began to wash his hands. 'Thank you for cleaning up here too. Do you feel able to stay another few hours? I need the help.' He gave me a smile that was wryly conspiratorial. 'Bridget means well but her idea of nursing is to boil water and scold patients.'

'I could work here for longer than that,' I said. 'If you were agreeable I could come several days a week.'

He was tired, but not that tired. He took me in from head to toe.

'What training have you done?' he asked.

'I'm self-taught and self . . . trained.'

'I'll be more explicit: what experience have you?'

I was silent for a minute; there was no good lying to this man.

'I've tended sick friends,' I said, 'and at my school in France one of the nuns, who had worked as a nurse in the Crimea, taught some of us what she knew. Also, I've been reading Mrs Fenwick's *Nursing Record* and . . .' I paused, debating what else to tell him, whether I should mention everything else I'd read as well as tell him I knew Daniel Casey and wanted to be a doctor.

I decided against confusing things and said, simply, 'I want to nurse. I'll do whatever you ask of me.' There was a knock on the door and a voice called the doctor's name. 'I'll work hard,' I added.

'You might be useful,' Dr Connolly said, 'you just might do us. Although, if I'm to be honest, you don't look the part.' He began to roll down his shirtsleeves. 'What is your name?'

'Alicia Buckley.'

There was another knock on the door. This time it opened

and the woman Bridget came in. Behind her in the waiting room I saw Sarah, pacing and white-faced with my bonnet in her hands.

'She delivered it then.' Bridget, eyeing the screen, was grim. 'Stillborn?'

Dr Connolly nodded. 'Sadly,' he sighed. 'Ask the boy to run for her husband, will you Bridget? He's just to bring him to the dispensary, not tell him anything. I'll do the talking when he gets here.'

Bridget sniffed. She was dressed in darkest grey with a crucifix on the end of a chain round her neck. If my guess was right she belonged to one of those groups of unmarried, older women who gave time to good works. Her expression reminded me of Mary Connor's.

'If he's like others of his kind,' she said, 'the husband's more than likely in the pub.'

'Tell the boy to get him, Bridget, if you would, and then make tea for Mrs O'Toole.' The doctor lifted his coat from a chair and buttoned himself into it. 'This young woman here has agreed to work with us a while. She's got knowledge and some small experience, or at least has gained some in the past hour.'

He ignored a rash of disapproving sniffs from Bridget and turned to me. 'Bring in the next patient,' he said.

When I hesitated, wanting to ask him if this meant we had an arrangement for me to work in the dispensary, he added a curt, 'Please.'

I brought a protesting Sarah back with me.

'I wanted to see Dr Casey,' she looked around as if expecting Daniel Casey to fall from the ceiling.

'Then I hope you're prepared to wait a long time,' said Dr Connolly. 'He's on a sick call. He's younger and fitter and more able than I am to climb tenement stairs. Wait if you want . . .' He waved her away.

'Sit down, Sarah,' I pulled forward a chair and she sat.

While Bridget gave tea to May O'Toole I told Dr Connolly, quietly as I could, what Sarah had done.

He drew up a chair and sat opposite her. 'What you did was both foolish and dangerous. You could have poisoned yourself as well as the foetus. I suppose you knew you might die?'

'Yes.' Sarah's eyes were bright with tears. She sat on her hands to stop their trembling.

'I'm forty years practising medicine and I'll never understand why young women risk all. Better to live and have hope, my dear,' he shook his head, 'better to live and have hope.'

'I am alive,' Sarah pointed out. She said nothing about her baby.

'I suppose the father's left you? No, don't answer.' The doctor held up his hand. 'Just so long as you're aware you could have killed yourself. From the look of you it's too early in your pregnancy for it to have done harm to the baby. Don't try anything like it again, though. You might not be so lucky the next time. If you *do* attempt it again don't come back here to me.'

Muttering and sighing he signed to Sarah to show him her hands. She took them from under her skirts and he held them in his own, examining them closely.

'Now your toes,' he said.

As Sarah, without a word, bent to untie her bootlaces he asked her what day it was, and what time of year.

'It's a Wednesday and it's the end of November and the year is eighteen sixty-seven. Do you think I'm mad, is that it?' Sarah pulled off her boots and glared at him, ignoring tears as they began to fall.

'My dear young woman,' the doctor said, sounding infinitely weary, 'because you've imbibed a lethal poison I am obliged to check your mental stability, as well as your physical well-being. Miss Buckley, bring us another chair, if you please.'

When I did this he put Sarah's feet resting on it and carefully examined her toes. 'I'm doing this,' he told her, 'to check whether or not the ergot might have caused a closure of the blood vessels.' He handed her her boots. 'You appear in good health. Am I to understand, since you're here, that you intend having this child?'

I handed Sarah a piece of damp lint and she wiped her face.

'I'm very glad the ergot didn't do any harm. I'm sorry I did what I did . . .' She bent to lace her boots. 'Will my baby be all right?'

'Probably. But I'll need to examine you.'

Because May O'Toole was using the bed Sarah stood while Dr Connolly felt her abdomen and listened to her heart. She held my hand all the while tightening her grip when he asked her when she'd stopped menstruating, if her breasts were swollen yet. He sat at last with a pad of paper.

'You're a healthy young woman and, providing you look after yourself, your baby will be fine. Get this tonic at the dispensary. I take it you're not married?'

Sarah, shocked by the abruptness of the question, could only shake her head, no.

'Come back in a month's time,' the doctor said, 'we'll find you a place to go to when your time comes.'

'I'll be married by then,' said Sarah.

He patted her on the hand. 'I hope so.' He turned to me. 'There's a man outside with a cut to his head. Bring him in to me, Miss Buckley.' He'd begun to mutter again as he went behind the screen to May O'Toole.

'How is it you always get what you want?' Sarah asked as she came with me to the man with the cut head. 'Dr Casey won't be pleased when he sees you working here.'

'I don't always get what I want and Daniel Casey doesn't own this dispensary . . .' I tapped the man with the cut head on the shoulder. He shook himself awake. 'Go on in to the doctor,' I said.

'I must go,' said Sarah, 'I'll be missed and there'll be questions asked. I hope my secret's safe with that doctor.'

'Doctors are bound by an oath . . .'

'And fish fly,' Sarah snorted.

The roars of the man with the cut could be heard, I'm sure, in the street. The cut was from a bottle and he needed stitches and the roaring began when I shaved the hair from the edge of the cut. It got even louder when Dr Connolly put in the stitches.

He made ten times the fuss May O'Toole, trying to rest behind the screen, had made. The small girl with the stone cut came next. I'd washed it with iodine and Dr Connolly was bandaging it when Daniel Casey arrived in.

CHAPTER TWELVE

Allie

My parents would have none of it.

'I'll burn the place down,' my father roared, 'I'll not have a daughter of mine catching typhus or cholera or others of the unholy diseases spread by the poor about this town . . .'

'Disease doesn't confine itself to the poor,' I said, 'there's typhoid on Clyde Road and Elgin Road.'

'Brought there by the poor.' My mother played gently with the cat's ears. He sat on her lap with his eyes half closed, wide awake as my mother, for all her languid air.

'The result of bad drains,' I said, 'the Medical Officer of Health and Dublin Castle have agreed.'

'I should never have allowed those medical books into the house.'

My father stomped from armchair to cabinet to secretary, bringing his fist down on the surface of each. We were in the drawing room, the curtains tightly closed and the coal fire fiercely burning. If my father felt frustrated then it was nothing to how smothered I felt myself.

'Disease has to be treated,' I said, 'and people made well. It's not the dispensaries that spread disease. It's expecting people to live like animals in the sort of squalid tenements to be found not a half-mile from here.' I paused. 'Have you been out and about in Ringsend and Irishtown?'

My father stopped, alarm all over his face. 'Have you been to those places too?'

'I don't have to.' I could barely keep my patience. 'The world knows how overcrowded the tenements are. How insanitary, badly ventilated, lacking in drainage. *The Irish Times* has written that not even natives on the west coast of Africa are worse housed than the residents of Ringsend, Irishtown *and* Ballsbridge, Dada. Why, in the cottages right behind us . . .'

'Disease, like the poor, will always be with us,' my mother yawned dismissively.

'It certainly will so long as it is not dealt with.'

'By others. Not by a daughter of mine.' My father stood with his backside to the fire. I worried that he would go up in flames but he didn't seem to feel the heat. 'I forbid you to go back to that dispensary.'

My mother yawned again and rested her hands in the cat's long fur. I decided on cunning.

'It's thanks to both of you that I've developed my interest in medicine.' I looked earnestly from one to the other of them. My mother ignored me, my father stared. 'It was you who brought Dr McDermott into my life and talking with him made me see what must be done.' His indifference had certainly goaded me. 'Think how useful this experience would be to me as the wife of a doctor, were that to happen.'

'It's not a wife's function to involve herself in her husband's life. And it's a wife Dr McDermott wants, not a work mate.' My father was not taken in.

'I agree.' My mother nuzzled Alfred as she spoke.

I wondered if my mother's lethargy was caused by the heat from the fire or by laudanum, or opium of some kind. It didn't seem natural.

'It could be,' I said, 'that I could bring myself to become the first if I was able, in some small way, to become the second.'

I'll never know where this line of argument, dishonest but resourceful, might have got me without the unwitting help of

Mary Connor. She arrived into the room just then, announcing herself with a small cough. Everything about her said she'd been standing outside the door, listening and waiting to interfere.

'Is the fire all right for you, ma'am? Does it need slacking up?' She stood in the shadows, her cap pulled more tightly than ever across her skull, her hands neatly crossed. My father frowned, my mother and the cat looked lazily pleased.

'The fire will do,' my mother said, 'but you might pour me a small glass of Madeira port. None for my daughter. She seems overly excited as it is.'

'I'll have a whiskey,' said my father and I swore inwardly. The alcohol would stir him up even more.

Mary Connor busied herself at the cabinet.

'I've invited Dr McDermott to dine with us on Friday,' my mother said.

'You might tell me of these dinners in advance, Harriet.' My father frowned. 'I won't be here.'

'All to the better,' my mother said, and shrugged, 'Maurice is sometimes inhibited by your company. It's our daughter he wants to see. In the meantime, Alicia, you are forbidden to go to that dispensary.'

She took the port from Mary Connor. My father finished the whiskey she gave him in one gulp. The housekeeper cleared her throat.

'It's not my place to interfere, ma'am,' she said, 'but since you're talking of dispensaries I heard only today that the one beyond in Ringsend is overrun with rats.'

My mother gave a small squeal and shiver of revulsion. But I knew Mary Connor had heard no such thing.

'You heard wrong,' I said, 'the dispensaries are very strictly policed by the sanitary inspectors.'

'You can't change the insanitary habits of the poor,' said the housekeeper,

'The dispensaries are not run by the poor,' I said, 'they're run *for* the poor.'

'But it's the poor who populate them and who bring their

habits in with them.' Mary Connor raised her voice. 'A dispensary is no place for a young woman from a good family.'

She'd overstepped her role. If my father had liked her he'd have overlooked this. He detested her.

'I'll be the one to decide the restrictions on my daughter.' His quiet tone was more chilling than his angry one as he held open the parlour door. 'I'd be obliged if you would leave us.'

For a few seconds I was almost sorry for Mary Connor. She stood like a small animal in a trap, fully aware she'd put herself there. Then she recovered.

'As you wish,' she said, 'but Miss Buckley will regret working in a dispensary.' She looked at me and I knew nothing would make her happier than to see the first marks of smallpox on my face, the dread flush of typhoid. Then she turned and sailed wordlessly past my father.

He waited until she had gone up the stairs before he said, 'I don't want you working in that place, Alicia, but I will not be told by that woman. If it will settle your mind and make you more kindly disposed towards Maurice McDermott then so be it. You may help out in Eccles Street for a few days a week from now until the new year. No longer.' He slammed the door behind him as he left.

'Before God I don't know how I could have given birth to you, Alicia.' My mother's voice was dreamy. 'A place in a Magdalen convent would be too good for you. We've done all we can, your father and I. You will marry Maurice McDermott or make your own way in life from now on.'

'Then I will make my own way,' I said.

She was staring into the fire and didn't seem to hear me.

Early the next day I took an omnibus across the city to the dispensary. It seemed to me more the thing than arriving by carriage. Late in the night before I'd removed the fancy trims from a Paris dress and was sober enough in navy blue. The rhythm of the horses' hooves over the cobbles soothed my nervous expectancy. It was a cold, sharp day but I sat on top of the omnibus so as to enjoy the spectacle of the city below.

Most of the people in the streets at that hour were servant women; you could tell by their dress and way of walking. I could see too into the baskets on the heads of the women hawkers; some filled with fresh cockles and mussels, others with fruit from the markets. There were boys and dogs everywhere, and soldiers and men in black topcoats on their way to work in offices.

I needed the diversion. My father had refused to speak to me as I left and Bess had told me angrily that what I was doing was an 'act of madness'.

All this and, at the end of my journey, a man who, to say the least of it, was disinclined to work with me.

Dr Daniel Casey hadn't been pleased to find me at work in the dispensary. After a tight-lipped greeting he'd taken me by the arm into the outer hallway. 'We had an agreement. We were to talk together about you working here. Nothing was to be decided until then.' His anger made him look less of a boy. He was flushed and I was careful not annoy him further.

'It's an accident that I'm here,' I assured him at my earnest best, 'I came with Sarah, hoping to see you. She needed to see a doctor. But a patient, Mrs O'Toole, was in labour when we got here and Dr Connolly needed assistance.' When I stopped and touched his arm he moved away from me. 'I didn't plan, or connive or conspire to come in here behind your back.'

'I've no doubt that's the way it happened,' he was still furious, 'and Mrs O'Toole has every reason to be grateful to you, I'm sure. But that doesn't mean you can stay and be a nurse to the rest of our patients. You're not—'

I'll never know what I was not because Dr Connolly came flapping into the hallway and cut him short. 'Sort out what's between the two of you some other time,' he was brusque, 'the waiting sick need both of you, now.'

I worked that first day for a further four hours, washing and putting cream or iodine on cuts, boiling water, taking the names and details of patients, boiling water, holding children still while their wounds were stitched, cleaning and washing, boiling water. I helped both doctors.

When Mrs O'Toole's husband came I carried her dead baby to her and she put it into its small coffin.

I was getting ready to leave when Daniel found time to ask me what had been wrong with Sarah. I saw no point in lying, or even in avoiding the question. 'She's going to have a child,' I said. 'She took poison in the night to end the pregnancy but was glad then when it didn't work. She came to be examined to make sure everything was all right.'

'Oh, God, not Sarah . . .' He stared into the basin of water on the table. 'That lovely young woman.' His expression was indescribably sad.

It wasn't the response I'd expected and I didn't try to say any more. I couldn't.

'What did Dr Connolly say?' he asked, after a while.

'That she should look after herself and everything would be all right.' I hesitated, then went on, 'Sarah says that Mary Ann came to her last night. They spoke. She believes it's thanks to Mary Ann she didn't lose the child.'

'She was hallucinating,' he was curt, 'the ergot will have been the cause. Of course Mary Ann didn't come to her.'

I wasn't so sure. Sarah believed it and Sarah wasn't fanciful, as a rule. Again, I said nothing.

'Is the father about?' Daniel asked.

'He hasn't replied to letters sent him. Sarah hasn't told her family. There's only you, I and Dr Connolly who know. Maybe the father, if he got the letters.'

Daniel Casey didn't ask me who the father was. 'Tell her I will help in any way I can,' he said.

When I left he walked with me to Berkeley Road, where there were horse cabs. The cold air, unfortunately, invigorated him.

'I must tell you again that I don't want you working in the dispensary. You're putting yourself at risk. You're young and educated. It's no place for you. You can surely find some other way to escape your parents' plans for you.'

'You're every bit as bad as them.' I stopped and turned to face him. Our breath made clouds in the cold air between us. 'Just like them you can't accept that I want a life in medicine. Who questioned you, Daniel Casey, when you decided to become a doctor? Who told you that you didn't know your own mind? No one, I'll wager, and all because you're a man.' I moved away. 'I don't need your approval. Dr Connolly wants me to work with him.'

I hoped he would come after me. I didn't want us parting on bad terms.

He did. 'My family put up a ferocious opposition to my becoming a doctor,' he said as he fell into step beside me, 'my father dying of typhus fever nearly destroyed my mother and sisters.' He was looking straight ahead. 'They didn't want the only other man in the family taken from them in the same way.'

The knowledge that he had a mother and sisters who loved him made him seem different to me. Made him a man as well as a doctor.

'It's not your place to worry about me, Daniel,' I said, 'not about my catching typhus fever or anything else. If anything happens to me it will be because I choose to take the risk myself.' I peered at, and assured, his stern profile. 'I'm the only one accountable.'

'You should at least know the facts.' He ran a hand through his hair, making it stand on end like a yard brush. 'Figures show the death rate among Irish medical practitioners higher than among army officers in combat. Fifty per cent higher . . .' He cleared his throat. 'The same figures show that twenty-five per cent of Irish doctors die in discharge of their duties.'

He stopped, leaning against an iron railings, waiting for me to speak. Paint flaked from the railings and fell about him like a small shower of soot.

'Why, with all these facts, did *you* decide to practise medicine?' I said.

'Because I see medicine as a practical art. I want to know about and use new means to cure or alleviate diseases.' He gave a small shrug and smiled. 'It's in my bones. It's all my father left me.'

'I see the practice of medicine as a practical art too,' I said, 'and what my father has given me is a great need to make a life for myself independently of him and my mother.'

We left it at that, for then.

Within a week it was December and the days had become colder, shorter and bleaker than in any December I could remember.

I worked hard in the dispensary and got used to Daniel Casey's quiet, stubborn company. He was the best of doctors. Even Dr Connolly, who'd worked, he said himself, 'with every kind of quack in the medical book', thought so.

Daniel Casey saw the worst of the diseases too. He was the one went out to the tenements to treat those stricken with smallpox and diphtheria and pneumonia and tuberculosis, all of them too ill to come to the dispensary themselves. He was a driven force, a living reminder of all that he'd told me about the chances taken by his dead father and every other dispensary doctor in Ireland.

Working in the dispensary didn't improve my tolerance for Maurice McDermott as a doctor. It was coming up to Christmas when I lost what little tolerance I had for him as a man, and as a happy consequence lost him as a suitor.

CHAPTER THIRTEEN

Allie

———◦◦◦◦◦———

The city was not at its best.

The snow which had fallen for two days left the streets piled with frozen slush on top of which animal droppings steamed.

I wasn't at my best either when I arrived home to find Dr Maurice McDermott waiting for me.

He, however, was in fine form. Flushed and beaming, he heaved himself out of an armchair by the drawing-room fire to greet me. The port bottle on the small table beside him was almost empty.

'I called to see your good father, Alicia,' he said with a small bow, 'only to find him away. When the housekeeper said you were expected home I decided to wait. I hope, Alicia, that you don't mind us being alone?'

The way he was forever using my name, with his Alicia this and Alicia that, made the skin of my scalp crawl.

'I trust myself completely in your company, Dr McDermott,' I said.

'And you're right to do so, Alicia my dear, absolutely right.' He rubbed his hands together. 'My intentions towards you are completely honourable.'

He was wearing a yellow vest with a spotted bow tie. He looked ridiculous but clearly thought he looked young.

'I haven't given any thought to your intentions towards me, Dr McDermott,' I smiled. I'd discovered that as long as I smiled

I could say anything I pleased and Dr McDermott wouldn't take offence. He didn't now either.

'I wondered, Alicia, if you would care to go to the Exhibition Palace to see Blondin perform?' He was rubbing his hands so hard I expected sparks to fly. 'He's the hero of Niagara, you know, and he's to perform on a high rope at the highest possible elevation . . .'

'I know all about Blondin, Dr McDermott, and I'm amazed you would think me interested in such nonsense.' I didn't smile.

'I see, I see . . .' He indicated an armchair I should use and sat into his own near the fire. The familiarity of this irritated me beyond belief. 'Sit a while and talk with me.' His encouraging smile made me want to run from the room.

'Will sad tales of dispensary work entertain you? It's all I have to talk about these days.' My yawning was not a pretence; I was very tired.

'Your interest in medicine is commendable,' he said, and pursed his cherry lips, 'but that northside dispensary is no place for a young woman of your sort. I can tell you anything you need to know about medicine.'

'I think not.' I took an armchair near the centre of the room. 'The most unpleasant things interest me. Disease, the spread of infection—'

His laugh cut me short; it was loud and unfunny. 'Nature has designed women to nurture the young, Alicia. It's their purpose, and a fine and noble one it is too. It seems to me, my dear Alicia . . .' he gave a small cough and dabbed his lips, 'that your natural, womanly urge to nurture has driven you to the extreme of nursing work in this dispensary. If you had younger brothers and sisters to occupy you, or a child of your own . . .'

He left the thought unfinished and his smile, this time, reminded me of a malevolent gnome. I looked at him with a dislike he was too drunk to notice.

'I've no wish to nurture,' I said, 'only to cure. I've decided to devote my life to the practice of medicine. I intend becoming a doctor.'

I'd said nothing to him about this before and it was a waste of my time saying it now. He looked mildly amused and not very interested.

'Women function better as the helpmeet of man, Alicia. Men, after all, go into the world to keep it a better, safer, place for all of us. Women should not be exposed to the horrors of medicine.'

'Medicine seems to me to be more about the miracle of healing.'

'The male is better equipped to minister to the horrors of the diseased body.' His eyes on mine were like those of a small, unpleasant animal.

'Horrors, Dr McDermott? You keep using that word. Surely the sick or diseased body is pitiful? Surely the horror is that we are so unable to make it well? And surely, too, women have a role to play in the care and healing of other women?'

'Women are made for beauty, Alicia, and to enjoy beautiful things. They are the opposite of us brute males, a leavening force in this cruel world.'

'Women give birth,' I pointed out, 'when they are lucky enough to go to term. Where is the beauty in the lives of the fifty per cent of pregnant women who lose their babies in Dublin each year? You must know that infant mortality in Dublin is the highest in Europe.'

'So they say.'

He took a cigar from his pocket and without asking my permission snipped and lit the end. I held my tongue. I was hungry and said a small, silent prayer that he wouldn't stay to dinner.

'*You* must know, my dear Alicia, that it's women of the labouring classes who lose their babies. It's nature's way of curtailing numbers.'

The door opened and Mary Connor, in a lace collar exactly the whey colour of her face, glided to the centre of the room. She showed not the slightest ill effects of her fall.

'I've had three places laid for dinner, Dr McDermott.' She ignored me. 'Since I presume you'll be dining here when Mrs Buckley returns?'

'Thank you, Mary, thank you, I'd be delighted.' He was immediately his bluff and hearty self. 'And maybe, while we wait, you might bring another bottle of port wine so as Miss Buckley could enjoy a glass? She's somewhat overexcited on the subject of women in medicine.'

He laughed. Mary Connor nodded. She still didn't look my way.

'Bring the port for Dr McDermott, Mary,' I said as I stood, 'I won't be having any. I'm tired and I'd like to eat in my room.'

Mary Connor made no move to go. I grew hot in a way that had nothing to do with the fire.

'Tell Bess to make up a tray for me when you go for the port, Mary.' I faced Maurice McDermott. 'My overexcitement would make me bad company at table.'

'I'll be most offended if you don't dine with me,' he said as he heaved himself out of the chair again. The beaming mask had gone.

'My mother will be delighted to have your company,' I said. 'I'm afraid that you and I have too many differences for us to make polite dining companions.'

'I'm sure we can find a subject convivial to both of us.'

'I'm sure we can do nothing of the sort.' As the last of my patience went I heard Mary Connor's tongue make its familiar click. 'You're the enemy of medical progress, Dr McDermott, the enemy of the poor and, though you may not know it, the enemy of women too.'

His hand, holding the cigar, shook. I knew I had gone too far but, on the principle that I couldn't take things back, I finished what I had to say. 'We're too different for a friendship between us ever to develop, Dr McDermott. We're in no way suited to one another.'

'I doubt, Miss Buckley, that you will ever find anyone suited to you.' He threw the remains of the cigar into the fire. 'I doubt you will make a doctor either, no matter your own ideas on the subject. You seem to have little to offer but rudeness and a dangerous anarchy you've brought with you from France.' The words came out of him in a loud torrent he'd probably been holding in. 'You'd do well to keep your views to yourself, miss, until they have been restrained by experience or altogether changed.' He raised his hand and snapped two fingers at Mary Connor. 'My coat, if you please, and my hat. And perhaps you would be good enough to tell Mrs Buckley I'll not be dining here again.'

I watched from my bedroom as he went down the front steps. He'd nearly reached the bottom when he stumbled, recovered himself and kicked viciously at the railing. The sight did me a world of good.

When my dinner failed to arrive on a tray I went to the kitchen and, eating my meal there, told Bess what had happened.

'You're storing up a lot of misery for yourself,' she said, 'if you'd any sense you'd have dangled him until he got tired of waiting your parents will tighten the rope on you now and no mistake.'

'They want me married. They will find someone else for me,' I said.

I wasn't altogether wrong. The someone else to pay court was a friend of my parents', though not one they'd chosen as a suitor.

Christmas came and went quietly, and so quickly there was a part of me still waiting for it to happen on the second day of January 1868.

I saw Sarah twice and she was well and managing to keep her secret. She hadn't yet heard from Jimmy Vance but was making plans to visit the Curragh camp when the days got longer.

My father, though unforgiving of my treatment of Maurice McDermott, didn't try to stop me going to the dispensary. He wasn't inclined, he said, to go back on his word during the season of charity and goodwill.

My mother behaved as if I didn't exist.

The weather changed in the New Year when the spell of cold, bright days which had seen us through Christmas came to a dramatic end on Small Christmas Day.

The sixth of January dawned dark. Around noon the lumpen, grey cloud hanging low over the city released a deluge of rain which went on for two days. The streets ran like rivers and the river Liffey swelled like an ocean. When the rain stopped the cold returned and then, within a day, more snow arrived.

If I'd ever had doubts about the grasp the hand of God had on the affairs of men and women, and I'd had plenty such, the weather that January did away with my uncertainties. That inclement time started a chain of events which led to the occasion which decided the rest of my life.

The rain caused a flood in Eccles Street and the dispensary was closed for four days. By the time it opened the snow was severely limiting the movements of both horse cabs and omnibuses.

An entire eight days went by without my crossing the city, or even leaving the house.

My mother was confined to the house too, which suited her even less than me since she didn't have reading to divert her. My father went about his business but the new maidservant, who was timid and fretful and grateful even to be allowed to breathe, failed to come to work. It was so difficult to move about that Bess had to spend three nights in Haddington Road.

Tempers in the house were short and seasonal goodwill a distant memory on the day Bess opened the front door to Ned Mulvey's knocking.

I was coming down the stairs when I heard her tell him my parents were out and would not be back for a while. He stepped inside anyway, stomping his feet and complaining of the cold saying he would warm himself by the fire before going on his way.

I came down the remaining steps.

'Alicia will keep me company.' He handed Bess his hat and

coat — grey with a velvet collar — and crooked his arm for me to take. 'Lead me to a warm fire,' he said.

'There are several,' I told him, 'but the drawing room is the warmest.'

I was glad of some pleasant company. Even Bess was in a bad mood. I was worried that Sarah was the cause but couldn't get her to talk to me.

'Maurice McDermott tells me you are fearlessly healing the sick on the northside of the city.' Ned Mulvey hunkered down and spread his long, white, manicured fingers to the flames of the fire.

'Does he, indeed.'

I stood by the mantel and studied him. He was in every way an indoor man, with the looks and manners of someone whose life was spent in salons and hotels and in travelling. He was very rich, according to my father, and a snob by my own reckoning. He'd shaken my hand but not Sarah's the day we met in the Shelbourne Hotel.

He was also bored, if my instinct that day was to be trusted. But he was diverting company.

'I doubt fearless was the word used by Dr McDermott,' I said when he moved back from the fire.

He was a lot taller than me and stood with his hands in his pockets. His suit was dark grey and his necktie pearl-coloured.

'Fearless is my word for you,' he admitted. 'Maurice thinks you mad, bad and dangerous to know.' He laughed and raised questioning eyebrows. 'He tells me he no longer calls on you.'

'That farce has ended,' I agreed.

'Unlucky Maurice,' he said.

'Nothing unlucky about him. We weren't suited and he knows it, now. I'm sure he'll find a suitable wife in no time.' I'd a vision of his bulbous eyes and overripe lips and revised what I'd said 'There's bound to be a woman in Dublin who'll find it fascinating to have the newspaper read to her by Dr Maurice McDermott.'

'He read the newspaper to you?' Ned Mulvey looked highly amused.

'*The Irish Times.* Maybe he thought I couldn't understand it for myself. Maybe he had no other conversation.'

'You didn't have to listen to him,' Ned Mulvey pointed out.

'Newspapers serve a useful purpose.' I didn't add that it was better than listening to Maurice McDermott's views on almost anything.

'They're of limited use. Do we really need to know that Viscount Lismore and suite have arrived from Holyhead?' Ned Mulvey asked. 'Or to be told the appalling story of the young man who threw himself on the railway track near Kingstown?'

'It's information about the world we live in. I suppose the news of Viscount Lismore's arrival is unnecessary . . .'

'Unnecessary to you, perhaps,' Ned Mulvey looked at me thoughtfully, 'but then you don't represent the thinking of most people.'

'I'm glad of that.'

'Then you must be prepared to take the consequences.'

'You sound like a teacher I had in Paris. She was eighty years old and a nun.'

He laughed outright. 'You are definitely not the woman for Maurice. Your patients must think an angel has come among them. An avenging angel.'

'Would you like tea?' I cut him short. He was immediately contrite.

'I didn't mean to trivialise what you do at the dispensary,' he said, 'and yes, I'll have tea. But only if you stay to share it with me.'

It was Mary Connor and not Bess who came when I rang the bell. She was out of breath and the tip of her sharp nose was red.

'You weren't expected,' she said to my guest 'or I'd have been here to open the door to you myself.'

'Why don't you rest, Mary, since you've just come back in?' I was civility itself. 'Ask Bess to bring us some tea.'

'Mr Buckley is away. Mrs Buckley will be back shortly.' Mary Connor ignored me.

'Then I will wait and see Mrs Buckley before I go.' Ned Mulvey sat into an armchair and crossed his legs. 'Tea would be nice in the meantime.'

'Perhaps you would help Mrs Rooney prepare the tray?' Mary Connor gave me a hard look out of pale, angry eyes.

'It would be rude of me to leave Mr Mulvey on his own,' I said.

She spun on her heel and left. I paced a little, unsure where to sit.

'Do you believe in Fate?' Ned Mulvey made a chapel of his fingers and looked up at me over their steeple.

'I've wondered about it,' I admitted, 'and I'm still not sure if I do or not.'

'I'm a great believer myself. I'm certain Fate brought me here today.'

He looked at me in a way that made me wish I'd worn something more exciting than my plain, and pale, green dress.

'I would be honoured, Alicia, if you would come as my partner to the Roomkeepers' Ball. My mother has something to do with the running of it and I'm obliged to attend. It's to be held in the Rotunda. He paused. 'It has a reputation as a very entertaining function.'

'This has been decided by Fate, has it?' I settled a cushion and sat into an armchair. It gave me a moment to collect myself.

'It has. I'm meeting with the person who has the tickets tonight and today,' he spread his hands, 'I meet with you. Will you come?'

I was flattered. I was also uncertain. Most of all I was curious – and aware of what curiosity had done to the cat.

Flattery won the day.

'They say it's foolish to tempt Fate,' I said. 'I'd be pleased to partner you. What charity is the ball in aid of?'

'One of the most deserving in the city. The Sick and Indigent

Roomkeepers' Society.' He turned as the door opened and Mary Connor came in with a tray. 'Thank you.' He took it from her. 'You needn't stay.'

She left, reluctance in every bone of her body. The door had no sooner closed than he took out and looked at his watch.

'I can't stay for the tea after all,' he said, 'will you excuse me?'

I let him out myself and watched from the door while he went down the steps. *He* didn't stumble. He didn't look back either.

I stood for a while after he'd disappeared along the road. I needed the cool air on my burning cheeks.

For such a small event, an afternoon visit and casual invitation, the repercussions were terrible. Like ripples from the centre of a pool they spread and lapped at the lives of everyone around. In my case I almost drowned.

The first victim was Bess Rooney. After a lifetime's service with us my mother dismissed her that evening. It happened as dinner ended.

'You took extra duties upon yourself this afternoon.' My mother had eaten hardly anything. Bess was serving a dessert of bread and butter pudding.

'Did I?'

Bess put a piled bowl in front of me. I'm fond of bread and butter pudding.

'You opened the front door to Mr Ned Mulvey,' my mother's voice rose, 'you allowed him in without either Mr Buckley or myself being at home. You encouraged him to spend time alone with Alicia in the drawing room.'

'That's not the way it was at all.' Bess defended herself gently enough. 'There was no one else about to answer his knocking and he asked to warm himself a bit by the fire before doubling back on his journey.'

'You had no business opening the door when there was no one at home.' There was an hysterical edge to my mother's voice. 'It's not your position to admit people. The task of admitting callers belongs to Mary Connor, who tells me she was out of the house for but one, bare hour. You should have ignored the doorbell while she was gone.'

My mother clenched her hands on the table. Bess and I watched her cautiously. When she'd returned from her afternoon's outing in a black mood I'd known that a row of some sort was likely.

'You have never known your place, Bess Rooney, never . . .'

'I was the one said Mr Mulvey should come into the drawing room,' I lied. 'I was sure either you or Dada would be home any minute. Asking a friend to step inside on a cold day seemed the civilised thing to do.'

'Was it civilised for a young woman your age to spend time alone with a man like Ned Mulvey?'

'But he is a friend of yours, and of Dada's. You didn't object to me being alone with Dr McDermott.'

This was completely the wrong thing to say. My mother went white in the face.

'So that's it!' She brought the palm of her hand down hard on the table. 'Having viciously dismissed Dr McDermott you plan to amuse yourself with Mr Mulvey. Well, you'll not do it, miss. I will see to it that you don't. Mr Mulvey is not a man to be trifled with.'

'Mr Mulvey has invited me to a ball,' I said, hearing Bess's intake of breath beside me, 'and I have agreed to go.'

Bess's shoes made a thin creaking as she walked to my mother with her dessert. It was the only sound in an electrifying silence.

'What ball?' my mother managed. She'd become rigid as a pillar.

'The Roomkeepers' Ball. It's to raise money for the Sick and Indigent Roomkeepers' Society.'

My mother stared. A muscle under her eye gave tiny, convulsive ticks and there were red spots high on her cheeks. Bess put the bread and butter pudding in front of her and she lowered her eyes to the bowl.

'Take that disgusting mess away from me,' she said, 'I will never again eat anything prepared by you, Bess Rooney. You've been the cause of untold damage and mischief in this house. I want you to leave. Immediately. Don't come back.' She lifted the bowl and, without looking at her, handed it back to Bess.

'You're telling me I no longer have a position here?' Bess took the bread and butter pudding.

'That's precisely what I'm telling you.' My mother lifted and shook the handbell on the table beside her. 'I should have got rid of you a long time ago. Before we moved to this house. You don't know your place and look where it has got us. None of this would have happened if you hadn't presumed to admit that man.'

'What exactly do you think has happened?' I tried to keep my voice level. 'We spoke. I accepted an invitation to a ball . . .'

'A ball? Don't play the innocent with me, miss. The ball you have agreed to go to is notorious, and well you know it. Last year's event caused outrage and was said far and wide to be nothing but a vulgar orgy.' My mother's glittering eyes held mine. 'The newspapers wrote of drunken men and women hanging together in maudlin embrace, of foolery and vice. It's not the place to bring a young girl. Or any woman, for that matter.'

'How was I to know any of this? I wasn't here.'

'You will not go.'

Mary Connor, in response to the bell, came into the room. Like a deformed shadow she attached herself to my mother's side.

'I've given my word and the tickets will have been bought by now,' I spoke loudly. The Roomkeepers' Ball seemed to me, suddenly, the most exciting event on earth. Also, if Bess Rooney was to lose her position then it couldn't be for nothing. 'I'm certain Mr Mulvey wouldn't have invited me if he thought it unsafe.'

'You will not go,' my mother said. 'But *you*,' she turned to Bess, 'will leave this instant. I won't have a mutinous servant in my house. Furthermore, I'll have the police remove you if you don't get out of my sight immediately. Mary . . .'

'There's no need for this carry-on Mrs Buckley.' Bess untied her apron. 'I'll be off.' She laid the apron on the table. As she passed she patted me on the shoulder. 'Take a good care of yourself Allie,' she said.

I wanted to weep.

CHAPTER FOURTEEN

Sarah

After twenty-one years working for the Buckley family, longer even than my own lifetime, my mother was dismissed by Harriet Buckley.

'That woman's a mad bitch from hell.' My father, full of drink, stood in the middle of the room and railed like the demented. 'She was always a mad bitch only now she's an evil one as well.'

'Well, there's an end to it now,' my mother said, 'and there's no good you bawling about it.' She turned her hands over and over in her lap, examining them. It was as if she thought this would somehow make sense of what had happened. 'God alone knows how we'll manage but we'll pray and He'll provide somehow.'

'You pray,' my father said, 'I'll go over and have this out myself with Leonard Buckley.'

'Do what you like but I won't be going back,' my mother said. She was sitting to one side of the fire, wearing her hat and shawl. The effort to remove them seemed too much.

My grandmother, sitting opposite her, had said nothing so far. I'd never known her so quiet. She'd been silent even before my mother came in and I was worried. There was an uneasiness about her, a waiting and a brooding in her silence.

'The judgement of God will strike that greedy, backsliding hound of a publican,' my father flailed the air with his crutch, 'or if He doesn't I'll strike him down myself. Hasn't he done enough to this family? Hasn't he destroyed me, ruined forever my chances of supporting my own? Isn't that enough for him?'

'It had nothing to do with Leonard and you know it,' my mother said as she got up at last to take off her hat. 'Harriet wants free of the past and wants nothing to remind her of Dominick Street and the way she was once a publican's wife.' She hung the hat on the back of the door but kept the shawl about her shoulders.

'She's free now,' she said.

'What happened?' I said. 'What led up to it?'

'I answered the front door and let that man friend of theirs into the house Mary Connor was out,' she took a breath, 'I couldn't turn him away he sat a while with Allie.'

'What man?'

'Ned Mulvey's his name you remember him pleasant enough by times.'

'I remember him.'

I wished, more than ever, that I'd told Allie my suspicions about Ned Mulvey. He was the reason my mother had been dismissed, I was sure of it; though Harriet Buckley wanting to be free of Dominick Street was a part of it too.

'I'll pray to God and His Blessed Mother and with their help I might get work tomorrow,' my mother said.

'Where was God when your other daughter died? Where was he today?' My father thumped the floor with his crutch. 'Where is He when I'm out looking for work? Answer me, God,' he shook the crutch at the high, silent ceiling, 'where have you been all my life, you bastard?'

His futility was a terrible thing.

'Stop it Cristy I won't have you blaspheming,' my mother stood in front of him, 'God's ways are not ours and we must accept and try to understand.' She held both of his arms. 'Things will get better we're over the worst of the grieving I'll get work and Sarah will get a good position one of the days . . .'

'There's no good you depending on Sarah.'

My grandmother spoke at last and I knew I'd been right to worry.

'She'll have enough to do looking after herself in the months ahead.' She turned to where I was sitting on my bed in the corner. 'Am I right, Sarah, in thinking you won't be around here for much longer?'

'Leave the child alone she'll talk to us in her own time,' my mother said.

I knew then that my mother knew too, along with my grandmother, about my condition. I wasn't very big; someone must have said something.

'You're soft, Bess,' my grandmother was harsh, 'too soft for your own good and for hers . . .' She jerked her head in my direction. 'She's lost to us. She's brought disgrace on a family with the best name of any in the streets around here. The Rooneys have always lived proper. She'll have to go.'

My father, rooted where he stood while my grandmother spoke, sank into a chair by the table and stared at me. 'Your grandmother's wrong, Sarah, isn't she? Or is it me that's wrong in understanding her to say you're with child?' He seemed to have shrivelled and grown smaller.

'There's nothing wrong with your understanding,' my grandmother said. 'Out with it, Sarah, and the truth, mind.'

'I'm five months gone.' I looked from my father to my mother, 'And I'm sorry for the shame it'll bring on you. I'll be going away. My plan was to go when the days got a bit longer but I'll go now, in the morning.'

'You won't spend another night in this house.' My father didn't look at me. It was as if he couldn't bear to.

'You'll leave now and you'll leave with the clothes on your back, not another stitch. Our good name was all we had in this family and you've lost us even that. You'd best get out of here and get yourself to one of the Magdalens. The nuns can look after you and your bastard when your time comes.'

'Let her stay Cristy,' my mother said, 'no one need know for a while yet and maybe with God's help we can manage somehow . . .'

'Every dog and cat in the city knows of her condition,' my grandmother said, 'isn't that the case, Sarah Rooney? All of them going in and out of the dispensary in Eccles Street knows. Allie Buckley does and so do the doctors. It was Biddy Moran told me. She saw you there. God knows how many others she's told.' She poked me in the shoulder and put her face close to mine. I could smell the decay from her rotting teeth.

'I've been watching you and hearing you get up in the mornings early. I've seen your middle thickening and your mother did too but she was too taken up with grieving your dead sister to do anything. You're a whore of the worst kind, concerned only with lust and depraved acts when you should have been grieving the dead child too.'

She spat on the floor at my feet. 'You've no place in this or any other decent family. We're disgraced, like your father says, and there's nothing for it but for you to redeem yourself in the convent. You've turned your face from God and your body to the devil. You'll earn your keep in the laundry. The nuns'll see to that. They'll separate you from your friend the devil too. You can forget about ever going to America now.'

'Five months . . .' My mother was sitting very still. 'Five months is the father gone Sarah is there no hope at all that he might . . .' she trailed off. 'Is he a soldier Sarah?'

She knew that he was. She was remembering my disappearances from the house in Haddington Road.

'He's a soldier, Mama, and my plan is to join him at the Curragh camp in Kildare. I'll go there tomorrow.'

My father gave a low, agonised groan. 'You've been misconducting yourself with a soldier of the British Army.' He put his head in his hands. 'You've betrayed your country as well as your family. The decent thing would be for you to kill yourself.'

'Stop it Cristy and stop it you too Martha in the name of Mary the Mother of God,' my mother said, 'have a bit of Christian charity what Sarah did was wrong but she's not the devil himself,' she shook her head, 'she's our child Cristy the only one we have now let her stay the night.'

My father left the table and dragged his useless leg behind him to the bedroom. 'Get her out of here,' he said, 'I want her gone within the hour. I don't care a toss where she goes.'

I knew where I would go. I pulled a valise from under my bed. 'I'll leave,' I said, 'but I'll take what's mine with me.'

The valise was not big but I didn't have a lot to pack. I made sure to take the Paris shawl. My grandmother watched in black silence and I wondered if she would ever forgive me. My mother's silence was different and, when I was ready, she walked down the stairs with me. It was cold and there was no one about. Our feet echoed hollow through the house. She put her arms about me in the hallway.

'You're my own child,' she said.

'Mama . . .'

'Shush now don't cry.' Her own eyes were dry. Mine were full of tears. 'When are you due?'

'In May, I think. Around the middle of the month.'

She held me against her and I felt her heart beneath the bones of her ribcage. She stroked my hair. 'I saved your christening shawl I'll get it to you where will you be?'

I told her and she let me go and made the sign of the Cross. 'Have you no place else?' she said. 'You'll be ruined entirely once you go there there'll be no coming back, ever.'

'I know that. But I'll only stay there a few weeks, just until I've enough money to get to one of the towns near the Curragh. I'll rent a room and Jimmy will come to me at once when he knows.'

'Jimmy.'

'Jimmy Vance is his name.'

'It's a nice name,' my mother said, 'it has a fine ring to it.'

Beezy Ryan herself answered the door to my knocking on the North King Street kip house. She took one look at me and opened it wider.

'So they drove you to me in the end, did they?'

When I stepped past her, into the hallway, she stood with her hands on her hips, studying me. Even in the gloom I knew she could see where the cold had frozen the tear tracks on my face.

'You look bad,' she said, 'and I suppose, since you're here with a valise in your hand, that you want a room?'

'I'm not asking for charity. I want the work you promised me as well.'

'You're lucky I didn't take on anyone else. I'd a feeling you'd be needing a place.'

In the weeks that followed I worked for my keep, and a small wage, in Beezy Ryan's kip house. I was driven by a need to be busy. Whenever I sat still my situation threatened to crush me so it was better, at first, to keep going all the time. In the mornings, while Beezy and her girls lay in their beds, I scrubbed and polished and cleaned. The place soon lost its foul, rank air and took on the genteel odours of Castile soap and lime. Beezy nagged me to take things easy, saying I would 'make the place too much like a church' and be the cause of the landlord putting up the rent. I ignored her.

I felt well and carried my baby low down. This was said to be a sure sign it was a boy but I knew in my heart, still, that I was carrying a girl.

She moved inside me on my very first night in the kip house. I put my hands over my belly and sat and talked to her about Jimmy Vance.

Beezy had given me the room at the back, off the kitchen, so that I wasn't bothered too much by the sounds of business in the night. Beezy's girls weren't that pleased to see me at first but I put work into being pleasant to them. I didn't want trouble and they were the sort would fight with their toes. Their lives had been hard and it was the only way they knew how to be.

To please them I got powder blue and cleaned the looking glasses until they shone like new. I made an orange flower paste for their hands and showed them, as my mother had shown me, how to whiten their teeth with a mixture of the juice of a lemon, burnt alum and common salt. I perfumed their underthings with a powder of cloves and cedar wood. I made perfumed bags for their drawers.

For Bernie Cole, who had the marks of smallpox on her face, I made a cold cream with sweet almonds and balm and rose water. To this I added powder of saffron, the ingredient needed to prevent the scars. It was too late to do much about Bernie's marks but it sweetened her temper towards me.

'You're right to go after the father and to keep your child,' Bernie said, 'but stay away from the Magdalens and the nuns. They'll take your baby. They took mine. A boy, he was. If I'd my time over again I'd not let them do it.'

'Easy to say that now,' Lizzie Early gave her snorting laugh, 'with your belly full of good food and a roof over your head.'

Bernie sighed. 'My baby had red hair,' she said, 'they took him from me after only two hours. I never saw him since.'

She never would see her son. Bernie Cole would be dead within six months, from pneumonia, just like Mary Ann.

My busyness served its purpose. After two weeks of agitated cleaning and scrubbing and wooing of Beezy's girls I became tired and calmed down. By then I was accepted in the house too.

By all but the beautiful Mary Adams.

Her face, with its eyes of pure, cornflower blue and perfect, snowy skin, was a source of wonder to me. But she was one of the strangest women I'd ever encountered. She followed me everywhere with those eyes.

She never left me alone for a minute with Beezy.

'Pay no heed to her,' Beezy advised.

But this was easier said than done and I told her so.

'She's not the full shilling but she's coming around,' Beezy said. 'Believe me, she's a lot better than she was, poor creature.' She shrugged. 'The men like her.'

The men liked Mary Adams because she was beautiful and didn't like them. Her coldness made them wild for her. She was the only girl some of them came to see.

'Why're you here?' she said to me one day.

I'd been in the house less than a week at the time and was

agitatedly rubbing grease marks out of the kitchen table with turpentine.

'I'm with child,' I said, 'I needed a roof over my head and I need to make some money to go to its father.'

'I had a child once. It died. It died in my belly when its father beat me. He was my father too.'

'When was that?' I was shocked.

'Three years ago. I married a man soon after but he beat me too and I went on the streets. Beezy found me. I'd be dead but for her. She's my saviour. She's like the Mother of God to me.'

'Beezy's a good woman,' I agreed.

'I suppose you think that your belly growing in front of you makes you better than the rest of us?' She stood very close to me. She smelled of lavender and her eyes were round and unblinking. 'You're the kind goes rutting with a man to make him marry you. That's the payment you were after and it makes you no less a whore than the rest of us.'

None of the bitterness of the words showed on her face, or on the pale, fine skin. She looked perfectly serene. Except for the fixed eyes.

'I don't think that at all, Mary,' I moved back, 'we're all dealt a hand in life and must play it the best we can.'

'Aren't you the wise one,' she was sneering, 'but just you remember it's *my* deal to have Beezy and I'm the one looking after her. Don't go thinking she's yours or that you can take her from me.'

'I'll be gone in a month, or less,' I said, 'and until then I'll be busy earning my keep.' I put sudsy water over the turpentine and began to scrub. She stood for a while watching me and then she left.

I told Beezy what she'd said later.

'I warned you about her already,' she reminded me, 'just humour her and she'll be all right. She's harmless.'

I wasn't so sure about the harmless bit.

There were no men allowed in the kip house before noon. The rest of the time, and into the small hours, there was a clamour. The brouhaha didn't bother me too much; it had never been quiet in Henrietta Street anyway.

Beezy had strict rules but the demon drink made it hard to keep them always. She didn't allow in bands of men – two together was the most and no more than four in the house at any one time. Men couldn't stay the night, they had to transact business with Beezy before going with a girl and Beezy turned away any man she didn't like the look of.

To deal with trouble she couldn't handle herself she had two men from the street.

They were great brutes of fellows and she paid them well. They came the minute she called.

I hated when uniformed soldiers came to the house, holding my breath until I checked the face above each jacket. It was never Jimmy Vance's. I never really thought it would be.

Though I'd heard nothing from him, not even at Christmastime, I still couldn't believe he'd rejected me. I blamed the army for keeping him away and knew that when I saw him again everything would be as it had been.

But for the most part I kept out of the way of the men, few of whom cared for the sight of a pregnant woman in a whorehouse. It reminded them of the wives they'd left at home in a similar condition.

I kept out of the streets too and went out only when I had to. One of the places I went was to the dispensary to see Allie. She was busy and happy enough.

'I'll get you money to go to the Curragh,' she said, 'when the time comes.'

I told her I was earning my own money but was grateful anyway.

I went to the pro-Cathedral to meet my mother too. She was there every day, wearing out her knees praying for me.

'Everyone in the street knows where you are,' she said, 'the child is one thing but going there has ruined you completely I hope your man will be there for you.'

'He will. I'll be going to him soon.'

'I wish you were at home with us shame and all your father misses you.'

'What you mean is that he was sober for a few hours and filled with remorse.'

'You did a terrible thing going to Beezy Ryan's.' My mother frowned at a statue of the Virgin as if expecting it to agree with her. 'It's not too late still to go to a Magdalen.'

'You know I won't do that,' I said, 'I won't work in their laundry and let them take my baby from me.'

'I pray that things will go well for you,' my mother said.

But God had never listened to my mother's prayers and he didn't this time either. I was the one opened the door to catastrophe when it came knocking in North King Street.

'Good day to you,' the man said and stepped inside quickly. All the grand types did that. They didn't want to be seen on the doorstep of a kip house. 'Get Beezy for me.'

He wore a top hat and carried a cane. It was darkening outside and he smelled of brandy. A carriage rolled away from the kerb as I closed the door.

'She's busy,' I said.

Beezy didn't jump for any man. She kept every one of them waiting. It was one rule she never broke.

'You can sit in the—'

He threw his hat on to the chaise and spoke to my belly. 'Tell her William Fleming is here.'

When I hesitated he looked up, into my eyes. His were like bits of gravel. He was a good-looking man otherwise.

'You'll have to wait,' I said.

'I'll find the whore myself.' He pushed me aside, 'Beezy!' His shout went through the house. I stepped in front of him and he made a fist of his hand and raised it to me. 'It would be better for the bastard you're carrying if you stood out of my way.' His voice was soft. 'I'm an impatient man.'

He was a violent one too, and pitiless. I was very afraid for Beezy.

'Even so you'll have to wait,' I didn't move, 'like everyone else.'

He caught my arm and threw me against the wall. 'I warned you,' he said, 'I'm an impatient man.'

'So impatience is what you're calling your bad temper these days?' Beezy came slowly down the stairs. 'Your impatience, William Fleming, will be your downfall. I told you not to come back here. Now I'm telling you to get out.'

Her hair was like a briary bush about her head. In the murky gaslight she looked taller and more forbidding than I'd ever seen her. I stayed where I was as she reached the hall floor and stood between me and William Fleming.

'Get back upstairs and into your room, Beezy,' he ordered her, his voice thick, 'I want to see you in your room.'

'Do you now?' Beezy was mocking, 'I'll see you in hell first, William Fleming. You've laid hands on one of my girls and for that there's no forgiveness, and no going back. If she's hurt in any way I'll have the skin off your back.'

'Don't threaten me, Beezy.' He whirled his cane and held it in front of him in his two hands. 'You're a whore and she's a whore. You'll do what I say and be glad to get your money.'

There was brutality as well as fury in him. In Beezy there was only fury. And she was sober.

'Get out, William.' Her cold-blooded tone was frightening. She was easily as tall as he was and she kept her eyes on his face.

'We're going to your room, Beezy,' he ran the cane between his fingers, 'so get yourself up those stairs and on to your back.'

'Why would I do that?' Beezy taunted, 'so as you can try again to prove yourself a man, is it?' She slipped her hands into her pockets and spoke very quietly. 'Take yourself elsewhere, William Fleming, with your sobs and your impatience and your withered excuse for manhood. I've done serving you.'

He was beside himself and she must have known it. She was too unafraid for her own good.

'We will go upstairs, whore.' He advanced a step and I could smell the hot sweat pouring from him. 'You will do for me what whores do.'

'I will do nothing for you, ever again. And you will not come here again and nor will you ever again lay a hand on one of the girls in my care.' She pulled her hand from the long pocket of her skirt. There was a bottle in it. I stopped a scream in my throat.

'Get out of my house,' Beezy raised the bottle and William Fleming's eyes widened, and cooled, all at once.

She might have got away with it, might have seen the back of him, if she'd resisted a final taunt. 'Take yourself and your useless cock out of here . . .'

I knew violence because I'd seen it, often, in the streets and in the pubs. I knew how quickly it could flare. Knew how the difference between life and deathly injuries could be a matter of seconds.

And still I was taken unawares by the speed of events that night.

I didn't see it go up but I saw William Fleming's cane come down and across Beezy's face. I screamed as she raised the bottle and lunged at him, pressing myself against the wall and holding my belly to protect the baby inside. I prayed in a way I'd often heard my mother pray, quick, desperate pleadings with God to do something to help.

Glass broke and the man gave a sharp, short yell and drew away from Beezy with a howled curse. He still held the stick in one hand but the other he held against the side of his face. Blood poured from between his fingers.

'You've cut me,' he said.

'Go now, William.' Beezy, as she spoke, relaxed a little. That was her second mistake.

William Fleming pitched forward, seized the bottle from her raised hand and drove it into the side of her face. Her scream was high and desolate and, as he drew back with the bottle in his hand, she fell to her knees.

I started to go to her but William Fleming, his face twisted like a bulldog's, moved between her and me and held the bottle to my face. 'Leave her,' he said, 'leave her to bleed, leave her to suffer.' He jabbed Beezy with his foot. 'You won't belittle me again, whore, nor any other man either.' He gave a half laugh. 'You'll pray for it, Beezy, from now on, beg for a man to even look at you.'

It was as he bent over her that I heard the sound on the stairs. By turning, just a little, I was able to see Mary Adams coming down and, behind her on the landing, the shadowy shapes of the other girls and whatever men had been with them.

Unaware, William Fleming went on, 'You'll remember me, Beezy, as long as you live. Every time you see yourself you'll think of me.' He poked at her again with his boot and turned to me. One side of his face was covered in blood. 'You'll keep your mouth shut, bitch, about what went on here tonight or I'll see that you never give birth to the child you're carrying. Do you understand?' He pulled me so that I was beside him when he turned again to Beezy. The blood was running over his collar and soaking the front of his coat. 'Take a good look at what happens to harlots when they forget their place . . .'

He heard Mary Adams too late. Before he could do anything she'd leaped from the stairs on to his back and brought the poker from the fire in her room crashing down on his poll. She jumped free as he fell backwards. He lay with his eyes staring sightless and dead, all fury and vengeance gone forever.

Beezy staggered to her feet. 'Sweet Jesus, Mary, what've you done . . .' One side of her face was a bloody pulp. The other side was grey as ash. 'You've killed him. He's dead, Mary, he's dead.'

'Death is too good for him,' Mary Adams said.

I went to Beezy. I touched her face, the bloody part near her eyes. The skin wasn't broken there. The eye wasn't lost.

'I'll go for the doctor,' I said, 'Daniel Casey will come.'

Beezy gripped my arms. 'Do that,' she said, 'but promise me something . . .' She gave me a small shake. It must have taken what strength she had. 'Promise me!'

'What is it you want me to promise?'

'Don't say a word of this to anyone on your way. This will be dealt with, justice will be done. It'll be my justice, and it'll be fair. Do you understand?'

'I do.' I wasn't capable of thought.

'I don't want you to even tell Daniel Casey about this man,' she gestured without looking again at William Fleming. 'There was a fight and I'm cut and need stitches. That's all you're to tell him. Do I have your word?' She gave me another, weaker, shake.

'You do.' I would have agreed to anything she asked of me.

I put a shawl about myself and left, running as well as I could, for Eccles Street and Dr Daniel Casey.

CHAPTER FIFTEEN

Sarah

———————⟨◦◦◦⟩———————

I ran and I prayed.

I prayed that Dr Casey would be at home and would come with me. I prayed that Beezy might not lose too much blood and live. That my baby might not be harmed by the shock and my journey. I even prayed for the immortal soul of William Fleming.

God was listening to at least the first of my prayers. Daniel Casey was at home and came with me at once, hiring a horse cab.

I told him only that Beezy had been wounded in a fight. He was gentle, telling me to be calm for the sake of my baby, that he would look after things. He even tried to persuade me to stay in his lodgings for the night but I would have none of it. Beezy would need someone to care for her.

William Fleming's body was gone from the floor of the hallway. There was a rug covering where it and his blood had been.

Beezy was on a chair in the kitchen with a red-soaked pad to her face. Mary Adams, full of efficiency, had water boiling and was tearing up a sheet for bandages. The other women were nowhere to be seen.

'I'm glad to see you, Dr Casey.' Beezy drank from a bottle of whiskey in her lap. It was almost empty. 'I'll need stitching.' she hesitated. 'Am I destroyed altogether?' She meant her looks.

'I'll do the best I can to see that you're not. I'll use a fine linen,' Dr Casey gently examined what the bottle had done to her face, 'I'll make the sutures fine as possible but you'll be marked. In time it won't be so bad. You've lost a great deal of blood. Do you feel weak?'

'I don't know what I feel.' Beezy raised the bottle. 'The best medicine there is.' She tried a smile but the effort was too much. 'Do it now before I fall asleep,' she said, then closed her eyes and gripped the arms of the chair as he began. 'Tell me again about how the marks will be . . .'

Daniel Casey, working with infinite care, didn't answer for a while. The cut was jagged, and half-moon-shaped, and the blood stopped running as he stitched.

'You'll have red weals but in time they'll become white.' He stepped back. 'They should be subtle enough.'

'What sort of time are you talking about?' Beezy opened her eyes. Her face was a patchwork, and bloodstained. She was an old woman.

'Six months. Maybe a year.'

'I'll have starved to death by then.' Beezy took a long slug from the bottle. 'May the man who did this and all who belong to him rot in hell.'

'Who did it, Beezy?' the doctor asked.

'I don't know,' Beezy said.

Dr Casey knew better than to persist. 'You'll recover, Beezy, but the wound needs to heal.' He placed gauze over his stitching. 'You must have peace and rest and eat well for at least a week or two.'

'It would be very bad for me to be seen like this,' Beezy agreed.

'Is there some quiet place you can go?' the doctor said.

'She'll be quiet enough here.' Mary Adams spoke for the first time. 'I'll look after her. You've done what you were brought here for. You'd best be going.'

Daniel Casey looked at her in silence for a minute. He turned back to Beezy. 'A man who did a thing like this might come back,' he said. 'Will you talk to the police?'

'The man is gone and he won't be back,' Beezy was curt,

'he was unknown to any of us here. It's over and done with.' She touched the gauze. 'There's none of us would know him again. But you're right that it would be better for me to go away. I'll go to the nuns for a week. It'll give them another chance to try saving my soul.' Her smile flickered again, and failed again.

'I won't let you go from me. I'll care for you here.' Mary Adams threw herself on her knees in front of Beezy. 'I'll be better to you than any nuns.'

'I couldn't rest here. There'll be comings and goings . . .' Beezy paused. 'It's best that I'm not here, on show with a wounded face. Bernie will look after things. It'll only be for a week. I'll be strong enough then to come back. The worst will be over by then too.'

'I don't want you to go,' Mary begged and clutched at Beezy's arm, 'I want you to stay with me.'

'I'll take you there now.' Dr Casey stepped between them and helped Beezy out of the chair, 'Sarah, pack some clothes for Miss Ryan. Let her go now, there's a good woman,' he prised away Mary Adams' hand, 'she's not strong enough for this.'

'Tell him to go, Beezy, tell him you're staying—'

'That's enough, Mary.' Beezy, brushing her aside, was harsh. She stood leaning on Daniel Casey. 'Sarah, see that this place is still standing when I get back. It's all I have between me and a pauper's grave. There's no need for you to know where I'll be. There's no need for anyone who comes looking for me to know either. Tell them I'm gone to a dying relative.'

She came with me to pack her things and, when it was done, got into a carriage with Dr Casey and rolled away.

I went into the yard behind the house and got sick. When I felt better I lay on my bed and tried to put visions of the man who'd been murdered out of my mind. It wasn't easy.

I knew his body had been taken away by Beezy's henchmen. That Bernie and the other girls had cleaned up the bloody evidence. I knew there would be an investigation, that the police would come. And I knew that not a person in the house, nor in the whole of North King Street, would ever talk about what had happened.

I never once thought about going to the police myself. I'd lived too long in the tenements, where people had to make their own justice. There would be no justice for Mary Adams at the hands of the police. She would spend the rest of her misfortunate life in the notorious Newgate prison or the madhouse. There would be no justice either for Beezy if the police were told, only ruin for her and her girls.

And there would be no justice for me, and no pity for my baby.

The police came anyway. Three days later. Bernie let them in and Bernie spoke to them. She denied everything. Carriages came every evening to deliver tall men in top hats, she said. They didn't give their names and they left after conducting their business. She'd never heard of a William Fleming, couldn't say whether such a person had ever been to the house or not. She told them Beezy was visiting a sick relative.

The rest of us agreed with every word she said. Not a person in North King Street said anything different.

The word on the street, though not for the police to hear, was that William Fleming wasn't greatly lamented by his family, who were bankers. He was childless and his wife was not inclined to spend much effort on a search for her missing husband. I thought the worst that could happen had happened, that it was over. I was wrong. Justice would have its terrible day.

The only man to come near the kip house that week was Dr Casey. He listened to my baby's heart with his stethoscope and asked me a lot of questions. He told me I was lucky to have such good health and that my baby was fine.

Mary Adams wandered about the house, day and night, mad-eyed and babbling to herself.

'She'll have to go,' Bernie Cole decided near the end of the week, 'there's not a customer will come near the place as long as she's here. She's a lunatic and there's no living with her.'

That night Bernie and the other women dressed themselves

and went into the streets for business. Mary Adams wouldn't go with them.

'If the mountain won't come to us then we must go to it,' Bernie declared as she threw a yellow fur about her neck, 'for the wolf must be kept from the door.' She laughed at her own wit as she went off into the street.

'May they never return,' said Mary Adams as the door closed.

It was a curse. I never saw any of them again and the next I heard of Bernie she was dead.

Mary followed me to the kitchen where I was making bread. 'There's just the two of us now,' she said, 'just the two of us alone.'

This was more than she'd said to me in days. I measured flour and salt. 'For a while anyway,' I said, 'until the others come back.'

I was frightened. Only six days before this woman had beaten a man to death with a poker. I abandoned the bread-making. 'I'm tired,' I said, 'I think I'll go to my bed early.'

'Bed's the best place for you,' Mary Adams agreed with a smile.

I lay on the bed thinking about where I could go if I left Beezy's house. There was nowhere. Allie would be at home now and the dispensary closed. I was less prepared than ever to be a laundress in a Magdalen convent, to have my child taken from me at birth by the nuns. But even if I'd had an option I felt honour-bound to stay in Beezy's house, keep it in some sort of order until she came back.

I was asleep when the fire started. I would have been burned alive were it not for Mary Adams insane need to be boastful about what she had done.

'I've put an end to it all.' Her hand on my shoulder and voice in my ear, shouting, woke me. 'Fire cleanses. You thought you would take Beezy from me but she'll know now I was the one to save her. I have cleansed this house of all that has happened here and she will thank me.'

'What have you done?' I fell from the bed. The smell of smoke was everywhere. When I got to the door I could hear crackling too. 'You've set fire to the place . . .'

'Fire drives out fire. All of the filth and evil will be driven away. Beezy will be free.' She left my room and went into the kitchen, clapping her hands and laughing. She was wearing a white shift and I had never seen anyone so beautiful, nor so mad.

I followed her. The crackling was like a forest burning when I got to the hallway. Mary Adams was climbing the smoke-filled stairs.

'We must get out of here, Mary, come down!' The smoke burned my throat as I screamed at her.

'Fire cleanses,' she cried again, 'we will all be cleansed by fire.'

She reached the landing and opened the door to Beezy's room. The smoke which billowed out was black and dancing with flames. She laughed as she walked into and died in the inferno she'd started.

I could have died then, too, if Beezy's henchmen, roaring and half-drunk, hadn't thrown the front door open and been brave enough to pull me from what, within minutes, became a burning hell. They fought the blaze until dawn but by then I was with Beezy.

Once out of the house I sent for Dr Casey, who came immediately.

'I must tell Beezy what's happened,' I said, 'and I must have shelter for myself and my baby.'

He took me to where Beezy was staying in a Magdalen convent in Drumcondra. We met and talked in a long, high corridor, sitting on a polished bench. Nuns passed silently by.

'It wouldn't have happened if I was there,' she said, 'I knew how to keep Mary from becoming light-minded. I'm not blaming you, Sarah.'

She put an arm about my shoulder, briefly. The stitches were still covered with a gauze and she was puffy-eyed but she seemed strong enough otherwise, and upright.

'I'm just saying what's true. I might have been better to leave her in the gutter when I found her there. She might have caused less harm. But we'll never know that.'

She was quiet for a while and I let her be. When she'd

thought things through she said, 'Mary lit that fire when the others were out. She came then to warn you. She didn't intend killing anyone but herself.'

I hadn't thought of this but it was probably true.

'Wait for me here,' Beezy stood. 'I must consider what's to be done.'

She walked away from me. I sat there, for maybe an hour, waiting for her to come back. It was very cold in the corridor. But it was quiet and the nuns didn't bother me and I felt safe. I don't know where Beezy went. She may even have gone to pray. Whatever, she came back full of purpose.

'I've made a plan. There's a place for you in it too so you'll need to understand how things stand.' She took my arm. We walked up and down, slowly, while she talked. 'There will few to mourn Mary Adams. There will be a commotion but the landlord has insurance so it won't be too great. Even so, it would be better if I were to be gone for a while, out of Dublin. The girls will have to fend for themselves, and so will you.'

'I'll go to the Curragh . . .'

'You'll go to the Curragh all right, but not yet. I brought my few jewels and money here with me.' When I showed surprise she gave a short laugh. 'Did you think I'd be foolish enough to leave all I have between me and the workhouse where a band of whores might lay their hands on it?'

'I didn't think about it at all,' I said.

'I pay the nuns for my keep,' she said, 'I prefer it to working in the laundry. I had enough of that as a child.' She shrugged and put a hand to her sore face. 'This is the convent I grew up in after my mother died. I'm a disappointment to the sisters but they'd never turn me away. They are forgiving, and so am I. They serve the God of Mammon too, just as I do. They will take you into the laundry to work until your time comes.'

'They cannot have my child. I'd rather go now, take my chances . . .'

'Are you mad? You would run around the countryside in the black winter with your belly swollen like that? Where will you birth your child if you don't find your man? If the army doesn't recognise you?'

'I'll find lodgings and a midwife,' I said. 'I'll pay for it with the money you owe me.'

But I knew she wouldn't give it to me and I was right.

'You won't get a penny out of me for such stupidity.' Beezy waved a dismissive hand. 'We will both stay here until your baby comes. Then we'll both go to the Curragh. I've heard tell of women who live in huts they've made themselves on the plains. There's a woman I know living there . . .' Beezy paused but said nothing more about this woman. 'They're known as bushwomen and some of them do business with the soldiers. When my face heals I'll do a bit of business too. We'll leave when you have your baby. I'll arrange it. The bushwomen will give you and the infant shelter until you find and set up with your soldier.' She took my arm. 'Come with me now.'

I followed her through a door at the end of the corridor, into the grey rooms of the convent. Somewhere in the distance I heard nuns' singing. My soul, for several minutes, was quiet.

'In the autumn, when my face is healed, I'll go to America,' Beezy said, 'there's ships going every week from Londonderry. I'll get myself a passage on one of them and go for New York. If your soldier fails you I've money that'll pay for a ticket for you and the child too.'

'He won't fail me.'

'You don't know. We don't know anything, you and me, about our futures,' Beezy said, 'but we can plan.'

I slept that night in a high, narrow dormitory with twenty other women. In the morning I went to work for my keep in a stone-built, steam-filled room, boiling and wringing sheets and towels.

I'd joined the women of the Magdalen laundry, something I'd sworn never to do.

CHAPTER SIXTEEN

Allie

———◄●●●►———

'It was one of the most debauched events ever held in this city. Decent people still talk about it with disgust.' My mother gave a tasteful, shivering indication of her own revulsion. 'Alicia cannot be allowed to attend. It's not even something I care to discuss.'

For the first time that winter my mother had got out of her bed early to breakfast with my father and me. The Roomkeepers' Ball was the only subject she'd discussed since joining us.

'I've agreed to go . . .' I began.

My mother crashed her cup loudly into its saucer. She glared at my father. 'I don't know what your friend Mr Ned Mulvey was thinking about when he invited her,' she said, 'the idea is entirely inappropriate.'

'He's attending for his mother's sake,' I said, 'and wanted a partner. There's nothing inappropriate in that.'

'And you were the only person in the city of Dublin that he could think to ask? Don't be ridiculous.' My mother, who hadn't actually looked at me yet, did so now. I'd have preferred not to face her cold dislike so early in the morning. 'You put yourself in the way of his invitation. You seem intent on living your life on the improper edge.' She gave another shiver of distaste. 'Is there no end to your brazen behaviour? You continue in that dispensary and insist on a ridiculous loyalty to that strumpet Sarah Rooney . . .'

'Sarah's not a strumpet.'

I saw no point in saying more. The terrible events in Sarah's life had separated us and I hadn't seen her since she'd taken refuge in a Magdalen convent a week before. But I would.

'I've spoken to Ned,' my father said as he finished the last of his fish with energy, 'his mother is one of the organisers of the Roomkeepers' Ball. He assures me that steps have been taken and that there won't be a repeat of last year's scandal.'

'You will allow her to go then?' My mother looked disbelieving. 'It will destroy what good name she has left, Leonard. She'll be on our hands forever, with a reputation that will repel any decent man.' She picked up and put down a piece of toast. 'This whole business has destroyed my appetite.'

'You well know, Harriet,' my father stole a quick glance at the wall clock, 'that the Roomkeepers' Society is a fine and worthy one and that it's in their interest not to have a repeat of last year's carry-on. Edith Mulvey's presence on the committee should be enough to assure you of that.'

He would have left the table if my mother, with a hissing intake of breath, hadn't stopped him. 'You will not leave, Leonard,' she said, 'until we have resolved this business.'

'Alicia may go. It's resolved.' My father pushed back his chair. 'Now I must go. I've got business to attend to.'

'If Alicia goes to the Roomkeepers' Ball then the very least we can do, as responsible parents, is go along too.' My mother gave a resigned sigh. 'She needs to be supervised. We will all go together, the four of us.' Appetite regained, she picked up her toast.

'You know I don't enjoy these events,' my father was querulous, 'she'll be perfectly safe with Ned.'

'The Lord Lieutenant has agreed to go,' my mother said.

My father grunted, looked at the clock again, cleared his throat. 'Since it means so much to you,' he sighed and walked to the door, 'then we'll go. But I don't want to hear another word about it.'

My mother and I finished our breakfast in silence.

Things didn't work out quite as my mother intended. Her

plan that we should all go together to the ball was changed when Ned Mulvey called for me in a carriage a full half-hour before the agreed time. He wore an evening suit with scarlet lining and a scarlet waistcoat. His necktie was red too, with a black stripe. He looked like a magician and I wondered if that was his intention. Beside him my father looked like a gouty parish priest.

'My mother has asked me to be at the Rotunda earlier.' He was apologetic.

'Understandable,' my father said, 'we'll follow in a second carriage.'

Ned Mulvey was preoccupied from the very beginning of the evening, a mood I hadn't seen him in before. There was nothing about him of his usual amused and mocking *bon viveur*.

We travelled across the town in a silence so complete I wondered if he'd forgotten he'd company in the carriage. I didn't point it out to him. There are some things a woman should never do, according to French etiquette. Reminding a male escort that you exist is one of them. I stared through the window and fumed; he didn't seem to notice this either.

I was wearing the best of my French style: a ball gown of straw-coloured silk with a puff at the back and looped at the sides with a garland of red roses. Another garland of roses draped the bodice. For all the attention Ned Mulvey paid I might have been wearing sack cloth.

My mother had thought the gown 'somewhat vulgar' and now, fingering the roses under my cloak, I wondered if she was right.

When we got to the Rotunda my escort came to life and smiled and took my arm. His attentions didn't last long. We were the first arrivals in the reception hall and I was still dazzled by the lamps burning in every nook and alcove when he said, 'I must leave you for a while,' and walked quickly away.

My eyes adjusted and I saw quiet, organising people coming and going through doors. One of them separated from the rest and came towards me. Ned Mulvey's mother, when she came near, dazzled too. She wore her usual black but with jet stones glittering at her neck and on her ears. When she moved her hands bracelets glittered at her wrists.

'Miss Buckley,' she stood three feet away, 'I'm told you're my son's companion for the evening.'

'I came with Ned, yes.'

'Where is he?'

'I've no idea.' I hated making the admission.

'Strange,' she raised her eyebrows, 'you struck me as an alert young woman last time we met.' She paused. 'You had a great many opinions then, as I recall.'

'I'd like to hand in my cloak,' I said.

'Of course.' She beckoned and another of the quiet shapes began towards us. 'Mr Craig will go with you.'

'There's no need . . .'

'There is every need, since my son is so neglectful.' She put a hand to the jet beads around her throat. 'You would greatly oblige me, Miss Buckley, if you would find my son and remain close to his side for the evening. It would be by far the safest thing. There was . . . trouble at last year's ball. We're anxious to avoid a repetition.'

'Thank you for your concern,' I was surprised, 'but I don't know that I'll be able to attach myself so securely as all that.'

'Find him, Miss Buckley, and do as I ask. My concern is for him, not you. Are you so terribly unaware . . .' She gave me a long, irritated look and sighed. 'I can see that you are.'

She left me with Mr Craig, a small man with an apologetic smile. He went slowly ahead of me to the cloakroom, waited until I was ready and then escorted me to the ballroom. Other guests had begun to arrive and the musicians were tuning and setting up their instruments. It was all very grand, with a great deal of natural foliage decorating the walls and even more lamps than in the reception hall. There were chandeliers too, large and hanging quite low.

Ned Mulvey was by the punch bowl with a noisy group. I waited for him to come to me and he did, after a few minutes, smiling and full of his old charm.

'I was looking for you,' he said, 'I thought you'd abandoned me.'

'The night is young,' I said and he raised his eyebrows in exactly the way his mother had.

'Are you threatening me, Alicia, with desertion?'

'You were the one deserted me,' I said.

'*Touché*,' he said and stood back to look at me. 'You're lovely and fair as the rose in May.' He kissed my hand but his flattery came too late. He'd been neglectful; I wasn't half as fascinated by him as I'd been before.

'Come, meet my friends.' He led the way back to the punch bowl.

His friends were younger than he was, but older than me. The women were pretty and underdressed, the men spoke loudly and were already well on in drink. They made me feel very young, an *ingénue* as the French would say, and made me aware of how unused I was to the night life of parties and balls.

I took a glass of punch. It was spicy and burned my throat but made me feel immediately more a part of the evening.

'Another?' Ned Mulvey refilled my glass.

'Your roses are . . . fetching,' a girl in an emerald dress said to me. She giggled.

'Thank you.' Her own dress was off the shoulder and almost off her bosoms. 'Yours is . . . effective,' I said. She stopped giggling.

'A word, if I may, Edmund.' Edith Mulvey's wintry tones carried from the edge of the group. She stood waiting as her son took my arm.

'You must meet my mother,' he said.

'I already have.'

'You will meet her again.'

There seemed no polite way to avoid another encounter with the stern widow. Edith Mulvey suffered herself to be kissed by her son. 'Are there many of those people here?' She eyed the group we'd just left.

'Many of my friends, Mother, is that what you mean? Not so many. I told you I would look after things.'

'Be sure that you do. I would prefer if none of that group were here.'

'It's a charity ball, Mother, you need all the paying guests you can get. I can't, in any event, stop people attending.'

'You could have discouraged them and I'm disappointed you didn't. I will not tolerate a repeat of last year's vulgarities on the part of you and your friends.'

'You're unfair, Mother . . .'

'I am worried.'

'You don't need to be.'

'We agreed, Edmund, that you would come in a spirit of atonement and to help,' she said as she looked around the ballroom. 'I will not forgive any misconduct tonight. If I'm shamed . . .' She paused. 'If the Society is shamed, I will hold you responsible. I will carry out my threat not to give you a penny piece towards your venture with this girl's father.' She gave me an irritated look. 'Now do we have an agreement?'

'We always had,' he replied, unruffled, 'and you're wrong about my friends.'

'I'm not wrong.' Her sigh was resigned. 'Please be more attentive to Miss Buckley.'

The musicians were playing and the room quite crowded by this time. My parents arrived and joined us and we chatted about the fact that the Lord Lieutenant would not, after all, be attending. My father, who was wearing a dark grey evening suit and already looked hot, disguised his disappointment well. My mother looked beautiful in burgundy-coloured velvet.

When the musicians struck up a waltz Ned Mulvey excused us and took me on to the floor.

'You dance well,' he said.

'Your lead is easy to follow,' I said.

'I doubt, my dear Alicia, that you could be led anywhere you didn't want to go.'

'That could be said of both of us,' I said and we danced in silence until I asked, 'What happened at last year's ball?'

'Very little. It was a great fuss about nothing, as is often the case in Dublin.' He whirled us from the path of a clumsy couple. 'This town can be too provincial by half at times. I'll be ending my business here soon and returning to London.'

Once he'd got money from his mother; he was becoming less and less charming as the night went on.

'It could be that you'll be happier there,' I said.

'Happy?' He gave a short laugh. 'Are you happy in your dispensary with the sick? Is my mother happy with her good works? Is your mother happy?' The music ended and we came off the floor. 'Are you happy tonight, Alicia? Am I?' He looked bored, and shrugged. 'I shouldn't have brought you here.'

'Why did you?'

'I thought it would be amusing to . . . excite passions. I was wrong. It's merely predictable. Boredom has yet again won out.' He looked around. 'I must leave you for a while.' He was gone, again.

He was missing for a long time. The punch had made me lightheaded and I sat by the wall and failed to think lucidly about what he had said. I watched my mother dance and my father talk with a group of men who all looked remarkably like himself. I saw Dr Maurice McDermott with his daughter Jane and a fat, powdered woman and wondered if he'd at last found himself a wife. I felt very apart from it all. When the music stopped my parents came to me.

'Alone?' my mother said.

'It's not right,' my father muttered. 'He shouldn't have left you like this.'

'It was an unsuitable arrangement from the beginning.' My mother shrugged. She looked pleased. Vindicated, I supposed.

'I'm sorry I came.' I knew this would please my mother, and my father, for their separate reasons.

But my regrets had nothing to do with them. My head was clearer now and I was feeling grossly humiliated. I didn't know how or why Ned Mulvey had intended to make amusing use of me and I didn't want to stay at the ball to find out. I wanted to be at home with my books, even with the dreaded Mary Connor for company. She, at least, was part of a world I understood and could deal with.

'Maybe you should leave,' my mother said, 'you've caused enough embarrassment. Your father will call a carriage.'

'You're right,' I said, 'I'll go home.'

'We'll all go,' my father said. 'Get your cloak, Alicia.'

My mother was arguing with him as I left for the cloakroom.

The smallest things can determine the course of a life. As I crossed the reception hall a current of crisp, night air gusted past and made me stop. A door to the rear stood open; my reeling head and hot cheeks decided the rest.

I stepped through the door and found myself in a private garden. It was wintry-looking and bleak, with skeleton trees and bare bushes. But there were walkways too and a bower and high hedging. When I rounded a corner I saw a waterless fountain. Gasoliers had been positioned about the place and guests from the ball were like figures on a stage, moving in and out of the shadows as they took the air.

After the ballroom it felt cool and clean in that garden. I walked along a path and when I came to a secluded wooden bench sat and closed my eyes and took deep breaths. The air on my face and in my lungs made me feel immediately better. I sat on. After a while a gong sounded for the buffet and I heard people begin to go back inside.

When I opened my eyes my mother and Ned Mulvey were standing in the shadows not ten feet away. My mother was holding him by the arms and speaking in a low, impassioned voice. He was smiling. After a minute he nodded, agreeing to what she asked, and held her to him. They kissed.

I did nothing for a minute. I couldn't. Things I'd never understood were becoming clearer than I wanted them to. My heart ached for my betrayed father, waiting in the hall for me and for my mother.

I stood and called to her. 'Mother . . .'

They turned together, then moved apart. My mother stood very still, staring at me. Ned Mulvey gave a low laugh.

'Were you looking for me, Alicia?' he asked. I shook my head and began walking toward the door to the garden.

'Wait,' he called.

I kept going. There was a rustle to my right and my mother hurried past along another path. Hoping to get to my father before I did, I supposed.

'I haven't been very attentive,' Ned Mulvey came up behind me and took my arm, 'but it's not too late to remedy . . .'

'There's nothing to remedy because I'm not the one who's ill.' I shook my arm free. 'I see now how I must have amused you. You and my mother are what needs remedying.'

I would have walked on but he stood in my way. We were alone, the only people left in the gardens.

'We have nothing to say to one another,' I said.

'You're a temptress, Alicia, though you may not know it.' His smile was the old, mocking one. 'You're like your mother in ways you don't even realise. That's why I liked you and why I invited you here.'

'I'm not at all like my mother,' I said, 'and neither do I share her tastes. You disgust me.'

His smile turned cold, then angry. He stepped closer to me. 'I don't disgust your mother,' he said.

When I moved back I found myself standing against a hedge.

'Nowhere to go, Alicia,' he smiled, 'but maybe it's time you learned that if you dance with the devil you'll be pricked by his horns.' He touched one of the roses on my bodice. 'What a pity you don't share your mother's . . . tastes. We're alone here, you know that.' He was almost on top of me. 'The evening has become quite interesting.'

'You said earlier it was boring,' I reminded him.

The door to the garden was closed. I wanted it to open and for my father to come through. I wanted to be a child again. I didn't want any of this to be happening.

'You're such a serious young woman, Alicia,' he said, 'you must try to see, and enjoy, the amusements in life.' His hands were in his pockets but I didn't trust him to keep them there.

When I tried to move sideways he moved with me. 'I would guess, Alicia, that you have never been kissed. Am I right?'

'That's none of your business,' I said.

'It could be that you've a taste for the sort of kiss your mother enjoys . . .'

'My father is at the other side of that door. I'll scream if you touch me. You'll be disgraced. Let me pass *now*.'

'You poor beautiful child,' he laughed, 'your father is already disgraced. Half the town knows about your mother's dalliances. Do you think I'm the first?' He gazed at me then shrugged. 'You knew nothing at all, did you? I could never be sure. You seemed sophisticated enough. I thought too that your friend from the tenements knew and would have told you.'

No. I hadn't known. I'd been too concerned with myself to know anything. This was what Sarah had tried to tell me as Mary Ann lay dying. I hadn't wanted to hear. I wanted to be sick. I asked a question instead.

'Does Mary Connor know about your . . . liaison?'

'The wicked dwarf is our postman,' he laughed without humour, 'her sister, who works for my mother, is the receptacle she delivers to.'

And my father the fool who paid her wages. My mother and Mary Connor made a rarer couple than I'd thought.

'I want to leave now,' I said again 'my father is waiting.'

I knew my mother wouldn't be. I'd heard what she said to Ned Mulvey. They were to be together that night.

'Don't fret so, Alicia.' He lifted a lock of my hair. 'I'm not going to rape you. I don't need to rape a woman, or even a girl, to persuade her of my charms. Still, now that it's looking as if I'll be returning to London sooner than I expected, it would be a pity to part on bad terms.' He ran two fingers down my cheek.

I spat into his face.

It was the wrong thing to do. He slapped me twice, quick, hard blows which stung my cheeks like lashes from a whip. My ears began a ringing and tears came to my eyes. I cried out and he snarled at me, wiping his face with the back of his hand.

'It would have entertained me to have mother and daughter but not any longer. You're still a child. A child playing among the dirt and disease of the slummers. You should stay there. You're not yet fit for society. You may never be.' He walked toward the door. When he got there he opened it and turned. 'Your father will have discovered tonight that he is a fool and a cuckold. I would spare him the news of our encounter, if I were you. He is already unhappy enough.'

The reception hall was almost empty as I collected my cloak and went into the street. I didn't see my father and didn't look for him.

I walked quickly for Sackville Street, putting my head back and taking deep breaths as I went. A bright moon had come out but clouds were moving to cover it. I felt both free and imprisoned. I didn't know how I would face my father.

I'd got as far as Findlaters when he came alongside in a carriage. I climbed in and sat next to him and we drove home through the mainly quiet streets. Neither of us mentioned my mother, or where she was. I ached for him to put an arm about me but he didn't, his own pain too great to help me with mine. Crossing Carlisle Bridge I remembered the day I'd arrived home and almost wept for its innocence. I closed my eyes and prayed for the journey to end so as I could be in my room, alone.

'Are you all right?' my father asked, once.

I nodded. 'Don't worry about me, Dada. I'm fine,' I said.

My face was hot and sore and beginning to stiffen. I felt sure there would be marks.

'Good,' my father said and I knew he didn't want to know what had happened in the gardens. My mother's betrayal was all he could deal with for now. Ned Mulvey had been right about that, at least.

I kissed my father lightly before going to my room. 'You should sleep,' I said.

'I'll wait down here,' he said, 'for a while.'

I put a cold cream pomatum on my face. It soothed a little

but my right eye, which was almost closed, would be worse before morning.

I lay for a long time without sleeping. The sky was lightening before I heard a carriage stop on the road outside and my mother let herself into the house. My father, still waiting in the parlour, came into the hallway and spoke to her. They exchanged two sentences, no more, before my mother climbed the stairs to her room. My father went back into the parlour and closed the door.

I stayed in my room all the following day. When the girl came with hot water for me to wash in I averted my face and told her to bring me tea, nothing more. My father came once to my door but didn't enter. He would be away for two days, he called to me, we would talk when he got back.

From my mother I heard nothing at all.

That night I packed all that I valued into two bags. I also packed some things I didn't value but which would get me money in a pawn or jeweller's shop. Into my purse I put what money I had and this journal.

I wrote two letters. To my father I said I couldn't any longer live with my mother. I told him where I would be, so as he wouldn't worry, but said he was on no account to come after me. I would let him know when I had decided a plan for my future. I wished him every happiness and I meant it.

In the morning early, before either Mary Connor or the house was stirring, I left quietly through the back kitchen door.

It was still dark but to make certain no one saw me I made my way to Mount Street Bridge through the warren of back lanes and poor cottages behind the big houses. I met only barking dogs and women beginning their long, daily walk to places of work.

On the town side of the bridge I got a horse cab.

CHAPTER SEVENTEEN

Allie

I arrived to join Sarah at the Magdalen convent as light broke on the first day of March, 1868. I left at an equally early hour on the last day of May.

In the months between I learned how to knead and wring clothes, how to iron and fold and hang them on drying lines. I learned to do without creams and mirrors and to keep my opinions to myself. It was not one of those Magdalens which insisted on penitents and others cutting off their hair and for this I was thankful; I couldn't have borne to lose my hair.

I also relearned what I'd known in the Paris convent – that communities of women have an inborn way of sharing and surviving together.

I could have lived without the lessons in laundering. Those about the fraternity of women would prove invaluable.

My arrival gave little joy. The nun who opened the door looked from my bruised face to the departing cab and back again with a sigh. 'Come in, child,' she said.

I gave her a version of my story designed to secure me sanctuary.

'My mother's depravity has made me afraid not just for my body,' I put a hand to my swollen face, 'but for my immortal soul too. I can't go on living in my father's house.' It wasn't hard to let a tear fall; I felt genuinely battered in soul as well as body. 'I'll pay for my keep and I'll work. I'll need to be occupied.' I opened my purse.

'You're not with child then?' She had grey eyes and was gentle.

'No . . .' I made it sound as if I was fearful even this might happen if I stayed on in my father's house.

'Come, child,' she took the money, 'we'll find you a cell.'

'I'd prefer to sleep in a dormitory with the other women,' I said. When she hesitated I added, 'For the company. I don't want to be alone in the night.'

'The women we have here are not, by and large, of your class,' she said.

'Surely we're all one in the eyes of God?' I said.

The grey eyes became thoughtful and I worried she might be seeing me as a postulant. After a minute she said, 'Very well then,' and led me to the dormitory.

I'd been fairly sure the nuns would find a place for me as long as I was willing to work. The city was full of public laundries and the Magdalens had to keep ahead or lose customers. Success in the laundry business meant they could give homes to women without places to go.

Offering money, as well as my labour, was a way of buying me an independence of sorts. It also ensured my father couldn't easily take me away, even if he wanted to. I'd deliberately said nothing about knowing Sarah. From experience I knew that nuns kept order, and control, by applying the principle of divide and conquer. Once they knew we were friends they would keep Sarah and myself apart. Either that or dispatch one of us to a sister Magdalen.

I couldn't have endured that.

By mid-morning I was drawing and boiling water in the heat and steam of the laundry. Without experience it was all, to begin with, I was fit for. All around me women scrubbed and kneaded over washtubs, or squeezed clothes through mangles. The windows were high up, ensuring light without views. The noise deafened. My face felt on fire.

Watchful nuns meant it was a while before I was able to talk with Sarah. When I found her she was in a corner under a window, almost hidden by freshly ironed petticoats, bed linen, shirts and frilled blouses. She was folding and packing them into baskets for delivery, a job which allowed her to sit.

She needed to, she'd grown large and looked pale and drawn. The dark blue dress she was wearing was the homeliest thing I'd ever seen on her.

'Hello, Sarah.' I sat under cover of the hanging clothes.

She looked at me in silence for a full minute. 'What are you doing here, Allie?' Her eyes had become very bright and she blinked. 'And what happened to your face?'

'I came to be with you and this,' I touched my eye, 'was on account of a disagreement I had with my mother's fancy man.'

'Ned Mulvey?'

'I know you tried to tell me about him . . .'

'I should have tried harder. But it seemed such a terrible thing and I couldn't say it without being sure. She's your mother, when all's said and done.'

'It doesn't matter now, anyway, who or what she is,' I said.

It mattered so much I couldn't bear to talk about it. It would always matter.

'Have you had word from Jimmy Vance?'

'Not yet . . .'

'Not *yet?*' I gave her a hard look through the swollen eye. 'Listen to me, Sarah.' I spoke quickly, trying to say as much as I could before a nun came. 'You'll have to make plans for yourself and your baby. I'm here now and I'll help you. Maybe it might be best to forget Jimmy Vance. When the baby's born we'll go away somewhere. To Paris, maybe. I'll teach. My father will give us money.' The ideas came to me as I spoke; I thought them inspired.

'You can't stay here,' Sarah automatically smoothed the shirt on her lap, 'a Magdalen is no place for you, Allie. It's full of . . .' she half smiled and shrugged, 'sinners like me.' She stared at my face. 'Your complexion is very red.'

'It's the steam,' I said, 'what do you think of my plan?'

'If they see us talking they'll separate us,' Sarah said. 'You'd better go. There's one of them coming. We'll talk later.'

I heard a swishing sound and out of the corner of my eye saw a nun's black skirts come to a halt beside us.

'Continue folding, if you please, Sarah,' her voice was businesslike, 'we have customers waiting for their clothes.' She tapped me on the shoulder. 'Pleasure and prattle are for when the work of the day, and God's work, is done.'

I looked up and saw that she was about my own age, with very freckly skin.

'If there's something you wish to know,' she said, 'the sisters are here to help.'

'I was curious to see the finished task,' I said.

'You've seen enough. The task begins with the drawing of water.' She moved away, clearly expecting me to follow.

'I have a plan already,' Sarah said quickly, 'Beezy Ryan is here too. This is the Magdalen she was reared in. We've a plan worked out together.'

I told the nun my face was bothering me and went and lay on my bed in the long dormitory. The rows of narrow, white-covered beds gave it the air of a mausoleum but at least I had it to myself and was able to weep alone. I wept as I hadn't been able to the night before, tears of lament for Sarah, who didn't need me any more, and of loneliness. I told myself I was a grown woman, that Sarah was too and that Beezy Ryan had helped her when I couldn't. None of it stopped me feeling desolate and cast aside. They were also tears for what I'd lost, for decisions taken, letters written and because I had nothing to go back to.

On my way to the Magdalen I'd posted a letter to Daniel Casey at the dispensary. In it I'd told him I could no longer work there, said I hoped all would go well for him and Dr Connolly and been thankful for all that I'd learned. It had been a harder letter to write than the one to my father.

I sat up and hugged my knees. Salt tears stung my face but the movement changed everything. The reality of the women who slept in the other beds came to me and self-pity retreated.

I got up and paced between the beds, touching the tightly pulled counterpanes as I went. They were so identically neat they might never have been slept in but were, every night, by women whose lives were in much greater states of desolation than my own. Those who sought refuge in the Magdalens did so because of drink or violence or poverty. Or because, like Sarah, they were with child. They had no choices.

I had. When I was less tired I would think about what those choices were. I climbed under my own immaculate counterpane and slept.

It was dark when Sarah shook me awake. 'The nuns said to leave you be or I'd have woken you before. You've slept enough, Allie. Get up now and wash yourself and put some cream on your face.' She was efficient and in charge and I did as she said.

'They know we're friends,' she answered my unasked question as she stood over me in the wash house, 'Beezy told them.'

'Why did she do that?'

'Because I told her we would have to help you too,' her belly brushed against me when she handed me a towel. She really was very big. 'I said I didn't want to leave you behind.'

She put her cool hand against my face. 'May he never see a day's happiness. May he be miserable for the rest of his life and your mother with him.'

I didn't tell her then what had happened between myself and Ned Mulvey. It was a week before I could bring myself to talk about it and when I did she said, 'You were right to leave. You'd be wrong to go back.' No further comment was necessary.

That night we sat on my bed, the other beds like recumbent spectres about us in the dark, and Sarah told me of Beezy's plan to go to the Curragh of Kildare.

We would have to keep it a secret, she said, because Beezy didn't want anyone to know where she was going. She needed to be out of Dublin, away from questions that might yet be asked about all that had happened in North King Street. We would live with the women who lived free on the plains, in huts they made themselves. Sarah would stay there until she married or settled with Jimmy Vance, Beezy would stay until the autumn, when she would go to America. And me?

'I'll be a nurse and doctor to the women and their children,' I said. 'In the autumn . . . I'll see.'

Sarah took my hand. 'I'm very glad you're coming with us,' she said.

'But Beezy doesn't want me,' I guessed, 'she told the nuns we were friends hoping to have me shifted to another Magdalen.'

'She doesn't know you like I do. She's afraid you won't be up to life on the Curragh.' Sarah began undoing her hair.

A moon had come up and the room was more ghostly than ever. Her face, when her hair fell loose, was like an oval sixpence in an inky frame.

'She says the women there won't take to you and that we'll have to look out for you all the time.' She shook her head tiredly. 'She was all for asking Mother Stanislaus to have you moved to another Magdalen.'

'Then why am I still here?'

'Because I said I would leave if you did and because of your father. He came today. Mother Stanislaus wouldn't have you woken for him but he stayed a long time with her in the parlour. I'd say money exchanged hands. I'd say too that you'll be well looked after while you're here.'

The news of my father was good. It meant he hadn't disowned me and that a plan, hatching in my head, might very well work. I would be twenty-one years old in October. I would go to my father and ask him for my birthright, or whatever amount it took to give me the independence to study medicine. In the meantime I would earn my keep.

'I'll work, like everyone else,' I said to Sarah. There was nothing unselfish in this. I was afraid that if I wasn't occupied I would slip into melancholy, as I had before. 'I learned a lot in the dispensary that I can use to help the women on the Curragh,' I went on, 'there's a great deal I can teach them to do for themselves too.' I paused. 'I'd like to.'

The days got longer, the weather milder and I got used to life in the Magdalen. We rose early, worked until seven and had two breaks during the day for food and rest. Each evening, after dinner, we were free to pray and look after our own clothes and needs until nine thirty. After that the dormitory was locked and the entire convent retired for the night.

'There's a peace here,' Sarah said one night before sleep.

'There's order,' I said.

We were both right; it was the predictability that made us feel safe. But I'd grown not to trust the calm periods in life. They usually heralded a storm.

By the time Easter came I was as used to the women in the Magdalen as I'd been to my student companions in the Paris convent and knew all of their stories. Most were with child. Some, escaping brutal men, had arrived at the convent beaten to within an inch of their lives. Others were there to cure themselves of drinking and others still were whores tired of a life on the streets.

They would all leave the Magdalen in time. They would nearly all return to the lives they had left.

Beezy Ryan didn't work in the laundry. It was said she spent her time working on the nuns' finances, on schemes that would help them make money. She knew some of the women from outside and wandered about, full of talk and gossip, when the mood took her. She spoke to me only when she had to but I knew the time would come when she'd have plenty to say to me.

She chose to do it on the drying green, on a day when Sarah's time was near. The drying green was a great square surrounded by high, bare walls with ropes strung between them. Miles of petticoats, bed linen, shirts, pinafores and pantaloons shifted and blew on the ropes as they dried in the wind and sun.

'You'd be better off leaving here alone and making your own life.' Beezy stood with the damaged part of her face to the sun. She was convinced of its healing properties and seemed to be right; the welts were fading. 'Your father will help you. You can rejoin respectable society. It's what you're fit for.'

I assumed she was sneering; the welts had created a distortion which made her expressions hard to read.

'I know better than you what respectable society has to offer.' I finished pinning a sheet and moved on. She moved with me. 'I'm going to the Curragh to be with Sarah and her child until she sets herself up.' I fumbled with another sheet; I could do nothing right when Beezy was around.

'You'll be no help to her.' Beezy took the sheet and laid it expertly along the rope. 'She has her life to live and you have yours.'

'We've been friends all our lives.' I kept myself from shouting. 'We'll always be friends.'

'Friends? Where were you, friend, when she was thrown out of Henrietta Street and had to come to me for work and shelter?' Beezy raised her voice so that others in the drying green could hear. 'The world knows you were dressing yourself in Paris gowns and playing at being a saint in the Eccles Street dispensary. Your type are ten a penny in this city, Allie Buckley. You're the kind dips your fingers into the stench of poverty and disease and leaves it behind you when something new comes along.' She dropped her voice again, to the annoyance of at least three women. 'You want to dabble now in Sarah Rooney's life, amuse yourself until you decide what to do with yourself. Take my advice. Go home to your father's house and live the life you were reared to.'

'Did the nuns rear you for a life of prostitution, Beezy? Or did you choose it for yourself?' I began pinning the sheet. 'Why do you want to possess Sarah?'

Beezy studied the rings on her fingers. 'You misunderstand,' she spoke slowly, 'I promised she could have her baby in North King Street but this is where she's ended up instead. Also, she stood by me in my spot of bother.'

I looked at her over the sheet, understanding what I hadn't before. Beezy had lost more than a kip house in the flames. She'd lost the women who'd worked for her and whose lives she'd governed. She only had Sarah now.

I finished pinning the sheet.

'Her soldier won't be there for her,' Beezy said, 'but I will be. She can go to America and start a new life there, her and the child. The three of us will go in the autumn.'

'Sarah's agreed to this?' She'd said nothing to me about America. All she ever spoke about was Jimmy Vance and bringing his child to him.

'No,' Beezy conceded, 'but it'll be the only choice left to her by the time the autumn comes. You'll see.'

'Tell me about the women of the Curragh,' I said.

'They're known as bushwomen, on account of the way they live. They're rough and they're hard and there's no place for you with them.'

This was as much as I could get out of her and it convinced me she knew very little. Like everyone else in the Magdalen she knew of the Curragh women only by repute. Not that it made any difference. Even if I'd been told all about them I'd have gone anyway.

I wouldn't have believed what I heard.

'You'll never find yourself a place in respectable society if you go there,' Beezy said.

I didn't believe this either.

Two other things happened before Sarah had her baby.

The first was my father calling to the Magdalen again. He was in a sorry state, sodden with drink and full of talk about my mother and the laudanum she was taking. He seemed to think I had become a postulant. I didn't disabuse him.

The second was the news, in a letter from Bess, that Daniel Casey had called at the house in Haddington Road. He'd been told by my father that I was a postulant. 'I let the hare sit and didn't tell him anything different,' Bess wrote. 'He seemed to me saddened.' She sent Sarah the shawl she'd been christened in along with the letter.

I loved Sarah's baby almost as much as she did from the day

he was born. She went into labour in the laundry and had to be almost carried to the sanatorium. The nuns, who were well used to birthing babies, wouldn't let me near her. She was nursing her baby when first I saw him.

'A boy,' she smiled.

'Are you sorry?' I touched his dark head. He was soft and very warm.

'He couldn't be better, or more wonderful. I'll call him James, after his father. I'll see he has a good life. One better by far than my own.'

James was the darling of the Magdalen until we left. It was rare for a baby to be there for more than a couple of days but James had two full weeks of loving attention from nuns and Magdalens alike.

Beezy persuaded the nuns to break all rules and Bess was allowed see him. She said she would pray that Sarah found her man in Kildare. Sarah told her nothing about us going to live in huts on the plains.

I don't know what Beezy told the nuns but they did nothing to stop Sarah leaving with her baby. They appeared sad to see us go, particularly Beezy.

'Maybe you're the one should become a postulant,' Sarah joked as we walked down the avenue.

'Do you think I haven't thought of it?' Beezy said. She seemed to be serious.

We took a train for the Curragh from Kingsbridge station, paying 2/1d each for second-class tickets. Sarah, as we waited for the train to come, pointed out a nearby boarding house. 'James was conceived in a front room of that house,' she said.

I was saved from making a reply by the arrival of the train. I wouldn't have known what to say.

It was the end of May and a good summer was promised. We were glad to be on the move and travelled hopefully — except for James, who travelled blissfully, smiling all the way, asleep in his mother's arms.

Part Two

CHAPTER EIGHTEEN

Sarah

———◁◦◦◦◦▷———

The road leading from the town of Kildare across the Curragh was rough, uneven and dusty. The horsecar we hired at the station had no springs.

Sitting behind the carman I watched the town's hovels and foul laneways disappear from view. When I turned to look ahead there wasn't much to reassure there either. Just the vast and rolling green of the plains. The fact of the sun shining on it all made it no less wild-looking. There was a sharp wind.

The size and emptiness of the place set my head reeling. Sandymount Strand was as far as I'd ever travelled from the shelter of the streets and high buildings of Dublin. Here, apart from low-growing furze, there was no protection anywhere. From either the elements or man. There was no army camp that I could see. No encampment of women either.

'Do we have far to go?' I said to the carman.

'Half an hour will do it.' He didn't turn. 'The women ye're looking for are on the southern slopes to the army camp, below the Gibbet Rath.' He straightened and pointed with his whip. 'The English massacred nearly four hundred men at that Rath in seventeen ninety-eight. The fairies play their music and dance inside it nowadays. I met a hunchback once was cured there of his hump.' He slumped into his seat again, chewing on tobacco. He was dirty and he smelled. But he was the only driver at the station would agree to take us – and then only when Allie paid him double the fare before leaving.

'I don't see any Rath,' I said.

'You'll see it soon enough,' he assured me.

James was protesting at the cold and wanted to be fed. 'Is it always so windy?' I asked.

'The northerly winds would cut you in half by times. The wrens have a rough enough time of it. But that's their choice.'

'The wrens?'

'The women I'm taking ye to are called wrens around here,' he spat and went on chewing, 'on account of they live in nests in the ground, like the bird.' He looked at Allie, who was sitting beside him, from under his hat brim. 'The wren village is no place for a decent woman.'

Allie ignored him. She was the only one of us he'd given a helping hand into the car. Beezy jabbed his shoulder with a finger. 'You've got your money. Keep your mouth shut and earn it,' she said.

We rattled along in silence after that. I didn't believe him about the nests. Men were forever twisting things, especially when it came to women who set themselves apart. I'd heard a lot of lies and foolishness about the women in Beezy's kip house before joining them.

The driver was right though about the army camp, and about the Rath. We saw both of them within minutes. The Rath, a good bit in from the road, appeared as a grassy circle on the top of a mound. The camp, when we first saw it on the horizon, was a long line of low huts with a clock tower and a flag on a flagpole.

James began to cry. I rocked him for a bit and kissed the top of his head. He cried more softly but didn't stop. The road became straight and the surface even.

'We'll have to follow along by the camp for this bit of the journey,' the carman said.

We passed a horsecar going towards Kildare. It was full of military men, all of them wearing the braid and buttons of officers. A little closer to the camp there were rank and file soldiers walking along the road in twos and threes, their red coats bright in the sunshine. Some made rough remarks as we passed.

Jimmy wasn't among them and I let go the breath I'd been holding as we left them behind. I didn't want to meet him like this, unprepared and with others around. I wanted to meet him alone, with my hair right and James in his best.

We left the road for a narrow track leading away from the camp. The plains, though dotted everywhere now with sheep, still looked to me pitiless. After less than a mile the car came to a sudden halt.

'Ye've arrived,' said the driver.

'Arrived at what?' Allie looked around.

'Ye're accommodation.' The driver removed his hat, mopped his brow and sniggered. 'What ye see before ye is what the wrens call their village.'

About five hundred yards in from the road there was a hollow. From where we'd stopped I could see the tops of thicker than usual furze bushes. There was nothing that resembled nests or huts of any kind.

'Drive on,' said Beezy, 'or by God I'll take the reins myself.' She meant it.

The carman shook out the reins and took us as far as the rim of the hollow. And it was from there, looking down, that we saw the wren village for the first time. It was sheltered in the hollow and a dozen or more women sat about, or stood talking, in the late evening sun. There were children too, four or five of them, though none as young as James. The children wore everything and anything but the women wore only petticoats. Their arms and feet were bare, their hair loose. Stretched here and there across the furze there were dresses and white, starched petticoats. There was something of how the kip house had been in the mid-mornings about it. The same air of abandon, and of companionship.

A woman crawled from under one of the bushes and stood watching us.

'That's the sort of shelter ye'll be living in.' The carman, wheezing like a bellows, threw our bags to the ground. 'That's a wren's nest.'

All of the women were watching us now. 'I wish ye joy of them,' said the driver. I blessed myself, but couldn't think of a single prayer to say.

Beezy got out of the car first, then Allie. Both of them helped me down with James. We picked up our bags, one for each of us. It was all Beezy had allowed us bring. We stepped over the ridge and into the hollow together.

CHAPTER NINETEEN

Allie

———◄━∞∞∞━►———

Under a blue sky, driven by a simian carman and with James crying softly in Sarah's arms, we arrived to live among the wrens of the Curragh. It was the ape of a carman who told us the women were called wrens by the local people. I thought at first it was meant kindly; I still had some innocence in me then.

Kildare wasn't much of a town; the low, fetid hovels around the station would have been rejected by even Dublin's poorest. Filthy children played listlessly and drunken men lay about in the sun. What I saw of the rest of the town looked drear and dank, even in the sun, with narrow, broken streets, a few shops and a hotel.

'You'll frighten the mare with that thing,' the carman said to Beezy as she lit up one of her noxious cigars.

'She can't be much of an animal so.' Beezy blew smoke his way as she helped Sarah into the car with James.

The carman handed me into the car after them. 'A woman like you has no business with the wrens,' he said.

His principles hadn't stopped him taking twice the usual fare for the trip. He wasn't quite the fool he looked.

Sarah gave a low, frightened moan when we first came in sight of the Curragh plains. But I'd travelled the flat, rolling fields of northern France and was less unnerved by their sweeping green acres.

After an uncomfortable half-hour or so the carman pointed first to a Rath and then to a long row of block huts and a clock tower on the horizon. There was a flag too, fluttering on a flagpole in the sharp wind.

'There's upwards of ten thousand soldiers in those huts,' the carman said, 'and more under tents round about.'

The notion of so many soldiers, like so many rats in cages, repelled me. Beezy would, no doubt, be pleased at the proximity of so much custom. I wondered how Sarah felt about searching through such a number for Jimmy Vance.

Closer to the camp there were red-uniformed soldiers in groups along the road and buttoned-up officers passing in cars on their way to the town. Sarah said nothing about any of them and when I turned to look at her she was rigid and white-faced.

The wren village was in a sheltered hollow, half hidden from the road. The carman would have had us walk the last stretch if Beezy Ryan hadn't threatened to drive his horse herself.

When we stopped at last on the ridge he spat and said out of the side of his mouth to Beezy, 'There's your wrens for you. You'll find plenty of your kind to keep you company in there.'

I'd never seen women like the wrens before. Not even among the poorest coming into the dispensary. They stood staring at us; hardened, half naked and unruly-looking as the plains they lived in. One had a bad cut to her forehead. Their children were dirty.

A sandy-haired woman crawled on her hands and knees from an opening under a furze bush.

'That's the sort of shelter ye'll be living in,' the carman said, 'that's a wren's nest.' As he reached for our bags I saw Beezy take the rings from her fingers and shove them into the long pockets of her skirts. The carman threw our bags to the ground and we climbed down after them. I grew an inch smaller as my heels sank into the spongy turf.

I'd given almost the last of my money to the carman. I'd made my bed. It was time to lie on it.

CHAPTER TWENTY

Sarah

———◆◆◆◆———

The horsecar went back across the plains at a canter. For a while after its tail disappeared from sight I could still hear the wheels, the whip cracking the air. Then there was silence. Even James had stopped crying.

The women stood watching us.

And we stood watching the women. The children came closer. They were curious and giggling and the oldest, a girl of about eight, touched Allie's dress.

'Did you make it yourself?' She fingered the flounce around the hem. Her fingernails were bitten to the quick and black with dirt. 'You must be very clever.' Her inky blue eyes followed the lines of the dress upward, past the pleating and fluted beading to the rows of blue velvet. 'And rich too.' She looked into Allie's face before touching the flounce again. 'It's a lovely thing.' She stepped back. Her admiration was matter-of-fact, not awestruck at all.

Allie's cheeks had flushed pink. I'm sure mine did too. Dressed in our best street clothes and facing those half-naked women and children, the three of us looked foolish. With the Paris shawl about my shoulders I felt like a Christmas tree but Allie, in her velvet and beading, looked even more at odds. The flush in her cheeks deepened. She said nothing.

'Is there a Nance Reilly here?' Beezy, smoking and calmly surveying the women, spoke loudly. Removing her rings hadn't made her any less conspicuous: if I was a Christmas tree then she, in her red satin with the silvery feathers, stood out like a lighthouse.

The thought came to me, cold and frightening, that the women watching us had probably been dressed as we were now when they'd arrived on the Curragh. They'd hardly planned to end up the way they were.

In the shelter of the hollow the smoke from Beezy's cigar hovered and coloured the air blue. The nests, now we were this close, were easy to make out. They were made from furze, piled into the shape of an upside-down bowl and with makeshift doors. Small fires smouldered in the doorways of most of them. Clothes were spread to dry on bushes everywhere.

'Who wants to know about Nance Reilly?'

The voice which called out belonged to the woman we'd seen crawling from a nest. She was tall and thin, with sandy hair and skin as worn-looking as her frieze petticoat.

'Beezy Ryan wants to know.' Beezy didn't move, 'I was told by Hannah Doherty you might be here. We need shelter for the summer months. She said the women here weren't the kind would turn us away.'

'How's Hannah getting on these times?' Nance Reilly watched Beezy closely. Scrawny and worn she might be but something in her reminded me of my mother. I think it was the way she held herself so straight.

'Hannah's not so good.' Beezy shook her head. 'Her baby died. She's with the nuns in a Magdalen. I was there myself, for a while.' She touched her scarred face. 'So were my companions.' She jerked her head sideways at me and Allie.

'Hannah didn't think of coming with you?'

'She was talking about coming later in the summer,' Beezy took a deep breath, 'but it's unlikely she'll make it, this summer or any other.'

'She's that bad, then?'

'She is. She'll see out her days in the Magdalen.'

'Hannah never did have much luck.' Nance Reilly moved her

gaze from Beezy to me and then to Allie. 'She was always too gentle for her own good.' She fixed her eyes on Beezy's face again.

'Too gentle for this world,' Beezy agreed and Nance Reilly shook her head, sighing. It was as if Hannah Doherty were already dead.

I remembered Hannah as witless and well meaning. When her baby was born dead all she'd wanted was to follow him to the grave. She'd been well on the way to doing that when we left.

'Your kip house was burned down,' Nance Reilly said. Beezy took a full minute to answer.

'It was,' she said at last.

'You're here to put a bit of distance between yourself and what happened, I suppose?'

'For a while.' Beezy touched her face. 'Until things are forgotten.'

'Who knows you're here?' Nance Reilly asked.

'No one outside of the two women with me. I won't be followed.' She hesitated, then asked, 'What did you hear?'

'Only that there was a fire.' Nance Reilly shrugged. 'There was talk too of a man who went missing around the same time.'

'There was a fire,' Beezy agreed, 'and if there's a man lost it's nothing to do with my misfortunes and the burning of my house.' She touched her face again. I don't think she even knew she was doing it.

'You'll be safer here than in most places,' Nance Reilly said.

Some of the other women began to move away. The small girl circled about Allie, studying her dress. Allie smiled at her.

'The Curragh's wide and there's plenty furze bushes,' said Nance Reilly, 'we'll help you build yourselves a nest. You're welcome to a share too in what we have — it's all for one and one for all here.'

'I ran my house along those same lines,' Beezy said, 'it was share and share alike.' She put a hand on my shoulder. 'Sarah worked for me and is no stranger either to give and take.'

'That's all right then,' Nance Reilly looked at Allie, 'because there's no one more special than anyone else here.'

'I haven't come to be a parasite on your community.' Allie was cool. 'I've got medical training. I'll do what I can to help with sickness and injury while I'm here.'

'We're our own doctors. We have to be.' The woman who spoke had a deep, but clean, cut across her forehead. 'There's none of the doctors from around here willing to attend on wrens when they're sick.'

'I can definitely be of use then.' Allie touched her bag with her satin-shod foot. 'I've brought ointments and medicines with me.'

'Miss Buckley plans on becoming a physician herself,' Beezy said and got the response she wanted when several of the women laughed. James, dozing peacefully in my arms, jerked fitfully at the sound.

'She's chosen a fine university then,' said a wren, 'we'll teach her a thing or two about disease, and about pain.'

'Just so long as you don't do us harm.' Nance Reilly, losing interest in Allie, turned back to Beezy. 'We've one of your girls here. You'll remember Lizzie Early?' When she raised her eyebrows her forehead creased like an accordion. 'It was she told us your story.'

Beezy, unprepared for this, was silent. The past staggered about us again, but this time more threateningly. Lizzie Early had not been the most dependable of the North King Street girls.

'Lizzie's here . . .' Beezy fanned herself with a hand. The silvery feathers danced. 'Is she well?'

'Well enough. She's into the drink in a bad way. She'll be getting up soon, getting ready for the night. You can see her for yourself.'

'Does she ever talk of Bernie Cole?' The welts stood out on Beezy's paled face. 'Or of any of the other girls?'

'She does.' From the way Nance Reilly said this I knew the word on Bernie and the others was not good.

The small girl touched Allie's dress again.

'Come away, Moll.' A black-haired woman with the same inky-blue eyes as the child pushed her way through the watching group. Her shoulders and arms were as powerful as a man's and her hair hung in matted curls down her back. When she was close enough she pulled the child by the hand away from Allie. 'My daughter's an innocent,' she held the girl behind her, 'and easily impressed. It's not often we get silk-dressed gentlewomen visiting us.'

'What's seldom is wonderful,' Allie said. When some of the women tittered the big woman turned on them.

'She'll bring trouble,' she shook a fist, 'and ye'll mark my words yet. There's no place for her here.' She turned away, the small girl held tight by the arm. 'No child of mine is going to simper over her dress either.'

Her child had other ideas. 'I'm doing no harm, touching her dress,' she said as she jerked her arm free, 'and there's one of her and many of us so what harm can she do?'

'You'll see, soon enough, what harm she can do.' Her mother glowered but made no attempt to recapture her arm. She turned instead and strode away through the nest village. Moll followed her, protesting loudly and ignored all the way to an outlying nest, into which her mother disappeared. I wondered what bad luck, or criminal act of her mother's, had brought the pair of them to the Curragh.

'There's been enough talk,' the wren with the cut forehead lifted my bag. 'I'll make tea.' She signalled that we should follow her.

The woman's nest was like all of the others, maybe a little smaller. Up close it was a fragile enough structure with, like all of the others, a small fire burning just inside the door. A pot pierced all over with holes sat on top of it as a guard. After removing the pot and fanning the fire the wren put a kettle to boil on it.

'No point your standing with the infant.' She pointed me at another, upturned pot and I sat on it and gave James the breast.

'What happened to your forehead?' Allie asked.

'I got a belt from a stick.' The wren's clever, foxy face assessed Allie. 'I kept it clean with salt and water and used iodine when it was at its worst. Would you have done any different?'

'No. You did the right thing.'

The wren looked at Allie for a silent half-minute. 'Sit down,' she said then, 'I've another pot if the grass isn't good enough for you.'

'The grass will do.'

Allie sat on the grass and Beezy, with more sense, sat on her travelling bag. Our hostess disappeared into the nest on all fours and came out in the same fashion but pushing four cups, a small bag of tea and sugar ahead of her. Her hair, which was exactly the colour of the freckles covering her face and chest, hung clean and shining to her waist. She might have been twenty-five or she might have been forty years old. It was that hard to put an age on her.

'Ellen's my name,' she told us while she placed the cups in a row. 'Ellen Neary. I came here from the county Waterford.'

Identifying themselves by the part of the country they came from was something all of the wrens would do. Most of them came from small villages and country places. It was as if they needed to remind themselves of the people they'd been before becoming wrens.

While Ellen Neary was making tea in a brown teapot Nance Reilly arrived carrying a pot. She turned this upside-down and sat on it beside Beezy Ryan. Beezy, smoking another cigar, listened without a word as Nance began to whisper in her ear.

'Tomorrow'll be another good day.' Ellen Neary squinted at the cloudless, but darkening, sky. 'You can set about building yourselves a nest. I've no milk. You'll have to take the tea black.'

She was liberal with the sugar and I liked the hot, sweet, smoky-tasting tea she gave us. I was having a second cup when the wrens who shared the nest with her, a couple of young women called Lucretia Curran and Lil Malone, joined us. Lucretia was rosy-cheeked and plump and not a day over seventeen. Lil, who told us she was eighteen, looked a bit like Mary Adams, though not as beautiful and without the mad, staring eyes.

'Where did you get a gown like that?' Lil felt the stuff of Allie's dress. 'Is it silk?'

'I got it in Paris and it's made of sultane,' Allie said.

'You were in Paris?' Lucretia stared. Lil did too. Ellen Neary grunted and refilled and put the kettle back on the fire. Allie slipped off her shoes.

'I was in school there, for a year.' She took off her stockings and stretched her feet in the grass.

Lucretia, after a minute, said, 'It's the loveliest thing I've ever seen on anyone.' She lifted the hem of the dress and examined the stitching. She stroked the velvet trim.

I could see trouble ahead on account of that dress.

'The countryside in northern France is quite like the Curragh,' Allie sad smiling at no one in particular.

'You must feel quite at home so,' Nance Reilly said.

'It's pleasant to be in any country place in the summer.' Allie went on smiling. The knuckles of her hand were white around the cup. She wasn't so calm as she seemed.

'You wouldn't want to be here for the winter.' Ellen Neary gave a short laugh. 'In the two winters I've spent on this plain I've served whatever time's coming to me in either hell or purgatory.'

Beezy took bread and fruit from her bag. We shared it round and talked of where we would make our nest in the morning. But Beezy was short-tempered and bothered-looking and after a couple of minutes got to her feet.

'You might be good enough, Ellen,' she spoke quickly, 'to tell me where I can find Lizzie Early.'

'She's to the west a bit, in number twelve nest,' Ellen pointed, 'you'll see a piece of green-painted wood over the door.'

Beezy, without a word to either myself or Allie, headed for Lizzie's nest. Nance Reilly followed her.

'Is Lizzie in a bad way, or what?'

I looked after Beezy as I put the question to Ellen Neary. She didn't answer at once and when I turned to her she gave herself a small shake. She was like her namesake the wren settling its feathers.

'It's my own view that she's too far gone in drink to be saved,' she said. 'I'd give her to the end of the summer, no more, the way she's going.'

'How long has she been here?'

'Two months, or thereabouts. She was bad when she came but she's a whole lot worse now. She's diseased from it, wasting away and vomiting when she eats even a morsel of food. And still she goes out most nights, looking for any kind of drink she can get. It's a terrible affliction and I've yet to see a woman cured of it. Or a man for that matter.' She turned to Allie. 'Have you come across a cure in your study of medicine?' She was very polite.

'The only cure is for her to stop drinking . . .' Allie began.

'Even the babe in arms knows that much.' Ellen Neary was all at once impatient, 'You didn't save too many drunken women in that dispensary of yours, from the sound of things.'

'No,' Allie admitted, 'no, I didn't. But if Lizzie Early's vomiting and wasting then there's more than drink wrong with her.'

'Maybe you should tell her that,' Lil Malone stretched and lay flat on the grass, 'maybe you should examine her.'

Lucretia Curran gave a snorting laugh and spluttered into her tea. 'That'd be a good one,' she said.

'How many nests and wrens are there in the village?' I was tired of them teasing Allie.

'There'll be sixteen when yours is built,' Ellen Neary set about rinsing the crockery in a basin of dull, brown water. 'We give them numbers, to help tell them apart. This is number seven.'

'How many people to a nest?'

'In the bigger ones as many as eight, but that's counting children.'

'How many wrens in the village altogether?'

'There must be upwards of . . .' Ellen Neary wrinkled her sharp nose and moved her lips, counting, 'sixty or so at the moment. When the wintertime comes we'll not be so numerous.' She shook her head as I started with another question. 'You'll learn all you need to know about the village soon enough. Better to see for yourself than listen to me.' She dried her hands on her petticoat. 'Will you let me hold the infant?' I handed James over to her and she cradled him in her lap. When she held out a finger he caught and held it.

'There were four of us in this nest until last week,' she said. 'Yourself and the child can take the place tonight of the wren's that's gone.'

'Where did the fourth wren go?'

'Disease and the workhouse took her. Her misfortune may as well be your good luck.'

'It'll only be for the night,' I said.

One night would be enough in a dead woman's bed. One week, maybe two, would be enough in the wren village. By then I would be with Jimmy and in an altogether different nest.

'What happens when it rains?' I said.

Ellen laughed. 'We wait for it to stop,' she said.

It was dark by the time Beezy came back. When she did I was sorry she hadn't stayed away. Lizzie Early was with her and she was drunk.

CHAPTER TWENTY-ONE

Sarah

———⟨∘∘∘⟩———

'The father never came looking for you then?'

Lizzie stood over me. I wouldn't have believed anyone could age so much nor so quickly. Her face had shrunk and her naked arms and chest were like worn sacking.

'No,' I said, 'he didn't come looking for me, Lizzie.'

She'd been slim and pretty, the last time I'd seen her, with rouge on her cheeks and her yellow hair curled.

'So, you came after him . . .' She gave a throat-clearing wheeze which turned into a racking cough.

'I did.'

Her laugh was like the death rattle. 'You're not the first and you won't be the last to come to the Curragh after a soldier. You'd better start praying, Sarah Rooney, that you'll have better luck than others around here.'

'Shut your mouth, Lizzie,' Beezy hissed, 'or, sick as you are, I'll shut it for you.'

'Better she knows than to foolishly hope,' Lizzie said, but the fight had all at once gone out of her. 'Bernie's dead.' She sat in a limp heap on the grass. 'She's dead two months now. Of pneumonia. In the fever hospital.'

'Pneumonia . . .' All I could do was repeat the word. Allie came and knelt beside me and put an arm about my shoulder. As she did, and as I stared ahead of me, I saw the dark-haired wren and her little girl Moll appear at the edge of our group. The

249

mother stood with her arms on her hips. She was anything but a comforting sight.

'Bernie took sick in the street one night,' Lizzie Early went on in a low whine, 'she was gone in a week.'

Beezy, standing by the side of the nest with her face in shadow, said nothing. I thought of Mary Ann, of all the help she'd got.

'She might not have been saved anyway,' I said, 'even if she'd taken ill in the kip house and been looked after.'

'She'd have had a better chance than in the street,' Lizzie said.

'It's time we were moving out, those of us that are for the hunting grounds.' Moll's mother didn't move, didn't even unfold her arms. But her voice carried hard and loud. 'Lil, get yourself ready. You too, Lucretia. Listening to this caterwauling for the dead won't put food in our bellies.'

'She's one of *our* dead,' Beezy didn't move, 'and has nothing to do with you. If we choose to lament her passing then so be it. You don't have to listen.'

Quiet as shadows the other women melted away. Even Moll disappeared. There was only Allie and myself to witness Beezy and the dark woman as they faced one another.

'Do your lamenting in private.' The dark woman threw out an arm. 'The plains are wide. We've the business of the night to be getting on with and if you're to live among us you'll have to fall in with our ways. This is no kip house. We're all equal on the Curragh. We've no madams here.'

'If you're all equal what gives you the right to speak for the village?' A moon shadow on Beezy's face gave a sinister slant to the scar.

'I'm saying only what the other women would say if they'd the courage.' Moll's mother took a step forward. 'Those of us who earn at night help feed the rest.' She looked at Allie, then me. 'Soldiers don't wait for ever and there are pickets about, forcing stray soldiers back to the camp. We must hunt when we can—'

'The women who came with me will not be joining your night raids,' Beezy said, cutting her short as sharp as flint.

'Only those who're used to the work go hunting,' Moll's mother shrugged, 'and those that won't frighten the soldiers away.'

Beezy didn't cover her face. She stood unmoving. She might have been a lamppost except for the fluttering feathers around her neck. The sight of her, proudly herself and strong, filled me with a terrible lonesomeness for Henrietta Street. I closed my eyes and bent over my baby, but even behind my closed lids I could see the buildings with their open doors and the women gathered on the steps on evenings like this one.

'We won't be a drain on the wren village,' Beezy said.

'Make sure that you're not.' The woman's eyes were cold. 'You've already been told that we share everything here.'

Did she think we had more money between us than we had? Could she know about Beezy's rings? About the few pieces of jewellery in Allie's bag?

'When what money we have is gone we'll earn,' Beezy said, 'Nance Reilly tells me there's a bit to be made in sewing for the country houses, and in laundering.'

'Maybe the doctor can open a dispensary,' the woman laughed, 'she'd find plenty of customers among the soldiers.'

'We came here in good faith,' Beezy said, 'we came believing shelter would be willingly given to women needing refuge.'

'You were told right.' All at once the woman turned away. 'But you need to know your place. We were all someone once. Now we're bushwomen and wrens. As you will be. You'll be helped build a nest tomorrow.'

'It's a hard life has no time in it to mourn the dead,' Beezy called after her.

'It is,' the woman agreed.

'It's a poor one too.'

'It is.' The woman turned slowly, and spoke slowly. 'I'll tell you Sally O'Hanlon's story and then maybe you'll know just how hard the wren's life is. Sally was taken ill in the night and was dead when the women on either side of her woke in the morning. A surgeon came. He examined her in the nest. There was an inquiry after and a great deal of questioning. It showed Sally had died of being in the open too much and from drinking water from the ditches. They gave us thirteen shillings to bury her and so we did, in Kildare churchyard. They send a water wagon out to us now, from the camp. Since then, when a wren is dying, the relieving officer comes to take her to the workhouse.' She shrugged. 'We live as best we can here, and when a wren dies we mourn her life, not her death.' She stopped, looking at Beezy in silence for a minute. She shrugged again and walked away, calling over her shoulder as she went, 'Lucinda, Lil – get yourselves ready. The night won't last forever.'

Beezy took whiskey from her bag and poured for herself and the two young wrens as they dressed themselves.

They might have been going to a ball. They gathered clean, starched petticoats and dresses from the bushes. To avoid the evening midges they dressed themselves close to the fire, laughing and talking as they helped arrange one another's hair. Lucretia put on a pair of white stockings. They both put on laced-up boots. They turned themselves into respectable young women.

'Be careful you're not caught by the military.' Ellen Neary draped a grimy petticoat over her shoulders. A chill had come into the night.

'Am I not always careful?' Lil Malone pulled impatiently at Lucretia, who was playing with a wakeful James. Lucretia got to her feet at once and they ran, hand in hand, after the other wrens trailing out of the village.

Beezy, taking the whiskey with her, had no sooner gone to sleep in Nance Reilly's nest than Moll appeared from the shadows.

'Mama says you can sleep in our nest,' she announced as she stood in front of Allie. In the darkness her face looked old as night, and far more knowing than those of the wrens who'd gone hand-in-hand to sell themselves.

'Your mother said that?' Allie looked uncertain.

'I asked her and she said yes,' the child amended. 'My name's Moll Hyland. My mother's name is Clara but she'll be gone for most of the night.' She hesitated. 'Maybe you'd let me hold your dress when you take it off?'

'Maybe I will,' Allie picked up her bag, 'or maybe I won't take it off at all.'

'You'll not fit into the nest with it on,' said Moll.

There was nothing more to be said. Allie, walking quickly and with Moll skipping beside her, disappeared into the dark.

Ellen Neary looked after them. 'That child will have what she wants, no matter the cost. Clara's a decent enough sort, but keep out of her way when she's got drink taken.' She shook her head. 'The drink makes a demon of her.'

'Will Allie be all right, sleeping in her nest?'

'She'll have to be. She has a lot to learn and she may as well begin tonight. It's time we got some sleep ourselves. We'll be woken by the women coming back.' She got on to her knees in front of the nest. 'Take your dress off before you come inside. It'll make a pillow for the night. Your underskirt will do for a blanket over yourself and the child.'

When I hesitated, looking about me, she grew impatient.

'There's only the other wrens to see you.' She parted the furze about the door and stood waiting. 'No one wears anything but a petticoat here. It saves our dresses from wearing out and it saves on the washing.'

I saw the sense of this, but still couldn't move. Dressed I was still decent, still had at least the cloak of respectability about me. Stripping down to my petticoat would make me a wren.

'You'll get used to it,' Ellen said, not unkindly.

'I'll never get used to it,' I said, 'never—'

'The first night's the worst,' Ellen cut me short without raising her voice. 'Think of the child and come inside.' She put the punctured pot back over the fire which, fanned by the breeze through the holes, burned red and cheerful. 'It'll light longer that way,' she said and crawled around it into the nest.

I took off my dress and petticoat and followed her.

It was warm in the nest, a home because Ellen and her companions had made it one. There wasn't a lot of room; four women lying side by side would have taken up all of the ground space. The earthen floor was scattered with straw and the roof so low there was no way of standing upright. There were no windows in the thick furze walls, and no chimney in the roof.

The smoke, that night, went out the door but it didn't always. There would be nights when wind and rain drove it back into the nest to swirl and choke and reek into the walls and roof.

A shelf ran along the back wall, supported by sticks driven into the floor. It held plates, the cups we'd used and the teapot as well as a candlestick and cutlery. Above it, hanging from the roof, was the mirror the women had used dressing for their night out. In one corner there was a wooden candle box, in another a couple of small saucepans. Hanging from pegs on the walls were a frying pan, bent poker, three petticoats and two dresses.

I sat, holding James, while Ellen Neary shook out the straw to make the bed big enough for all of us.

'We'll leave the space inside the door for Lil and Lucretia,' she said briskly, 'that way they'll not disturb us too much when they get back.' She rested on her hunkers, her small, foxy face smiling. 'Lie down there now with the child.'

I lay, holding James and thinking that, with a different throw of the dice, Ellen Neary would have made a schoolteacher, or kept a bright, polished kitchen.

'You haven't arrived in the Valley of Death, Sarah Rooney.' She lay beside me. 'Outcast we may be but you'll find we look after our own. You have your son. Be glad of that much at least.'

She was so small, sighing and settling herself, that she reminded me of Mary Ann. 'What brought you here, Ellen?' I said.

'Love for a man, same as brought you here.' She stopped and I waited for her to tell me her story. It took a while but she did in the end, speaking in a curious, flat voice.

'I had a baby of my own, once,' she began, 'a boy, more fair-haired than your lad. He had the neatest hands and fingers you ever saw. I called him Victor. He died when he was four days old in this nest, in my arms, in the middle of the night.'

'I'm sorry for you, Ellen.' James squirmed and I loosened my hold on him.

'I never knew my mother,' Ellen went on, 'nor my father either. My aunt kept a whiskey store in Cork and I grew up with her. There was just the two of us and she worked all the hours. She was hard but I never wanted for anything. I think she was my mother's sister. When I was seventeen an artilleryman came to the store. He was a big man and he lifted me up on to the counter and laughed and asked his soldier friends if they'd ever seen a living doll like me. He came back when the store was closed.'

She stopped, sighing. I waited in silence until she went on.

'He'd been ordered with his regiment to the Curragh by the time I found I was carrying his child. I followed him when my aunt said she'd have none of me. She didn't want the bastard child of an English soldier under her feet in the store.'

She turned her back to me and was quiet for another few minutes. I wanted to ask her to spare me the rest of her story until after I'd found the father of my own child. I couldn't do it, any more than she could have stopped telling me.

'I found him in the camp. It wasn't easy. You'll see that for yourself. When I did he was a different man altogether from the one I'd known in Cork. He ridiculed me in front of his companions, calling me a whore and worse. He took his hand to me and would have kicked me when I was on the ground too but for a soldier who stopped him saying it was shameful to hurt a woman who was with child, or any woman. I was nearly the nine months gone. My brave lover told me then that I should join the wrens in their bush houses like others of my kind.'

She fell silent again and I waited, watching the fire dancing red under the saucepan. I told myself Jimmy Vance would not have changed.

'My child was born in this very nest,' Ellen Neary went on. 'The birth was hard but the women were good to me. They were good to my little Victor too but he was born feeble and he couldn't feed. He was a good baby, very quiet. He never cried, not even once. I kept thinking that if he cried he'd be saved. But he didn't and he died in the evening of the fourth day.' Her voice dropped. 'I would have died myself but for the wrens. They saved me and I stayed on in the village. There wasn't a whole lot else I could do.'

'And his father never knew he'd a son?'

'Never, any more than my child ever knew it had a father. He was sent away from here and bad cess to him, wherever he is.' She sat up, hugging her knees. 'When I lost my good name I lost everything. Everything.'

My grandmother's voice, telling me to guard my name, echoed in my head. 'Is it hard,' I said, 'living here?'

'It's hard all right.' She looked down at me, then around the nest. 'It's hard in the wintertime, with the bitter winds to contend with. It's hard when the rain goes on for days and weeks together. The beating of the one and the pelting of the other destroys the nests. Sometimes they fall in on top of us. When they do we build them again and keep some sort of shelter going for the bad months. The snow is the worst. It covers the plains and sometimes cuts us off from the camp and the towns. We lose wrens every winter, to sickness and the workhouse.' She shook her head. 'But it's man who treats us the worst.'

'What do you mean?'

'You'll see for yourself,' she said, 'and it'll be time enough then for you to know.'

'Why do you stay? Wouldn't you be better taking your chances in Cork, or even in Dublin?'

'The wrens are my family now. We hold for one another. I never had that before.' She inched towards the wooden box in the corner. 'In any event, I might as well wait here as anywhere.'

'What're you waiting for?' I said.

Without answering she took a bundle of letters and a photographic portrait out of the box. She put the portrait into my hand and brought the candle closer. A soldier with a round, open face looked out at us. He was wearing a bandsman's uniform.

'I met him one day on the road to the camp,' Ellen said. 'He's a different kind to the other. We were together twice and then they sent him to Malta. He'll be gone for six years. He writes letters to me.' She put the picture back into the box.

'When did you last see him?'

'I walked to Dublin to see him before he sailed. He wanted to see me one more time before going. He was heartbroken as I was when his ship left harbour.' She looked at the letters. 'Can you read and write?' she asked.

'I'm not bad at either,' I said.

'You might help me make a better hand of my next letter to him so . . .'

'I will,' I said.

I wished I had a likeness of Jimmy Vance to show her. While she put the letters away I told her about my letters to him.

'The army's a funny thing,' she said when I finished, 'it may be that he never got them. Then again he might. You'll have to go careful when you set out to find him. There's extra soldiers on guard on account of fears about the Fenians.' She sighed. 'There's bad feeling about the wrens in the camp these days too, with fines and imprisonment for women from the village caught in the camp. They blame us for—'

'They can say what they like,' I'd heard too much, 'and do what they like. I'm going to the camp in the morning.'

Something was happening outside. The sounds were familiar enough: the screaming laughs and howled obscenities of drunken men and women, the roars and thuds of drunken fighting. I'd heard it all before, on bad nights in the kip house. Sometimes too in Henrietta Street. It got louder and nearer by the minute.

'The women are back early,' Ellen was calm, 'and they've got soldiers with them. Things could go well enough or they could turn bad. We'll be all right as long as we stay inside the nest.'

The nest was fragile. The plains were lonely. I felt a sick fear for James, stirring in his sleep and making small, grunting sounds like an old man. I sat up, wanting to rush from the nest and run with him.

'Stay where you are.' Ellen was sharp.

Then I heard the gunfire, five shots in all, each one sounding closer to the nest. I sat and rocked James.

'Lie down, in the name of God, and stop your caterwauling.' Ellen Neary squeezed my arm. 'It's only a picket from the camp out looking for the soldiers. If you keep that up you'll have them in on top of us, poking around and destroying the place with their bayonets.'

I stopped. I'd never been the type to whinge and cry but motherhood had changed me. I worried about James as I'd never worried. I anticipated danger as never before.

I hadn't anticipated the bayonet's shining point before it came through the door. It stood in the air for a shining, terrifying minute before it was followed by the face of its soldier owner.

'Are you alone in there?' He didn't shout, just looked from me to Ellen and then James, who had started to cry.

'You can see for yourself there's no soldiers here,' Ellen said.

'Sorry,' he said and his head disappeared.

There were no more gunshots and the shouting, though it didn't stop, became less. The violent mood died slowly into occasional, muttered oaths. Ellen crawled to the door of the nest and called, 'How well did ye do?'

'Well enough,' Lucretia Curran's voice came from close by, 'the summer weather had them in generous mood.'

Ellen lay down again. 'We'll be able to stock up on market day so,' she said.

She was asleep and gently snoring long before I got James stopped crying. Before Lil and Lucretia, stripped of their gowns and back in their frieze petticoats, fell into the nest and wormed themselves into comfortable positions for the night. Before sleeping myself I whispered to James that his father was close and promised to find him the next day.

It was as well he couldn't understand. It's bad to make promises to a child that you cannot keep.

CHAPTER TWENTY-TWO

Allie

———⟨∘∘∘⟩———

Moll was turning the pages of Gray's *Anatomy*. She couldn't read a word of it, but her sharp eyes devoured the drawings. Her absorbed face was guileless, but I wasn't fooled. It was a trick of the morning light. There was nothing innocent, and not very much that was young, about Moll Hyland. She was a child of her rearing and I couldn't help liking her.

All around us wrens were beginning their day. Moll ignored them. She ignored her mother too, who was briskly washing and spreading clothes to dry. Clara Hyland looked none the worse for her drunkenness and fighting in the night.

'What's this?' Moll looked with magnificent distaste at a skeleton. 'Is there a disease can take the skin from a man?'

'None that I've heard of,' I said. 'That's a drawing to show how the body's made up. It's called a skeleton.'

She traced the drawing with a finger. 'So the doctors know everything that's inside of us then?'

'They should,' I said.

'You can have your old skeleton.' She dropped my precious *Anatomy* on the grass, 'I don't like the look of it at all.' She took the point lace handkerchief I'd given her earlier from her pocket. Her look calculated its value and I'd no doubt she would sell or trade it at the first opportunity.

'I've never heard tell of a lady doctor,' she said.

'You will.'

'I think it would be a much grander thing to work in a big shop, selling lace and other finery.' She folded the handkerchief. 'That's what I'll do with myself, when Mama dies.'

'When your mother dies?' I stared at her.

'Are you a doctor or not?' With her hands on her hips she looked like a miniature of her mother. 'Don't you know that the drink kills women? I've seen plenty of them die. Mama's often in a worse way than she was last night.' She stared past me. 'Your friend's going somewhere, the one with the infant. She has her town clothes on her.'

Sarah, less than ten feet away, was headed purposefully our way. She was carrying James and dressed as she'd been the day before. Her face was pale and set. I went to meet her.

'I'm off to look for Jimmy and I want you to come with me.' She stood frowning at my petticoat. 'If you get dressed and carry your parasol, we'll pass for respectable women. I'm afraid that if I walk in alone, with James . . .'

'That you'll be stopped,' I finished for her. 'Of course I'll come with you, but it would be better to wait until later in the morning. At this hour there'll be very few about and we'll be noticed.'

'Put on your clothes, Allie, please . . .'

'Do you have a plan for finding him?' I said.

She was shaking, and jiggling James to disguise the fact. 'I hate to see you in your petticoat.' She went to where my dress and underskirt were stretched across a bush. 'We'll go now. I can't wait any longer. We'll make up a plan on the way.'

The sun was still low in the sky and the dew wet and cold under my feet. The air was filled with birdsong. An early morning mist, hovering low over the plains, blurred the outlines of the army camp and reminded me of a shroud.

'It's too early,' I said, gently as I could.

'They'll see you coming,' Moll was scornful, 'do you think soldiers stay in their beds once the dawn is up? They'll see you carrying the baby and it won't matter whether there's one or twenty of you they'll know you come from the village. You'll be stopped. You'll have to wait till the Saturday market. That's when they let the wrens in.'

'You should be with the other children, or tending to your unfortunate mother.' Sarah looked at Moll as if she saw a deviant, or freak of some kind, in front of her. 'You're only a child.'

'I may be a child but I know more than you do about what'll happen if you go off to the camp now.' Moll gave a pitiless shrug. 'You'll be caught by the hair of the head and thrown back out on to the plains. Allie will be thrown with you and all for going there because you asked her to. Go on your own if you want to find your soldier that much.'

'That's enough, Moll,' I said as Sarah stared at her, speechless. Ellen Neary arrived and stood coiling her hair into a topknot as the argument went on.

'I'll go on my own.' Sarah's eyes were far too bright.

'You'll be sorry,' said Moll.

Sarah, fight and courage leaving her, sank to the ground with James. She sat weeping and rocking to and fro.

'We'll go in a little while,' I promised as I knelt and held her, 'we'll go in a little while.'

Ellen Neary sat beside us. 'I told her much the same things as Moll but she wouldn't listen. I hope to God he's a decent sort, this soldier of hers, that he's not a bastard, like a lot of the others.' When she reached for James Sarah let him go to her. 'You're her friend,' she said to me, 'talk sense to her.'

'Maybe it would be better to wait until the market day.' I held Sarah's shoulders. 'The weather's good. We'll be all right here until then. It's what we planned, after all, to stay with the women until you found a way of working things out. We'll build our nest today and tomorrow and then it'll be Saturday . . .'

'Two days!' Sarah wailed. 'I've been without him for nearly a year and now that I'm half a mile from where he is you want me to wait another two days!' I hadn't seen her so distraught since Mary Ann's funeral. Her eyes were wild and she was trembling as she pulled herself to her feet. 'I'll find him. Myself and James will find him . . .'

She took the baby from Ellen and walked up and down with him. He sensed her mood and began to cry, which made her walk faster.

She might have gone on like this for a lot longer, might even have taken off across the plains in spite of my and Ellen Neary's best efforts, if Beezy Ryan hadn't come briskly through the bushes.

'You're putting yourself before your child.' She stood in Sarah's path. 'Go if you must but go alone. It's not right to risk harm coming to him. You don't know how harsh they'll be, nor what might happen. Give him to me,' she held out her arms, 'and be on your way.'

Sarah stood very still. She'd never been parted from James. The fire and panic went out of her. 'What am I going to do . . .' she said. 'What am I going to do?'

We made tea and had some bread with it. The day got brighter and warmer and the village became a hive of the sort of tasks you'd expect in any household. There was washing and sweeping going on and some wrens even sat sewing. There was a peacefulness about it all.

'I hate this place,' Sarah said in a low voice as we sat, a little apart from the others, with our tea and bread. 'It's uncivil and it's heathen. I want my baby and myself to be out of here. I want you out to be of here too.'

'We're free here,' I said. 'We've no one behind us, telling us what to do and what to think . . .' I stopped.

'You're romanticising it,' Sarah was hard, 'all we've done is ally ourselves with a pitiful, shameful community of outcasts. The freedom you feel is rejection. We're unwanted, as these women are unwanted. What we have here is not freedom, Allie. We're slaves, we're without choices.'

I could understand how it was different for Sarah. She had her baby to worry about and she had her crippling love for Jimmy Vance tying her down. Her plight might have been what brought us to the Curragh but I was the one liberated and she the one repulsed by the women and free life we'd found there.

'We have choices, Sarah,' I said. I couldn't see, then, how right she was. To do so would have made a cripple of me too.

Beezy joined us. 'We've to decide on a spot for our nest,' she said, 'we'd best put what money we have together and go into Kildare for utensils and such.'

We chose a corner, not far from Ellen Neary's nest, where there was a depression already from an earlier nest.

'We'll have to walk to the town,' Beezy said, 'and take a horsecar back with our purchases.'

'I'm not taking James into that miserable hole.' Sarah was sullen and stubborn. 'You can go without me.'

It was enough that she'd agreed not to go to the camp; there was no point arguing with her further. The idea of making the trip alone, with Beezy, didn't appeal to me at all.

'Maybe you'd come with us,' I said to Ellen Neary, 'we'd be grateful for your advice about the best stores to do business with.'

'They're all much the same when it comes to doing business with wrens,' Ellen shrugged, 'in Kildare and Newbridge both. If you dress up grand enough you mightn't be taken for wrens and could get some civility. I'll come with you to point out the worst of the stores.'

I wore the lilac dress I'd travelled in and carried a parasol of the same shade. It was the finest of the three dresses I'd brought with me. Beezy wore her feathers, which I thought foolish but said nothing. Beezy Ryan would never have *savoir-faire*. She also put kohl around her eyes, and rouged her cheeks. This made the welts on her face more noticeable.

Ellen Neary got herself ready too. She looked neat and trim in a yellow cotton dress. I had no idea, and nor did she say, how much I'd asked of her.

The sun got warmer and the grass dried under our feet as we walked along. Beezy and I carried our footwear; Ellen Neary thought this uncivilised and wore her brown button boots all the way.

'We're not the savages people around here think we are,' she said. 'The army's wrong too, when it blames the wrens for the disease in the camp.'

'There's syphilis in the camp then?' I said.

'Give it the name we all know,' said Beezy, 'she's talking about the pox, Ellen. Is the pox in the camp?'

'All over it, they say. The army and local people both blame it on the wrens. You'd think that none of themselves ever did wrong.' She kicked so hard at a tuft of grass that it flew through the air and landed near a startled sheep. 'Sarah'll need to be careful. There are new powers allowing the authorities to lift women wherever they find them,' she waved an arm, 'on the highways, in the street, makes no difference. They can arrest wherever they like. I tried to tell Sarah this morning but it was like talking to the deaf.'

'It's the Contagious Diseases Act gives them the powers you mention.' Beezy was sour. 'I know all about it.'

'Wrens have been fined and put in prison already for being caught in the camp,' said Ellen. 'Some were taken away for examination and when some of them were found to be afflicted they were put in the Naas Union Workhouse and kept there for months, or until the doctors decided they were cured.' She knelt to loosen her boots. 'It's a while since I wore these and I'd swear my feet have spread.' She looked up at me. 'The doctors don't seem so good at curing the pox. Even with their mercury and God knows what else they don't seem able to fix it, do they?'

'They do sometimes,' I said.

I knew about syphilis. I'd read about it and knew there were many cures and none and, if I was honest, even the thought of it frightened me. If I was to be a doctor then I'd have to get over my fear.

I'd once seen a woman with syphilis. Sarah and I had watched as she was carried, screaming, from a house in the Broadstone when we were about ten years old. She'd been covered in rotting lesions and completely mad in the head. I still saw her sometimes in my dreams.

Ellen Neary hadn't finished what she had to say. 'It's said that suffering girls are smothered in the Lock hospitals, to put them out of their pain,' she said darkly, 'so on Sarah Rooney's own head be it if she goes into that camp.'

Beezy Ryan and I put our stockings and shoes back on when we reached the road into the town. The mood in the narrow, rutted streets was no more cheerful than it had been the day before and we passed rows of thatched cottages and a ruined cathedral without meeting a single friendly face. The only acknowledgement we got was from a gaggle of dirty children with red-rimmed eyes who called names and followed us for a while.

Ellen brought us at last to a wider street where there was a hotel, barber, baker, public house and provision store. It was busy enough, carts and men on horseback and pedestrians for the most part. She brought us straight to the provision store, where the name painted across the window read Cummins & Co., Spirit Grocer and Hardware. The money we'd put together to spend on the nest didn't amount to a great deal but then we didn't need a great deal. Cummins & Co. looked as if it could just about supply our needs. I was keeping my jewellery, and what I could raise on it, for a far rainier day than this one.

'The owner's a Christian woman, but old,' Ellen said, 'she won't turn you away though her son might, if it's one of his bad days. It's the only place in town sells to wrens.' She gave a half-laugh. 'Even then it depends the kind of wren. I'll stay outside, in case I spoil your chances. I'll try for a horsecar to take us back.'

We were hot from the walk and glad of the murky cool of Cummins & Co. A man behind the grocery counter watched silently as we came in.

'Good morning.' I smiled and approached him. Beezy went to examine the saucepans and ware at the other end of the shop.

'It's not a bad morning,' the shopkeeper agreed. He had a round, pink face that extended into a round, pink, bald head. 'Have ye travelled far?' He looked at Beezy.

'From Dublin,' I said, deliberately misunderstanding. If he

wanted to know whether we'd come in from the plains then let him ask outright. 'We need provisions and we need candles, some were . . .'

He ignored me, eyes still beadily on Beezy. It was as if he expected the shop to combust about her. I became brisk.

'I'll have sugar and tea to start with. My friend will make a selection from the hardware. We'll need saucepans, a kettle, a looking glass . . .'

'A looking glass!' His eyes, when he swivelled to face me, were dancing in his head. His face colour had deepened to red. 'It's the face of God you and your kind should be looking at, not at your own brazen—'

'What kind am I, Mr Cummins? You are Mr Cummins, I presume?'

'I'm Cornelius Cummins and don't you take that tone with me,' he sniffed and looked at me as if I were a stinking shoe. He was a small man, and not very clean. 'Your airs and graces don't disguise you,' he rocked on his heels, 'the company you keep says it all.' He spat on the floor behind him. The spit sizzled in dust which hadn't been swept for weeks. Months, maybe.

I gave him a look of my own. 'Judge not lest you be judged, Mr Cummins,' I said as I surveyed his shop. His goods were as dusty as his floor. Cummins & Co. were shopkeepers to the poor; the local rich no doubt bought in Dublin, or perhaps Naas. We would be spending more money than the rest of his customers in a week. I took my purse from my pocket.

'I'm here to exchange money for goods, Mr Cummins, nothing more. Nothing less, either.' I put the purse on the counter. The coins made a healthy jingle. 'If my money offends I can take it elsewhere.'

'Where else would—' He stopped too late to hide his greed and alarm.

'I'll get what I need from the army stores, where money is money and business business.' I felt Beezy at my side and jabbed her with my elbow. She stayed where she was.

I put a hand on the purse. It was made of brown velvet, with a handle of plaited silk cords and tassels. It looked opulent on that dusty, wooden counter and Cornelius Cummins' splayed fingers almost touched it as he estimated the money inside.

'I'll do business with you but not with that harlot.' He kept his eyes on the purse, his neck bulging greasily from his flannel collar. 'She's the kind spreads her evil wherever she goes, contaminating the society of good people . . .'

'Half the money inside here is mine.' I opened it so that he saw the coins and inclined my head in Beezy's direction. 'The rest belongs to Miss Ryan.' I buttoned it shut again. 'But if it offends you it might be best for all concerned if you kept your candles and crockery for more God-fearing customers. Their money is no doubt worth a lot more to you than Miss Ryan's.'

I turned for the door and Beezy turned with me. There was nothing else she could have done. Behind us, Cummins' voice rose to a whine.

'I'm a shopkeeper. I do business with all sorts. I've a family to feed and times are hard. Money is money.' His voice almost broke and he cleared his throat. 'My son will attend to you.'

I went back to the counter. Beezy stayed where she was. 'I agree with you, Mr Cummins, that money is money. And good manners are good manners. I hope your son's are better than your own.'

His eyes, mad with hate, held mine. He would never forget, never forgive. He was very likely a vengeful man too. With a stifled oath he disappeared through a door behind the counter.

'You're your father's daughter, after all,' Beezy said softly as we waited for the son to appear. 'You did well with that fat *amadán*, I'll give you that.'

'I did,' I agreed.

'Doesn't make you a woman though,' Beezy said.

'No more than spreading your legs to make money from men makes a woman of you.' I meant to shock Beezy Ryan and I did. She was silent for a minute before giving a great screech of laughter.

'We might make a woman of you yet,' she said and for a short while, until the door bell jangled and two women came in, there was peace between us. The women who came in kept a silent, watchful distance.

'What can I get for you?'

The son, when he appeared, was taller than his father but just as fleshy. He had hair too, though not a great deal. It was gingery and there was more in his ears and on his arms than his head.

One of the women behind us spoke in a loud, firm voice. 'I'll have my bag of yellow meal, Joseph, if you please.'

'I have it made up for you . . .'

'We've been waiting awhile,' I cut him short, 'so we'll take our turn first, if you don't mind.'

The woman was firmer, and louder. '*I* mind. I mind that you're here at all.'

I turned to look at her, at her yellowed skin and small, black eyes. She came closer to me and raised a bony finger.

'Keep out of this town. Respectable women shouldn't have to stand behind the likes of you to get the necessities for their families. Hunger and starvation are too good for you.'

'I've no intention of starving,' I turned my back to her again, 'and no intention either of spending more time than I need to in this place.'

Joseph Cummins put a bag of Indian yellow meal on the counter. The woman threw down a coin, lifted the bag and with her companion left the shop as if propelled by a gale force wind. She was another Kildare citizen who wouldn't forget.

'She's a good customer.' Joseph Cummins' explanation was almost an apology.

'So might I be,' I said.

I bought eggs, bacon, cheese, tea, sugar, milk and what passed for sweet cake in the Cummins' emporium. The cake was nothing but soda bread with a few sultanas and caraway seeds added and Bess would have left it where it was. I kept a careful count of what I spent; it came to nine shillings and eightpence-halfpenny. When Beezy added a bottle of whiskey I said nothing.

I wasn't going to give the shopkeeper's son the satisfaction of seeing us argue in his shop.

We selected the rest of what we needed and put everything on the counter. Joseph Cummins, doing his sums in a notebook, said nothing until we came to the end.

'We've cups and saucers better than those,' he said then, 'only where ye'll be using them I doubt the style will matter much.'

'Why is that?' I said and he giggled like a girl.

'Ye're unlikely to be receiving society people in a nest on the Curragh. It's all the same what you drink out of in one of those holes in the ground.' He giggled again and bent his head over his figures.

In the darker recesses behind the counter a door opened and a very old woman came through. She stood like a waxwork beside Joseph Cummins as he started to go over his figures with a pencil.

'You seem very familiar with the wren village,' I said, 'have you visited?'

His head shot up. 'I have not.' He looked more than ever like his father when his face reddened. 'No God-fearing man would be caught in or near that place. You owe me four pounds and four shillings.'

'We owe you three pounds and nineteen shillings,' Beezy said.

'Three pounds and nineteen shillings,' I echoed. I didn't for a minute doubt Beezy was right. Beezy didn't make mistakes about money.

Joseph Cummins looked from one to the other of us. 'Ye're very good at the arithmetic,' he sneered. 'But I've it written down here and four pounds and four shillings is what you owe me.'

Beezy leaned across the counter. 'You're mistaken.' She took the notebook from his hand and stepped smartly out of his reach. 'The big saucepan is two shillings, not six,' she went briskly down the columns of figures, 'and the provisions come to something over nine shillings, not ten. You'll find that accounts for the extra five shillings.' She laid the notebook on the counter. 'It's easy enough to make a mistake with sums,' she shrugged, 'if you're not careful.'

Joseph Cummins' hand was shaking when he picked the notebook. He said nothing for a minute or two, breathing heavily as he studied his figures, rapping the counter with his free hand.

'I know my sums . . .' he began.

'Give it to me.' Without warning the old woman held out an arthritic hand. Her eyes, holding mine, were bright as a bird's as Joseph Cummins passed her the notebook. She gave me a small nod and began to quickly scan the figures. It was a bare half-minute before she said, 'Take three pounds and nineteen shillings, Joseph,' and began wrapping a cup in newspaper. 'It's what they owe.' She looked from me to Beezy. 'Ye're paying dear enough at that price too.'

Joseph Cummins picked up and threw down the notebook. 'I did my sums,' he shouted, 'they were—'

'Wrong,' said the old woman, 'you were wrong, Joseph.' To me she said, 'My grandson didn't take time enough to do things right.'

She held out her crooked hand and I put the money into it. She pocketed it and then, together with myself and Beezy, packed everything into a couple of empty candle boxes. Everything but the bottle of whiskey. For this she refused to give us paper, or wrapping of any kind. Beezy, without a word, slipped it into her long skirt pocket. It was where it would have ended up anyway, where it would remain until emptied.

'I'm against the drink,' said the old woman, 'it's the divil's own work and I've seen it destroy too many in my own and other families around here. I'd not have served it to a woman.' Her bird's eyes held mine again. 'Keep away from it. You'll survive everything but the drink.'

'You're right,' I said. The woman nodded and gave Beezy a hard look.

'May God and His Mother look after you,' she said, 'may They look after the both of you.'

Ellen Neary was sitting on a stone block, waiting, when we came out of the shop with the two boxes. She complained about the time we'd taken and said the few carmen about had either ignored or been surly to her.

'The fellow from yesterday's down the street a bit,' she pointed, 'I'd say he'll do the journey if you ask him, Allie, rather than me.' She eyed the parasol. 'He's sure to remember you.'

I left her and Beezy with the boxes and went looking for the carman. He wasn't so friendly as the day before but he agreed to take us.

'Times are bad,' he echoed the shopkeeper's son, 'and business is business. But don't come to me again. I'll be getting myself a name.'

'As a friend to the wrens?'

'That's it. Your friends aren't popular in this town. You'd not have been served in Cummins if it wasn't for the old woman holding the power there . . .'

There was a scream, followed by a roared obscenity. I spun in time to see a thickset man lash with his boot at Ellen Neary, who was on the ground in the middle of the street. Beezy, still standing outside the shop with our purchases, saw what was happening at the same time as I did. We started running towards Ellen together. Beezy had a saucepan in her hand.

'Don't cross my path again, whore, and don't come into this town again either. Stay outside on the plains with the beasts of the fields, where you belong.' A hobnailed boot caught and tore at the arm Ellen had thrown protectively about her head. 'We don't want your kind of filth on our streets.'

I reached them just as Beezy did. Ellen's arm was pumping red blood. I could see the marks of the man's boot on the back of her dress too. She would have more than an injured arm.

Beezy raised the saucepan above her head as the man moved back to position his next kick.

'If you so much as lift your boot once more I'll flatten your head into your body.' She might have been remarking on the weather, her voice was so calm. The man stopped in mid-kick and spun to stare at her. His face was disbelieving.

'I should have known. Her kind of animal travels always in a pack. I'll kill you . . .'

He took a step towards Beezy. His mouth was rimmed with white spittle and he clenched and unclenched a pair of thick veined hands. Beezy, who was taller than he was, didn't move and didn't lower the saucepan.

A small crowd had gathered: men and women and a few children. They stood in a silent semi-circle. When a dog among them barked a child hushed it.

'You'll have to kill me too.' My voice was high and twittering. I cleared my throat and would have tried again but for the blazing look Beezy Ryan gave me. I stepped around the man and bent to help Ellen.

He didn't turn as I lifted and helped her to where our purchases sat piled. None of his fellow citizens came to help. I sat Ellen on one of the boxes, where she could lean against the shop front. She was cold and shaking, her freckles a ginger rash in a whey-coloured face. The arm was in a bad way. A large sliver of flesh, ripped by the hobnails from the flexor muscle of the forearm, hung in a bloody pulp. Her back and ribs would be another story, one which would have to wait until we got back to the village. For now, I tore the frill from the end of my petticoat and bound the torn flesh tightly back into its place. Ellen Neary didn't complain. She didn't even flinch. Her blood destroyed my dress and I cursed the vanity which had made me wear it.

While I was doing this Beezy delivered herself of a tongue-lashing to the bully-boy.

'Lay a hand on me and I'll have you in court.' Her voice carried in the hushed street. 'I've as many rights as the next citizen and I'll exercise them. There's two of us, apart from the wounded woman herself, who're witness to what you did.'

'It'd be the word of a band of whores against that of a church-going citizen.' He was sneering but less sure of himself. 'There's not a judge in the land would believe you, never mind listen to you.' He was bluffing and knew it; he was a man realising the consequences of an outburst of bullying rage.

'Oh, we'll be listened to all right,' Beezy said, 'and the word will go round. You'll make a name for yourself as the church-going citizen taken to court by three bushwomen.'

'May God strike you dead,' the man roared, 'I'd do it myself but I wouldn't have you on my conscience.' He shook a fist in the air. 'God *will* have His vengeance on you, and on your kind.'

Beezy gave a short laugh. 'I've never known God be too generous with His kindness so His vengeance will be no great thing.' She lowered the saucepan. 'Go home, little man, and say your prayers.'

She'd almost reached where I knelt bandaging Ellen Neary when the man made a frenzied rush and stood in front of her. His voice was low and thick but I heard every word he said.

'I don't forget things so keep an eye to your back from now on, madam, wherever you go . . .' He rubbed the spittle from his mouth with a sleeve. 'Not even the black of the night will protect you, nor the nest you lie in.'

'You're a brave man,' Beezy said, 'brave with your fists and feet against the weak, brave under the cover of darkness too it seems.' She leaned closer to him. 'You'd best keep out of my way because I'm not afraid of cursed and cowardly curs the likes of you.'

'You'll remember you said that.' The man turned abruptly and pushed his way through the crowd, which dispersed, some of them looking disappointed.

Our carman had to be persuaded all over again to drive us. I paid him one shilling and sixpence, which was again double the usual fare, but he wouldn't have taken us otherwise.

In the village I used salt water and iodine on Ellen Neary's arm and bound it with gauze. I gave her laudanum for the pain.

'It'll mend,' I said, 'but you'll have a scar.' I wasn't as sure as I sounded about it mending.

'I suppose it will.' Ellen gave a small grin and closed her eyes. 'It's only the good die young.'

Half a dozen women, including Clara Hyland and Nance Reilly, helped us build our nest. It was finished and furnished before dusk fell. It was warm, just big enough for the three of us and James, just strong enough to last the summer. There was no nest numbered eleven in the village so we gave ourselves that number.

That night's band of hunting women were leaving the village as we lay to sleep for the night.

'We might as well be dead as far as the rest of the world is concerned,' said Sarah.

'We'd be better off if that was true,' Beezy said, 'but the world has no intention of leaving us alone. More's the pity.'

CHAPTER TWENTY-THREE

Allie

———◦❮❍❍❍❯◦———

I woke in the night to find Sarah crawling from the nest.

'Where are you going?' I sat up. She had James with her.

'Go back to sleep,' she hissed as she disappeared through the doorway.

It was hot and clammy in the nest, like the night outside only worse. I crawled after them. Sarah was dressing, already in her underskirts. James lay sleeping by the side of the nest. I'd never known a baby enjoy his sleep so much.

'What you're planning is futile and feeble-minded.' I lifted her dress from the ground. 'You'll get yourself barred from the camp altogether.'

'I'll find Jimmy first.' She reached for the dress. I held it away.

'How're you going to find him in the middle of the night?'

'The middle of the night's the best time. The camp will be quiet and I can talk to the sentries. It was sentries helped me meet him before, when he was in Beggar's Bush.' She held out a hand. 'Give me my dress, Allie.'

'You don't know the sentries here.' I took a step away from her. The moon was high, and bright, creating shadows all around us. Sarah stood like a half-dressed spectre in its light. I spoke quickly, afraid she would take James and run as she was to the camp. 'The camp is as big as a town and it's forbidden to wrens. It's a bright night. The sentries will see you coming with James and know you're from the village. It's market day tomorrow, Sarah, and the women who go will ask for you . . .'

'They might destroy my chances altogether.'

'They might, and they might not. It's better to wait and see what they have to tell us. We have to plan, Sarah. One more day's waiting isn't going to make any difference.'

'It will . . . I *can't* wait.' She crumpled and slid to the ground, hugging herself. 'You've no idea what it's like, Allie, being without him when he's so close . . .'

'Just as well too,' I was harsh, 'one of us needs to think straight.'

She lifted her head. 'What does your straight thinking tell you then?' She was full of hostility.

In a minute, if I wasn't careful, she would be up and making for the camp again, with or without her dress.

'I think you'll lose him altogether unless you go about finding him the right way.' I sat beside her, careful to keep the dress to the other side of me. She seemed calm enough. 'If you're thrown out of the camp you may never get back in again . . .' She looked about to protest so I completed the picture, 'You'll end up like Clara Hyland, rearing your child on the plains.'

I'd gone too far and immediately regretted it – not least because it was disparaging of Moll. The child had attached herself to me and had even, and miraculously, cleaned my dress of Ellen Neary's blood.

Sarah jumped up. 'Have you lost your reason, Allie?' She glared down at me. 'Clara Hyland's a drunkard. That's why she came here and that's why she stayed. I won't be keeping James here any longer than a week. I won't have him made into a savage.' She paused. 'I won't have myself made into one.'

Sarah was right about one thing. Clara Hyland was a drunkard. She wasn't the only drunkard in the village but she was one of the worst. Lizzie Early was different; there was something more than drink eating away at Lizzie's body.

'What're you going to do?' I said.

'I don't know,' Sarah was calmer, 'yet.'

'It's time we decided something,' I said.

The plan we made that night to bring Sarah and Jimmy Vance together seemed, to me, as sure as death and taxes. Sarah had doubts, but then she never had my certainties about anything.

It was surprisingly easy to persuade Sarah that it would be wiser if I was the one to make the first approach to the camp. I would dress in my best, speak in my most elocution-trained tones and would take Moll Hyland with me. A woman with a young girl in her charge would be a lot more acceptable than a woman alone. I would be the most respectable and reasonable young woman ever to come seeking a meeting with the camp's commander.

Sarah's doubts were about the chances of arranging such a meeting. But I've always believed in venturing to gain and knew that someone in a position of power could produce Jimmy Vance.

I left for the camp with Moll early next morning, well ahead of the wrens who would be leaving later for the market.

The camp, as I came close to it, was more sprawling and less imposing than it had looked on the skyline. In the centre, a clock tower rose high above the rest of the buildings. The Union Jack, defeated by the windless humidity, hung limp against a flagstaff nearby. To the right and left of these high points there were two churches while everywhere else, far and wide and further than my eye could see, stretched rows and rows of wooden huts.

It was the huge number of wooden huts which made it easy to believe there were more than ten thousand soldiers stationed here. Sarah would never have found Jimmy Vance just by wandering about the camp.

There was a dull chorus of horses neighing and soldiers drilling as Moll and I joined the stream of country people on the main road into the camp. Most of them, driving donkey carts, were bringing produce to sell at the market. Others, on foot like ourselves, were hoping to buy.

Moll, skipping like the blithe innocent she was anything but beside me, was in great good humour. We'd made sure too not to approach the camp from the direction of the wren village, walking almost to Kildare so as to come at it from the other side. Moll had been glad to come with me, her mother less so.

'She can be giddy. I don't want her going near the horses,' warned Clara, red-eyed and pale-faced, 'nor anywhere near the soldiers either.'

I didn't see how either of these could be avoided but nodded agreeably. Clara had been given a full bottle of whiskey by a soldier the night before; she was drinking the last of it as we spoke.

'Go inside for a lie down.' Moll took her mother's hand. She was matter-of-fact. 'I'll bring you something sweet from the camp stores.' She gave me a grave look.

'We won't forget her, will we Allie?'

'We won't,' I said, 'we'll bring back bonbons . . .'

'I'd prefer raisins,' said Clara Hyland, 'or currants. It's a long time since I tasted either.' She looked from Moll to me, jealous and hurt at the friendship her daughter was bestowing on me. Moll, instinctive creature that she was, threw her arms about her mother's neck and hugged her close and kissed her blanched cheek.

'I'll have ten thousand things to tell you,' she said.

Moll walked with my parasol high above her head as we crossed the plains. When we left the grass, which was scrubby and worn from the hoofs of the army's horses, she handed it to me. 'While we're on the road and in the camp we should be proper,' she said. 'It doesn't look right to have a child with a parasol.'

In her best blue and white striped dress and with her hair tied with one of my ribbons she was close as she'd ever be to looking like an ordinary nine-year-old. I needn't have worried; we might both have been children for all the heed the sentries paid us as we walked with the country people into the camp.

'We'll buy Mama's raisins first,' Moll said when we got to the marketplace, 'in case we don't get a chance later.'

She meant in case we were thrown out when I started to ask questions. Moll never rested her vigilance. Ever.

The donkey carts, *sans* donkeys, were lined up and displaying everything from eggs, meat and poultry to soap, razors and blackening brushes. Other vendors sold much the same goods from rough, uncertain-looking tables. The donkeys, looking lost, unhappy and dirty, wandered about the place.

I stopped at a table selling perfumery and opened a bottle. The stench made my head reel.

'Buy it,' Moll sniffed too, 'it's a beautiful scent.'

'It smells of cabbage with lavender,' I said, 'and someday you'll choose better for yourself.'

'I might,' said Moll, 'and then again I might prefer not to wait.'

There were no bargains on the market stalls so we bought the raisins in one of the army stores. They cost eightpence for a pound and for an extra threepence I bought a pound of currants too, to keep body and soul together as we went back across the plains. The shopkeeper was talkative and asked if we were enjoying our visit to the camp.

'We are indeed,' I said, 'we're finding it both hospitable and friendly.'

He gave Moll a fat fig for herself. 'Enjoy your stay,' he smiled.

'Where do we go now?' Moll darted between store windows, stopping to stare into the baker's.

'Eat your fig,' I said.

It was dusty in the camp, the ground all dug up by horses' hoofs and the boots of parading soldiers. My skirt hems were already well soiled by the time I led Moll away from the market, into the rest of the camp. There were enough army wives and children about, as well as idling soldiers, for us to go unnoticed.

I marched us along with a purposeful air. As soon as I could be sure I had the right building I would march with the same directness into the headquarters offices and ask to meet the commanding officer. I was prepared to lie, and to flatter; I didn't think about failing.

The camp was less sprawling once I got a sense of how it was laid out. The soldiers' huts were in squares separated from each other by high, sod fences. Lines of larger huts in front of them housed officers, many of whom sat in the sun playing card games. Some of these huts had flower gardens and fencing and a reassuring homeliness about them.

In the raised centre of the camp stood still grander huts as well as the two churches, one Catholic and one Protestant, and the flagstaff and clock tower we'd seen from the plains. The clock tower had a weathervane and spire. On a height, with a commanding view of it all, I could see another lot of buildings.

I stopped a boy of about ten, running past with a dog. 'Are those the camp headquarters?' I pointed at the building which overlooked the camp.

'Who wants to know?'

'Answer the question.' I gave him a penny.

'That's them all right.' He took his penny and went after the dog before I could ask him in which building exactly the commanding officer had his office. He mightn't have known anyway.

'A halfpenny would have done him,' said Moll, 'what do we do now?'

'Be patient.'

I knew, from talking with the wrens, that the commanding officer was one Major General Ponsonby. He didn't much fraternise with rank and file soldiers or local people and all any of them knew about him was that he was a stickler for discipline and rules. I was hoping that this meant he would also be courteous and mannerly enough to listen while I presented Sarah's case.

To get to him, though, I needed to be able to walk directly and confidently to his door. Wandering uncertainly in front of the headquarters building would get questions asked, might even prevent me ever getting inside. I would have to speak with someone who could give me precise directions to his office.

'We're going to admire some of the gardens by the officers'

huts,' I told Moll, 'and while we're doing it I want you to be seen
and not heard. Do you understand?'

'You don't want me to speak because I won't sound like you
and I might give you away,' Moll said.

I straightened the ribbon on her hair. 'That's right,' I said, 'I
want you to play the role of a shy, well-mannered child.'

Moll said nothing.

Youth, my father had always said, is not so corruptible as age.
I remembered this when we dawdled by a florid garden tended by
an officer who looked to be in his forties. As one of the
corruptible aged he would be suspicious if I asked for directions.
I had better set my sights on a younger man, or men.

There were plenty of them about. The card players we'd seen
earlier were younger. There were four of them, sitting on chairs
and laughing. Not a very serious game then. I studied them from
under the parasol's fringe. Their uniform jackets were open and,
in the case of three of them, so were the top buttons of their
shirts. One was smoking a cigarette and two had the thin
moustaches of young men trying to look old.

It was the moustaches made up my mind for me.

'Good day to you.' I stopped; not too close, not too distant
and carefully not standing in the way of the sun. 'I'm sorry to
interrupt your game. I seem to have lost my way . . .'

Hesitant and apologetically smiling, I held Moll's hand and
caught the grey eyes of an officer with a scar over an eyebrow. A
little suffering might have made him more sympathetic than the
others.

'Where were you headed for?' He half stood, bowed and sat
again with his cards face down on his knee.

'I thought we were on our way to Major General Ponsonby's
staff quarters,' I made a vague gesture, 'only now I'm not so sure . . .'

'Who is looking for him?'

The officer who asked the question sat forward in his chair.
He had a narrow face and was the one with his shirt buttoned up.
His eyebrows were quite a distance above his eyes and gave him
an imperious look.

I smiled at him cautiously. 'My name's Alicia Buckley. I'm visiting the county from Dublin and promised my father I'd call on the major general.' The lie came easily. 'I'd hoped to find his office and make an appointment there to call on him. If you could direct me . . .'

'Your father did not write to the commander in the first instance?'

The man's eyebrows came together as he coldly scrutinised Moll, beginning at her feet and working up to the ribbon in her hair. She stood very still, her hand in mine like a dead thing, knowing that he saw her poverty and despised her for it.

I went on smiling. 'My father's a practical man and not much given to the use of pen and ink,' I said. 'We agreed I would simply make myself known to the major general while in the area.' I stopped smiling, tilted the parasol, and gave a small curtsy. 'I shouldn't have disturbed your card game.'

I nodded to the group and, holding tightly gripping Moll's hand, stepped quickly around them. The narrow-faced officer was definitely trouble. It would have been both stupid and dangerous to prolong the contact.

'You're headed in the wrong direction, Miss Buckley,' the voice of the officer with the scar followed us, 'you'll find the shortest route is back the way you came and to the left.'

'Thank you.' I turned, slowly.

I had the advantage of him now, of them all, since the sun was in their faces and behind me. The scarred officer shaded his eyes with his hand.

'Go to the end of this block and turn,' he said. 'Swing with the road and it's a six-minute direct walk.'

'Thank you,' I said as I began a businesslike retracing of our steps, 'we've been wandering in the heat too long. It's confused us.'

'So it seems.' The narrow-faced soldier put his hat on his head and looked at me under its brim. 'You've wandered quite a distance from the main road, Miss Buckley. It would have been better to come escorted. Your small servant can't be of much help to you.'

'Moll is not my servant.' I squeezed her hand, praying she would keep silent, 'she's the daughter of a friend. But you may be right that I should have waited to be escorted through the camp.' I looked at them all in turn. 'I decided instead to trust in the natural courtesy of the British soldier.'

The man smoking the cigarette put it behind his back.

'*Touché*, Miss Buckley.' The scarred officer dropped his cards and clapped his hands together, twice. 'And you're right, of course. A young woman should feel safe among the men of Her Majesty's army.'

It was hard to know whether or he was laughing with me or at me. 'To prevent us wandering off course again,' I was crisp, 'I'd be glad if you would tell me in which of the buildings I might find the commander.'

'Your trust in the gentility of the soldiery is commendable, Miss Buckley.' The other officer's mouth, under the shadow cast by his hat, curled slightly. 'But Major General Ponsonby is another matter. He may wonder, as I do, about the *bona fides* of a young woman arriving unannounced and unescorted.'

I'd been right. He suspected me. He probably disliked me too. He probably disliked all women.

'You seem, sir, to imply that in some way I am not to be trusted,' I was the essence of dignified offence, 'it's not a response I'd have expected from an officer.'

'Your trustworthiness is not the issue, madam,' his face was hot now with more than the sun. Moll pulled at my hand. 'At issue is your right to be here. I think it would be best if you were to leave the encampment and have your father make an appointment in writing with the major general.'

'Are you afraid, sir, that I'm here to plant a Fenian bomb?'

Moll pulled again, much harder, at my hand. 'Come away, Allie, please do . . .' She was shrill and frightened, both for and because of me. It was so easy to forget Moll was a child.

'We'll go at once.' I put my hand about her shoulder and

pulled her to me. I'd never in my life regretted losing my temper so much. 'We can only hope that the major general will be more civil than some of his officers.'

We began walking away again, Moll's small body stiff and shaking under my arm. Behind us I heard a short, sharp exchange between the soldiers, then quick footsteps over the dusty ground.

'Allow me make amends for my fellow soldier,' the scarred officer said as he fell into step beside us. 'Captain Browne takes an overly serious view of life, and of the army.' He buttoned his jacket, pulled it straight and ran fingers through his short, fair hair. 'Will I do for an escort?' He stepped in front of us, grinning. 'We can ramble *à trois* to the commander's office.'

He might be as suspicious as his fellow officer but he didn't dislike me. He was relaxed, the kind of man who liked all women. There was no harm in that, up to a point. I smiled at him.

'That won't be necessary,' I said. 'Directions are all we need to make our own way.'

'You might get lost again. You might meet another Captain Browne.' He stepped closer and spoke softly to Moll. 'I'm sorry to say there are a great many Captain Browne's about the place. Far more of them than there are Captain Ainslies.' He bowed and Moll stared at him, unblinking. He stared back.

'Is your name Ainslie then?' she asked.

'Captain Alexander Ainslie,' he confirmed with a nod and Moll gave him another careful look before she said, 'It's not up to me whether or not you walk with us where we're going. It's Allie will have to decide that. I'm only a child.'

He looked surprised. 'Are you sure?' he said gently.

'I'm sure,' Moll said, 'and there's no good you playing the fool with me either when it's Allie you really want to talk to.'

'You're right.' He straightened and brought his hand to his forehead and saluted.

'My name is Alicia Buckley,' I frowned, flustered and wary, 'and my companion is Miss Moll Hyland.'

'Am I to call you Alicia then? Not Allie?'

'There will hardly be a need to call me anything if the journey to the commander's quarters is as short as you say it is,' I said.

'May I call you Moll?' He looked gravely down at the child, who sighed.

'I suppose so.' She slipped from under my arm and took my hand. 'We might as well go with him, Allie,' she said.

He pointed to this and that as we went along. The post office, which he said was 'a haven of military precision and regularity', the savings bank, telegraph station and fire engine depot. He told us that the clock tower had an internal staircase which allowed people out on to an encircling balcony and that there were two hospitals as well as racket and ball courts. He had the bronzed fingers of a man who'd spent time under a sun a lot hotter than that summer's on the plains of Kildare.

'You seem less than fascinated by our encampment world,' he said when I didn't respond to a mild joke about the six pieces of cannon guarding the flag of England.

'On the contrary,' I said, 'I'd even like to know how the rank and file soldiers live. There are so many of them. Ten thousand, I'm told. How is it that war doesn't break out in the camp?'

'We're permanently at war,' he said, 'hostilities and faction fighting enliven camp life enormously.'

'What about the women who live here?' I asked, 'the wives of the soldiers, and their daughters? How is life for them?'

'It's not a bad life. For many it's better than the life they left behind.' He hesitated, seemed about to say something else, then changed his mind and said, with a shrug, 'There aren't a great many soldiers' wives in the camp. The accommodation is not ideal and the pay is bad. I would never bring a wife or children here myself.'

This left me wondering if he was without a wife in the camp because he didn't have one, or because he disliked the accommodation.

'You're very frank,' I said, carefully, 'about the army, about . . .' I made a vague gesture, 'all of this.'

'Why not?' He stopped. 'We've arrived.'

Soldiers stood guard at each of the three doors to the headquarters building. 'Thank you for escorting us,' I said, 'now maybe you could tell us which one of these doors leads to Major General Ponsonby's office?'

'You're a very single-minded young woman. I hope you get what it is you want from the commander,' he spoke lightly.

Far too lightly; he wanted to know my business, why I was intent on visiting his commander. He didn't believe my story of a casual call to please my father.

'I'm sure we'll have a pleasant meeting,' I said.

'You'll find the major general's offices through the second door. He may not be there at this time but is almost always there in the mid-afternoon. Perhaps you should wait until then?'

'Moll wouldn't like that.' I was firm. 'We'll take our chances now. I'm grateful to you,' I held out a hand and he took it briefly in his long, brown fingers.

'Are you staying close by?' he said.

'Quite close,' I said.

'Perhaps I could escort you home, when you've finished with the commander?'

'We've a car and driver waiting,' I lied.

The headquarters building, inside, was dark and smelled of polished wood. The commander's office, with his name on the door, was directly ahead of us as we went in. A young soldier, small and slight as a cane, stood guard. He looked worried.

'You've no problem telling lies,' Moll said softly as we went down the corridor towards him, 'only you're not so good at it as you think.'

'Be quiet,' I hissed and she looked sulky. She'd been well-behaved too long and the strain was telling.

We stopped in front of the soldier, who came nimbly to attention. His ears were too big for his head and rose in points on either side of his hat.

'We'd like to see Major General Ponsonby.' I was briskly polite. He looked confused. His training hadn't equipped him to deal with direct young women. He was also shy.

'He didn't tell me anything about . . .' He cleared his throat. 'I don't know as I can let you go in, miss.'

'I'm certain the major general will be glad to see me—' I was cut short, and the soldier put out of the misery of his uncertainty, when the door behind him was pulled roughly open.

The man who filled it was clearly Major General Ponsonby. He wore gold at his neck, in a high collar which looked in danger of throttling him, and more braided across his erect and very wide shoulders. His buttons were twice the size of the soldier's.

I dropped a quick curtsy. 'Major General Ponsonby,' I held out my hand, 'my name is Alicia Buckley. I wonder if we might speak?'

'Miss . . . er . . .' Taken aback he might have been, but he was no young and unformed soldier. 'What did you say your name was?' His irritation vibrated in the corridor.

'Alicia Buckley.' I dropped my hand. He didn't seem to notice. 'I'd hoped you might be able to help with a matter of importance to a friend.'

He stared at me without blinking. He didn't look at Moll at all. 'Do you know anything about the business of armies, Miss Buckley?' he demanded.

'Very little,' I admitted.

'I thought as much.' His brows, when he brought them together, obscured his eyes. 'Commanding officers are not common soldiers, Miss Buckley. If you wish to speak with one you must proceed through—'

Moll's sudden wail was not so much anguished as heart-broken. She buried her head in my skirts and began a pitiful, muffled weeping.

'What's wrong with that child?' The commander looked startled.

'I'll remove her, Major General, sir.' When the soldier stepped forward Moll howled and held on to me as if drowning. A door further down the corridor opened and another gold-braided officer appeared. Then another door opened. Moll gulped and shuddered and went on crying.

'She'd hoped, Major General, as indeed I had myself, that you would give us some few minutes of your time.' I spoke in my most polished tones and loudly enough for everyone in the corridor to hear.

'She shouldn't be here.' Some of the fight had gone out of the commander.

'I realise that, now,' I was contrite, 'please put our incursion down to the ignorance of a city woman. I'm visiting in the locality, from Dublin. It was my father suggested you might be of assistance.' I smiled ruefully. 'Both my father and I mistakenly thought a camp on the plains, such as this, would be less formal than those in Dublin.'

He watched my face carefully as I spoke. When I stopped he rubbed the side of his nose and grunted. 'Your father was not completely wrong.' His smile was paternalistic and revealed large gaps between his teeth. But he'd relaxed. He'd found a role he could adopt with me. 'Unfortunately, I have a busy schedule and cannot speak with you now. Come back tomorrow, in the afternoon at three o'clock. I'll give you fifteen minutes then. Don't bring the child with you.'

He bowed, stiffly, and walked past us without another word. The young soldier followed him at a military trot from the building. The open doors along the corridor discreetly closed.

'You can take your head out of my skirts now,' I said to Moll.

We got out of the camp as quickly as we could, avoiding the officers' huts and Captain Browne. Captain Alexander Ainslie was nowhere to be seen.

'You shouldn't have been so quick to lie to that captain about us having a carman waiting,' Moll sniffed as we began a tired trudge across the plains. 'He might have given us a drive back.'

'I'd have had to tell him where we live,' I pointed out.

'He very likely knows anyway. I told you — you're not the great liar you think you are.' Moll looked back at the camp and stuck out her tongue. 'When I'm a woman I'll have nothing to do with soldiers. I'll have nothing to do with any man. When Mama's dead I'll go to America and live my life there.'

'What do you know about America?'

'I know that it's far away and that it's a rich place.' She opened the bag carrying the currants and took out the bottle of scent she'd admired on the donkey cart. 'I'll have perfumes for every day of the week when I'm in America.' She dabbed her throat and hair liberally.

We ate the currants as we went. I said nothing about her stealing the perfume. I was only sorry I hadn't bought it for her.

CHAPTER TWENTY-FOUR

Allie

———◆◇◆———

'I can't leave him. I'm doing it for his sake.' Sarah stared at James, on a blanket in the afternoon sun, as if she was being asked to abandon him to hell's fire.

'You're doing it as much for yourself as you are for him. What he hasn't got he won't miss.' Ellen Neary picked the baby up and laid him gently across her knees. James kicked his legs when she tickled him. 'It's not as if children saw much of their fathers anyway.'

This might have been true of children in general, and of Ellen's childhood in particular, but it was not the way to persuade Sarah to leave James in the wren village while she went with me to meet Major General Arthur Ponsonby. Sarah had never been good about taking advice. She had to learn everything the hard way.

'My child *will* know his father,' she insisted as she lifted James from Ellen's knees, 'and I *will* take him with me tomorrow. The army won't have the heart to deny him once they see him.'

'Innocence is one thing, Sarah Rooney,' Ellen stood, 'but stupidity's another. There's an excuse for the first but none for the second. Your stupidity will lose you your man.' She left us where we sat by our nest, her petticoat whipping about her brown feet with every angry step away.

James began to snuffle and then to cry. 'You can see how I can't leave him,' Sarah said, 'he can't be without me . . .'

'He won't even know you've gone,' I said, 'Ellen will take care of him, and Lucretia and Lil.'

'I won't have that Lil Malone near my child,' Sarah's voice rose, 'she reminds me of someone . . .' She took a steadying breath. 'It's better if I take him with me. I won't feel easy without him.'

'The camp's commander is full of pompous self-importance, Sarah,' I said patiently, 'we'll have to work up to telling him about James. It's my guess he'll be furious if presented with a baby.'

'I can't leave him. He's all that I have.'

'You've lost your reason, and you may well lose your chance of meeting your soldier too if you go on like this.'

I took a book to the other side of the nest to read. My hands, turning the pages, were brown. My arms were turning brown too, and my face, from being in the sun without a hat and wearing only a camisole. It was the same with Sarah. Soon we would be no different from the other wrens.

But it was good that the weather was holding; I didn't want to imagine what life in the village would have been like otherwise.

When the sun cooled I took my medical bag and went to see Lizzie Early, who'd been vomiting again. I was fairly certain that Lizzie had a tumour and that there wasn't a lot I, or anyone else, could do for her. I gave her laudanum and Beezy gave her whiskey. It made things bearable, nothing more. She would soon have to go to the workhouse. She didn't want to, maybe because she knew she would never leave it alive.

Sarah dressed carefully for our trip to the camp. She washed her hair and dried it in the sun. She stretched her petticoats on the grass in the sun too, to whiten them, and shook out her blue sprigged cotton dress, sprinkling it with water to freshen it. When her hair dried she caught it up with combs. She looked beautiful. She went to just as much trouble getting James ready. When she'd finished he looked merely disgruntled.

'I'm sorry, Allie,' she said as we walked along, 'I didn't mean it when I said I'd nothing but James. I have you.'

'I understand,' I said, and did.

I understood her feeling that she'd lost everything – her family and lover to circumstance, her sister to death. I understood because I sometimes felt I'd lost everything myself.

We walked slowly, not wanting to be overheated and perspiring when we stood in front of the commander. A sentry stopped us just inside the camp. I gave him my name told him about my appointment. He told us to go ahead. No one else stopped us.

The clock in its tower was striking three as we stepped into the headquarters building. The young soldier of the day before was on guard at the commander's door. His face took on a tormented look when I appeared with Sarah.

'I'm sorry, ma'am, but you'll have to wait outside,' he told her and stood in her way.

'She won't do that,' I said, 'so you might as well let me go ahead and tell the commander she's here.' I gave him a rueful smile. 'In that way I'll be taking the responsibility. None of the blame will be on you.'

He stood to the side, reluctantly, and knocked on the door and opened it. Together, in one quick movement, Sarah and I slipped past him and into the commander's office.

Major General Ponsonby stood, disbelieving. 'Miss Buckley!'

The picture of the Queen behind him on the wall trembled as he brought his fist down on to the writing table in front of him. It was a big room, with wood panelling and a high ceiling. His anger filled it.

'This is an outrage. You were to come alone. But instead of yesterday's snivelling child you have brought an infant and . . .' he hesitated, 'nurse . . .' his second hesitation was longer, 'or mother. This is not a nursery. You are in a British Army station. You have abused the privilege of the meeting I agreed to. I must ask you to leave.'

He stopped. The outburst had taken energy. His hair,

magnificently black still with white sideburns, rippled with agitation.

'Please allow me speak before I go.' I stood in front of the table, trying to distract his gaze from Sarah and James – a waste of time since Sarah moved to stand beside me.

'I forbid you to say another word.' He turned his back and stared at the picture of his Queen. 'Be so good as to leave the camp and take your companions with you.' He lifted his hand and smoothed the folds of the Union Jack hanging to one side of the Queen's picture. 'Private Lynch,' he said without turning, 'please escort these females out of here.'

The soldier, who'd come into the room on our heels, stepped between Sarah and me. I'd seen more imposing figures doing card tricks in the Broadstone.

'Come along now,' he cleared his throat, 'you'll have to leave.' He took hold of our arms. He wasn't gentle.

'I'm here for a purpose. I'll not go until I've said what it is.' Sarah shook her arm free and strode the few steps to the writing table. 'I cannot believe the great British Army would deny justice to the child of one of its soldiers,' she said. 'I cannot believe you would deny a soldier the right to know he has a son.'

The commander didn't turn. He didn't speak either, just continued his study of Queen Victoria's picture. In it she was young and wearing her coronation robes, looking a lot more regal than she did in the widow's weeds she'd taken to wearing since Prince Albert's death. She had a calming effect on the major general, who was quieter when he at last turned.

'Any man, whether soldier or civilian, would know his child if he was married to its mother.' He looked over Sarah's head. 'I take it you are an unmarried woman?'

'My child's father and I had planned to marry. His regiment was moved to the Curragh unexpectedly from Beggar's Bush Barracks in Dublin to—'

'Yes, yes, it's a familiar story.' He was suddenly impatient. 'Women of your kind follow the army wherever it goes. You must understand that I am an officer in charge of men and that it is my duty to protect them. I don't want you, or your kind, in my camp. I cannot help you. This business . . . is between you and your soldier.' He still didn't look at either Sarah or James.

'You could help all right, if you wanted to,' Sarah said flatly, 'but you don't. You may disparage me all you like but commanding this camp doesn't give you the right to deny my child his father. Have you no shame? Have you no decency?'

Major General Ponsonby looked at her then and it was clear Sarah had lost her battle. He was the righteous, she the sinner. He reached behind him for a bell rope and pulled it viciously.

'You will be removed forcibly from the camp, madam, you and your friend, Miss Buckley, both.' He spoke with the barest movement of his lips. 'You talk to me of shame and decency? You who have seduced a soldier, or soldiers, for God alone knows how many men you've known. You impose yourself upon me in a flagrantly deceitful manner . . .' He leaned forward, so stiffly I thought he would topple. But he put his hands on the table and steadied himself. 'I command a fine body of men, madam. I have no intention of delivering one of them up to a whore. My men are diseased because of creatures like you. You peddle your filth and they are but men and lonely and avail of you out of need and you leave your curse with them. It's spread throughout the camp. We're in the midst of making the men clean again and I don't want your kind about the place.'

Sarah stared at him. 'I am not a whore,' she said slowly, in a whisper. The door opened and two soldiers came in. They stood wordlessly to attention by the wall.

'You are a whore and your child is a bastard.' Their commander permitted himself a grimly virtuous smile. 'Those are the facts of it. You had best repent your sins and put yourself at God's mercy. The army cannot help you and it cannot help your child.'

James began to cry. I looked at the standing clock, ticking in the corner. We'd been in the room less than fifteen minutes.

'I pity you, sir,' Sarah said, 'and I pity the Queen you serve if you are the best can be found to command her army. There's a name, where I come from, for men like you.' She turned for the door. 'I won't waste my time saying it.' She gave the soldiers a contemptuous look. 'I hope you're proud of yourselves, and of how you earn your shilling.' She walked past them, and through the door, before turning. 'I'll find my child's father, Major General, and I'll find him without your help,' she said then.

'Assist Private Lynch in the conducting of these women out of the camp,' the commander sat at the writing table, 'make sure they are outside the boundaries.' He called my name as I started to follow Sarah. 'Miss Buckley.'

I turned, slowly. He'd made a steeple of his fingers. They were surprisingly fine and delicate fingers, their tips pressed so hard together they were blue-white.

'Major General?' I said.

'You were wrong to bring that woman here,' he spoke in clipped, militaristic fashion. 'You seem a respectable person. No doubt you thought you were doing good. You were duped. You heard her yourself. She is a wanton harlot. She is insolent to boot.' He collapsed the steeple and dismissed me with a flick of his fingers. 'You may go, but first some advice . . .' He leaned forward, his eyebrows low over his eyes again as he slipped into the paternalistic role of the day before. 'Nine trains leave the town of Kildare each day for the capital. Seven leave from Newbridge. Take the first one you can this evening and go home to your father. Have nothing further to do with that woman.'

'That woman is my best and oldest friend.' I nodded good day and left, moving quickly to catch up with Sarah. The soldiers followed close behind.

'Don't tell me I should have listened to you.' She didn't break her step as I came alongside. 'Don't tell me I brought this on myself. Just be pleased with yourself that you were right.'

I trotted beside her in silence, two of my steps matching every one of hers. There would be no talking to her until she'd flogged herself a good deal more.

People looked at us as we went along. We were a lively procession, two women and an unhappy infant being escorted at a quick march through the camp. The roads were rutted and sudden holes threatened to swallow us every few yards. I stumbled a few times and had to clutch at Sarah, whose shoes were sturdier than mine. She steadied me but didn't stop. James cried all the way.

'What's the name you would have called the major general?' I said when we were well clear of the headquarters building.

'I'd have called him a— tin God from Hell. It's too good a name for him.'

'Much too good,' I agreed.

We were passing the Catholic chapel when Captain Alexander Ainslie stepped into our path. He was buckled into his uniform and wearing his hat and looked a lot less amiable than the day before. Our escorts saluted and he saluted in return; he gave Sarah a swift bow before turning to me,

'How was your meeting with the major general?' he asked.

'Educational and disagreeable.' I made to move on.

'May I walk with you?'

'We're leaving the camp,' I pointed out.

'So it seems.' He glanced at our soldier chaperones and for a minute I thought he would dismiss them. He didn't. What he said, with a smile and before falling into step by my side, was, 'I was going that way myself.'

I wished, suddenly and childishly, that he would take off the hat. There was far too much of the soldier about him with it on.

Sarah hadn't so much as acknowledged him and resumed walking at an even faster pace. Captain Ainslie gave me his arm; with the rutting and holes becoming worse as we neared the boundaries of the camp I was glad to take it.

'You didn't go alone to see the commander?' he said.

'You ask a great many questions,' I said.

'Only when a situation isn't clear to me. I understood you wished to make a social call on behalf of your father?'

'That was a lie.'

'Do you tell many lies?'

'I lie when the truth is not enough to get me what I want.'

'Expedient lying. I do it myself.'

'There's nothing admirable about it. I'm not proud that I've become a liar. Just sorry our society is such that devious means are often the only way a woman may get justice.'

'Is our society so different to that which went before it?'

'It's no better and it's worse in many ways. We hold truth as a virtue but it's not rewarded. We're more concerned with the appearance of things than we are with the reality. Greed and acquisition are values, friendship and learning are not.'

'Do you see yourself redressing some of these wrongs?'

'Some wrongs, yes.'

'What a passionate young woman you are, Miss Buckley.'

'What a patronising man *you* are, Captain Ainslie.'

He laughed and for a minute I thought he was going to remove the hat, but he merely touched the brim in mock salute. 'You're right that I've patronised you,' he agreed, and slowed down. 'Forgive me.'

He was holding my arm still, which forced me to slow down with him. Sarah went relentlessly ahead, the soldiers with her. Captain Ainslie nodded at her retreating back. 'It seems you failed to redress the wrong done your companion and her child?' he asked.

I thought for a moment before I said anything. Both Captain Alexander Ainslie and his commander seemed to think me a respectable woman given to good deeds. Not a bad thing. The captain might well be a gift horse; it would be foolish to look him in the mouth.

'The commander was unwilling to help her find the father of her baby, yes,' I said, 'but *she* is unwilling to give up the search. I'm not going to give up either.'

'And the child you had with you yesterday, is she another of your causes?'

'People are not causes, Captain Ainslie.'

'They can be,' he shrugged, 'what will you do now that the commander has refused to help?'

'Seek help elsewhere.' I looked at him questioningly. For a

moment he looked startled, then he laughed outright. One of the soldiers with Sarah, a good bit ahead by now, looked back uneasily.

'I was right about you,' he said, 'you're a woman who will have her way.' He glanced down at me, half laughing still but more thoughtful. 'You expect me to help you find that young woman's soldier lover – even though my commander has refused and has more than likely told her to leave and not come back. Am I right?'

'That much is obvious,' I said. 'I'm asking because you struck me yesterday as a man who was aware how harsh army life and rules could be on soldiers as well as wives and children.'

'This is not about a wife . . .'

'It *is* about a father and his son,' I said quickly, 'and about two people who planned to marry but were parted by the army.'

'Tell me what happened.'

I told him Sarah's story then. I gave him Jimmy Vance's name and told him he was a private with the Royal Welsh Fusiliers. I told how he and Sarah had met and grown to love one another. I told him of Sarah's need to be with him after Mary Ann's death, how their friendship had deepened and how, weeks after the regiment had been sent to the Curragh, she discovered she was carrying his child.

I told him all of this because there was no point expecting him to help unless he could be made to understand how things had happened, and sympathise. It was easy to tell him. He'd the air of a man more diverted by life's calamities than shocked by them.

'Sarah wrote to Private Vance three times,' I said.

'That doesn't mean he got the letters. Mail is often intercepted for reasons of censorship and discipline.' Captain Ainslie shrugged. 'The case of the young woman you've taken up is not unique. The army doesn't encourage—'

'I know about the army's position,' I cut him short, but politely. I needed to know if he was going to help, or not. 'Sarah is certain her soldier will move heaven and earth to have them together once he knows about his son.'

'She may be right,' he said mildly. He didn't once suggest that Jimmy Vance might not be the father of Sarah's child. His manners would always be impeccable.

As we stood talking Sarah and her retinue came to the boundaries of the camp. The soldiers said something which she ignored and, head high, walked quickly on in the direction of the wren village. After several hundred yards she turned and, seeing me still in conversation with Captain Ainslie, began to pace back and forth, an expression of hopeless fury on her face. I waved to reassure her; her expression didn't change.

'How did you come to hear of Miss Rooney's case?' the captain asked.

I'd been waiting for this question. 'She was in service in my family home, which is close to Beggar's Bush Barracks, when she met Private Vance . . .' I allowed my voice to trail away, as if this fact explained everything.

'Do you often take on the burdens of others?'

'Now and again,' I said. After a while, when he didn't say anything, I said, 'Will you help find Private Vance?'

'I might be persuaded to,' he said. 'There will be a price, however.'

So he knew I was a wren. He'd been playing with me all along. 'I've very little money,' I said stiffly. 'But you're welcome to what jewellery I have with me.'

'I think, Miss Buckley, that you're being deliberately disingenuous.' His tone was still light but now it was impatient too. 'What I want in exchange is some of your time. I would like to meet with you again; your conversation is entertaining.' He smiled. 'I haven't been so entertained since arriving here.'

'I haven't been called entertaining before,' I said, 'and you might find on a second meeting that my conversation is not so interesting as all that.' I didn't for a minute believe his desire was for conversation, he'd admitted to being a liar, after all.

'We can meet then?' he said.

'It seems the least I can do in return for the favour of finding Private Vance.'

'Good.' He became brisk. 'Come back tomorrow, alone. No airy little girls, no unhappy young women. Come by the entrance closest to the marketplace. The sentries there will expect you. Be at the clock tower by one o'clock in the day. Tell the sentries you've a meeting with me. I'll see that you speak then with Private Vance, if he's in the camp. You can make whatever arrangement suits for him to meet with the mother of his child. After that,' he gave a mocking salute, 'I will expect you to begin fulfilling your part of our bargain.'

I shaded my eyes and looked down the road at the pacing Sarah. 'Miss Rooney will be pleased,' I said.

Once Sarah and her Jimmy were together I would worry about my deal with Captain Ainslie. Once he knew I was a wren there would be no deal anyway.

Unless, as I suspected, he knew already.

CHAPTER TWENTY-FIVE

Allie

———————⋖∘∘∘⋗———————

Life has a way of making its own decisions, of upsetting the plots we draw up ourselves.

Sarah, when I told her of my conversation with Alexander Ainslie, was caught between wild hope and a creeping despair. She had me go over and over everything he'd said, examining and reexamining words and phrases: Had he said absolutely that I would meet Jimmy Vance in the morning? Did I believe him? Why was he doing it? Was it all a trick, a cruel joke?

'Is he a good man? Does he really mean to help?' She searched my face, as if the answer was written there. 'Or is he a trickster of some sort?'

'I don't know what he is,' I said.

Sarah would have gone on all night if it hadn't been for Lizzie Early. Beezy, tired of a conversation in which she had no part, had gone early in the evening to Lizzie's nest. There was always drink to be had there.

It was close to midnight when I heard Beezy's voice, in the distance then quickly and loudly coming closer, calling my name. Her head appeared in the doorway. Lizzie was bad, she said, and needed my help.

'I don't know as there's much you can do for her,' she said, her hair like an orange veil in the candlelight, 'but get your bag and come anyway.'

Lizzie had crawled from the nest and was lying a few feet

from it, on grass already moistening with dew. The state she was in the damp wasn't going to affect her very much.

The place stank. Lizzie had lost control of her bodily functions and was lying in her own vomit. She lay gasping and jerking, her hands clawing at the ground and her bony feet dancing to a demented rhythm of their own.

But it was her face told me everything. Her sunken eyes and sharp nose. The tormented grinning of her exposed teeth, the yellowy-green colour of her skin, apparent even in the fitful moonlight. I knew what I was looking at: I'd come across descriptions of the Hippocratic facies often enough, the facial appearance of impending death as described by Hippocrates.

All in the space of two days. I hadn't thought she would go so quickly.

I knelt beside her. The stench unsettled my stomach and I had to close my eyes and swallow and hold myself rigid against an attack of nausea.

'Lizzie, can you hear me?'

But Lizzie, consumed with her pain, couldn't give me a sign. I went on talking to her, feeling her poor, swollen stomach with my hand. It was rock hard. Her breathing was very shallow, and it was rapid. Her skin, when I felt it, was hot and dry.

'I'm going to give you laudanum, Lizzie.' I spoke close to her ear. 'It'll calm you, give you some peace until we get you to the hospital.'

'They won't take her into the hospital.' Clara Hyland, standing with the circle of wrens about, was adamant. 'They'll only take her into the workhouse and she won't go there. She said that if she's to die it might as well be here.'

The moon disappeared behind cloud and the first rain for weeks began to fall in heavy drops. Three of the wrens, with the speed and efficiency of practice, brought sticks and sacking and erected a canopy over the dying woman.

'Where's the God poor Lizzie prayed to now?' said one of them as she hammered. 'You'd think, after all the praying she did to Him, that He'd at least give her a dry night to die in.'

'He wasn't much good to her in life,' Nance Reilly spread the sacking, 'so why would He look out for her in death?'

I gave Lizzie the laudanum from a spoon, not easy with her vomiting still. But I got it into her at last and she managed to keep it down. She became still, but no better, just dying more quietly. Some of the wrens began to pray.

'I can't do any more,' I said.

'You did what you could,' Ellen Neary said.

Lizzie needed to be in hospital, or at least in the shelter of the workhouse. I'd no idea how to convince the wrens of this. I tried to pray, but couldn't. God had never seemed so far away.

'We should get her a priest,' said Beezy, 'she'd want a priest.'

'There's none of the local druids will come out here,' Nance Reilly said.

'She'd be seen by a priest in the hospital,' I said, 'and by a doctor who might be able to do something to make her more comfortable.'

'You'll have to accept, Allie, that the hospital won't take in a wren that's gasping her last.' Ellen Neary was impatient.

She was also the answer to the prayers I couldn't say. She faced Clara Hyland. 'We can't let her die here,' she said. 'There'll be another inquiry and it'll be worse than the last one. We'll be turned out of our nests and have no peace for weeks.' She knelt with me at Lizzie's side and took one of her threadbare hands. 'She won't thank us but we'll have to get her into the workhouse. We've no right to deny her a priest for the end. She's sinned. She'd want to be forgiven.'

'She's suffered enough for whatever sins she has,' Beezy said stubbornly, 'she came here to keep out of the workhouse. She knew she hadn't long to go.'

The rain got heavier and the trampled ground around Lizzie began turning to mud. A pallet came from somewhere, made from pieces of timber and more sacking, and was slipped under the dying woman. Furze bushes were put leaning against the canopy of sacking. In minutes she was housed in a makeshift nest.

I went inside and bent over her. 'A proper doctor might do something,' I said, 'maybe save her. We've no right to deny her a chance of life.' A hospital of doctors wouldn't save Lizzie — but I would never be party to the barbarity of allowing her to die in in the rain and mud.

'I'll go to Kildare for the relieving officer.' Lucretia Curran, who'd been whispering with Ellen Neary, broke ranks with the other wrens. 'He'll bring a cart to carry her to the workhouse.' She blessed herself. 'Let ye pray she lives until I get back.' She left running. She was already wearing her boots and dress, all prepared to go hunting.

'Lucretia's an innocent and a fool,' Clara Hyland said as she added more furze to the makeshift nest.

'What's innocent and foolish about her?' I was angry. Lucretia had gone, alone in the dark and rain, for help. Courageous and good were words I'd have used.

'She's innocent to believe the relieving officer will come any sooner than daybreak,' Clara said, 'and she's a fool for the same reason. He's paid thirty pounds the year, and so were those that went before him, for relieving sick and destitute women. But I've never known one of them willing to put himself out. Not for the sake of wrens, at any rate.'

'When she tells him how it is with Lizzie he'll come at once, surely?' I didn't try to keep my voice down. There was no way Lizzie could have heard us; I doubted she was even aware of our existence.

'You're as simple-minded as Lucretia.' Clara Hyland kicked the furze into place. 'The facts speak for themselves. It's not long since a wren died in a ditch because of neglect by the relieving officer. She wasn't the first and she won't be the last.' She swore at the rain, added yet another clump of furze and said, 'God and the relieving officers are together in wanting to see the lot of us dead. And that's another fact.'

She left then, to see to Moll, she said.

'To see what's left in the whiskey bottle, more like,' Ellen Neary observed with a shrug.

'Tell me what happened to the wren who died,' I said.

Ellen frowned at Lizzie and smoothed the hair from her forehead. She blocked a hole where the rain was coming through. She reached a hand from under the canopy. 'The rain's stopping,' she reported.

I waited. When she was ready she told me about the dead wren. 'Her name was Rosanna Doyle. She was in a nest with three others on the far side of the camp from here. She was taken ill and a Curragh caretaker by the name of Greany was asked for help. He waited a full day before going to the police and when he did the police didn't kill themselves with speed either. One of them left a note for Patrick Cosgrove, the relieving officer. But Cosgrove, and Bergin the carrier, waited yet another full day before going for Rosanna. By then, if you've been keeping track, she'd been two days dying in a ditch.

'They finally put her in a donkey cart on top of straw, covered her with a sack and drove the three hours to Naas and the workhouse. She died as soon as she got there. There was an outcry and an inquiry.' Ellen peered from under the sacking again. 'The rain's stopped altogether. Lucretia's innocent but she's no fool. She'll knock on doors until she shames them into coming out.'

The rain stopped and started many times during that long night. Lizzie Early seemed to die and come back to life many times during the hours we waited for Lucretia and the relieving officer.

Sarah came to help but was sent back to the nest and James. All of the women with children stayed away. All except for Clara who, like the rain, came and went. She was drunker each time.

It was getting light, and the rain had passed on at last, before a wren came running to say a covered car was on its way, that she could see Lucretia in front with the driver. We'd been waiting six hours. The relieving officer had insisted on finishing his night's sleep after Lucretia had called him.

'Lizzie'll be all right now,' said Ellen Neary. She didn't believe it any more than I did.

But Lizzie Early, a complainer all her life, was conscious and quietly accepting as she was loaded into the car. It had springs, so her journey would hopefully be bearable. I said I would go with her; since the doctor at the workhouse would need to know she'd been given laudanum and how much. Clara Hyland said she would come too; there was no stopping her.

Clara slept for most of the three-hour journey to Naas but I was glad to have her with me anyway. Moll's mother was more eagle than wren. She might be troublesome and troubled but she would protect to the death those who needed her help.

Lizzie Early was taken from us at the workhouse and put in a ward set aside for wrens. I had never before, and have never since, felt the poverty of spirit I felt in Naas Union Workhouse that summer morning. It was a debased place, and demeaning.

The ward into which they put Lizzie had twelve beds filled with grey and dying women. A young doctor, so tired-looking he seemed ready to take a place in one of the beds himself, was looking after both them and the rest of the sick and indigent. He reminded me of Daniel Casey.

When he examined Lizzie he confirmed what I'd diagnosed myself. Lizzie Early had a tumorous growth in her stomach. To be as big as it was it must have been growing, he said, for a couple of years.

'Her pulse is thin and thready and the bowel's obstructed. It's hopeless . . .' He rubbed a hand across his forehead. 'Laudanum's about all you could have given her. It didn't do any good but it didn't do any harm either. I'll do what I can for her, but it won't be much. The twelve pounds a year we're given to pay for the medical care of wrens and prostitutes doesn't buy a great deal.'

'Twelve pounds . . .' I echoed him, wondering if I'd heard right.

'That's what they give us,' he nodded. 'We get another three shillings and fourpence a week each for their maintenance.' He scratched his face, the unconscious gesture of a man whose nerves were rattled beyond normal endurance. 'We get ten pounds too to rent auxiliary buildings for those who aren't sick, just destitute.' He realised what he was doing and dropped his hand, blushing. He might have been Daniel Casey's brother. 'Take a look at what the ten pounds is spent on on your way out,' he suggested, 'if you can bear to.'

He went back to his work. He didn't ask me how I came to have medical knowledge nor how I came to be delivering a dying wren to the workhouse. A man whose priorities were screaming and in pain in dismal wards on all sides didn't need to know such things.

The auxiliary buildings were separated from the main workhouse by a high wall. I thought at first that we'd made a mistake and were looking at some ruined and empty hovels. They were low to the ground with sagging roofs and wayward walls but they were lived in, by women and children both. Their beds were bags of foul straw. The air inside smelled and was musty. The earthen floors from the rain the night before were sodden underfoot.

The women in them were sick or tired or both. They were all defeated. Even the children seemed to be living to die.

We stayed just long enough for me to understand why those who could preferred to live as wrens on the Curragh.

'In the wintertime,' said Clara as we walked away, 'when great numbers of women leave the plains, this place, it's a great deal worse. Better to die with a bit of dignity intact, in the open, I always say.'

I tried to imagine anything worse and couldn't.

The carrier drove us back to the wren village. He didn't want to but Clara was sober now and wanted to get back to Moll and threatened him with an inquiry. She would see to it, she promised, that the authorities knew about him going back to his bed after Lucretia calling him and telling him there was a woman dying out on the Curragh. His job could be taken from him, she said.

'I'm not a well man,' he sniffed.

'Then give your job to someone strong enough to do it,' Clara gave her hard laugh, 'give it to a woman.'

I slept fitfully on the journey. Each time I woke it was a shock to find myself in the car. Once I'd dreamed I was back in the French convent. The next time I was in my bedroom in Haddington Road.

I was so tired when I climbed down at the village that I was surprised to find my legs still able to support me.

Sarah was frantic. 'There's a curse following me,' she said as I washed and made myself decent for our visit to the camp. 'Of all the nights of the year why did Lizzie Early have to choose last evening to get sick? Why not tonight, or tomorrow?'

'It wasn't a choice,' I said, 'and your bad luck is nothing compared to Lizzie's who may be dead as we speak.'

'I know, I know all that. I'm half mad with selfishness and worry . . .' She took the brush from my hand and began to smooth my hair. 'Motherhood and missing Jimmy Vance have turned me into my grandmother. I expect the world to turn on its head to suit me and everyone to do what I want them to.' She gathered my hair into her hands. 'Let me make it into curls like I used to. Let me at least do that.'

It wasn't a style I liked any more but it was restful having her do it. I was less tired setting off for the camp.

There was no sign of Captain Alexander Ainslie by the clock tower. I stood for a while at its base and, feeling conspicuous and alone when he didn't arrive, began walking slowly in the direction of the churches.

At fifteen minutes past one o'clock I was standing outside the Protestant church and there was still no sign of the captain.

I was working out a way of telling Sarah we'd been betrayed when I saw him, sauntering towards the clock tower as if time, as well as I, would wait all day for him. I stayed where I was. It took him three minutes to spot me.

'A much more suitable meeting place,' he smiled as he approached, 'in the shelter of God.'

'I've been waiting fifteen minutes in His shelter.'

'My apologies.' He didn't look sorry. 'I was busy on your friend's behalf and was delayed.'

'You had a shorter distance to travel here than I.'

'Where exactly have you travelled from, Miss Buckley?'

I was *very* tired. 'I've walked here from the wren village in the hollow below the Gibbet Rath. You might know it better as the home of the bushwomen.'

'A longish journey.' He didn't flinch. He was English and an officer, after all. 'I can see why you're tired.'

'It's a pleasant enough walk,' I amended.

I leaned against the side of the church door and couldn't think of a thing more to say. Captain Ainslie's *sang froid* didn't fool me. Dimly, through the layers of my tiredness, I could see that he was shocked. It was why he'd become so quiet. He really hadn't known I was a wren. He hadn't known Sarah was one. He was discovering that he'd agreed to deliver a soldier colleague to one of the wanton harlots of the plains.

'It's not really the way you think it is . . .' They were the last words I said before the world circled about me and an icy chill made me clutch at the door jamb. The sky was sinking to meet a crazily dancing clock tower as I slid to the ground.

'You lose consciousness quite elegantly, Miss Buckley.' Capt Ainslie's face was hovering over mine when I opened my eyes. When I coughed and shook my head, he stoppered the bottle of smelling salts in his hand. 'We're inside the church.' The low, vaulted beams overhead told me as much. It was bright in the church and smelled of polish. There were flowers everywhere: on the altar, fixed to the end of each pew, on high stands by the walls. I was at the back, supported by a bed of cushions. The captain left my side and sat in a pew.

'Are we the only people here?' I said.

'No one but me saw you collapse,' he was wryly reassuring, 'the soldiers are in the canteens. Meal times are strictly observed in an army camp.'

I sat and then stood. He made no attempt to help me and I was glad. I needed to gather my thoughts together. Not easy since I still felt chilly and shaken.

'You'd better sit down.' He moved along the pew, making room for me to sit beside him. I did, but not too close.

'Thank you,' I looked straight ahead, 'for your discretion and your help.'

'Have you eaten today?' he said.

'Of course.' I didn't look at him. I'd had tea, made by Sarah, before leaving the village. She'd wanted me to take bread, and fruit, but I hadn't had the stomach for it. I wished now I'd taken it regardless.

'So it wasn't hunger made you faint,' he said. 'I don't believe it was your walk on the Curragh either. I suppose,' his sigh turned into a cough, 'that you're with child? Is that the reason you're living with the bushwomen?'

I thought I was going to faint again. He thought so too and put an arm about my shoulder as I swayed. We sat for several minutes with him holding me hard against him while I took deep breaths and gathered myself, and my senses, together.

'It's natural enough that you would think that,' I said eventually, 'but I assure you, I'm not with child.'

'I believe you,' he said and it was my turn to be shocked; it hadn't occurred to me that he might doubt me.

'I'm feeling well now.' I moved away from him. 'Will you still keep your promise to bring me to Private Vance?'

'You know that the wrens are forbidden the camp?' he said.

'Yes.'

'So why should I hand a soldier over to a wren?'

'Because you promised and an officer's word is his bond. Or so we're told . . .' I paused. 'I've always believed it to be true.'

I believed no such thing. What I believed was that honourable people kept their word. Their position in life had little to do with it.

'I would be defying my camp commander,' he pointed out. 'That would be dishonourable too. And it could be ruinous to my career.'

'Of course.' Looking down I saw the ugly roughness of my hands and folded them into my skirts. Alexander Ainslie wasn't going to bring me to Jimmy Vance. 'Tell me one thing.' I looked up. He was watching me closely. 'Is Private Vance here, in the camp? Or is Sarah's journey, and her wait out on the Curragh, all a sad waste of time?'

He said nothing for a minute or two. I'd convinced myself he was working out a way to politely throw me out of the camp when he said, 'Private Vance is here in the camp. I've already told him how things are. The news appeared to give him great joy. Since I didn't know myself I was not, however, able to tell him where his lover is presently residing.' His eyes were cool. 'The price of bringing you to him has gone up since yesterday.'

'You'd better tell me what it is then,' I said. I would lie. I would cheat. I would find a way out of whatever it was he wanted.

'The truth.' He was brisk. 'I want to know why someone with the manners of a respectable young woman is living on the Curragh.'

'You don't think I'm respectable then?' I said. 'Only that I have the manners of respectability?'

'Manners are learned and you have been an apt pupil. Respectability is a way of mind, a belief in a righteous way of being.'

'I thought to be respectable was to be of good social standing. That it was a question of being virtuous and upright. You don't think I'm those things?'

'I am sure you are of good social standing,' he waved a dismissive hand, 'that's why you have learned your manners well. You may well be virtuous and upright too. You miss my point, Miss Buckley, deliberately and cleverly.' He paused. 'What has brought you to live with the wrens?'

'I'm here because society wouldn't give me what I wanted while demanding from me things I couldn't give.' When he looked puzzled I said, shortly, 'The circumstances of my life.'

'Then we have that in common. The circumstances of my life have brought me here too.' He gave a short, humourless laugh. 'What I'd like by way of payment for Private Vance is for us creatures of circumstance to meet again and continue our conversation.'

'You want to talk.' I thought I would faint again, this time with relief.

'What did you think I wanted?' He was mocking.

'My family don't know where I am.' I eased my grip on the pew. 'I came here with Sarah, to help her find Jimmy Vance. I'll be leaving as soon as she's settled.'

'Where will you go, now you've been a wren?'

It was the question any right-thinking person would ask and I couldn't resent him for it. What the captain knew, as well as I did myself, was that by throwing in my lot with the women of the plains I'd forfeited forever my place in respectable Irish society.

For a few minutes, before I answered him, I saw myself with his eyes and understood, in a new way, exactly what I'd given up, and the consequences. It's true that we don't appreciate the value of what we have until we've lost it. Or maybe it's that some things don't actually *have* a value until we've lost them.

'I'll go to America,' I said.

'I'd never in my life before thought about going to that continent. But if Moll Hyland, at nine years old, could dream of escaping to the New World then why couldn't I?

'You'll go to America . . .' he echoed me, shaking his head. 'And why would you go to America, Miss Buckley?'

'To become a doctor.'

Why else? Why not? There were women doctors in America; Elizabeth Blackwell, twenty years before, had been the first.

'You're an original,' the captain said. By this I supposed he meant I was half mad. 'But you made a mistake aligning yourself with the women who live in the furze.' By this he meant I would never become a doctor.

'I *will* practise medicine,' I said, 'I've already begun . . .' The icy chill spread more slowly this time, the blood draining from my brain and bringing a cold sweat to my forehead. 'Could I have the smelling salts, please.' I clutched again at the pew.

He held me against him and I sniffed. I revived almost instantly and, pulling away from him, tried to get out of the pew.

'It's my very amateur diagnosis, doctor, that you need food and rest.' He put an arm round my shoulder and helped me out of the pew and to the church doorway. We stood there with his back to the sun, my face in the light. 'You're chalk white . . .' He gave me his arm. 'Private Vance will have to wait. You'll need to be fed before meeting him.'

His quarters, in a hut not far from where Moll and I had met him playing cards, were presentable enough. There was a fireplace with a clock on the mantel, two smallish windows, a table, three chairs, a chaise longue and sideboard. It was ordinary, orderly and and very clean. Only the chaise longue, on which I sat, carried the whiff of another Alexander Ainslie, of a life beyond army life.

He went behind a screen and I heard him moving crockery about. To keep myself from falling asleep I said, 'Your accommodation is more pleasant than I'd have expected in an army camp.'

'How did you imagine soldiers live?'

'In more spartan conditions. The chaise longue is pretty.'

'It was my brother's.' He came from behind the screen with a glass of milk and a plate with cheese and soda bread. 'He served here before me and brought it and the candlesticks, as well as a picture or two.' He put the food on the table. 'I inherited his quarters.'

'As well as a family tradition of joining the army?'

'Yes. Will you sit to the table?'

He watched while I ate. In his shirt and with his hat off he looked younger and I felt less unnerved by him. He was tall but I saw now that he was also slight and, when he asked if he might smoke a cigarette and I said yes, please do, he looked amused.

'Most women would be outraged,' he said.

'Most of the kind of women you know would be outraged,' I corrected.

'*Touché*. Tell me why you are so hungry and tired. Are things so very bad with the bushwomen?'

'I spent the night and morning with a dying woman.' Let him have the facts if he wanted them. 'I went to the workhouse with her. There was no time for sleep before coming here and I didn't feel hungry.'

'What was she dying of?'

'She had a growth, a tumour. There was nothing could be done for her,' I said. I knew he feared syphilis.

'You're sure?'

'The doctor at the workhouse confirmed it.'

'Why are you doing this thing to yourself?' He studied the tip of the cigarette. His voice had become harsh. 'It can't all be for the sake of friendship.' He raised an eyebrow. 'Could it be that you see yourself as an Irish Florence Nightingale?'

I pushed the food away. 'I'd be obliged if you would take me to meet Private Vance now,' I said.

'You're offended.' He seemed surprised.

'Offended . . .' I thought about this. 'No. Merely irritated that you, along with most of your compatriots, must always see this country, and its people, as a pale reflection of your own. I'm an Irish woman who wants to become a physician – and that is all that I am. I've no desire to fill the footprints of any other woman, English *or* Irish.'

'My apologies,' he said. He still looked surprised.

I stood, waiting. 'Private Vance is expecting to meet me,' I pointed out. 'And you promised.' I paused. 'We've had our conversation.'

'We've had some intriguing chit-chat.' He stood facing me. He was smiling, a little. 'I still want to know why you have put yourself outside society.'

'Maybe it's more that I've retreated for a while, much as you could be said to have done yourself by joining the army.'

'The comparison isn't a good one, Miss Buckley,' he spoke softly, 'you've turned your back on everything. The army, on the other hand, gives me rank and power and a role to play for my country.' He smiled. 'It has brought me to this fair land of yours.' He shrugged himself into his tunic. 'I don't at all think I've got anything like enough payment for my kindness. Nor for the risk I'm taking.' He began buttoning buttons. I told myself it was my imagination that he became more officious with each closure. 'I'm sticking with my condition that we meet again. When you're more rested and we have more time.'

'You want me to come back to the camp?'

The lines of huts, the towers, churches and rutted roads – they all at once seemed to me part of a spider's web, ready to trap me if I came in from the plains to meet this man.

'Is the prospect of spending time with me so terrible?' he said.

'Of course not.' I put spiders and webs out of my mind. 'It's just that I won't be around. Once Sarah and her private make arrangements to get married I'll be––'

'Things may not happen as quickly or as easily as you imagine, Miss Buckley.' There was a warning in his voice. 'I'm not asking you to be my mistress, though that would be pleasant, I'm sure. I'm merely requesting your company.'

'I'll meet you in two days' time,' I said, 'by the Gibbet Rath at midday. We can walk on the plains.' I felt sure he wouldn't agree to this.

'And if it's raining?'

'We'll talk in the shelter of the Rath.'

'I'll be there. Do you ride?' he said.

'No.'

'A pity.' He buttoned the last button and straightened his shoulders. 'Now, as you've been reminding me, Private Vance awaits.'

Walking through the rows of identical huts, each one identified by a letter of the alphabet, I asked if he really hadn't known, when he asked where I'd travelled from, that I lived with the wrens.

'No,' he said, 'I asked because you looked on the point of collapse. I would have believed whatever you told me.'

'How long have you been stationed in the camp?'

'Three months. I was in India before. It's very different.'

'I'm sure it is.' I didn't want to hear about India, or about his career in the army. I just wanted to meet Jimmy Vance and go back to the nest and sleep there for two days.

'He's in Row D,' said Captain Ainslie, more observer of tired irritability than mind-reader, 'just a few minutes more.'

The ground underfoot was muddy and to keep my balance I took his arm. 'The men complain that the camp is as bad as Sebastopol when it gets like this,' he said.

Soldiers sat on the steps of the wooden huts, which were long and low and not nearly so solid-looking as the single hut occupied by Captain Ainslie. I was trying to keep my skirts clear of a water-filled hole when my companion said, 'Private Vance, you have a visitor.'

A soldier, tall and slim and very young, lifted his head from the piece of wood he was whittling. He stood, staring at me and twisting the half-carved whistle in his hands.

'Miss Buckley, tell me how Sarah is.' He spoke as he came towards us, ignoring Captain Ainslie. 'Tell me about my son.' When he stopped I thought for a minute he would take me by the shoulders and shake me.

'I think it would be better, soldier, if we went inside.' Captain Ainslie was sharp. Jimmy Vance hesitated. Then he nodded and turned and led the couple of steps to the door of a hut which he pushed open. We followed him inside.

Instead of a fireplace this hut had a lopsided stove with a hole in the roof for a chimney. The windows were smaller and there was no way the men who lived there, and slept on the straw pallet beds, could have had the remotest privacy from one another. Even on that mild day I felt a breeze blow through the planks which made up the walls. But it was clean and we were the only people inside.

'Excuse me, Captain, sir,' Jimmy Vance hurriedly saluted his officer and turned to me. 'I know you're her friend from childhood. She spoke of you all the time. I'm glad to meet you.'

'And I you.'

He took my extended hand and I took a proper look at Sarah's love. He had a pleasant, open face with hair that curled as if to spite the short haircut. It was easy to imagine him a beloved son and brother. Far easier than it was to see him as the father of James.

'How old is my son? What did she call him? Why didn't she tell me she was carrying my child? Is she well?' His questions fell on top of one another as he dropped my hand.

'He's nearly six weeks old and he's called James,' I began.

'She gave him my name . . .' This fact seemed more than he could deal with and he set his jaw and walked to the window. He stood there for a full minute, a small muscle ticking at the side of his eye. 'I'm sorry.' He left the window and pulled three chairs close together. 'We should sit.'

Captain Ainslie refused the chair offered him, preferring to lean against the wall, but Jimmy Vance and myself sat opposite one another while I told him as much as I thought he should know of Sarah's story. Sarah could fill in the details herself.

'I got letters from her all right,' he said when I'd finished, 'but none telling me she was with child.'

'She wrote telling you three times,' I said.

'I got three letters,' he agreed.

His hands hung loosely between his knees, the half-carved whistle in one of them. He became very quiet. A long silence stretched. A soldier came in, took a look at Jimmy Vance's face and went out again; the mood in that hut was not good and it got worse. Jimmy Vance moved at last, folding his arms and looking me in the eye. 'I can't read,' he said, 'Sarah's letters were read to me.'

'Were they censored?' Captain Ainslie moved to the window and stood with his back to us, looking out.

'There were no lines through them, if that's what you mean.' Jimmy Vance brought his hands together and snapped the whistle in two. 'They were misrepresented to me,' he looked at what he'd done, 'by another soldier. A man who wouldn't want me staying behind if the regiment goes to India.'

'This man is a friend of yours?' said Captain Ainslie.

'He was,' said Jimmy Vance.

There was another silence after this. The same soldier came back into the hut. Detecting an even worse mood he saluted Captain Ainslie and went out again quickly. Jimmy Vance dropped his broken handiwork to the floor.

'I've nothing to bring my son,' he said. 'Where is he?'

'With his mother,' I said, 'in a shelter on the plains. They're both waiting for you.'

'Sheltering on the plains? What do you mean?' He said the words slowly. His upper lip was beaded with perspiration.

'They're with the wrens,' I said, 'or maybe you know them as bushwomen.'

For an eternity of time he stared as if at a grave into which he intended flinging himself. He was seeing me as I really was, my tiredness and dishevelled state, and he was at last understanding how things really were.

'What have I done to her . . .' He seemed to grow thinner and younger as he stood there.

'She came to the Curragh to find you. She's waiting,' I said.

He stood to attention. 'Captain Ainslie, sir, I'm glad for what you've done for me so far. But you would have my gratitude for life, sir, if you would . . .'

'You know the commandant's views about soldiers who keep company with bushwomen?'

'As well as you know them yourself, Captain.'

'Go to her, Private Vance,' Captain Ainslie said, 'and repay your debt of gratitude by seeing that Miss Buckley gets safely to her own shelter in the wren village. I'll get a horse car to take you both.' He moved from the wall and his voice hardened. 'I want you back here in an hour, soldier. Any longer and you will create difficulties for me. You wouldn't want to do that.'

Alexander Ainslie came with us to where the carmen were lined up waiting for hire. He chose a driver he knew and paid him enough for the man not to protest about the destination. He spoke in my ear as he helped me up into the car.

'Until the Gibbet Rath,' he said.

I nodded as Jimmy Vance got in beside me.

'Sarah was on the plains for last night's rain?' said Jimmy Vance as we moved quickly out of the camp.

'She and James have been there for more than a week now,' I said.

'I wrote to her too,' he stared ahead, his hands cupping his knees, 'the man who wrote my letters for me was the same one who read Sarah's to me. He took them with his own letters for posting. Did she get letters from me?'

'Never.'

'Sarah never trusted John Marsh. She thought him all for himself.'

I looked back as we left the camp. Captain Ainslie, standing where we'd left him, raised his hand in salute.

CHAPTER TWENTY-SIX

Sarah

The days, then weeks, of that summer became altogether different once I was with Jimmy again. I knew I was fooling myself. That the mornings were no brighter, the nights just as dark and the great sea of green no more a lily pond than it was the Atlantic. I didn't care.

I saw him coming, the day Allie brought him back to me, when he was a good half-mile away. The rain in the night had sharpened the green and flattened the dust. So I was able to see him quite clearly, sitting upright beside Allie in a horsecar, wearing his soldier's uniform.

I walked out of the village to meet him. When he saw me he jumped from the car and ran the last bit of the way.

We stood in the road while he held me and James close against him. Even James was silent for those few minutes. I felt Jimmy's heart, and his breath on my hair. I thought that if lightning struck us down, or God's hand, we'd be together forever, the three of us. I almost wanted it to happen.

What happened was that James, who'd been fretful and colicky since early morning, began to cry. Jimmy took him from me.

'He's got a look of my mother about him.' he said.

I'd always thought James resembled Mary Ann. He was becoming fairer by the day and his face was round and mostly smiling, as hers had been. He wasn't smiling for his father. His face was distorted with the pain in his small stomach.

'So your mother suffers from colic, does she?' I said.

'I don't blame you being angry at me,' Jimmy put James across his shoulder. 'But there wasn't a day I didn't think of you, Sarah, and that's the God's truth.'

'I know it is,' I said.

I did too. All I'd needed was to hear him say it. The rest of the truth could wait a little longer.

Allie travelled on to the wren village in the horsecar while Jimmy and I, with James still across his father's shoulder, left the road and walked out across the soft grass. There was nowhere else for us to be alone; the sheep couldn't be counted as company. When we found a sheltered spot by a low hillock I took James and comforted him until he was quiet again.

'I was wrong.' Jimmy examined his son's peaceful face. 'It's me he looks like.' I hadn't the heart to take this away from him so I said nothing. I still thought James looked like Mary Ann.

We sat on the drying grass and Jimmy took off his jacket and put James lying on it. He liked it there and lay quietly, kicking his legs. I put my head on Jimmy's shoulder and he put his arms round me and his face in my hair again. We said nothing for a long time.

Then Jimmy said, 'You can't go on living with the bush-women. There's talk about them in the camp. They're not . . .'

'They took me in when I came here to look for you,' I said.

It was one thing for me to find fault with the wrens and the way they lived. It was another for Jimmy to do so.

'They did,' he agreed, 'but we're together now and you must leave them. I'll find lodgings for you in Kildare town. You can stay there until we're married.'

'When will that be?' I trusted Jimmy. I did not trust the army.

'I'll go straight away to the provost marshal, tell him I want leave to marry the first day I'm not needed for a parade or route march. We can do it by licence or after banns, whichever you prefer . . .' He saw my distrust and stopped. 'It'll be all right, Sarah, I promise you.'

Jimmy had always made things sound easy. 'I've been in Kildare town, Jimmy,' I told him, 'wrens aren't welcome there.'

'Newbridge then,' he said, 'we'll go to Newbridge tomorrow and find you a room.'

'And Allie? What about her? She came here on account of me. I can't leave her alone in the wren village.'

'We'll find a room for Allie too. She's been a good friend to the pair of us.' He stopped, remembering something. After a minute, sounding like someone not sure that he'd heard right, he said, 'She told me the two of you went visiting the major general.'

'We did,' I assured him, 'and if I ever see that *amadán* again it'll be too soon. He's not worth our time talking about.'

But Jimmy insisted and so I told him a little of what I thought of his major general, and of his army's attitude to the mothers of its soldiers' children. He didn't disagree with me. He said the major general had a wife who dressed in black to be like the Queen. Unlike the Queen they had no children.

'He took command a year ago and he's a great discourager of wives and families in the camp. But the provost marshal's a good sort and if Captain Ainslie sticks with us we'll be all right, in spite of Ponsonby,' he said.

'Why would Captain Ainslie turn against us?' I asked.

'Because he's an officer. Officers do what they please and when it pleases them,' Jimmy said. 'What amuses Ainslie today, Sarah, may be of no interest to him tomorrow.'

'You're talking about Allie, aren't you?' The sun might have gone in, I felt so chilled.

'He's very taken with her,' Jimmy agreed.

I knew he was. 'Allie's not taken with him.' I prayed I was right. 'She'll be gone from here as soon as we're married.'

Jimmy turned my face up to his. 'You don't have to look out for her on your own any more, Sarah,' he said, 'I'm here and I'll be a friend to her too. I owe her.'

The sun warmed up again.

'Do you know the wren village?' I said. 'Have you ever been there?'

Jimmy reddened and sat away from me. 'If you mean have I been a caller there, Sarah, then the answer is no, I have not.' He was stiff with insult.

'That's not what I meant.' I shook my head. 'I just wondered if you'd ever stopped in passing, as some soldiers do, or driven out with the water wagon.'

I swatted a bee hovering near James. The Curragh was alive with insects of all sorts. Ellen had told me the butterflies everywhere were Wood Whites. She was very interested in that sort of thing. I didn't notice Jimmy's upset until he stood up.

'How could you think, Sarah, that I'd go with a prostitute?' He took a cigarette from his tunic pocket. He hadn't smoked when I knew him before. 'I was always waiting to get back to you. I've never even thought about another woman, not to mind a prostitute . . .'

'Prostitutes are women, Jimmy,' I pointed out. 'It was a prostitute took me into her kip house when my father put me out in the street. That same prostitute gave me work when no one else would. And none of the women in the wren village, prostitutes or others, have ever made me feel ashamed of our child in the way your commander did.'

He said nothing for a while, just stood pulling on his cigarette, the smoke making a thick cloud in front of him. It would be hard for Jimmy to accept women like Beezy and Clara Hyland. Or the girls in the kip house, if he'd ever had to meet them. None of the women I knew who were prostitutes had much regard for men. Men sensed this very quickly too and, depending on their type, were either frightened or wary of them. Jimmy, who was a boy in many ways and saw life plainly, would find them more frightening than most.

I watched my baby watching the butterflies and waited for his father to say something.

'It was a soldier fought in the Crimea gave me my first one of these.' He spoke at last, examining the cigarette as he did so. 'He got the habit from the Turks.'

'Beezy Ryan uses cigarettes,' I was not having him change the subject, 'and she got the habit from a soldier too. It could even be that he fought in the Crimea.' I paused. 'Beezy's the prostitute gave me a home and work when I was carrying James.'

'I don't want to fight with you, Sarah.' Jimmy dropped the cigarette and ground it with his heel into the grass. 'All I've thought about these months was seeing you again and getting you to change your mind.'

'Change my mind about what?'

He sat beside me again, but a little apart and without putting his arms about me. 'About wanting to finish with me. That's what I thought was the matter, that you'd grown tired and didn't want to see me.'

And so, at last, I heard and understood how the wretched John Marsh, Jimmy's best and jealous friend, had conspired to keep him away from me.

John Marsh had read to Jimmy, from my letters, that I wanted to end our friendship because my father had found out about us. In John Marsh's version of my letters I told Jimmy that in any event my feelings had changed.

John Marsh had also, as a good friend would, sat down with his pen and written Jimmy's replies asking to meet me. God alone knows what he'd really put down. Or even what he'd done with the letters. Written rubbish and burned them, most likely. Jimmy had even gone to Dublin and haunted the house in Haddington Road for two whole days, hoping to see me.

'Why didn't you tell me you couldn't read?' I said.

He looked away. 'I thought it more important to tell you you were the only woman I could ever love.'

'Tell me again.' I took his hand and made him look at me. His eyes were bright with tears. 'Tell me again that you love me,' I said.

A good while later, when James became impatient with us, I told Jimmy everything that had happened to me. It was hard to get him to understand how fine a person Beezy was, how good, in their way, the girls in North King Street had been to me. How companionable the women in the Magdalen.

'That's all in the past, Sarah,' he said when I'd finished. 'You can't go on living with outcast women.'

'I'm an outcast woman myself,' I pointed out.

'You didn't choose to be.'

'Do you think the wrens choose to be as they are?' I tried to hold back my anger. 'They did not. They were decent, most of them hardworking, before disaster and poverty and abuse left them without choices. For some of them life's kinder here, living free on the plains in the summertime, than anything they've known.' I paused. 'The winters are different. The winters are hell itself and the women who stay on have no place else to go.'

'They could go to the workhouse.'

I remembered about what Allie had told me of the Naas Union Workhouse. 'You don't know what you're talking about, Jimmy,' I said.

Two days later we went to Newbridge together to get me a room. Jimmy was to pay for it. He said he'd heard from soldiers in his regiment about a row of cottages in which there were rooms for rent.

I said nothing to Allie or to Beezy Ryan about going to live in Newbridge. Time enough when the deed was done. That would be the time too for Allie to leave the village. I'd an idea growing in my head also about how I might help her do what she wanted with her life.

Jimmy arrived to meet me with a swollen nose and blackening eye. He'd sorted out things with his treacherous friend in the way that men do.

'I hope John Marsh didn't get off so lightly,' I said.

'He won't be writing letters for a while, or doing a lot of reading either,' Jimmy said.

'Will you be punished?' I was worried about him being put in a guardhouse.

'They'll have to find me out first,' Jimmy grinned and rubbed his sore nose, 'and that's not going to happen. That lying swine never had many friends but he's got none at all today.'

Jimmy didn't come into the village to meet me, preferring to wait at a distance in the horsecar. Allie said he was wrong to do this, that he would have to get to know the women sooner or later, that it might as well be sooner. I said it would have to be later and kissed her and ran to the horsecar.

The cottages Jimmy had been told about ran along one side of Francis Street. Across from them stood the barracks and a row of high trees. The road in between was wide and stony, with yapping dogs and a great deal of traffic. The cottages straggled in a low, uneven row and once, in some distant past, might have been decent and whitewashed.

My skirts raised clouds of dark dust as we walked and counted the doors to the cottage Jimmy had been told to look for. A woman with pale eyes opened the door a narrow crack to his knocking.

'What do you want?' She spoke to the buttons on his tunic.

'We're looking for a room,' Jimmy said.

'For one of you or the both of you?' She didn't raise her eyes. She didn't open the door any wider either.

'For my fiancée,' Jimmy said.

'Will she be staying long?' The woman opened the door another couple of inches. Her smile revealed a single, large tooth.

'Until we get married,' Jimmy said.

'A couple of weeks,' I added.

The door opened, wide. 'Ye might as well come in.' The woman turned and went down a dank, dark hallway. We stepped through the door and followed her. It was hard to see anything at first, after the light outside. The smell was another thing. It seeped from the walls and ceilings, smothering in the dank air. I'd been in an abattoir once and it had smelled only slightly worse than the hallway of that cottage.

'You can't stay here.' Jimmy reached for and held my hand.

'Maybe it's cleaner at the back of the house,' I said, 'maybe there's a drain or something causing the smell in this part.' I wasn't hopeful, just desperate to be settled in a room with four walls around myself and James.

At the end of the hallway we went through another door into

a kitchen. It had a dirt floor and some tubs of water, a table and chairs, an unlit open fire and shelves with crockery and utensils. Everything was filthy or broken or both. The smell was no better.

The woman who had let us in was talking to another, older woman. They turned when we came in.

'We've a room all right.' The older woman had hair on her upper lip and chin. 'But you'll have to share it with two others. There's great call on the rooms we have here.' She sniggered and nudged the other woman who showed us her tooth in another grin. They were alike enough to be hell hag and daughter.

'I won't be staying,' I said, 'I've changed my mind.'

'We're not good enough for you, is that it?' The first woman narrowed her eyes. This made it impossible to see where she was looking.

'That's it,' I agreed, 'and your house isn't good enough for me either.'

'You'll not get anything else in Newbridge,' the woman sneered, 'there's nowhere will take the likes of you and your bastard child.'

I ignored Jimmy's hand on my arm, urging me out of there. The woman wasn't the kind worth losing my temper with. I would have kept it too if she hadn't insulted James.

'Then I'll stay where I'm living,' I was loud and sharp, 'there's decency among the wrens, at least. There's not a nest on the Curragh as foul as this hole.'

'A wren! The dirty jade's nothing but a wren!'

The daughter spat at my feet. Her mother moved back as if I was diseased.

'You come in here full of airs and graces and you're nothing but a bushwoman,' the daughter screamed. 'Get out.' She advanced a step, her eyes like a cat's when it's ready to fight. 'Get out before I lay hands on you.'

'There's no need for that,' Jimmy put an arm about my shoulder and held me and James tight against him. I could feel him shaking and knew he was having a hard time with his own temper. 'A mistake's been made. We'll go now.' He turned me towards the door.

'A mistake's been made all right,' the mother's voice snarled behind us, 'the mistake was in thinking that we'd take in a strumpet from the Curragh.'

'The cottages might have the name of being a she-barracks,' the daughter's voice followed as we went back along the stinking hallway, 'but the women who stay here aren't savages.'

The dusty street, with its grey barrack wall and trees, might have been a palace garden, it felt so good after that house.

We walked in silence until we got to the railway station. Then we kept on walking because I wanted to be clear of the town. To rest in a place where I would feel clean. When we came to a river we sat on its bank. Jimmy took off his tunic and laid it down again, this time under a bush, for James to lie on. A bird was singing and I asked him what it was.

'Would it be a swallow?' he guessed. Jimmy was a city person like myself.

It seemed more like a linnet to me. I didn't know much but I knew that the swallow lived among buildings and the linnet in the countryside where he sang like a canary.

'I miss the goldfinch we had in Henrietta Street.' My eyes blurred with sudden, scalding tears.

Jimmy took my hand. 'I'm sorry I brought you to such a place as that,' he said, staring into the river, 'I should have known better, should have known there's only one kind of house will take in an unmarried woman with a child.' He tore a clod of earth from the bank and threw it violently into the water. His face was red from the neck up. 'I've ruined your life, Sarah, I've destroyed something that was beautiful and free.'

I put my hands into the river and cupped them full of water and threw it over his face. 'I was never free,' I said, 'and are you telling me now that I'm no longer beautiful?'

He looked at me for a minute, the water dripping from his nose. 'There's nothing compares to you on this river bank,' he grinned.

'And I know the difference between a linnet and a swallow too,' I said.

We stayed a long time by that river. When I put James to the breast Jimmy watched as if some miracle were happening in front of him. He'd seen his mother suckle his younger brothers but it was very different he said, when the baby was your own and the breast belonged to the woman you loved.

'What's a she-barracks?' I asked. Jimmy frowned and hesitated but I insisted he give me an answer.

'I heard the name in Dublin first,' he said, slowly, 'it's given usually to houses where women of bad habits lodge.'

'Prostitutes and such?' I laid James down again on Jimmy's jacket.

'Every kind. Women who marry soldiers without leave, drunken women, thieving women.' He leaned over James, watching his sleeping face. 'We won't marry without leave, Sarah. When you're my wife you'll have all the respect due a married woman. You'll never again, as long as I live, be treated like a bawd or harlot.'

'Are you expecting to die soon then?' I joked. He took me seriously.

'I'm a soldier,' he reminded me.

'The world is full of soldiers living long and healthy lives,' I was impatient, 'and there's no war in this country for you to fight.'

'There are the Fenians . . .'

'The Fenians are not going to attack the Curragh camp.'

'Maybe not,' said Jimmy, 'but we might be sent to attack the Fenians. A soldier must go where he is sent, serve where his army tells him to.'

'Even when he has a wife?'

'It makes no difference.'

I was tired of army talk, and what might happen. 'I'll stay with the wrens until we marry,' I said. 'Compared to Francis Street the wren village is decency itself. It's closer to the camp anyway and the weather looks set to hold for a couple of weeks more.'

I took off my boots and then my stockings and put my feet into the river. The water was cool and curled about them like silk.

'The wrens are decent, many of them,' I said, 'and Allie and Beezy Ryan are in no hurry to leave.'

Jimmy put his feet into the river too and we sat and watched the quick water while I told him about how Allie was trying out her medical skills on the wrens.

'You told me she wanted to be a nurse,' Jimmy remembered.

'She wants now to be a doctor.'

Jimmy had more sense than to challenge this. She'd brought us together and the least he could do was respect her dreams. All he said was, 'She seems to make her own rules.'

I was glad to be returning to the wren village when we crossed the Curragh in the late afternoon. Much as I'd wanted to be out of it I'd had worries about Allie staying on there without me and about forsaking Beezy Ryan. A lot had happened in the months without Jimmy. Allie and Beezy had been with me through it all.

I'd good reason to worry about leaving Beezy alone in the village. She was drinking more than I'd ever known her to and had taken to talking to herself in a way I'd never seen her do before either. It didn't need a crystal-gazer to see she was brooding about the fire and all that had happened in North King Street. Lizzie Early going to the workhouse had made her worse.

I told Jimmy as much of this as I thought he'd understand as we came closer to the village.

'You can't stop her drinking,' he said, 'and she wouldn't thank you for telling her what to do with her life.'

He was right, of course.

There were a couple of things on my mind about Allie that I kept to myself though, and didn't discuss with him. There seemed no point, yet, in telling him I felt she was becoming too bound up in the village. The arm she'd stitched up for Ellen Neary was healing fine. She'd stopped Lil Malone's vomiting two days before. She'd cured another wren of a crippling earache and she'd treated a child's fever. All of this made her feel important and needed, as well as which she was all the time adding the wrens' own cures to her store of knowledge. She watched and learned as she saw them use a stinging nettle against insect bites and feverfew for headaches. When Beezy took dandelion tea, saying it was 'very effectual for obstructions of the liver', Allie agreed it could do good.

But when the worst happened and she was unable to do anything for Lizzie Early her distress had been terrible.

'There should have been something,' she said over and over, 'it's because I know so little that I was able to do so little. But I'll learn here. I'll learn by observing the women and testing what can be done.' She stopped when I looked disbelieving. 'It's called empiricism,' she snapped.

'I don't care what it's called,' I said, 'it sounds to me as if you're making an experiment of the wrens and their illnesses. It's not right.'

'Why? I'm helping. I'm doing good. If I learn in the process what's wrong with that?'

I could have argued that there was no future for her in the wren village. She wouldn't have listened.

I didn't tell Jimmy either that I was worried, and hurt, by Allie's secrecy over a meeting she'd had at the Gibbet Rath with Captain Ainslie. They'd been seen there by two of the wrens.

I said nothing because I knew she would tell in her own time. She always did. But I wondered about it and was hurt anyway.

CHAPTER TWENTY-SEVEN

Sarah

The weather continued fine. Everyone said it was a miracle and that the devil, at last, was looking after his own. By his own they meant the wrens.

The sun rose, and set, in glowing orange in a cloudless sky. The days in between were long and lazy. Not even the army, with all its rules and disciplines, could get its soldiers to drill and parade with any energy.

One thing, however, did cut through the idleness of that summer and it affected me and Jimmy. When word came that the Prince of Wales was to visit the camp all marriage leave was cancelled until after he'd gone.

I railed against the Prince daily, wishing he would stay at home and amuse himself in England, something the newspapers said he did with great zeal. Jimmy said the visit was an honour and that the commander and his staff were in a state of 'high anticipation'. He would plead, he said, for ours to be considered a special case and ask if Captain Ainslie would help. Jimmy had great faith in Captain Ainslie.

The wrens enjoyed that time of grace and sunshine for the respite it was. There wasn't a woman in the village didn't know from experience the calm that will always come before a storm.

None of it mattered to Lizzie Early. She lived on for two weeks after going into the workhouse, but without ever being aware of where she lay dying. The prayer in the village had been that she might never know she'd been taken to Naas Union. God, for once, listened to the wrens. They say He listens to the prayers of sinners. Lizzie had no next of kin but a good half of the wrens went to her burial in Kildare churchyard. Beezy paid for a deal coffin and spared Lizzie the final shame of a pauper's funeral.

The priest was young and came from the workhouse. His thin brown hair hung to his collar and he was full of Christian charity. 'We bury our sister Elizabeth Early,' he said, 'in the full and righteous belief that she is at peace at last with her Heavenly Father. The sins of her short, painful life are all forgiven now. We will remember her in our prayers.'

Things would have been all right if he'd left it there but he added a homily.

'Her friends, gathered sadly here on this most wondrous of God's days, must learn to pray that they will be guided to the path of righteousness, the path that poor Elizabeth failed to find.' He opened his arms wide, as if to embrace us all. 'You have only to ask. God's mercy is infinite and generously given.'

Clara Hyland said loudly what most of the wrens felt. 'We've seen plenty of God's mercy. We saw it in the way He listened to Lizzie's prayers, and she said plenty of them.'

'Despair is a sin against God's goodness.' The priest's pale face lit up at the prospect of saving a soul. 'You must fight against it. We will pray together.' He fell to his knees by the open grave and raised his arms. 'Send enlightenment, Almighty God, to the friends of Elizabeth Early . . .' He gestured that we too should kneel.

'Cover her,' Beezy, nodding to the grave diggers, was curt, 'cover her good.'

I left the graveyard with Beezy. We were the only two there had known Lizzie in her other life, when she'd had her health and been what Beezy called 'a decent hard-working whore'. Beezy knew her better than anyone.

Allie stayed talking to the doctor from the workhouse and Clara Hyland waited with her. From being sworn enemies they'd become companions of sorts, at least in the matter of Lizzie Early.

'I blame myself,' Beezy said as she turned for the Curragh. She hated Kildare and every other country town. She said they were nothing but cesspits of ignorance and cant. 'I should have seen Mary Adams for what she was and left her where I found her. I should have put my girls first and then there would have been no fire. No deaths.' She walked fast, swinging her arms, her rings flashing in the sunlight. She'd worn every ring she had for Lizzie's last outing. She hadn't had a drink all day either. I had James in my arms and found it hard to keep up with her. Though there was no talking to her in the mood she was in I tried anyway, calling after her.

'You might as well say you're sorry you took me in, Beezy Ryan,' I cried, 'I didn't bring you much luck either.'

Beezy stopped. 'I wanted you to do work for me, and you did it. You more than earned what I paid you. I wasn't looking for luck, or any other kind of unearned reward. Not from you and not from Mary Adams. Taking Mary Adams in wasn't even a kindness. It was business. I knew the men would like her and I was right. They came after her like dogs in heat. Lizzie was the one said it was wrong.' She started to walk again when I came up beside her. She went on talking. 'She said it to my face that Mary Adams was demented and would destroy us all. I told her that if Mary Adams went on account of her that I'd put her out too.'

Beezy faced me. She'd got older-looking since coming to the Curragh and her hair wasn't the shining mop it had once been. But the sun had at least faded the scar on her face.

'Now they're both gone. Three people dead and my house burned to the ground and my girls on the streets and for what? For what, Sarah?'

'It wasn't your fault, Beezy, and Lizzie dying was nothing to do with any of it either. You're not seeing things straight since we came here.' I shook my head. 'Taking Mary Adams in was a great kindness. How were you to know what would happen? You've worked all your life, Beezy, and here on the Curragh you've too much time on your hands. You're brooding on things that are past and done with and can't be undone.'

She was more like stone than stone, standing in the road, looking at me without seeing me. I touched the scar on her face and she blinked and came to herself.

'Listen to me, Beezy,' I said, 'what happened was terrible but you can't bring William Fleming back. Mary Adams was mad before you ever met her and Allie says Lizzie had a growth inside her for a long time. It could have been there a couple of years, she says, before even she came to the kip house. She knew by the feel and size of the swelling in her stomach.'

'Allie Buckley is not God.' Beezy was snappy. But she was listening so I went on.

'The countryside doesn't suit you,' I said, 'you're a city woman, used to working for yourself. You're too independent-spirited for this place. It's driving you to melancholy.' I stopped, deciding not to say anything about the drink. I might lose her if I did, now that she was listening.

'You're right that I'm a city woman and you're right that all this space and emptiness is making me uneasy. But the Curragh'll have to suit me until the autumn.' Beezy began walking again. 'I'll go to America then. There's no good my going back to Dublin. The past and all that happened would catch up with me sooner or later and I'd really be finished then.'

We walked on slowly, friendly now in the way we used to be. We were getting on so well that after a while I took a chance and mentioned the drink. I felt I had to. She'd taken to going some nights with the hunting party, coming back to finish the night snoring and grunting, and often calling out, in her sleep.

'You won't be going to America or anywhere else if you keep on drinking the way you are,' I said. 'You've seen for yourself, often enough, what it does.'

'It gets me through the days,' she retorted, sounding surly.

'And the nights. It's like having a hog in the nest by times, the noises you make after drinking.' The whiskey might help her forget but it didn't help her in any other way.

'Enough, Sarah. I don't want to talk about it. You don't need to worry about me and the drink. I'm no Clara Hyland. The drink won't control *me*.' She shrugged. 'If it'll please you I'll stop. You'll see then that there's no need to worry about me.'

She took James and held him as we went along, tickling him until he laughed. She never failed to get a laugh and a smile out of him.

'I often thought that if I'd a sister she might have been like you.' She didn't sound sad, but she didn't look at me.

'Because we're of a height?' I said.

'Maybe that's all it is. Or maybe it was that I wanted to be part of a family and you and Bess were always there, friendly and talking to me.' She put James across her shoulder, so that the sun didn't shine in his eyes. 'I've always wanted the best for you.'

'Jimmy's what's best for me,' I said.

Beezy gave a long sigh. 'Was there ever a woman born, apart from myself, that could live without a man . . .' She gave me a quick, sidelong glance. 'I'm not so sure either about your Jimmy. I've not made up my mind about him yet.'

It didn't surprise me that Beezy didn't trust Jimmy. There wasn't a man on earth she trusted. She did like him, however. All of the wrens liked Jimmy. It would have been hard not to.

He came regularly to the village now, his caution around the wrens making him go out of his way to please. He brought gifts when he came, and told funny stories about barracks life. He helped too with small jobs, like buying a plank of wood and mending the door of Clara Hyland's nest. I never knew if this was a clever or innocent act on his part. The result anyway was that no one dared say a cross word about Jimmy Vance in Clara's hearing.

Cigarettes were hard to get so he brought Beezy plug tobacco and a clay pipe. She wasn't the only wren to smoke a pipe and she shared it around. I thought the habit a filthy one myself, though I had to admit the smoke in the evening times kept the clouds of midges at bay.

Preparations for the Prince of Wales's visit were so frenzied that Jimmy was able to slip out of the camp, unnoticed, most days. Sometimes he stayed a half-hour or less, other times he was with me until the last post sounded in the camp at nine thirty in the evening. As the time went on I was noticing small ways in which he'd changed. His face wasn't so soft as it had been and he'd got thinner. He looked older, more a man. The boy I'd known was going.

Beezy questioned Jimmy a few evenings after the funeral. We were sitting on the soft grass in front of the nest. The water wagon had come that day and Allie, Beezy and myself had washed almost every stitch of clothing we owned. In the dark, stretched over the furze to dry, they looked like ghostly, floating things. The sounds of drum and trumpet and parading came clearly from the camp. A great show of military manoeuvres was to be put on for the Prince of Wales.

'Tell me how it is in the camp for the married soldiers and their wives,' Beezy quizzed. Since she'd stopped drinking she was greatly concerning herself with my affairs. It made me want, sometimes, to put a cup of whiskey into her hand.

'They're not the best,' Jimmy said. He'd told me as much. 'But better than in the barracks in the towns where two or three families share a room without even a screen to divide them.'

'Answer me straight,' Beezy jabbed him with a finger, 'where in the camp will you live with Sarah and James?'

'There's a couple of huts for married soldiers in my own barrack square.' Jimmy stopped and Beezy went on looking at him, waiting, the smoke from her pipe standing in the air between them. 'There's a wash house with boilers and wooden troughs.'

Beezy nodded.

'There's a common cook house,' Jimmy cleared his throat, 'and privies for the women.'

Beezy nodded again. 'What else?'

'There's no place right now for a couple to move into,' Jimmy admitted, 'but once we're married . . .'

'I've heard a great number of wives spend the early months of marriage lodging in rooms in Kildare or Newbridge,' Beezy said, 'is that a likely fate for Sarah?'

'Sarah and James will live with me in the camp.' Jimmy was firm.

Beezy nodded. 'I'm glad to hear it. It would be a bad thing, after her coming all the way from Dublin, if Sarah had to live with her baby in the she-barracks in Newbridge or in one of the back streets of Kildare.' She paused. 'It would be a very bad thing.'

'That won't happen to Sarah and James,' Jimmy spoke stiffly 'as my wife things will be different for Sarah. She'd have her pick of lodgings.'

'I won't be needing lodgings, good bad or indifferent.' I sounded a lot calmer than I felt. I'd been more than a month with the wrens. I'd hoped to spend no more than a week. 'I'll be married and moving into a place in the camp as soon as the visit by the Prince is over.' I gave Beezy a hard look and spoke loudly enough for Allie to hear me. 'It'll be early autumn then. Time for yourself and Allie to be moving on your own plans.'

'Don't you worry about my plans,' Beezy took a deep drag. Allie, sitting a bit away reading one of her medical books by candlelight, gave not the slightest indication that she'd heard me.

'You'd imagine that officer friend of Allie's could do something to hurry things along,' Beezy said in a raised voice.

'There's not a lot anyone can do at the moment,' Allie heard this all right, 'not until after the royal fever has ended.'

I watched her carefully. She hadn't raised her head. She didn't seem to miss a line of her reading either.

It was hard to know if Captain Ainslie meant something, or nothing at all, to her. They met once, sometimes twice, a week and went walking together across the plains. He never came into the village, arriving either on foot or on horseback and waiting a short distance away for her to join him.

When she did they walked slowly, keeping a decent space between them and as sedately as if they were parading the footpaths of Ballsbridge or Merrion Square. Allie always wore a dress, and sometimes a hat. They were never gone for longer than an hour and never out of sight of the village.

Beezy Ryan and the other wrens watched them too. No one said anything to me but I knew they were talking and wondering what was going on.

Wondering was all I could do myself because, though Allie gave me facts when I asked for them, she *told* me very little. I knew, for instance, that he rode a large, bay horse called Sam and that he liked the countryside around. I *didn't* know what he expected of their friendship, if anything.

'Your Captain Ainslie seems fond of you,' I said to her later that night. We were lying side by side in the nest trying to sleep. It was hot inside and noisy outside where a hunting party was getting ready to leave. Beezy was going with them.

'He's bored with life in the camp and wants diversion,' Allie said. 'All he hears there is talk of the Prince and the honour he's doing the camp and what's to be done to impress him while he's here.'

'What do you think of him?'

'I've not given him much thought,' Allie yawned, 'they say he likes to travel and to be amused. Alexander says he's been to the Curragh before, for military training, and that he made an ass of himself—'

'I don't want your thoughts on the Prince,' I interrupted curtly, 'it's Alexander Ainslie I wondered about.' I stressed his name.

'He's passable company.' She yawned again, putting great effort into it. 'His conversation is interesting because it concerns things I know nothing of. He talks to me about the part of England he comes from, about how the people live there.'

'Why does he stay in the army if he's so bored by it?'

'He's obliged. It's tradition in his family for men to spend time soldiering. It's all to do with money and honour.' She laughed. 'Have you noticed, Sarah, how money and honour are never too far separated?'

'What do you think of him?' I wasn't going to have her changing the subject.

'I don't think of him,' she was brisk, 'except to give him polite attention when we're together.' She tossed on the pallet. 'I'm tired, Sarah. Goodnight.'

I let it go. Any more questions and she'd remind me that I'd kept Jimmy Vance a secret from her until it had suited me to tell.

At the core of my need to know was the nagging worry that Allie had put herself in debt to Captain Ainslie for helping bring Jimmy and me together. I hoped her walks and talks with him – and wherever they were leading to – hadn't to do with a repayment of that debt.

Beezy and Nance Reilly came to me one day as Allie left to meet her captain outside the village.

'What's Allie Buckley up to with her officer?' Beezy stood with her hands on her hips watching as they walked away. Her bare arms and chest were freckled and she'd been wearing her rings since Lizzie Early's funeral. There had been no comment about this from the other wrens; no one in the village questioned Beezy any more.

'You can see them for yourself,' I said, 'they're just walking together.'

Beezy made a sharp, clicking sound with her tongue. 'Don't talk to me as if I was a fool. Walking's the least of what they're doing,' she said, 'I thought life had knocked some sense into that silly woman but now I'm not so sure again.'

'She says there's nothing to it,' I said.

'What else is she going to say?' Nance Reilly sat on an upturned pot and poked at the fire. I was boiling water for tea. 'He may be able to play a patient game but he's no different than the rest of them. He'll have his way with her in the end. She'll be nothing but the leavings of an officer when that happens and may as well forget her notions of becoming a physician.'

She was right. Captain Alexander Ainslie might well be a decent man but he was an officer in Her Majesty's army. His place in society was ordained by God and bound by class. By allying herself with the wrens Allie had put herself beyond the prospect of a respectable friendship with him. Beezy and Nance Reilly were right too in saying that he would make her his mistress, if she would have him, and leave her when his time in the army ended.

'He's taken with her,' Beezy said. She was never wrong when it came to the affairs of women with men.

'That's only because he hasn't had her yet,' Nance snorted.

'I thought the officers had their own diversions? I heard there was a kip house serves them the other side of the camp. A grand country house, was what I heard.'

Beezy began to pack her pipe. She'd been short-tempered for a couple of days and it seemed to me she was missing the drink.

'I don't know how grand it is,' Nance said, 'but it's big and there's a fair number of girls in it all right. A lot of trouble too. The madam isn't as diligent as she might be.'

This last was to mollify Beezy, who snorted and dragged on her pipe. 'It's hard to avoid trouble,' she was sour, 'even in the best-run places.'

'There was a lot of gossip about the Prince of Wales and an actress the last time he was here,' said Nance. 'He brought her to his rooms.'

'There always was and always will be one rule for the rich and landed and another for the rest of us.' Beezy squinted into the distance. 'Your soldier has joined Allie and her officer,' she said quickly, 'there's a lot of talking going on. It looks to me as if he's got news of some sort.'

I settled James and walked down the road to join them. Listening to Beezy and Nance had made up my mind for me about taking action on Allie's behalf. I wanted her happy before I settled for happiness myself and had become more than ever certain that Daniel Casey would make her content. He would help her find a role in medicine. He would marry her, if she would have him. He would always care for her.

I would write to him and this time make sure nothing came between them.

I was quite sure of my reading of the two men. I didn't once think about which of them Allie herself might want.

CHAPTER TWENTY-EIGHT

Sarah

Captain Ainslie had arranged a day at the races.

He would be Allie's companion for the day. Jimmy would be my escort. The four of us would travel to the Punchestown meeting in a brougham. We would picnic there too. Captain Ainslie would see to everything.

It had all been agreed between Jimmy and the captain by the time I got to where they stood talking. Allie was doubtful, shielding her eyes against the sun and, under the cover of her hand, giving me a warning frown as I drew near.

I was doubtful myself when I heard the plan. The Prince of Wales would be there, and the Princess, along with anyone worth inviting in county Kildare and a good percentage of Dublin society too. There was a chance of someone seeing and recognising me and of the past opening up. I didn't want anything to come in the way of my plans to quickly and quietly marry Jimmy Vance.

There was also James to think about. He'd been with me, waking and sleeping, since the day he was born but I couldn't bring him to a racetrack meeting. I was weaning him from the breast but he would be distressed without me anyway. *I* would be distracted without him.

I said nothing, and neither did Allie, as the men talked about the racing.

'Steeplechasing's what they do at Punchestown, sir, so I'm told.' Jimmy rubbed his hands together, grinning.

'They go over the jumps at Punchestown all right,' Captain Ainslie nodded, 'and the racing's promised good. There's five hundred pounds in the pot for the inaugural of the Prince of Wales's Plate. The day will be an enjoyable one,' he pulled a face at a few straggly clouds, 'unless it rains.'

It was hard, in the face of Jimmy's shining delight and Captain Ainslie's generosity, to argue the case for not going.

And so it was agreed that we would go to Punchestown Races.

The brougham hired by Captain Ainslie had two white horses. Its hood was down and the sun shone on its leather upholstery when it arrived to collect Allie and myself. Jimmy and Captain Ainslie climbed out and stood, side by side, as we walked towards them.

Jimmy was buttoned into his best tunic and wore his hat. It would have been hard to find a more handsome man anywhere. The captain wore a great deal of braid and a larger hat. But the way they stood, stiff and self-conscious, made them both look like boys.

You couldn't blame them. Allie and I were followed from the village by two-thirds of the women, all of them laughing and calling as if it was a fair day or procession of some kind. Beezy wasn't with them. Beezy was with James, in the nest.

'You'll be getting us a good name.' Clara Hyland stopped the parade at the edge of the road. 'More of this kind of carry-on and the hoi polloi will be coming to take tea with the wrens.'

'Take me with you.' Moll tugged at Allie's sleeve. 'You won't know I'm there. I won't talk. I won't breathe, hardly. I'll follow at your heels like a faithful dog.'

'If I wanted a dog I'd get one,' Allie said, looking annoyed, 'and stop your carry-on. I've promised that you and I will have another outing, another day. Your mother has agreed . . .' She raised her eyebrows at Clara who looked from Allie to the brougham before taking her daughter's hand and heading back towards the village. Allie lifted her parasol and walked quickly on.

If Allie felt bad about leaving Moll behind it was nothing to the way I was feeling about leaving James. No matter how often I went over the facts that Beezy would guard him with her life, that he would very likely sleep most of the half-dozen or so hours I would be away, the hollow at the pit of my stomach remained. The umbilical cord might have been cut that morning.

Jimmy and Captain Ainslie helped Allie and me into the brougham. We sat, two polite couples facing one another, and drove away. I tried not to look back, but my neck swivelled of its own accord. I will forever see the Curragh as it was when I did: the yellow-flowered furze bushes against the green, the lazy white of the sheep and the paint-like dabs of red and blue that were soldiers walking in the distance. Most of all I will see the wrens in their petticoats and bare, waving arms wishing us joy and the best of days.

I'd never seen anything like the racecourse at Punchestown, and never seen so many people in one place.

The course itself was laid out in a semi-circle and separated from the racegoers by a fence. The horses which were to run were kept mainly to one end; everywhere else was black with people: police and soldiers and men and women in their best finery. The Grandstand towered over it all, flags flying from its white-painted, curved iron supports. A German band played loudly.

The Prince of Wales was there, riding a white horse and wearing a black top hat. He was surrounded by dukes and lords of every kind, all of them on horseback but none on a white animal like the Prince. The Princess of Wales and the Vice Regal party were distant figures, high in The Grandstand.

'That's as much as we'll see of any of them,' Captain Ainslie laughed, 'a refreshment room's been built on to the back of the Grandstand for the royal party.'

'I've seen as much as we want to see,' Allie said.

'So have I, my dear,' said the captain, 'so have I.'

It was unspoken between us that it would be a bad thing if

the captain ran into Major General Ponsonby. The commander could hardly fail to recognise myself and Allie and he hadn't struck me as a man with a forgiving nature. Nor one who would overlook an officer ridiculing his orders.

Allie and I had done the best we could with ourselves and certainly looked no worse than many of the women there. We looked, in fact, a lot better than some I saw. Wealth and fine feathers do not a lady make, my mother used to say, and there were plenty examples, that day at Punchestown, of her wisdom.

The horses at Punchestown were nothing like the horses I'd all my life seen drawing carts and carriages. They were sleek and proud and dangerous-looking. They wouldn't have survived two days on the streets of Dublin.

Jimmy, who'd sworn he wasn't a betting man, put money on three races and won on two of them.

'What sort of soldier would I be if I didn't put something on the Irish Grand Military Steeplechase?' He put an arm about my waist after he'd collected his winnings.

'A prudent one,' I said.

Captain Ainslie bet on every single race, often on several horses. It didn't seem to matter to him much whether he won or lost. Twice, when he put money on animals of Allie's choosing and they won, he insisted she take the winnings.

'But it was your money to begin with,' she protested.

'I was prepared to lose it,' he said, 'it was your choice turned it into winnings.'

Allie, pink in the face, took it. 'A fool and his money are easily parted,' she said.

We picnicked in the late afternoon, under a row of trees a bit away from the hot and bother of the racecourse. There was cold meat and cheese, fruit and sweet cake. There was wine too. Allie had a glass and so had I. All it did was clear my head.

'I've been away from James too long,' I said as I stood, 'I want to go back now to the wren village.'

'All in good time,' said Captain Ainslie, 'there are a few races to go yet.'

He didn't understand. He clearly had no children.

'I'll take the brougham and send it back from the village for the rest of you,' I said. 'I can't stay here a minute longer.'

Jimmy got to his feet. 'We'll go together.' He put an arm about me. 'My winnings will pay for a horsecar.'

'It's time we were all leaving.' Allie put her wine glass carefully into the basket.

'The little fellow needs his mother,' Captain Ainslie said, and caught her hand, 'and his father. Surely you can bear to stay with me until the end of the meeting?'

'I've seen as much as I care to.' Allie pulled her hand from his. 'And heard as much too. That German band is making my head ache.'

The band was a distant tinkle. 'In that case we had definitely better leave.' Captain Ainslie looked for a moment at the remains of the picnic. 'A pity . . .'

'I'll pack up, sir.' Jimmy stepped forward, soldier-fashion, and went on one knee by the basket.

'Leave it, Private,' Captain Ainslie's command was clipped and icy, 'it's not important. Time is what matters here and clearly we've spent too much of it.'

Jimmy looked at the food, at the uneaten cheese and fruit, a second, unopened bottle of wine, the scattering of cutlery and napkins. 'I'll be quick.' He lifted the bottle of wine.

'I gave you an order, Private.' Captain Ainslie moved the basket out of Jimmy's reach with his foot. 'We will leave, now.'

Allie had already begun to walk back towards the racecourse. The captain, putting his hat on his head, followed her. We stood, Jimmy and I, for uncertain minutes by the remains of the picnic. Good food, left like that. Alexander Ainslie was either rich enough to be careless or wounded enough by Allie to be angrily indifferent.

'The cutlery's better than anything we have in the nest,' I said.

'Leave it,' Jimmy said.

The brougham was with a lot of other horsecars at the other side of the racecourse. It was a long walk through the crowds, and a slow one. Allie held her parasol high and spoke in a light voice to the captain, who was equally composed-sounding. They walked about a foot apart.

Jimmy and I followed close behind, so close our shoulders touched. After a while I felt for and held Jimmy's hand, tightly.

'James'll be all right, Sarah,' he said, 'Beezy's a good woman. She'll have looked after him well, you'll see.'

We couldn't have been any more than five hundred yards from the waiting horsecars when a couple of officers stepped from the crowd and hailed Captain Ainslie.

'You've been keeping your charming companion to yourself, Captain.' A black moustache and missing tooth gave a villainous look to the one who smiled at Allie.

'Indeed I have, Captain Fetherston.' Captain Ainslie nodded curtly and would have moved Allie briskly on if the second officer hadn't stepped smartly in front of them.

'I do believe we've met before, your companion and I.' His small, sharp nose twitched as he stared at Allie. 'You interrupted our card game, as I remember, you and some ragamuffin child.' He leaned forward on his cane. 'I've forgotten what you said your name was . . .'

'I remember yours.' Allie spoke in a clear, sharp voice. This was not a good sign. I moved to her side. 'You're a Captain Browne,' she went on, 'you weren't disposed to help me find my way through the camp.'

'I had a difficulty with your free and easy attitude to army procedures,' he corrected, 'but Captain Ainslie would appear to have no problem with your lack of manners.' When he sneered his narrow face turned in on itself and his eyes met by his nose.

'Fortunately,' Captain Ainslie, with a smile, took Allie's elbow, 'and fortunately too we were just leaving.'

He nodded pleasantly to the two men and moved on. Allie, by his side, stared straight ahead and kept step with him. The officers looked at one another, then after Captain Ainslie's retreating back. Jimmy, as we started to follow, gave a brief salute.

'Did you enjoy the racing, soldier?' the officer called Fetherston asked.

'I did, sir,' Jimmy said.

We didn't stop. The officers fell into step on either side of us, the smaller, narrow-faced one closest to me. He reeked of port.

'Did you enjoy the meeting, Miss . . . ?' He waited for my name.

'Rooney.' I didn't look at him.

'Rooney.' The sound of my name seemed to amuse him. 'Did you enjoy the races, Miss Rooney?'

'Very much.'

'A shame we should meet as you're leaving,' he said, 'we might all have shared a drink and a bet on the last couple of races.' He raised his voice. 'Any chance you and your party could delay your departure, Captain Ainslie? Captain Fetherston and myself would be greatly entertained if you could.'

Captain Ainslie stopped and turned slowly. 'The races will be more to your taste,' he said, 'than any entertainment my friends and I could provide. Private Vance, perhaps you would lead the way to the brougham? I've forgotten exactly where it was we left it.'

As Jimmy moved forward, with me by the hand, the gap-toothed Captain Fetherston laughed out loud. 'Not walking today, Ainslie? The word in the camp is that you've taken with great vigour to exercising on the plains . . .' he bowed mockingly toward Allie, 'with your fair friend here. Are you not worried, Miss Buckley, that you will run foul of the wild life in the furze bushes?'

'*Au contraire*,' Allie said, 'I feel safer there than I did when visiting the camp. I've found nothing on the plains to compare with the rudeness I experienced in the barracks.'

'Indeed.' Captain Browne's eyes merged with his nose again. 'You mistake rudeness for an army officer's natural defence of his realm.' He sniggered, then cleared his throat. 'I'm sorry if you were offended. A soldier's duty is never done, I'm afraid. Am I forgiven?'

'It would be easy to forgive you, Captain Browne,' Allie said, 'if I thought you were sincere.'

People, all around us, continued to laugh and talk. No one in our group said anything. Captain Ainslie looked amused but Jimmy, by my side, stiffened.

Captain Browne's voice, breaking the hush, was thin and tight. 'Captain Ainslie may have a use for you,' he shrugged, 'but it's my view that he's making a sad mistake encouraging you and your kind.'

'It would be a sad mistake on your part, Captain Browne, to continue with this display of ignorance.' Captain Ainslie, putting Allie behind him, looked for a minute as if he might knock his fellow officer to the ground. He didn't, of course. Officers in Her Majesty's army don't do that kind of thing – so Jimmy told me later. Not the civilised ones anyway and Captain Ainslie was, at the very least, civilised.

'The ignorance, Captain Ainslie, is on your part,' Captain Fetherston displayed his missing tooth in another leering grin, 'women like these are fit playthings for India-bound soldiers such as Vance. They are not—'

'What sort of women are we exactly?' My eyes were on a level with his when I faced him and cut him short. He looked shocked.

Allie stood beside me and we faced the Captains Browne and Fetherston together. A small crowd was beginning to gather. Some were army officers.

'Captain Fetherston meant nothing by the remark.' Captain Browne ran a finger round the inside of his collar. 'An idle and misunderstood pleasantry is all . . .'

'Then let him answer Miss Rooney's question,' Allie said, 'and explain what idle and pleasant thing he meant by his remark about "women like these".'

'You know the answer to that yourself, miss,' said Captain Fetherston, who was not so intimidated by the crowd as his companion, 'you are no lady, madam, and you furthermore do not know your place. Your friend, at least, confines herself to the ranks but you—'

'Oh, be quiet, Fetherston.' Captain Ainslie raised his voice hardly at all. It was enough, though, to raise a couple of supportive 'hear, hears' in the crowd. 'You're boorish and a fool and doing both yourself and your regiment a grave disservice. I'd insist you apologise if I thought Miss Buckley would accept.'

He took Allie's arm and brought her to his side. She looked coldly and silently at the Captains Fetherston and Browne, then turned on her heel. Captain Ainslie, with exquisite courtesy, and a small bow to the rapt crowd, took her arm again and gestured that Jimmy and I should follow them.

'You're amusing yourself with that woman, Ainslie, and you're a liar and scoundrel if you're pretending otherwise,' Captain Browne's voice followed us. 'She is no lady and you, as an officer, should have left her in her dung heap on the plains. It's you, sir, who are doing your regiment a disservice.'

Captain Ainslie didn't turn. His tone didn't change. 'I will not challenge you now, Browne, and nor will I bandy words with you. You are, as too often, inebriated. We will talk again. Good day to you.'

I wished we'd never come to the races and said so to Jimmy.

'I must apologise for my fellow officers,' Captain Ainslie turned, 'it's an unfortunate fact that there are as many fools and knaves in the army as there are in civilian life.'

'That's a matter for debate, sir,' Jimmy said, 'and I'm not so sure how well the army would win the argument.'

As an attempt at temper calming this worked. Captain Ainslie laughed. But if Jimmy meant to assuage the offence felt by Allie and myself then he failed altogether.

The driver, asleep in his seat, was waiting with the brougham. We were on the road when Allie, with apparent sincerity, said, 'That was a most enjoyable day. Thank you, Alex.' She paused. 'I'll certainly remember my time at Punchestown Races.'

'For the best of reasons, I hope,' said Captain Ainslie.

'For all sorts of reasons.' Allie smiled at him, her head to one side.

'We must discuss them,' he said.

The journey back seemed to go on forever. The rhythm of the wheels, as we went along, repeated three of Captain Fetherston's words over and over. India-bound-soldiers, they said, India-bound-soldiers, India-bound-soldiers. When I couldn't stand it any longer I asked Jimmy what he'd meant.

'Are there huge numbers being sent, or what?' I asked.

'There's talk of a regiment or two going all right,' Jimmy said, 'but it's talk only. Just as it was talk only in Beggar's Bush.' His grip tightened on my hand. 'Don't think about it, Sarah.'

I was reassured enough to hear the message change in the wheels. For the rest of the journey they seemed to say talk-only, talk-only, talk-only.

The days had been shortening with terrible speed since the beginning of September and the village, when we drew up on the road, was a series of hulking dark shapes in its hollow. It gave me a shivery premonition of what winter might be like on the plains.

Allie said her goodbyes to Captain Ainslie and he took the brougham back to the camp. Jimmy walked into the village with Allie and me.

It was Jimmy who saw Beezy, pacing with James in her arms, when we were still fifty yards away from the nest. I got to Beezy before he did.

'He's feverish. He wants feeding . . .' She was trembling and white as paper when I took him from her. 'I thought at first that he was lonesome for you but as the day went on I knew there was something wrong. I did everything I could, Sarah.'

James was hot as a furnace in my arms. His breathing was tortured, coming in long and short whistles through his mouth and nose. He whimpered and coughed when I rocked him, whimpered and coughed even more when I kissed and held him against me. Even his hands were hot.

I cursed the races and myself for leaving him. I stopped when I heard myself cursing his father.

'When did this start?' I tried to be calm when I spoke to Beezy.

'About noon. You weren't gone more than an hour or so. We tried to bring the temperature down. Ellen put a herb poultice to his chest. It gave him some peace, but not for long'. She turned to Allie. 'We've been waiting . . . all the time hoping and praying you'd know what to do.'

'Maybe he'll feed . . .' I opened my dress and tried to feed him. All he would do was throw his small head from side to side. The coughing becoming worse all the time. He was like a rasping saw. The hot glaze over his eyes terrified me.

I held him out to Allie. 'Please help him,' I said.

Jimmy stood with me while she examined him. We had made a child and brought him into our perilous world. I had left him in that world, and at such a tender age, to pursue my own pleasure. It was my fault entirely he was ill.

Allie said nothing and she took an age. James wasn't still for a minute, full of convulsive movements and every so often coughing. She listened to his back with her ear and tried to examine his throat. To me it seemed she could do nothing and was doing nothing. He needed a proper doctor.

'What's to be done?' I almost shouted at her.

'He's got croup but it's not severe,' Allie said, 'I'll bring down the fever and there's a bottle can be made up. Jimmy, will you go to the apothecary in the camp?'

'Give me a note,' Jimmy said.

'He'll be all right,' Allie said to me gently.

'Easy for you to say when he isn't your child,' my panic turned to fury, 'I've seen what coughing and the croup does to children . . .'

'Then you've seen them get well. I won't let him die, Sarah.' Allie signalled to Ellen Neary to bring James's bed out, into the open. 'I'll take good care of him. You must trust me.'

'I should never have left him . . . this was brought on by my leaving him.'

'This has nothing to do with you going to the races, Sarah,' Allie said with a hard look, 'this is an illness. Not a curse. It can and will be cured. He needs ipecacuanha syrup . . .' She paused. 'And he may need a doctor.'

'One of the camp doctors will come,' Jimmy said. 'I'll raise one of them. I'll go to the apothecary too.'

'Go to the apothecary first and come straight back with the syrup mixture I'm going to write down for you. Ask someone else, Alexander if you can get him, to raise a doctor.'

While Allie wrote out for Jimmy what she wanted him to get I crawled into the nest and found a piece of paper wrapping. I smoothed it as best I could and wrote Daniel Casey's address and a message.

As Jimmy left I walked with him to the edge of the village. When we were out of Allie's hearing I told him to telegraph the message to the address on the page. He said he would do it. He would have exploded a cannon gun if I'd asked him just then.

Daniel Casey, if he was still at the Dorset Street address, would come instantly, I was sure of that. He would come for my baby's sake and he would come to see Allie.

I prayed it wasn't too late for James.

CHAPTER TWENTY-NINE

Allie

James lay against me gasping for breath.

I'd stripped him naked and was sponging him all over with a cloth dipped in water. The wrens kept replacing the water with colder, fresher pots. His small stomach staved in with every intake, the rasp in his throat got coarser.

'It's definitely not pneumonia?' Sarah said. She got the words out slowly.

'No,' I assured her.

'It's not typhus either, is it?'

'It's not typhus. You know I'm right, Sarah. You know that it's the croup.' I was finding it hard to be patient, though I understood her feverish agitation. I would have been much better able to look after James without her pacing up and down in front of us. 'It'll take its course,' I said when she knelt and took the sponge from me and began wiping him. He went into another bout of hoarsely croaking coughs. 'You know that too.'

She nodded. 'I do, I do. I can hear the sound of the croup in his coughing. I just want to be sure. I've never seen anyone get better from pneumonia or typhus and I've seen people with both diseases look the way James does . . .'

Jimmy Vance had been gone more than an hour and a half. The syrup I'd asked him to get could be made up in minutes so the delay was probably in finding the apothecary.

But even allowing for this he was taking a long time. He must

359

have gone looking for a doctor instead of, as I'd asked him, coming straight back with the syrup. I swore at him, and at all men, for the way they were never able to believe a woman right.

'We'll take him inside,' I said when the night began to cool. 'I'll go in first and light candles and make a corner ready for him.'

When I'd done this Sarah brought James into the nest after me. Beezy, in her wisdom, had moved the fire away so that I was able to make a bed for him close to the door. This ensured him relatively clean air as well as shelter. Beezy had made sweet tea too, cupfuls of which she kept pressing on myself and Sarah. She was taking whiskey herself and, in between times, walking out to the road to see if Jimmy Vance was coming.

The curses she rained on his head weren't silent like my own.

Sarah, saying it was the softest thing she had, put the shawl I'd brought her from Paris under James. For a while after that he seemed less tortured. It didn't last, of course, and he began to gasp and writhe again, jerking as if he would break in two.

'It's destroying him.' Sarah's eyes followed every wrenching movement. 'It's tearing his body apart.'

'The syrup will make him well.' I prayed it would and that I was right about his croup not being the most severe kind. If I was wrong, and if the illness was gone too far, an airway would have to be created to allow him breathe. To do this an opening would have to be made into the trachea from the front of his neck. I couldn't do that for him. Only a trained doctor could.

Jimmy Vance came at last, running like a dervish, and he brought the syrup. 'No doctor,' he was terse handing it over, 'two of them that serve in the camp aren't back from the races yet and the third says he can't leave the barrack hospital before morning.'

'Did you speak to Alexander Ainslie?' I said.

'I sent a soldier with a message to look for him.' Jimmy went on his knees at the nest opening. Inside his son continued to rasp and wheeze, his mother to make endless soft, soothing sounds.

I checked the ipecacuanha syrup before moving Jimmy Vance out of my way and going inside with the bottle. I poured some on to a spoon and while Sarah held James still as she was able I eased what I could into his mouth and down his throat. He resisted the strange taste and feel of it but I kept at it until I'd got enough into him to do what it was supposed to do.

There was nothing could be done then but wait, and watch.

It didn't take long. In less than a minute James was consumed with a coughing so bad that he began to vomit. When he expelled what looked like a piece of muslin I let go the breath I was holding.

'Oh, God. Oh Holy Mother of God, what's that? What's he brought up?' Sarah gathered James to her, held him as he went on coughing, but less horribly, more like the tired exhaustion of someone clearing their throat.

'He'll be all right now,' I said.

'Why will he be all right? What's happened?' She rocked James. There were tears on her cheeks.

'He's got rid of the membrane in his throat,' I said, 'he'll be able to breathe more easily now. He'll sleep after a while.'

James did sleep, thought not as soon as I'd hoped. He cried, weakly, and gave occasional dry coughs as Sarah paced up and down with him outside the nest. But at last, grumbling and sighing like an old man, he slept. Jimmy Vance went back to the camp then, prepared for the worst and a punishment for not being with his regiment in time for the last post.

I burrowed deeper into the nest and slept myself.

When I heard my name being called I groaned, full of sleepy protest. It was dark. It wasn't morning. There was no need to waken or get up. Then through the folds of sleep I remembered James and sat up.

'What is it, Sarah?' I said, 'is he all right?'

She sighed and didn't answer. James slept, peacefully as his mother, in the crook of her arm. The voice calling my name was Beezy Ryan's and she was outside the nest.

I crawled to the opening.

'Visitor to see you,' Beezy said as my head appeared, 'I found him on the road when I was stretching my legs.' Walking off the whiskey more like. Drinking made Beezy restless.

Alexander Ainslie, in full uniform and with his hat on his head, helped me to my feet as I came out of the nest. 'I came to see how the child is. If needs be,' he nodded at the horse he'd tethered to a bush, 'I can ride back for a doctor.' He went on holding my arm, even after I was standing. I was in my petticoat and my arms were bare. My hair was loose to my shoulders. I had no shoes on my feet.

'You've caught me unawares,' I said.

'Your neighbour tells me the child is recovered?' He still held my arm.

'Beezy shares the nest with us, usually, and she's right. James is much better. He'll be himself again in a day or two.' I pulled my arm, sharply, and he let it go. 'It was good of you to come,' I said.

'I brought this,' he said with an apologetic shrug and held up a bottle of brandy. He looked defenceless, something I'd never seen in him before. I took the bottle.

'Thank you,' I smiled, 'I'll use it for purely medicinal reasons.'

'If there's anything else . . .'

'There's nothing, thank you. James will be fine now.'

'How are you?'

'Tired, but that's easily remedied.' How I was, really, was acutely aware of my petticoat, of my bare arms and chest and general state of *déshabillé*. 'I'd best get back to my bed.' I held the bottle against my chest. There was no way of covering the bared rest of me. 'Thank you again for coming, Alexander.'

'I'm sorry I didn't know earlier about the child.' He stepped back, stiffly. He looked at the nest, at the opening I'd come through. 'How can you sleep in there?'

His tone, and his face, were full of an uncomprehending wonder. He'd never come close enough to truly understand how the village was before; now he was right inside it and all the questions he'd asked me were being answered at once. I laughed, but softly so as not to waken Sarah and James.

'You'd be surprised where a person can sleep when they're tired,' I said, 'and when they're—'

'You don't have to sleep here, Allie.' His tone was modulated again, nonchalant in the way it usually was. 'You know that I can arrange a room for you in the country home of friends. It's a good-sized house. You'd be left alone. You could call on your companions here as often as you wished.'

'I was also going to say, Alex, that a person can sleep well when she's among friends. You mean well but I'd prefer to stay with Sarah and James until things are settled with Jimmy Vance. You know that.' I stopped. 'I'm comfortable enough here, for the moment. I'm using my time well.'

Both of these points were true. But I was worried too, and growing more so by the day. The winter was approaching and the weather showing signs of changing. Sarah and Jimmy Vance would have to settle on a marriage date very quickly. Beezy was restless and muttering more and more about America. The comforts of a country house, and daily visits to the village, would have suited me well, but only if Sarah and James could come with me and that was not what I was being offered.

In any event, Alexander Ainslie's idea of 'good-sized' meant the house was most likely a mansion. His friends would patronise me and he himself, though he'd been monk-like in his correctness so far, would expect more than polite conversations from me in such a situation.

'I'd like you to think about it, nevertheless.' He gazed over the furze bush roofs, 'and perhaps tell me tomorrow if you've changed your mind.'

'I won't do that, Alex,' I said, 'and I'll say good night now. Thank you again for coming.'

He reached out and lifted a length of my hair. For one, very gentle, minute he held it between his fingers. He let it fall back on to my shoulders then, and smiled. 'Until tomorrow,' he said.

I watched and listened until he'd ridden out of sight.

He was a good man and I felt reasonably safe with him. He was also full of pride and would never force himself on a woman who didn't want him. He was a creature of the light to Ned Mulvey's monster of the dark.

I wasn't altogether surprised at him coming to the village, even though he'd never expressed a wish to do so and I'd seen no point exposing him to jibes and coarse humour. Or in exposing the wrens to his scrutiny. But things had begun to change between us a week before and his visit seemed a natural enough extension.

'I would marry you if it weren't that I would be destroyed socially,' he'd said to me on an afternoon about six days before.

I laughed. 'I'm flattered. But there are others reasons why you'll never marry me, Captain Ainslie. In the first place your fiancée in England would not have it.' I paused, put my head to one side and considered him carefully. 'In the second place, I would not marry you.'

'Not even if I told you that I believe myself to be in love with you?'

'Love!' I was scornful. 'I have only to look around the wren village to see the effects of love.'

'What you see in the village are the effects of lust and loneliness and romantic delusion.'

'And your feelings are, of course, much superior?'

'Obviously,' he said, 'or I would succumb to them.'

We were in the sitting room of the hut which was his quarters. I'd walked there from the village, alone and without telling Sarah or Beezy or any others of the wrens where I was going. Even to have told Sarah where I was going would have opened a flood of questions I didn't have answers to.

I knew that I'd been observed coming into the camp though, and that those who'd seen me go into Alexander's hut suspected I was behaving as all wrens were believed to behave.

'Perhaps you would like to be my mistress instead?' He seemed half serious.

'Since I don't want to be a wife why would I want to be a mistress?'

'A mistress has freedom. She's not shackled to a husband and conventions in the way a wife is—'

'I've been offered the role of mistress before,' I cut him short, 'and it appealed to me no more then than it does now.'

'Pity,' he unfolded himself from his chair, 'because it's all I can offer you.'

'I don't know why you feel the need to offer me anything,' I said.

'Because I don't want to lose you.'

'You don't possess me so you can't lose me.'

'But we're friends, are we not?'

'We have a friendship, yes. But it's one which you're half ashamed of . . .' I shrugged, 'and you don't respect my aspirations for my life.'

'You're hard on me, Allie.' He rubbed the scar to the side of his eye, which was what he always did when he became agitated. It was the only indication he ever gave of inner turmoil.

'Just honest,' I said. 'I don't disregard your life plans, your ambition to be finished with the army and rearing cattle on your family lands.'

'My life's plan is a conventional one,' he said, 'and easy to accept. Yours, to be a lady doctor, begs both admiration and scepticism.'

'In what sort of measures?'

'Equal, I would think.' He came to where I was standing by the desk, a copy of the work of Charles Darwin in my hand. He quickly and lightly brushed his lips across my forehead. 'On the other hand,' he walked back to the table and lifted his hat, 'you're quite likely to do anything you decide to do.'

'Thank you for that,' I said.

For a minute, as we looked at each other across the room, the gulf between us was sad and deep and neither of us knew how to bridge it.

It was Alexander who ended it by saying, 'I'll walk with you to the road to the wren village.'

On the way through the camp I brought up the subject of Charles Darwin. I didn't want to part with an awkwardness between us and it was always easy to get him talking about topics of the day.

'He supports his ideas with huge evidence,' I said about his conclusions that man had evolved from lower animals. We'd read *On the Origin of Species* in the convent in Paris – mainly because we were told not to by the nuns. It made sense to me, for the most part.

'I think Darwin is right,' he said. 'But I also believe that man will eventually destroy himself and everything else which lives on this planet.'

'How can you possibly believe that?' I laughed and wished I hadn't. He was looking very serious.

'Because man is so immensely certain of his superiority,' he said.

'Indeed he is,' I said, 'but woman is not and so there is hope still for the world.'

'You may be right.' He smiled and the tension between us lifted.

I'd made sure not to be alone with him, or to encourage intimate conversation, since then.

James was crotchety and pale next day. But he wasn't sick.

'You're better than any doctor,' Sarah said to me, 'I want you to know that I believe that, no matter what happens.'

'I'm coming to believe it myself.' I grinned at her and reached for James. She gave him to me reluctantly and I held him for a minute only before giving him back to her. 'A few years in medical school and I'll be as good as the best of them,' I said. I didn't ask her what it was she expected to happen. If I had, and if she'd told me, it would have prepared me. But it wouldn't have changed anything.

I was sitting in that afternoon's sun, reading, when I head the sounds of a horsecar pulling up on the road. The shorter days meant the sun cooled earlier and earlier. James was beside me in the small crib his father had brought for him; soon it would be too cold and too dark for either of us to sit outside. Sarah had gone for a short walk with his father.

I looked up from my book and saw Daniel Casey standing in the road as the horsecar drove away.

I saw the village as he must have: peaceful at that time of day, a primitive situation in which a community of women tried hard to preserve decency. Some wrens were washing clothes and others adding furze to the roofs of their nests. A group stood talking, children ran about. Everyone, of course, wore only petticoats and most, like myself, had draped a second petticoat or underskirt over their shoulders against the chill.

I hoped that Daniel saw the village for what it was and not as I'd seen it myself, the first day. What I'd seen, and so had Sarah, was a series of low, furze-covered hovels into which those who lived had to crawl, animal-like. I hoped he wouldn't see the wrens simply as half-naked women with matted hair, the children as out-of-control wantons.

I stayed where I was as he came towards me. I couldn't have walked to meet him to save my life. It was unlikely I could even have stood steadily. I knew at once that Sarah had sent for him, that she hadn't trusted me to make James well. I didn't blame her; I wasn't a mother, as she'd pointed out. I wasn't even a qualified doctor.

But I was hurt, nevertheless.

Daniel looked much the same but was somehow more of a man than when I'd last seen him. He carried himself with more assurance and looked older. Working in the dispensary would do those things to you; dealing with poverty and sickness was aging and left no time for self-consciousness. He was wearing a tweed suit with a dark waistcoat and his hair, which had always been short, was longer and unruly over his forehead. He carried his doctor's bag.

'I'll have a look at the child, Allie.' His manners hadn't improved. He said not a word of greeting before putting down his bag and crouching beside the crib.

'Of course.' I lifted the covering. 'You'll find he's recovering well.'

He picked James up and gestured that I should spread the covering on the grass. He laid James there and began to examine him, listening to his chest and back with a stethoscope and testing his temperature and looking at his throat. James protested, loudly and healthily.

When he'd finished I put the child back in the crib and rocked it with my foot. 'Sarah sent for you?' I said.

'She telegraphed me. You've looked after him well. He's a fine baby.'

He put his instruments back into his bag; he still hadn't looked at me directly. I thought this was because of my state of undress but saw that it was more than this when he turned and stared at me and said, 'You're well yourself?'

He was awkward and embarrassed and it was all he could do to get the words out. He'd always been like that, I saw now, only I'd been too preoccupied with myself to notice. Or care.

'I'm very well.' I smiled to put him at his ease. 'The simple, country life suits me.'

'You've been here since leaving Dublin?' He looked around him.

'It's not so bad as it seems,' I said gently. A gust of sudden, sharp wind lifted the cover from James's cot. 'It's less smelly than Dublin and the sun has shone almost every day.' I secured the cover around James.

'The sunshine's coming to an end.' He looked skywards. I didn't follow his gaze to the clouds I knew were gathering there. 'The winter's coming in.' He paused. 'Come back with me to Dublin, Allie. This is no place for you.'

'I'll make us some tea,' I said, 'by the time it's ready Sarah will be back to share it with us. She'll be getting married soon.'

'What will you do then?' He knew me well.

'I'll go back to Dublin.'

It didn't seem the time to add that I would be moving on from there. America, since my first, vague thoughts about going to that continent, was becoming more and more a definite plan in my head. There were medical schools there, with women students; I hadn't forgotten how discouraging Daniel had been of my plans to study medicine.

I filled a pot with water and put it on the fire. We talked

about the dispensary and Dr Connolly and about Daniel's mother, who'd been ill but was better. Daniel had spent a month in Galway, looking after her and his younger sisters. He would always be caring for someone, it seemed to me.

'You were good to come to see James,' I said.

'I came to see you too. Her telegraph said you were here.'

'How long will you stay?'

'Until you come back with me to Dublin. I've taken a room in Kildare town.'

'Then you could be waiting a while. It's not at all certain when Sarah will be married. What about your work at the dispensary?'

'I've made arrangements.' He paused. 'Have you no gown to put on, Allie? It's getting cold.'

I flushed. The more I became aware of my hot cheeks and neck the more they burned. I lifted my dress from the furze and slipped it on over my petticoat.

'Am I more respectable now?' I said.

'I hope you're warmer,' he said.

I moved James in his crib into the nest and got the cups and made the tea. Sarah and Jimmy Vance returned just as it was ready and we sat drinking, the four of us, and talking, pleasantly but of nothing much. After a while Beezy appeared from Nance Reilly's nest. She sobered very quickly when she saw Daniel; he looked just as shocked to see her.

'Your face has healed well,' he said.

'It was a good doctor treated me.' Beezy watched him closely as she spoke.

'The word is that you've gone to America,' Daniel smiled, 'they say you're making your fortune there, running a big house in New York City.'

'Will you be telling them any different when you go back?' Beezy didn't take her eyes off his face.

'There'll be no need for me to mention your name to anyone,' Daniel said.

'There's no one looking for me, then?'

'There's no one looking for you, Beezy.'

Beezy stayed silent for a while. Then, very slowly, she said, 'What they're saying will be the truth soon enough then. I'll be gone to America . . .' She looked at Sarah. 'before the winter.'

It was the first time she'd mentioned her plan, either to me or to Sarah, since coming to the Curragh. I saw relief, and a smile, cross Sarah's face.

Jimmy Vance left for the camp, saying he would send a horsecar to take Daniel to his lodgings in Kildare. The dusk was deepening but Daniel said he would like to take a walk with me anyway, while waiting for the horsecar.

I knew he wanted to talk.

I told him everything that had happened, or almost. I didn't tell him about Alexander Ainslie. He wouldn't have approved or understood and, in any event, it would have been making too much of a small thing.

The dark closing around us made it easy to talk about everything else. It was better not seeing Daniel's face; it was as if he were a priest and we were in the confessional. And like a good priest too Daniel said nothing, holding his counsel while I was speaking and for several minutes afterwards.

When he did at last speak his voice was low and cold. He clenched and unclenched his hands in a fury beside me. 'Mulvey should be hung from a rope until dead. Unfortunately, it's unlikely that will happen. The swine is in London.'

'You know him?' I was surprised.

'I called to your father's house three times, looking for you. Mulvey was there on two occasions.' He paused. 'Later I heard the talk about him and your mother, then that he'd left for London. I thought you'd gone to be away from the scandal about town . . .' He paused. 'I'd no idea Mulvey had—'

'It's in the past,' I cut him short, 'and I've put it behind me. How is my father?'

'Well enough.'

'He's drinking?'

'He is.'

We left it at that and walked silently if not, on my part, peacefully, for a while. My guilt about my father was huge but assuaged a little by the certainty that his drinking was because of my mother. If I'd stayed on living in the Haddington Road house things wouldn't have been any different.

I was worried too about my reception when I went back. In just a little more than three weeks I would be twenty-one. Hopefully, Sarah would be married or have set a date by then and I would be free to go to Dublin and see my father. I still believed we would come to an arrangement about my birthright, and future independence.

I'd said nothing to Sarah about any of this because I didn't want to increase the pressure she felt about setting a marriage date. My and Beezy's futures depended on her nuptials; neither of us would leave her unmarried and unsettled in Kildare. She knew this; it was the reality we all lived with.

I was thinking how much I liked and admired Daniel and how safe I felt, by his side in the dark of the Curragh, when he said, in the caustic way he sometimes had, 'Do you intend pursuing your studies to become a doctor on the Curragh?'

'I've been thinking about going abroad.' I was short. I don't like being laughed at.

'It won't be easy, wherever you go, and you're not helping your cause by staying here,' he said.

'Not easy? It will not be impossible then? Have things changed so much since we last spoke?'

'Yes. I'm prepared to help you gain admittance now. I wasn't then.'

'Why?' His honesty would be his undoing. And yet it was one of the things I admired most about Daniel Casey. 'Why are you prepared to help me now?'

'Because of what has happened to you, because I don't want you to go on living here. It's primeval. It's unhealthy. It's . . . dangerous.'

I didn't ask him why he wouldn't help me before. I didn't want to be told it was because he cared for me and had wanted to protect me from the adversities I was bound to experience as a woman in medicine.

Soon after that we saw the horsecar coming from the camp and went back to the village. Daniel, before he left, said he would be at the village at ten next morning to check on James.

'And to check on you, too,' said Sarah as he drove away. 'Have you told him about Alexander Ainslie?'

'You're the one asked him here. Maybe you should be the one to tell him.' By way of a softener for my curtness I added, 'there's nothing to tell, in any event.'

'You know that's not true,' said Sarah.

CHAPTER THIRTY

Allie

By noon the next day I knew that it was not Daniel who would have to be told about Alexander Ainslie. Alexander would have to be told about Daniel.

By that time Daniel had asked me to marry him.

'I'll make you a good husband,' he said, 'and we'd be compatible in many ways. I could help you with your medical studies.'

Everything he said was true. He was a good man and a kind one. We had interests in common. And he could definitely help with my studies.

'I don't want to marry,' I said.

'Married life couldn't be any worse than the one you're living at the moment,' Daniel said, 'it would get you away from here.'

'I don't need to marry to leave the Curragh.'

'I know that.' He paused. 'The truth is that I'm fond of you, Allie. Very fond of you.' He sighed. 'I love you.'

'I know that,' I said.

I'd known the day before, when we were walking on the Curragh and he'd fulminated about taking Ned Mulvey's life. Such wildly irrational talk from an avowed rationalist had to have its root in something as fallible as love.

'Love is not rational,' I said, 'there's no reasonable test to prove it's—'

'Don't tease me, Allie. I may deserve it but don't do it

anyway.' He looked so miserable I put my hand over his on the table.

We were drinking tea in the Prince of Wales Hotel in Newbridge. It was a dreary place, all got up in brown velvet and dark green paint. But the tea was strong, in the way I'd grown to like it on the Curragh, and the scones were served with sweet blackberry jam.

Daniel, as he'd said he would, had arrived at ten o'clock that morning to check on James. Afterwards, when he'd asked me to come to Newbridge for a drive with him, I'd been glad to say yes. There were things medical I wanted to discuss with him.

I'd been enjoying myself until he brought up the subject of marriage. Now I was uneasy. I took my hand away and reached for another scone.

'I've become a bit of a rationalist myself,' I said. 'It comes from observing love and its effects on the people around me. Take Sarah. Her judgement's gone completely. She thinks this world will become a heaven when she marries Jimmy Vance when in fact she'll be sharing space in the camp with English women of the lowest and loudest sort.'

'I didn't think you were a one for superior airs, Allie,' He raised his eyebrows.

'Neither am I,' I snapped, 'but the wrens are an aristocracy compared to some of the wives I've met in the camp. They live cheek by jowl in the married quarters with their children so I suppose their tempers are stretched.'

'What brings you to the camp?'

It was an innocent question, prompted by simple curiosity. Daniel Casey didn't have a devious bone in his body. I discovered I had a fairly lively set myself.

'There's a market there two days a week,' I said, 'and I've been there with Sarah, when she went looking for Jimmy Vance.'

All true. The lie was in what I omitted; I'd no intention of telling Daniel about Alexander Ainslie. He would be hurt and he would be confused and there was no need for him to be either.

Alexander was merely a casual friend; there was nothing to tell Daniel about him.

But Alexander would have to know about Daniel. I would have to explain to him that my time would be taken up from now on and that I couldn't any longer meet him for walks, or even for tea in his quarters. I'd no worries about ending my friendship with him. Daniel was a friend to whom I owed loyalty and his intentions towards me were entirely honourable. Alexander's were not. I was a diversion, as far as he was concerned, a distraction in an army posting he found boring. He liked me, I knew, and his vanity would be pricked by my going. But he would move on, spend more time with his friends in their big houses, forget me quickly.

'Maybe you'll let me come with you to the market next time?' Daniel took a scone himself. 'I'd be curious to see the inside of the camp and how it operates.'

'Maybe I will,' I said.

We munched on our respective scones and I tried to make sense of what was happening.

Daniel would not go away, and I didn't want him to. There was a reassurance in having him about. I'd have preferred him not to talk about marriage but knew that he was as stubborn as he was pragmatic and would pursue the idea to a conclusion.

I hadn't said I would marry him and might never say I would marry him. Then again I might.

I certainly wasn't as appalled by the idea as I would have been five months before.

'Do you care for me at all, Allie?' Daniel asked the question lightly, apologetically almost.

'Of course I do,' I said.

I smiled at his earnest face and dabbed some blackberry jam from the side of his mouth and thought about the ways in which I cared for in him. I respected him, certainly, more than any man I knew – though I didn't know very many to measure him against. I was certainly glad to see him again. And I'd missed him, and our talks about the dire injustices in life and medicine.

'I missed you,' I said.

'Why didn't you write to me then?'

'Because I didn't want you to come here,' I said, 'I didn't want you telling my parents where I was. I wanted to stay away from Dublin.'

All true. But it was also true that I hadn't missed him *enough*. I'd been preoccupied and occupied and feeling freer than I'd ever felt in my life before. And, if I was honest, Alexander Ainslie had been another reason. Had been.

'I won't force you back to Dublin any sooner than you're ready,' Daniel said, 'but I'll be coming to the village every day. We'll get to know one another here, in the countryside, in a different way. You'll see that I'm indispensable to your life.' He had a dreamy look about him.

A swift, hard apprehension gusted through me. My father, in love with my mother, had pursued her and offered her marriage as an escape from her circumstances. My mother had accepted and never grown to care for him.

I put the thought away, and finished the last of the tea, and remarked airily to Daniel that I'd like to see his lodgings in Kildare. 'The day is only half over and it'll be a pleasant drive back that way,' I said.

The weather was changing and the air sharp. We trotted sedately past roadside trees on which the leaves were beginning to turn. The light too, had lost most of the luminous quality it had displayed in high summer.

Daniel's room was in a two-storey house on the road into the town, his landlady a round, busy woman who was most impressed to have a doctor for a lodger. 'They say it's better to have a doctor than a priest in the house,' she thrilled, 'though I hope we'll never have to call on your services, Dr Casey.'

'I hope so too, Mrs O'Neill. I'd like you to meet a friend of mine, Miss Buckley. I'm hoping that she'll be a visitor here, from time to time.'

'We've no parlour suitable for receiving.' Mrs O'Neill's gaze, when it fixed itself on me, had lost a lot of its welcome. 'But you being a doctor I'm sure it's all right for your friend to visit you in your room for short spells. In the daylight, of course.' Why Mrs O'Neill thought doctors could be trusted in rooms alone with young women, even in daylight, I'll never know. In Daniel's case however her judgement was sound.

It was clear she didn't know I was a wren. She would soon enough. Her delight in her doctor lodger would wane, if not vanish, when she discovered his 'friend' lived among the wanton harlots of the Curragh. But it was unlikely she would ask him to leave, given his profession.

I said nothing of this to Daniel. Better to take each day as it came.

His room had one window and it looked out over the edges of the Curragh. It had yellow walls and a small, white-painted fireplace filled with turf. There was a narrow, cast-iron bedstead, an easy chair, a desk-table and pitcher with jug.

I stood looking out the window. 'Sarah was intimidated by the size and greenness of the plains when she first saw them,' I said, 'but I thought it liberating. That's what I think of now when I look out over the expanse of it. I think of freedom.'

'You haven't seen it in winter,' Daniel the countryman said, 'with raw gales and rain blowing over it.'

For a brief, hot moment I felt furious at him. He was right, of course, but that wasn't the point; I'd wanted him to feel with me the abandon of the plains and he hadn't. I wondered if he would ever fly with me, ever leave the ground. And if it mattered.

I turned back to the room, facing him. 'I'm aware that I haven't seen it in winter,' I said, stiffly.

'That was small-minded of me,' he said, 'I'm just stupidly jealous of all that you've had here that I've had no part in.'

I liked him all over again. Daniel always had the capacity to surprise me. And himself, I sometimes thought.

'Stay here with me, Allie, don't go back to the wren village.' He made the invitation sound as if he were offering to make tea.

'I can't do that, Daniel, and you know it,' I said crossly.

He sighed and said nothing and pulled out recent copies of

The Lancet which he'd brought for me to read. We sat at the table and went through them, disagreeing about an article on the health hazards of tobacco. I held, with the article, that the dangers were the same whether tobacco was taken in by smoking or chewing or sniffing it in snuff. Daniel held that smoking was the most potent danger because of tar and carbon monoxide formation. We exhausted our combined knowledge and still couldn't agree.

I stayed the best part of an hour and then said I must be going. It was early evening and he would have come with me but I told him no, I would take the horsecar back to the wren village alone. He had letters to write, his absence to explain, and was easily persuaded.

He went to the window and searched the street for a horsecar. 'I'll come to the village in the morning.'

I lied then, outright. 'Don't do that, Daniel,' I was firm, 'the water wagon came today so tomorrow Sarah and I do our washing.'

'The afternoon then.' He turned, agreeable and unsuspecting. 'I'll come at four o'clock.'

There was no reasonable or convincing way of putting him off. I would have to visit the camp and Alexander Ainslie and be back in the village by that time, or a little later.

'Five o'clock,' I said.

Daniel nodded, smiling. 'I'll bring food. We'll have supper together, you, me, Sarah and Beezy Ryan. A reunion.' He looked eager, pleased with his idea.

'We'll have supper.' Agreeing, I crossed my fingers. Deceit did not suit me. My mouth felt dry, my stomach hollow.

'You're pale.' Daniel, frowning, came and stood beside me. 'Staying out there is madness, Allie. Mrs O'Neill might have another room . . .'

'No,' I was sharp, 'in the first place she would find out soon enough that I'm a wren and then we'd both be without a place to stay. In the second it will not be much longer until Sarah marries. I'm not going to desert her.'

I could have added a third – that he hadn't the money to be paying for rooms for both of us – and a fourth about my own lack of money.

Alexander Ainslie was a fifth reason. He deserved to be told before I moved into rooms with another man.

'You'd better go then before it gets any darker.' Daniel took my hands into one of his own and studied them, separating the fingers, stroking each one as he did so. He looked very serious and very young, his red hair almost into his eyes and his thin face, in the gloom, not so ordinary at all.

'Is everything in anatomical order?' I joked to quash a sudden rush of tenderness. He was, still, so very much, a boy trying to be a man.

'Beautifully so,' Daniel answered without looking up, 'despite the rough work you've put these small fingers to . . .'

'I must put them to more work this evening.' I jerked my hands and he let them go at once.

'I'm sorry,' he said stiffly, 'I didn't mean to frighten you, or to offend.'

'You didn't,' I touched his cheek, 'it's just that I'm no better than you are at . . .' I stopped.

'At what, Allie?'

'At courtship, I suppose.'

'Are we courting then?'

'We might be.'

'May I kiss you then?'

'You may.'

We kissed twice. The first kiss was timid, a feathery, hesitant, brushing of lips against lips, an exploration of possibilities.

The second kiss was a kiss. It even started off differently, with an insistence in the way our mouths came together, a turbulence in the moulding then clinging together of our bodies. I closed my eyes and allowed myself to feel, only to feel, not to think or see or even hear. Daniel's hands were in my hair and on my back, holding me hard against him. His mouth forced my lips to open and I felt his teeth, then his tongue against my own. I felt myself melting, losing all control of my responses which were urgent as his were, demanding more of these feelings, more of this pleasure.

Then other feelings reasserted themselves. A shiver of fear, a tremor of caution. I came to my senses.

'No, Daniel, we can't . . .' I pulled away and he let me go, but almost at once reached for me again. This time he held me against him gently, with all the careful tenderness I'd seen loving parents bestow on their children.

'We *will* be together, Allie,' he vowed into my hair.

Even then I didn't, couldn't, reassure him in the way he wanted.

'I'm glad you came to the Curragh,' I said and took him by the hand, quickly, out of that room and its intimacy.

I walked to the camp to see Alexander early next morning; I'd no arrangement made to see him that day, nor indeed for two days following, so had to hope against hope that he would be free to see me. Arriving, unannounced, to meet him in the camp was something I hadn't done before; I didn't stop to think how wise it was to do it now.

Sarah had watched, in silence, as I dressed and fixed my hair.

'You're going to meet your captain, aren't you?' she said.

'He's not *my* captain.'

'Did you tell Daniel Casey about him?'

'It won't be necessary to tell Daniel anything after this meeting.'

'Why are you taking such care then, if it's to be a goodbye?'

'Because it *is* a goodbye,' I said.

It started to rain when I was more than halfway to the camp. It fell lightly at first, no more than a shower really. But then the drops became bigger and a sudden wind blew up and the drops began to beat down in fast and faster torrents. There was nothing to do but go on; the camp was nearer than the village and there was no shelter in either direction.

I was wet through and through by the time I arrived. The rain kept most people indoors but the few soldiers who were out and about in the deluge ignored me as they rushed past in their oiled capes. No one offered me cape or cover of any kind. To be so wet I'd need to have walked a good distance; they probably knew where I'd come from.

But the rain was a blessing too. Its suddenness, and ferocity, had sent most soldiers to their quarters; Alexander was in his hut and opened the door in seconds to my knocking.

'Allie! What in God's name . . .' He reached for me and pulled me inside and kicked the door shut with his foot without letting go of my arm. 'What's wrong? What's happened?'

'Do you have a towel? Something I could use to dry my hair?'

I stood in the middle of the familiar room until he brought a towel, and with it a heavy, dark blue wool overcoat.

'You'd better put on something dry,' he nodded to the screen, 'and tell me what's happened while you do so.' He was frowning. I began to dry my face and hair.

'I won't be staying long,' I said, 'there'll be no need for me to change my clothes.'

'As you please.' He watched me closely. He was still frowning.

I gave him back the towel and stood in front of the small, log-burning fire. I knew I must look like a half-drowned cat and hated to present such a sorry spectacle for our last meeting. I was cold too and clenched my teeth to stop convulsive shivers as I held my hands open to the fire.

'A friend has arrived from Dublin,' I said, 'he came to see to Sarah's baby, James. He's a doctor . . .' I gave him a quick look but he'd turned away and was standing with his back to me, studying a map of the Curragh pinned to the wall. I willed him to turn, even a little, so I could see his scar. The scar, which was prone to involuntary tics and shudders, would tell me how he was taking my news. He went on studying the map. 'He's a very good doctor. He works in the dispensary I spoke to you about.' I paused. Alexander's silence was louder than ever.

'He was of enormous help to me.' I hardened my voice when I went on. I'd nothing to apologise for. I'd in no way deceived

Alexander Ainslie, had never pretended an affection I didn't feel. 'He's proposed marriage to me. I came to tell you that our walks and meetings will have to end.'

'Have you accepted him?'

'No.'

'Then why do we have to stop meeting?' He turned as he said this. The scar was giving a very small flutter.

'Because he would not understand that we can be friends and not lovers.' It was the simplest way I could put things. 'He would be hurt.'

'His hurt matters more than our friendship?'

'It does.'

'Do you love him?'

'I care for him. He's a good man.'

'Ah . . .' he raised his eyebrows. 'The good man! Such a creature will always win the lady's affections.' The scar was quite lively now, its mood angry. 'What's this good man's name?'

'He's called Daniel Casey.' I paused, then added for want of something to say, 'He's from Galway.'

'I don't care, Allie, if he was born on the islands of the Pacific Ocean. He's taken you from me and it's my own fault. I should have had more courage.' He shrugged and smiled, his anger evaporating as quickly as it had blown up. Then he sighed. 'I'll always regret you, Allie. But I wish you happiness.'

'I wish the same for you, Alexander.'

I was so cold I'd stopped shivering by the time he helped me into a horsecar. The rain had stopped but he insisted anyway that I wrap myself in his greatcoat. I did so to please him but it didn't help much. The cold and wet had gone through to my bones.

When I was seated Alexander gave a curt, sharp order to the driver to go safely. Then he tipped me a brief salute and walked quickly away. This time I didn't turn once as we drove out of the camp.

CHAPTER THIRTY-ONE

Allie

———◄∞∞►———

The wren village, in my absence, had become a different place.

The rain, and more especially the wind, had torn it apart. Nests had collapsed in on themselves, others had been blown sideways or had furze lifted to make huge gaping holes in roofs.

There were no bright dresses on bushes, no children playing, no chatting groups of women. Robbed of colour and sun the place looked wretched and so desolate I wanted to turn and run.

I walked into the village slowly. The ground around and between the nests was thick with mud. Wrens, slipping and cursing and mud-splattered, struggled everywhere with the job of rebuilding them.

'We weren't prepared. It came too sudden.' Ellen Neary didn't stop gathering furze as I came up to her. 'Usually we'll see a storm like that coming and tie down the nests, do what we can.' She stood still long enough to look me up and down. 'You're a sorry sight,' she said.

She didn't look so good herself. 'I wasn't prepared for a storm either,' I told her.

Our nest hadn't been so badly hit as some of the others. Beezy claimed credit for this, saying it was because she'd had the foresight to tie the first layer of furze when we were building. She may well have been right. Between us we made it dry and secure as we could again. But nest number eleven was not as it had been before. Nothing was.

More than the structures of the village had changed; the mood had too. With this sudden, vicious ending of the long drawn-out summer the harshness of winter had arrived before anyone was ready for it. The wrens, salvaging what they could of dignity and their homes, were poor, pathetic creatures, shrunken and older and grim-faced.

And this was only the beginning; it would be impossible from now on to keep clean, to be dry and warm. There would be no way of avoiding disease if it struck — because to stay healthy in conditions so dank and foul and poverty-stricken would be impossible.

Daniel Casey arrived in the very late afternoon with food, enough for a banquet compared to the meagre rations we'd been allowing ourselves for weeks past. He brought Limerick ham, currants and raisins, fresh soda bread, cheese, milk, lemonade and a flask of old French brandy. He'd gone to every shop in the town and asked his landlady to bake him the bread.

'Doctoring is a powerful profession,' Beezy said drily, 'it'll get you anything and anywhere.'

'Almost true,' Daniel agreed, 'providing you don't run foul of the enemy within and of politics.'

'The enemy within?' I pricked up my ears.

'The watchful and controlling in the ranks of physicians,' Daniel half smiled, a habit when he had something serious to say, 'they're what put the brakes on the activities of such as myself.' He paused, looking about the nest for something on which to place the ham. 'And will on you too, once you make your move to enter their ranks.'

'I'll deal with them,' I said and thought I could, then. Considering all that had happened, and the way we were now living, anything else seemed to me child's play.

'I won't stay here any longer with James,' Sarah announced.

There was no need to ask why. The nest smelled bad. The not unpleasant headiness of freshly cut furze had disappeared and the walls, in drying out, were giving out all sorts of odours.

Though it was only five o'clock it was so dark we needed three candles to have enough light to eat by.

'It's a death trap,' Sarah went on, 'I'd be putting James in the way of every disease known to man if I stayed on here. Jimmy agrees. I'll be moving out in a matter of days.' She looked me in the face, then looked at Beezy too. 'There'll be no reason for either of you to stay on after that.' She leaned forward, her face all shadowy hollows in the candlelight. 'It's my fault we're still here. My fault entirely.'

We'd all come for our own reasons so I ignored this last. On the other hand, I wasn't at all sure Jimmy Vance was prepared for Sarah to move so suddenly. I said as much.

'Will you marry within the week so?' I asked.

'It'll be arranged, don't you worry.' She was short, taking a breath before adding, even more shortly, 'Whether or which.'

Jimmy hadn't visited in a week. He'd been confined to barracks and given extra sentry duty after being caught slipping into the camp after curfew time. This hadn't so much to do with his crime as with an army fear that Fenians were infiltrating the ranks and a great deal of resulting high security. There were fewer soldiers in the camp too, since many had been sent off to reinforce numbers in barracks around the country against what an army notice called 'the ferocious and irregular warfare practised by the Fenians'. The camp, as a result, had become fortress-like.

In the circumstances, I couldn't for the life of me see how Jimmy Vance could have set about arranging his and Sarah's wedding.

'What do you mean, whether or which?' I watched her carefully; so did Daniel. Beezy, pouring for herself from the old French brandy, kept her eyes fixed on the liquid.

'You know what I mean or you wouldn't be asking.' Sarah looked stubborn. James, behind her in his corner, made a small sound and she turned to him, gentling him with her hand.

'I want you to tell me what you're planning,' I said.

'She's going to marry without leave,' Beezy took a long slug from the cup, 'without getting the army's permission. That's the case, isn't it, Sarah?'

Sarah kept her hand on James and her head averted. 'That's what I'm going to do,' she agreed, 'there's many have done it before me. James should have his father's name.'

'But the army won't house you if you do that.' I said this in as neutral a voice as I could manage. Sarah, even in these extremes, wouldn't take being told what to do. 'You'll have no choice but to take lodgings in Kildare or Newbridge.' With a will of its own my voice went up an octave. 'I wouldn't give you much chance of happiness in either place.'

I could have added that I didn't hold out much hope either for James's well-being and reminded her too that she wouldn't see a lot of his father. But she knew these things already.

'The army will find a place for us soon enough once we're married.'

'The army will leave you to rot and you know it.' Beezy poured brandy for Daniel. She offered none to either myself or Sarah. 'You've waited this long so you might as well wait the extra few weeks for your soldier to sort things.'

'I've the name of a priest that I'm going to talk to tomorrow,' Sarah said. 'We'll be married on the Saturday after Jimmy's finished his punishment.'

'I've to go to Kildare myself tomorrow,' Beezy was brisk, 'I've a bit of business to attend to. I'll come with you to see the priest.'

'I don't want you to come to the priest with me, Beezy.'

'Afraid he won't marry you if he sees the sort of company you keep?'

'Yes,' Sarah said.

'Well, I'm of a mind to test the Christianity and charity of this man of God you've been told about,' Beezy snorted. 'So I'll come with you.'

'You can put your trip off till the next day, Beezy,' Sarah said, 'and leave me to get on with my business tomorrow.'

'I've done a lot for you, Sarah, but I won't put off my trip,' said Beezy.

'I'll go the next day so,' Sarah said.

It rained again in the night, after Daniel had gone; I listened to it falling steadily on the furze and marvelled at how none of it got inside. I thought of Daniel, caught in the open carriage he'd hired to collect him, and hoped the carman provided oils for cover. I didn't want to think of him catching a chill on account of me. I didn't want to think of anything bad happening to Daniel Casey.

I thought about him a lot before I fell asleep. I thought about the way he'd held my hand as we walked out on to the plains after supper, how easy it had been talking to him. We spoke of things which mattered to us: the dispensary, his mother and sisters in Galway, my concern for my father, a little of Sarah.

We said nothing at all about ourselves, not a word about the growing feelings between us. They mattered too much to even whisper about.

I promised him I would to go to Kildare with Beezy next day and that I would call at his lodgings before midday.

The rhythm of the falling rain lulled me into a state of reverie, to thinking lazily about how it never rained but it poured and how the dead it rained upon were blessed. As if this wasn't enough a piece from the Bible, about rains descending and floods coming, popped into my head. It was from Luke, if I remembered rightly, and finished with how 'the winds blew, and beat upon that house; and it fell: and great was the fall of it.'

I cursed my memory for woeful things and curled myself smaller. I was almost asleep when Beezy began to snore and James to cry. But the rain, at least, had stopped.

I was already awake when a grey dawn inched its way slowly through the covering we'd hung at the door.

Beezy's tale of business in the town had been just that – a tale. 'It was all I could think of to stop Sarah seeing the priest,' she said as we crossed the Curragh next day. 'It's hard but she'll have to wait for her soldier to arrange for things to be official.' She hitched her skirts higher and walked faster, finishing the bottle of brandy that morning had given her a great burst of energy.

Crossing the plains was, in any event, a lot easier than walking in the streets of Kildare. 'There'll be nothing but ruinous poverty ahead of Sarah if she marries without leave,' she went on, 'that's if her soldier marries her at all.'

I had to make a fast trot to keep up with her. 'Why do you say that?'

I only asked because I'd my own, and growing, doubts about Jimmy Vance and wanted to hear Beezy's. Maybe she knew something I didn't; in any event she knew men better than I did.

'He's torn in two, that's why,' Beezy said. 'He wants Sarah and he wants to be off adventuring across the world with the army. He can't do the two and knows it. It's my feeling the army will win him in the end.'

'He loves Sarah. And James . . .'

'He loves the army and its promises more.'

'What promises?'

'Promises of India. Of freedom. The smells of the Orient are in the air in the camp and filling his nostrils. The talk there is of men fighting for their Queen. If he goes he'll have the companionship of boys like himself, all of them growing into men together.' Beezy stopped as, panting, I fell behind. 'You'd no business putting on so many petticoats. Anyone would think you'd a fancy for Daniel Casey.'

'How do you know the army's promised him India?'

'How do you think I know?'

Beezy didn't expect an answer and I didn't give her one. I didn't pursue my own question either; I didn't want to be told when and how her soldier clients spoke with her.

'Sarah and James will take his freedom from him,' Beezy went on, 'and freedom's what our soldier boy's heart is set on. It's what every boy's heart is set on.'

'Sarah will make a man of him,' I said.

'You're right about that at least.' Beezy gave me a surprised look that was most insulting.

'I'm right about a lot of things . . .'

'Oh, be quiet,' Beezy gave a snort, 'my head's not up to your whining this morning. Just take it from me that Jimmy Vance has been promised India and is a torn man. He's honourable enough to want to do well by Sarah but he craves India. He thinks if he waits a solution will present itself. It won't.'

'What good will putting her off seeing the priest today do?'

'It'll give me a chance to talk to Daniel Casey, ask him to visit the camp and talk with Sarah's soldier.' She paused. 'It's better to know than not, in my experience, and maybe the doctor can help him decide his mind.'

'Daniel will agree to see him,' I said, 'but I'm not sure how much good it will do.'

'It'll flush his intentions into the open,' Beezy said.

We crossed the Curragh in silence after that.

The wind and rain had not improved Kildare town. Beezy and I were ankle-deep in mud within minutes of entering the place and had to cling to one another to stop ourselves from slipping and falling into the worst of it.

It was a good half-hour after midday, which was the time I'd told Daniel I would call, when Beezy stopped outside Cummins & Co. in Kildare's Main Street. 'I'll wait here while you go on to the doctor's lodgings.' Beezy squinted through the grimy glass of the window as she called after me, 'There's something I want to get inside.' She was going to buy whiskey. I knew it. 'It would be best if our good Daniel's landlady remained unaware of his connections locally.'

She waved me on, grinning, her eyes flashing green through the kohl painted around them. There was a lot of the old, outrageous Beezy Ryan in that grin and I will always remember it.

It was the last time I saw joy of any kind in her face.

'Get out of this town! Go, and go now or I'll help you on your way . . .'

The man bearing down upon her was a priest. He wore the cloth and he wore the collar but there was nothing priestly about his face. It was red and roaring and filled with an apoplectic rage. He was a big man too, more than six feet tall and broad. The horse he'd dismounted from stood several yards away and he was carrying a whip.

'My money's as good as another's.' Beezy, standing her ground, was cool. 'And if the shopkeeper feels I'm a threat to his soul he can refuse to serve me.'

'There's not a merchant in this town will take money earned in fornication and filth.' As he came closer to Beezy I moved closer to her myself. Passing townspeople stopped. 'But neither should temptation be put in their path. I'm here because of a report made to me about your parading through the town. I've a duty to rid the town of you and your kind. Out,' he held the whip between his hands, 'take yourself away from here back to the degenerates you came from.' The whip, of black, shining, leather, quivered.

'Come with me, Beezy,' I came up behind her, 'there's nothing to be gained—'

'I'm as entitled under God to have my say as this black-hearted divil is.' Beezy, shaking off my hand and staring into the priest's bulging eyes, was too brave by half. Either that or she was too foolish.

I would never have defied those eyes myself; they were half mad with hatred and rage. The other half was filled with a disbelief that he was being defied, and by a woman.

'God will not be mocked in these streets.' The priest spoke slowly, each word ringing out. 'And nor will He be denied.' He turned to the growing crowd. 'You see in this woman the devil come among you to do his work . . .'

'You're more of a divil than I'll ever be.' Beezy's folded arms held her scarlet shawl across her chest. The crowd, mostly men, took a breath.

Beezy's head was high and her back straight. With her hair piled high, washed in rainwater the day before and in shining coils on top of her head, she was almost as tall as the priest. The scar on her face twitched but she was magnificent anyway, brave beyond anything bestowed by the brandy.

'I've met your kind before,' Beezy went on, 'I've had them in my own bed and seen them panting around the girls who worked for me. The single difference between your kind and other men is that your kind are the greater liars. Ye're even the greater hypocrites . . .'

The priest lunged. With a huge hand he grabbed most of Beezy's hair, twisting and pulling at it until he threw her to her knees where she screamed at him in the name of God to stop. Holding hard on to her hair he brought the whip down across her shoulders. When the shawl fell away he stopped long enough to tear away the dress too. Then he grabbed her hair again and resumed his work with the whip on her bared flesh.

It all happened with a speed that froze my heart and stopped me where I was.

'Foul harlot,' the priest was hoarse and gasping, 'you will not defile these streets again.' He danced on his toes, the whip came down faster and faster. 'Whore . . . you will take God's punishment for your moral depravity.' He was a great and frenzied black crow, with a fiery head and frothing beak. He was wheezing now too; nothing stopped him. 'You will be cast out. *I* will cast you out . . . whore . . . whore . . .' Beezy's blood spurted on to his prancing boots.

'In the name of God let me be.' Beezy's cry, as she tried to catch the flailing whip, was thin and pleading; not at all like herself. Still the priest didn't stop. There was a low moan from the crowd but no one stepped forward.

I pitched myself at the priest and grasped at the arm with the whip. I held on when, with an oath, he would have shaken me off.

'You'll kill her,' I screamed.

He turned the whip on me then. My arm felt as if it had been sliced as the leather cut across it, two, then three times. I let go. I heard a cry in the distance that sounded like my name. I didn't look round. My arm was numb and I wanted to go to Beezy.

She had begun to stagger to her feet, but the priest wasn't finished with her yet. As she dropped her hands to the ground and attempted to push herself upright he grabbed her hair again.

Pulling on it cruelly he cast aside the whip and produced a pair of scissors from his pocket.

'God will be served.' There was a ferocious calm about him as he knelt in the mud in front of Beezy. And a righteousness. He brandished the scissors. 'I have come prepared to do God's work. You must know His punishment for the shameless,' the scissors cut through Beezy's hair, 'how He would want the wanton to be chastened . . .'

I was afraid to throw myself at him again, to even draw his attention on me. I didn't know what else he might do to Beezy with the scissors if I provoked him.

Beezy's hair, in all its glorious redness and curl, he threw into the mud of the street behind him. It landed at the feet of some of the men in the crowd. They didn't look down.

He stood then and looked at Beezy. She was a pitiful, shorn bundle at his feet. Almost casually he picked up the whip and poked her. He still held the scissors in his other hand.

'You won't come back here,' he said, 'and you will have respect for the priests of the Church from now on.' He nudged her again with the toe of his boot. 'Get up out of there and be on your—'

I moved then; I couldn't stay still any longer. But I wasn't alone. Daniel Casey's arm went about my shoulder at the same time that he seized the scissors from the priest's hand and slipped them into his pocket.

'In God's name, man,' he said, 'what have you done?'

The suddenness of the movement and of Daniel's appearance confused the priest. But only for a moment. 'I have carried out God's work.' He drew himself up. 'He has been well served here today.' He looked around the swollen crowd. 'Get a cart to take her out of here.'

A small man separated himself from his fellow citizens and ran, sideways like a crab, down the street to where a common cart and horse stood tethered to a post. He untied the animal and began to lead it and the cart back towards us.

'You call this God's work?' Daniel said.

His fingers had found the cuts made by the whip in my frock.

He turned me gently and looked at the damage to the exposed skin. Then he turned me again so that I was facing him. He was white as a bed sheet, his eyes flint-cold. But he was very, very controlled and he had command.

The crowd shifted and gave a mutter or two but didn't interfere. The priest glared at them but was silent. I'd no doubt everyone knew Daniel was a doctor; this was a small town and Daniel's landlady would have been talking.

'You'll be all right,' he said to me, 'I'll look after you. Beezy too. I'll see to it that justice will be served,' he jerked his head in the direction of the priest, 'for what has happened here.'

Dropping to his knees beside Beezy he lifted her so that she half sat, half fell across him. With her head lolling on his shoulder he examined the torn flesh of her back, then her head for damage where the hair had been shorn. Beezy, while he did this, was utterly silent.

I gathered her hair from the mud and bundled it deep into my pocket.

'God's work?' Daniel asked the question quietly as he stood and lifted Beezy with him. I helped him support her as the cart trundled to a halt at the outskirts of the crowd.

'God is served in many ways, doctor,' the priest said over his shoulder as he headed for his horse, 'and we must each do what we are ordained to do. You, sir, must look to man's temporal body. I will tend to his soul.'

'You call the merciless beating of women looking after the soul?' Daniel's voice, in the dreadful silence, carried after the priest. 'You think a Christ who preached love and forgiveness would condone this?' He held up a hand red with Beezy's blood. 'It's you and your kind who are damned, not this unfortunate woman. You are no Christian, sir, and should look to your own soul, if you have one, and beg your God's forgiveness.'

The priest, who had reached his horse, stood with his back to Daniel, listening. He put a foot into a stirrup and spun himself elegantly into the saddle before turning the animal and staring coldly down at Daniel.

'She defied me and she is a whore,' he stated as he jabbed the whip in Beezy's direction, 'it's for the good of all that I was able to cut short her visit to the town. Let today be a lesson to the vultures she lives with on the Curragh, a warning to them to stay out of the streets of Kildare.' He pointed the whip at me. 'Keep your own whore out of this town too, doctor. None are welcome.'

'You will burn in hell.' Daniel's quiet ferocity shook even the priest. 'But before that happens I'll see you're dealt with by whatever justice there is in this world.'

I helped him lift Beezy into the cart and we sat on on either side of her as it rattled out of town. The driver, who had refused to help with Beezy, said nothing and drove fast. When I looked back before turning out of the street the crowd had broken up. Smaller groups of twos and threes looked after us and there was an air of gloom about them, as well there might have been, and maybe even a hint of remorse. Or I may be giving them credit for more humanity than existed in that miserable town.

'Slow down,' Daniel said as we bumped in and out of potholes, 'or, by God, I'll hold you responsible if this woman bleeds to death.'

We stopped at Daniel's lodgings for his medical bag and a blanket for Beezy. The landlady was unhappy about the blanket but Daniel assured her he would pay for it. This didn't greatly improve her humour but Daniel took choice, and the blanket, out of there with a sharp word to the driver.

He did what he could with Beezy's wounds while we moved along. Between us we made her as comfortable as possible. I held her while he dabbed my own gash with iodine.

'Thank you,' I said and we sat without another word and watched the green of the Curragh pass on either side. It was easier than looking at Beezy, with her shorn head and blanched face. I wanted to take her lovely hair from my pocket and show it to her but couldn't.

'I didn't think you believed in hell's fire? Or in God?' I said when the silence became unbearable.

'There are times . . .' Daniel didn't finish and I didn't press him; there are times too when explanations are a waste of that time.

It started to rain as we came up to the village. The driver refused to wait for Daniel, who paid him and told him to get to hell back where he came from. Nance Reilly said Sarah and James could have Lizzie Early's bed for the night, so leaving room in nest number eleven for Daniel and me to lay Beezy Ryan on her stomach in her own bed while we bathed her back with borax in warm water. When we were sure it was thoroughly clean I tore strips from a petticoat and soaked them in salt water. We laid the cloths carefully over the wounds.

'They'll need to be replaced every few hours until healing begins,' Daniel said as he prepared and gave Beezy laudanum.

The cut to my own back was nothing much. My dress had been torn and the skin beneath broken but the result was no more than a deepish scratch. Daniel bathed it with the borax in water and covered it with another strip of soaked petticoat. It would cure within days and never give me any trouble.

Though Beezy's beating was a bad one she seemed more affected by the loss of her hair.

'Give me a drink, for God's sake,' were her first words when she broke her silence.

Her first action was to cover her head with her hands.

'I should never have left my house that night,' she said as tears coursed down her face. I had never seen, or thought to see, Beezy Ryan weep. 'It was the most foolish thing I've ever done in my life and I'll pay the price forever, and wherever I go. There would have been no fire and Mary Adams and Lizzie Early would be alive still if I hadn't fled . . .' She stared sightlessly, rocking back and forth where she sat. 'The priest is right. What happened today is God's judgement.'

'Your hair will grow again, Beezy,' I said, 'I've ribbons and a scarf that'll make something of it while it's short.'

'You can keep your ribbons and scarf,' Beezy said, but not

unkindly, 'it's of no interest to me whether it grows back or not. I won't be needing long hair where I'm going.'

Daniel Casey and I stayed the night with her. We held hands for most of the time and we talked, very low, about a great many things. We kissed, once, a short kiss but warm.

Beezy slept fitfully and didn't speak again.

CHAPTER THIRTY-TWO

Allie

Beezy refused to get well; what happened to her was as simple as that. The day after her whipping at the hands of Father Mangan (the wrens knew immediately who her torturer had been; it wasn't the first time Father Henry Mangan had used a pair of scissors on a wren), she objected to having her wounds dressed afresh.

Daniel would have none of it. With the help of Clara Hyland and myself he held her down while he examined her back and put on clean cloths. She had surprising strength for a sick woman; her will had always been iron.

She found a way of imposing that will on the situation. She asked Nance Reilly to bring her whiskey from the camp. Nance, as well as being Beezy's friend, was the longest living in the village and had ways and means of doing and getting things. She brought Beezy the whiskey. Three bottles of it. She said there would be as much available as Beezy wanted.

I knew then that Beezy had money hidden somewhere and was paying her.

By the end of the second day after her beating Beezy was drunk and obstreperous and absolutely refusing to allow the wounds to be treated.

'Your back will turn septic,' Daniel warned, 'your blood could become poisoned. You're endangering your life.'

'Endangering my life, am I?' Beezy, sitting propped against

the inside wall of Nance Reilly's nest, into which she'd insisted on moving, was mocking. She tried and failed to focus on Daniel's face. 'It could be, Dr Casey, that I'm not all that fond of my life, or of life itself, any more. Or it could be that I know full well you're wasting your time and that *my* time on earth's running out anyway.' She shifted and winced and said, quietly, 'I'm not going to get better from this. I know that I'm not. You might as well stop wasting your time and what's left to me of my time.' She made a dismissive gesture with an almost empty bottle. 'Get out of here and leave me be. I didn't ask for your help.'

Beezy had decided to die.

I knew this because she wouldn't move from Nance Reilly's nest and, after one long talk with Sarah, turned away even from her when she came with James to sit and watch over her. She wouldn't even greet James, whom she'd loved and cherished since the day he was born.

Sarah was distraught. 'We can't let her do this to herself.' She held and shook me when I crawled from Nance Reilly's nest after another attempt to look at Beezy's wounds. 'She's in pain, Allie. It's in her eyes, not even the drink can kill it. She's sick and she's sore and she's full of a noxious portent about her death.'

'All true,' I said, 'and it's the last that's making it impossible to cure her. She talked with you so tell me – why is she so sure she's going to die?'

'I couldn't make much sense of it. Her mother died when she was twenty-eight years old, the age Beezy is now. Beezy was three years old then and the nuns took her in and reared her until she was eighteen. They wanted her to stay on in the convent but she left them. She says now that the shearing of her hair is what would have happened to her if she'd become a postulant and that it's God's wrath on her. She chose another path and failed those in her care, Lizzie Early and Bernie and the rest of them. She's not right in her head, Allie. The Curragh's done it to her.'

Drink had a lot to do with it too but I didn't say this. There was no point in us fighting over it.

Beezy's wounds got worse. On the third day, when she fell

unconscious with drink, Daniel and myself were able to have a look at the swelling and terrible redness spreading out and beyond the weals. She was feverish too, and weak, and Daniel and I knew, as well as Beezy herself must have known, how quickly the horrors of poison and rot could follow. We did what we could but the next day it was worse. When I began to think that Beezy had a knowledge about her time on earth that the rest of us didn't I told myself the Curragh was getting to me too.

And on top of all this it rained for most of every day and all of the nights. The space between the nests and the common ground we all shared became mucky and oozing. The nests remained dry enough inside but we spent our time trying to dry out clothes. Tempers grew short under the relentlessly low and pouring grey sky.

'It was like this last winter.' Moll, sensing change in the air and terrified we were all going to leave her, was full of assurances, 'but it got dry again quickly. The village is built solid enough.'

'Of course it is.' I held her against me and kissed the top of her black curls. 'And you're right that it can't rain forever.'

'It does get cold though,' she admitted, looking worried.

'So why don't you add a layer to the furze of your nest? Better to do something than live in dread.'

But she went on looking worried. Like all of us she regretted the life of the summer falling apart. In her case though it opened up a void; she had no idea what would happen to herself and her mother in the months ahead.

I worried about Moll. I also worked hard at putting out of my mind the fact that I would have to leave her.

Daniel came every evening and stayed until early night. The rest of the time he campaigned for justice.

'That malignant cleric will go to court for what he did,' he'd sworn quietly during the night we sat with Beezy after the attack, 'I'll see to it myself. He'll never do to another woman what he did in that street today.'

'You've great faith in the system of justice,' I said.

'I don't know that I have. It's more that I believe the facts, being so horrendous, will win the case when presented.'

'You believe right will win the day then?'

He paused. 'In this instance, yes, I do.' He looked down at the fretful, silent Beezy. 'We have the evidence.'

'You'll be depending on witnesses. I wouldn't rely too much on any of those citizens who were there coming forward.'

'Given the law of averages there's bound to be some decent folk among them. In any event, you're a witness too.'

'I'm a wren. The court's not going to take my word for anything.'

'They'll be obliged to,' he was tight-lipped, 'in any event we have other evidence.' From his pocket he produced the scissors used to cut Beezy's hair. 'I've got these and you've got the hair itself.' He lightly touched my back where the whip had opened the skin. 'We'll see him punished,' he said.

'I hope you're right,' I said.

Since then, whenever he wasn't in the village, he was dividing his time between a lawyer and four people from the crowd he'd somehow found and persuaded to speak in court. The witnesses, two men and two women, needed encouraging and coaxing; the women said they'd been fearful of being whipped themselves if they'd stepped forward on the day. The lawyer, Tim Kilgallen, was from Naas and starting out in his career. He was decent, and opinionated; he also believed that a notorious case would do him no harm.

'One of the men has come forward because he has a grievance against the priest,' Daniel said, 'but we'll deal with that when the time comes. The other's a good man, truthful but timid.'

'And the priest?' I said, 'will he allow his parishioners to speak against him?'

We were walking along the road, a good twenty minutes away from the village. Since starting his campaign against the priest Daniel was finding it hard to hire horsecars and came to the village on foot. I'd taken to walking part of the way with him when he went back to Kildare each evening.

His landlady hadn't yet thrown him out, probably because he'd paid his rent to the end of the month.

'Mangan will make it hard for them to speak against him,' Daniel admitted. 'He's not liked but has great power and denounces people from the pulpit at a whim. His zeal against prostitutes is infamous.'

'Notorious, more like,' I said, 'Ellen Neary's told me stories . . .'

'All true, I'm sure.' Daniel didn't like to be interrupted; his own zeal for justice and the cause he'd taken up had him taut as a cat ready to spring. 'She'll probably have told you that a few years ago he got help from the army to burn down shelters a group of women had built against Newbridge barracks wall?'

'She told me that,' I said impatiently. I didn't like being cut short myself. 'She told me too that he's already shorn the hair of four wrens and from at least two other women.'

'But did she tell you about Mangan's earlier court appearance?' Daniel caught my arm and turned me to face him. His passion for what he saw as his cause was so boyish that I hadn't the heart to continue being annoyed at him.

'No . . .' I shook my head and he moved us on, talking and walking quickly.

'Mangan was taken to court by the soldier husband of a woman he chastised and struck. It happened late one night in a street in Newbridge and the priest claimed he mistook her for a prostitute. The Petty Sessions fined him a pound and costs. It caused a great scandal at the time and Mangan's been more cautious with his whip and scissors since. Until he met Beezy, that is. She was more than he could tolerate and the long restraint boiled over.' He put an arm round my shoulder and slowed us down. 'He's sick in the head, not rational.'

'He doesn't have to be rational,' I said, 'he's a man of God.'

Ellen Neary thought Daniel mad. 'He'll be lucky if he's not attacked in the street worse than Beezy was,' she said as she helped me make Beezy comfortable later that night. 'I hear he's been spat at more than once. He didn't tell you that, did he?'

'No. He didn't.'

'There's plenty in that town share the priest's hatred of wrens. Your doctor is a stranger, not one of themselves. That alone is enough to provoke them. You can be sure too that the priest is whipping them up.' She paused, remembering. 'Not that they need encouraging, the Cornelius Cumminses and others of them.'

She pulled a brush gently through Beezy's short hair. It had settled into a halo around her head. When I'd told her this earlier she'd smiled. If it hadn't been for the pain etched into it her face, with the short curls framing it, would have been girlish-looking. As it was she was flushed, almost unconscious from drink and looking about sixty years old.

'Your doctor had better keep an eye to his back.' Ellen, as we turned Beezy on to her side, was doleful. 'He'd be well advised to stay out of the streets of Kildare after dark.'

The pus I'd dreaded had begun to fester in the weals on Beezy's back. Though she'd become increasingly feeble about resisting the cleaning and dressing of her wounds, nothing seemed to halt the worsening infection. The swelling had spread and filled with pus well beyond the marks of the whip. There was a smell too, like rotting meat. These effects, known as corruption by physicians, meant Beezy's blood was poisoned. There was nothing I could do for her. It was up to Daniel now, and a miracle.

Sarah sat with Beezy through that night. It tore at her heart, seeing Beezy the way she was, but Sarah couldn't seem to keep away from her. She was rarely absent from Beezy's side and would sit talking to her for hours. Beezy's replies, whenever I stopped to listen, were either monosyllabic or a matter of two or three words. Sarah's talk was mostly of Henrietta Street and the streets around it, about people they both knew and tales of their lives.

She was homesick and she was sick with worry about Beezy. She was worried too about Jimmy Vance who would be free of his punishment and able to see her at the end of the week.

Daniel arrived early, and on foot, the next morning.

He drew off as much of the pus as possible and spread fresh gauze and boracic ointment over Beezy's back.

'If I was a praying man . . .' He shrugged.

'The women are praying,' I said, 'some of them.'

'Tell them to pray harder,' Daniel said.

He didn't tell me about the threats. I might never have found out about them if it hadn't been for Clara Hyland arriving at our nest as Sarah made tea for the three of us. Frost had replaced the rain and the grass underfoot was a crunchy white where the sun hadn't yet caught it.

'There's a lot of talk going around about your war with the priest.' She was bleary-eyed and white-faced. She'd been on the hunt the night before and would usually have been in bed at that hour.

'Good,' said Daniel, 'we need all the support we can get.'

'They're not behind you in that town. They're against you and you know it,' Clara narrowed her eyes at him, 'and the talk is about harming you and getting rid of you. Sending you back where you came from in a box was how two brave lads out sporting in the night put it.'

'Talk is cheap,' Daniel said.

'There's more than talk going on, by all accounts,' Clara said.

'Tell me,' I commanded when Daniel, with a dismissive wave of his hand, would have changed the subject.

'There was a poster nailed to the door of our hero's lodgings.' Clara rubbed her nose with the back of her hand and sniffed. 'It warned him to go back to Dublin if he didn't want to be buried in Kildare. It said the diseased birds on the Curragh would suffer along with him if he didn't go.' She shrugged. 'It's one thing to risk himself. It's something else entirely when he puts all of us here in danger. We've enough to contend with.'

'I'm with him.' Sarah looked from Clara to Daniel and then at the wrens gathering round. 'There's a time when a stand has to be made to have a wrong put right. Beezy would agree, if she was in her right mind.'

'In her right or in her wrong mind Beezy Ryan wouldn't want anyone hurt on her account,' Clara said, and this was true.

But Beezy was ill, maybe dying, and not in her right mind. There was no point Daniel dying too.

'You must delay things,' I said, 'we'll be leaving here soon enough, in a week or two perhaps. You can fight Mangan from Dublin. You'll be safer there.'

'It's too late for that. If we back away now we've lost,' said Daniel, 'I've Kilgallen prepared and the witnesses are firm. It's to be heard in the next sitting of the Petty Sessions.'

It was too late for a lot of things.

The night was cold and starry when Daniel arrived back in the village that night. He'd gone to Newbridge, to call on the lawyer Kilgallen, and come back to find his bags on the doorstep of his lodgings. Mrs O'Neill, in a state of hysterics behind the door, would neither open it to him nor listen to what he had to say.

'She'd had a visit from some of the town's stalwarts,' Daniel said as he sat on the bag containing his belongings and held his hands to the fire. 'Emissaries from Father Mangan, from the sound of it. She said she couldn't risk her children and her home by having me go on staying there.' He was apologetic and smiling. But he didn't seem to me all that worried. 'I'll be fine here by the fire for the night. I'll keep the blaze going and it'll be cheerful enough.'

'You won't be saying that by three or four in the morning.' Sarah was impatient. 'You'd best squeeze yourself into Beezy's old corner.' She grinned. 'James and myself will be chaperones to Allie for the night.'

'I'll have a look at Beezy first.' Daniel took his medical bag and left.

I waited for him, walking in a circle around the nest; he wasn't gone long. There was nothing to be done but keep putting the soaked cloths on Beezy's wounds. He didn't say how she was. He didn't need to.

'I gave her some laudanum,' was all he told me as he crawled after me into the nest and made himself comfortable as he could where Beezy used lie.

Having him there didn't seem in any way strange. We were all of us behaving as if life had been suspended and we were in a time of waiting – for Sarah to marry, for Beezy, by some miracle, to get well, for the court case against Father Mangan to be over. When all these things happened life would become normal and we would begin living again.

In the meantime, and in the circumstances, Daniel sleeping between us in the nest seemed neither strange nor improper.

The righteous and the good of Kildare town didn't think so. They arrived for him at two in the morning, when the village was asleep. A wind had come up and the moon and stars had been obscured by heavy rain clouds. The rabble came across the Curragh with blazing torches, about a dozen of them. We heard them coming and were out of the nest long before they came crashing and roaring into the village. So was Daniel, in spite of pleadings and warnings on the part of myself and Sarah. The mob bellowed its way past the first few nests and stopped not far from Clara Hyland's. I thanked God for our place at the far end of the village, and the fact that we weren't revealed by the torchlight.

'Give us the renegade doctor and we'll be out of here,' Cornelius Cummins, who appeared to be their spokesman, demanded, 'we know ye're hiding him. There's nowhere else would give shelter to his kind.'

'Save yourselves,' said a fat man with no teeth, 'we'll have no choice but to burn him out if ye don't hand him over.'

They were a vision from hell. Between them they were holding high a half-dozen torches, great orange-red fires that lit up the sky and showed us the enemy we faced. They'd worn their heavy boots, hobnailed most of them, for their trip across the plains. Some carried sticks. There were no women but every age of man was represented, from a boy of about sixteen years to a looming, white-whiskered fellow of seventy or so. From the leery, wild expressions on their faces it was clear every last one of them had drink taken; my guess was that their breaths alone would have kept the torches burning.

All of the wrens were out of their nests now, all of the children with pale, frightened faces holding their mothers' petticoat skirts. The smaller ones cried. The women themselves looked no less terrified, some of the younger ones clinging together and whimpering.

'You're a brave lot of men.' Daniel moved forward quickly into the light. There was nothing I could have done to stop him. 'It takes courage to come into a community of women with sticks and burning torches. You could have spoken to me, any one of you or all of you, in the streets of Kildare in daylight.'

'Daylight and civility's too good for the likes of you.' The fat man shook a stick and moved several steps closer to Daniel. 'And by God we'll do with you what should have been done with you the first day ever you came to Kildare town.'

'And what might that be?' I heard my own voice before I knew I'd spoken. 'Would you have taken a scissors and whip to him as your—'

'Stay out of this, Allie,' Daniel, turning his head, was furious. He waved at me to get back. 'Stay with Sarah and the baby. The police will take care of this when we get to Kildare.' He faced the mob again. 'I'm ready to go with you. There's no need for you to terrorise these women.'

'Women!' A voice from the mob spat the word and guffawed. 'These are not women. The harlots you live among aren't fit to walk the same earth, let alone inhabit the same parish, as decent women. There's no place for them in Kildare. They should be driven off the plains. They've made a disgrace and laughing stock of the county.'

This speech was greeted with a harsh chorus of agreement and a clashing of sticks in the air.

'You filthy coward!' Daniel's voice was loud with a cold fury. 'It's not enough that you come in the night! You have to hide yourself too in the belly of your fellow spineless curs to hurl abuse. Come out of there and face these women with your insults.' He took a step forward. 'Come out or I'll pull you out myself.'

'It's your own skin you should be worrying about.' Cornelius Cummins held a silencing hand over his followers. 'It's you is the cause of us being here. You'd better come with us now and take your punishment.'

'Punishment for what?' Daniel walked towards him.

'The whore was dealt with no worse than she deserved,' Cummins was shouting, 'you've no business questioning the just chastisement of a priest of the church.'

'You'll be dealt with yourself now . . .'

'Our priest will stand in no court.'

'You were warned . . .'

The men surged forward and the women screamed. I ran to Daniel and clutched at his arm but he turned on me, white-faced and and full of that cold fury. 'Get away from me, Allie,' he said, 'this is my battle and I don't want you near me.'

'It's my battle too.' I hung on to him.

'They're drunk and they're mindless and you're a fool if you think they'll have regard for your womanhood. Get away from me.' He pulled his arm violently from my grasp.

The mob were all around us. I could feel the heat from their torches and their rank, whiskey breaths and stinking body odours. There was an animal howl from them as hard hands took hold of my shoulders and threw me to the side, many feet away from Daniel and the sticks battering down upon him.

I screamed. Still screaming I got to my feet. Standing, I saw Clara Hyland and Nancy Reilly throw themselves at the mob of men, begin tearing at their backs and necks and arms, anywhere they could lay hold of.

A man, more sober than the rest and so less anaesthetised, snarled in pain and rage as Clara drew her nails down the side of his face. She scratched him again as he turned on her. That was when I saw Daniel again, on his feet and flailing with a blackthorn stick he'd somehow got hold of. He flailed in a circle about him with a desperation, and courage, fuelled by the need to survive that was more powerful and concentrated than the drunken viciousness around him.

'Get him! Any of yis, one of yis!' Cornelius Cummins stabbed the air with his torch. 'Don't let the devil have his way . . .'

'The devil is everywhere, within us and around us!' The white-whiskered man's shriek was demented. 'He's not just in the doctor. The bushwomen are sheltering him! He's here, in their hovels!'

Whirling and dancing like a lunatic, a stick in one hand and burning torch in the other, he made for the nearest nest which, as it happened, was Ellen Neary's. When he was still six feet away he lunged madly with the torch, travelling with the blazing weapon until it was embedded in the roof of the nest. The furze was ablaze in seconds.

Daniel broke loose from the shocked, and momentarily transfixed, mob. He reached the nest and began a frenzied beating of the flames.

'You'll not protect him, by God you'll not!' the whiskery man roared, all reason lost. 'You'll not protect Lucifer and you'll not protect the whores either. You'll burn with him!' Dancing and screaming he threw himself at Daniel. 'Into hell's fires with you!'

The first drops of rain began to fall as Daniel, turning too late, was caught on the side of the head by the madman's stick. He looked surprised. Then he toppled backwards and I couldn't see his face any more as the flames lapped about him and he collapsed with the roof into the inferno that had been Ellen Neary's nest.

CHAPTER THIRTY-THREE

Allie

Daniel looked as he always had when he was laid out in Naas Hospital; not broken, not mutilated or burned at all. He seemed younger to me, more like a boy than a man, with a boy's thin body and untidy red hair. His face wore its usual, thoughtful expression and his lips looked ready to speak. But they were cold and dead as he was and would never move again.

The pain was like a blade in my chest as I sat uselessly waiting, knowing that no matter how loudly now I told him I loved him, how often I said I was sorry to have been the cause of his death, he would never hear me. Ever.

I turned and stared at the window where the sun shone. He would have been pleased at how rational I was.

He would have been less pleased at the short time it lasted. Being rational didn't ease the searing pain in my chest, the numbing desolation in every other part of my body. Being rational didn't make any less bearable the fact that the one, the only good man I'd ever known was gone from me – and from a world that had needed him and that he'd wanted so much to make better.

And what, in the end, had his good life amounted to? The filth and poverty and disease he'd worked so hard to alleviate would go on. And how was it that Daniel was dead when men like Cornelius Cummins and Maurice McDermott were still alive? I would have choked on bitterness if I hadn't been so forlorn and aching, aching for him to move and touch me, for a smile to lighten his still, cold face. I wanted to weep but couldn't.

I turned again to look at him. I thought about gathering his beloved body against me until, by some miracle, the life that was mine might pass to him and he might breathe again. But I couldn't do this either so I touched his hands instead, where they'd been crossed on his chest by the hospital priest. The atheist in him would have hated the pose but *rigor mortis* had set in and there was nothing I could do about it. I would not break Daniel's bones.

I traced the outline of his mouth with my finger. I touched and tidied his hair back from his forehead. He'd have liked me to do such things when he was alive. I never had.

I closed my eyes, tightly, against the unbearable sight of him. In the shining black behind the lids I imagined him beside me, lying warm and alive, imagined the way we could have been if I hadn't been so blind and so arrogant for so long. I would pay, for the rest of my life, for that arrogance. But pain was a thing to be borne; I'd learned that much at least from the wrens. There was no good running from it. It had to be embraced.

I did then what I had to do for myself, if not for Daniel. I climbed into the bed and lay with him, my heart breaking. Holding him as I never had in life, I wept at last and told him all that I would always feel for him, whispering to him that he was my one and true love. Cradling his poor head, his hair wet with my tears, I lay with him for a long time.

No one disturbed us.

When I was at last able to let him go I stood again by the bed and rearranged his hair. The hospital doctor had told me about seeing a case like Daniel's before, where a man had been unmarked by a terrible fire. He said it meant Daniel had been unconscious going into the flames and had lain on the floor of the nest, breathing in smoke. He would have been suffocated within minutes, the doctor said, and suffered little. I knew he was right and that that was how it had happened. I knew it because Daniel had been pulled from *under* the nest, his face and hands blackened by smoke, the only burns to his back. Standing now by his bed I was able to give thanks for this, small, mercy.

His body had been so very still under the falling rain when they stretched him out on the grass. I'd shaken and shaken him but nothing I did could revive him. Cornelius Cummins had shaken him too and when he stopped I'd tried again, calling to Daniel to breathe, not to go from me. I only stopped when Clara Hyland lifted me bodily away from him.

'He's gone.' She held me against her while Moll took my hand. 'There's nothing you can do to bring him back. There's nothing anyone, doctor or priest, can do now.' She held me tighter. 'He was the best of men. May they burn in hell, those that murdered him.'

Some of the mob had sobered up when they saw Daniel go into the fire. Cornelius Cummins and two others had run with sticks and beaten at the flames while a fourth man, who'd disappeared into the dark immediately afterwards, pulled him by the feet from the burning nest. When the police and a doctor arrived an hour later it was because the fourth man had alerted them. But none of it had been enough to save Daniel.

I was waiting now by his bed for his mother to arrive from Galway. There could be no wake without her, and no funeral. I'd found her address in his medical bag and telegraphed her. It was a hard, cruel way to let her know of her son's death but there had been no alternative. The wrens, and even some townspeople from Kildare, had been and paid their respects to him but it was more than I could bear to leave him alone.

The hours went by without my noticing. The room was narrow and cold and I know that night passed into day and that night came again before a thin woman in black stood beside me. Hannah Casey put her hand over her dead son's eyes and said, without looking at me, 'I know who you are. My son wrote to me saying he'd come to Kildare because of you.'

I didn't correct her, tell her about him coming to the Curragh because of James too. She was right in that Daniel had stayed on because of me – and that was what had made all the difference. It made me responsible for his death.

I stood and gave Daniel's mother my seat and said nothing at all. After a while a nurse attendant brought a second chair and I sat opposite Mrs Casey, on the other side of Daniel. She didn't touch her son again.

When she took the shawl from about her head I saw a woman with a worn face and heavy, dark grey hair caught back in a bun. She looked nothing like Daniel so his looks must have come from his father. Her back was very straight and she stared without seeing at her dead son; she didn't weep either.

'He was . . . a good man.' It wasn't what I wanted to say.

'He was too good for you,' Daniel's mother said.

'He was,' I said.

'You were everything to him. I knew by the way he spoke of you. Because of you he's dead and you . . .' she looked at me out of bleak, cold eyes, 'are alive. There is no God.'

We didn't speak again. If her grief was impenetrable then so was mine. I had no way of escaping my pain so as to help her with hers.

Not that she wanted or would have allowed me to. Daniel's mother despised me. She'd come alone and was quick about arranging Daniel's funeral; he would be buried in Galway, beside his father and a dead sister and the generations of Caseys who'd gone before the three of them.

By the end of the day of her arrival in Kildare Hannah Casey had Daniel coffined. She had also booked for him to go first thing in the morning on the train with her to Dublin and from there to Galway.

While she was away doing all of this I stayed by Daniel's bed. He was much less like himself now, growing waxen and hollow-looking, his soul as well as his life departed. I wanted to lie alongside him again. I would close my eyes and, as long as I didn't touch his cold, stiff limbs or face, could pretend we were together at last in the way he'd wanted.

But I wasn't completely deranged with grief and knew I would have been thrown into the street if I attempted such a thing. Instead I sat and remembered every minute of every hour I'd spent with him since the first time I'd met him by Mary Ann's sick bed. I remembered our talks and our walks, in Dublin and on the Curragh. I remembered his quick hands and the way they healed patients in the dispensary and his quick tongue when he had something worth saying. I recalled his decency and kindness: to Mary Ann and Sarah, to James and to Beezy.

To me. There had never been a man so patient and under-standing of me. He was the only man I'd ever kissed.

Jimmy Vance came to pay his respects in the late afternoon.

'He came when my son was ill.' He stood with his hat in his hands. He looked tall and awkward in the narrow room, and very ill at ease. 'What I knew of him I liked.' He looked at Daniel for a long time. 'I knew about the threats. I should have looked out for him. I should have looked after Sarah and James better too.' He lifted his gaze to the iron barred window and stared at it. 'I don't want her staying with those women. It's dangerous and indecent. I want her to go back to Dublin. I'll follow her there as soon as I can.' He was very stiff. 'Will you persuade her that's the best thing?' He didn't look at me.

'Why is it the best thing?' I wasn't thinking straight. But I knew enough to know that what he was suggesting was odd, and wrong. 'I thought you were to be married?'

'We'll be married.' He looked at me at last and he was firm. 'Don't for a minute doubt that Sarah and I will be married. It's that I don't want her staying out on the Curragh, or even in one of the towns round about, until it's arranged.'

'You'd better tell her yourself.' I'd no energy left to deal with his and Sarah's predicament. I hadn't even the energy to care.

'I'll do that,' he said, 'but I'll need you to back me up.' He stopped. 'She'll listen to you.' The thought didn't seem to give him much pleasure.

'Go to her and talk to her now,' I said.

I was alone again with Daniel when his mother came back. It

was past eight o'clock and I'd somehow fallen asleep in the chair. A nurse attendant had earlier brought me some bread and sweet tea; I'd taken the tea.

'You can go now,' Daniel's mother said loudly enough to wake me up. 'They'll be here with the coffin in an hour. I'll sit the night with my son alone.'

My head reeled when I stood up. 'Please believe that I cared for him.'

I'm not sure why I wanted her to know this. Maybe some part of me wanted her to be assured that his fondness for me had been valued, and returned.

'It's of no interest to me whether you did or not.' In the light from the oil lamps her eyes were grey as a rain cloud; there were still no tears in them. 'From what he told me you led him a dance and now he's dead. Because of you.'

'He told you that? That I led him a dance?' I felt icily cold. To support myself I held on to the iron of the bedstead.

'He told me he'd met the woman he wanted to marry. The rest wasn't hard to make out. He wasn't wise to the ways of women like you. All he knew how to be was faithful and honest.' She sat with her eyes on her son's dead face. They were very bright now. 'He was too good for you,' she said for the second time. She sat so rigidly I thought she would keel over; she was exhausted.

'I'll get you some tea,' I said.

'I'll take nothing from you,' she said, 'and I don't want you or any of the women you live with to be at the railway station in the morning.'

There was no danger of the wrens seeing him off because they wouldn't know he was being taken on a train so early. The village was too far away, and it was in any event too late for me to get there now to let them know.

I sat on a bench in the hospital corridor. An hour had barely passed when two men went by with a pine coffin. I followed them and stood at the door of the narrow room while Daniel was coffined. His mother had dressed him in a clean suit of clothes and shirt and the coffin, inside, was plain. It was what he'd have wanted. The men left the coffin open and Hannah Casey put a candle at its head and knelt at its foot in prayer. The men left.

I went back to the bench in the corridor. Someone, in the night, threw a blanket over me and I slept for a while. The cold woke me at around five o'clock and with waking came the memory, like a blow to my stomach, that Daniel was dead.

The men came and nailed him into his coffin at six o'clock. When a horsecar began for the station with him and his mother I followed behind on foot. I didn't care about the indignity. I couldn't let him go. Halfway through the town Hannah Casey had the carman stop and allowed me to climb into the back of the car.

At the station, after Daniel had been put on the train, she turned to me. 'Take this,' she handed me his doctor's bag, 'there'll be no more doctors in my family.'

The train took a long time to disappear from view. When I couldn't see it any longer I could still hear it, hooting and whistling in the quiet morning as it went down the tracks.

When I told a carman at the station that an officer would pay him well at the other end he agreed to take me to the army camp.

CHAPTER THIRTY-FOUR

Allie

Alexander's manners were, as always, impeccable. He gave no indication that the hour, the state I was in or the carman demanding money were in any way an inconvenience. He got me a small glass of brandy and when he laid me in his bed to sleep it was still warm from his own body having been there.

I slept for three hours. When I woke Alexander was in the room, sitting in a chair by the bed, reading. I studied him for a few minutes. He was leaning forward with the book, which was about birds, holding it in both hands in front of him. He was dressed in trousers and shirt and hadn't shaved. I wondered if this was because he'd been afraid of waking me. His face looked kind, but unreadable.

'Thank you for taking me in,' I said.

'The pleasure's mine.' He put the book down, smiling. 'You'd no doubt like some tea?'

'Thank you,' I sat and swung my legs from the bed. 'The doctor friend I told you about is dead.'

'I heard.'

He went into the main room and was poking at the fire under the kettle when I came up behind him.

'You know then what happened in the village?'

'I do.' He nodded but didn't turn round.

'His mother has taken him back to Galway to be buried.'

'The best thing, in the circumstances.'

'Yes.'

The kettle began to hum and he rinsed the teapot and put in two spoons of tea. For a man he was very adept at domestic tasks.

'Another for the pot,' I said and he looked at me. 'An extra spoon of tea for the pot is supposed to be lucky,' I explained.

'As you wish.' He added another spoon.

We drank the tea in silence, sitting at the small table. He seemed disinclined to talk and I didn't know where to begin telling him the reason I'd come.

'Your friend was taking a priest of the Kildare parish to court,' Alexander said at last.

'You knew about that?'

'It was the talk of the camp. He'd a great many on his side but not many willing to stand and be counted. Not even Private Vance, who was worried about what the consequences might be for Sarah and his child.' He shrugged and went to the window and looked out. 'Your friend had courage.'

'He had conviction.'

'The courage of conviction then.' He continued to look out of the window. 'He should have taken you back to Dublin and left Kildare and everything in it to rot. In his place that's what I would have done.'

'Will you make love to me?' I said.

'Why?'

He turned. With the light from the window behind him it was impossible to see his expression. His voice was curious, nothing more.

'To make me better. To warm me. I'm so very cold.'

He came to me and held me against him. 'Cry if you want to, Allie,' he said.

But I couldn't have wept, even if I'd wanted to. All I wanted was to feel alive, to stop thinking about Daniel's surprised face as he fell into the burning nest, to empty my head of visions of his still, cold body and his lips that would never speak to me again.

'Love me.' I lifted my face to his and he kissed me.

It wasn't like Daniel's kiss and that was a good thing. It was bleak and hard but I didn't care. Bleak was how Alexander felt and the hardness was his safeguard. I understood how he was because now I knew how much I'd hurt him. I knew too that he wouldn't hurt me, ever. That was why I was there.

He lifted his head and looked at me. 'Will you be sorry, after?'

'Will you?'

'Never.' He ran a finger down the side of my face, 'I'll be glad, whatever your reasons . . .' He moved away from me, towards the bedroom. He didn't take my hand or try to touch me. I followed him and he shut the door behind me. We stood together just inside the door. Even then he didn't touch me.

'Do you still want me?' I took his hand and kissed the palm and held it to my face.

'I want you,' he was smiling, rueful, 'come . . .' He led me to the bed and I sat on its edge. He sat too and turned me by the shoulders to face him.

'You are confused and grief-stricken.' He shook me gently, as you would a child, 'these are not reasons to make love.'

'Why not? To be close to someone, a friend, is what I need. We're friends . . .'

'And now you want us to be lovers.' He was not so cool as he was pretending to be. I could feel a tremble in his hands and see the intensity in his eyes. It made me feel powerful. 'Making love will not take away the grief,' he said, 'you'll have to wait for time to do that.'

'Let time do it then. But this is what I want for this time, this moment. I will at least have crossed a barrier. I will be a woman. I will be different.'

'Maybe you'll be a woman,' he put his hands into my hair, 'but you will be no different. You may even be lonelier.'

I put my hands on either side of his head and covered his ears. 'No more talk,' I said as I closed my eyes and let out a slow breath, 'kiss me.'

This time, as he kissed me, he loosened my hair with one

hand and held me tight against him with the other. I felt his teeth against mine and stiffened. He took his mouth from mine.

'Don't be afraid,' he whispered, then began to open the buttons of my dress. As he went he laid his lips against my bared neck, moving his mouth lower with each opening until he was kissing my breasts. 'Such beauty.' He lifted his eyes and uncovered my breasts and shoulders and arms as he eased my dress to my waist. He held me close and now I was the one trembling; so hard I could feel my heart beating against his chest. Quite quickly he removed all of the rest of my clothes. Quite expertly too. I was glad of it. I liked his sureness. It compensated for my own lack of experience.

I lay with my eyes closed while he took off his own clothes. I didn't open them when he stretched himself beside me and when I felt his hands on my back and waist, pulling me into him.

'You knew I wouldn't resist you,' he half whispered, half groaned, into my ear, 'I've wanted you every time we met. You're so lovely, and so fragile.'

Dimly, I was aware that there was something I should say to him. All I could think to say was, 'I'm not fragile.'

I pressed my bared body against his, feeling his skin, surprised at its softness, at how warm his body felt. Softness and warmth weren't things I'd expected from a man's body. I felt his male part, hard against my stomach, and lower in my own stomach, at the very pit, felt a lurch, and then a long quivering.

His hands went about my waist and he turned me and laid me on my back. He was whispering, I couldn't hear what, into my ear again. He parted my legs and began to kiss me, putting his tongue into my mouth this time. His fingers between my legs were doing what his tongue was doing in my mouth, so gently insistent my initial trepidation turned quickly to a wild torment.

'Take me,' I said, 'take me now.' I wanted the act of love to happen. I wanted everything else in the world blotted out.

He came into me slowly and gently and I felt myself slipping away, losing myself in the feel of him. His breathing became faster and so did my own. I heard myself moan too, and whimper, and put my hands into his hair as he moved in and out of me, slowly at first and then faster, faster.

'Allie . . .' He said my name once before, in a frenzy of deep, final thrusts, he spent himself in me.

He didn't leave me at once and when he did at last roll away he put his arms about me and stroked my back and hair.

'Are you all right?' he said.

'I am.'

I wasn't and he knew it. Making love hadn't made me feel better. Just lonelier for Daniel and desolate that it wasn't him lying beside me.

'It's not your fault that he's dead,' Alexander said, 'he died because he was the sort of man he was.'

'He wouldn't have been there, in the street to see Beezy Ryan beaten, if it wasn't for me.'

'Another man would have walked on. He responded as he did because of the sort of man he was.' Alexander was insistent. 'He had courage, of a foolish kind, but courage nevertheless.'

I said nothing. I would never think Daniel foolish. He'd been brave and passionate and committed to justice and rights for all. That he'd fallen foul of man's savage inhumanity didn't make him foolish. His courage was what separated him from Alexander Ainslie.

'How did this happen?' I touched with a finger the scar above his eye. 'Is it a battle wound?'

'Nothing so interesting.' He smoothed the hair back from my forehead. 'I fell out of an apple tree as a boy.' He paused. 'My life's been a protected one, Allie, and privileged. I've known women, some respectable, some not. The woman I was to marry when I go home – well, I haven't the heart for it any longer.' He lay on his back, looking at the ceiling, holding me against his side. 'I could take you away from all of this, Allie. I could marry you.'

'You'd be found out,' I said, 'it would be said that you married a whore, a barbaric Irish woman who lived in the wild.'

'Not if I leave the army and we marry quietly in England.

You could change your name, begin all over again.' He propped himself on an elbow and looked down at me. 'What will you lose by leaving Ireland, Allie? What is there you want to stay for?'

The question was a good one and the answer dismal enough. I'd long ago lost my mother. My father might very well have given up on me by now too. My reputation was gone. My best and lifelong friend would soon be gone as well, married to her soldier and living God knows where.

And the man I'd loved too late, who would have made me his life's companion and helped me become a doctor, was dead.

'Not a great deal,' I said.

'You'll marry me then?' he said.

I might have said yes if he'd been more like Daniel. I liked him a great deal, even if I didn't love him, and we'd have got along well enough. He lacked Daniel's courage and would doubtless live by my side to a ripe, and safe, old age.

But while Alexander wanted us to run and hide and deny my life Daniel had accepted me as I was, even been glad of what I was.

I held Alexander's hand when I gave him my answer. I was grateful to him; he'd shown me love and helped me see what I had to do. He lacked Daniel's courage but he would find someone like himself to be happy with. He would never be truly happy with me, nor I with him.

'I can't marry you, Alex, but thank you for—'

'Spare me the courtesies, Allie.' He released his hand from mine, left the bed, covered me with a blanket and got dressed. He left the room and came back with water and toiletries which he left for me on the washstand. He did all of this in a matter-of-fact, unhurried fashion.

My body, as I washed, looked the same as it always had been. I wasn't sorry for what I'd done. I wouldn't be in the future either. I was no different to the other wrens now. I was prepared for the life I'd chosen.

Alexander was in his uniform when I came into the other room.

'Duty calls,' he smiled. 'What will you do now?'

'I will nurse Beezy back to health. I'll be a doctor and nurse to the wrens and their children and to any other woman who calls on me.'

'You're as foolish as the man who died,' he observed as he put on his hat, 'you do that and you won't be thanked and you'll probably die of some contagious disease yourself.' He took my arm and led me to the door. His tone and manner were almost lighthearted. 'I'm letting you go, for now, but only because I can't restrain you. You won't escape me, Allie, and I won't let you destroy yourself.' He opened the door and helped me down the step to where a horsecar stood waiting. 'This man will drive you back to your wrens – but we'll be reunited before long.'

He was wrong. I knew that we would never again lie together.

CHAPTER THIRTY-FIVE

Sarah

Daniel Casey's dying changed everything.

Or so it seemed at the time. When I looked back on it later, with a bit of a distance between me and the Curragh, I could see that all he'd done was arrive into the middle of change. What his dying really did was hasten the end.

The biggest change was the weather. The end of summer revealed the countryside as the ugly place I'd always known it to be. The village began to fall apart. The nests fell because of the battering by wind and rain, the numbers of wrens when women began leaving to spend the winter elsewhere. Lucretia Curran and Lil Malone left. Better to take their chances on the streets of the towns and cities, they said, than die in the cruelty of the open.

Those who stayed, like Ellen Neary and Clara Hyland, were either waiting for soldiers or far gone in drink.

If Allie blamed herself for Daniel's death then so did I. He died because he became caught up in the terrible, ruinous course my and Allie's lives had been following for a long time. Maybe since we were children together, for all I knew. All that was left to do was pray that the worst had happened.

The police were conducting a big inquiry – into what had led up to Daniel Casey's killing, as well as the death itself. The hope was that justice, in the fullness of time, would be meted out to the priest and to the cowardly, murdering members of his flock.

Allie's grief over Daniel was terrible. She was desolate and forlorn and wouldn't speak about it. I knew she was full of bitter regrets for the times she'd been cool with him, at her slowness in letting him be close to her, at the loss of a love that had just begun to grow.

I knew all of this because I knew her so well and not because she shared any of it with me. She didn't share her grief with anyone. After Daniel Casey's mother came and took his body away to Galway she developed a detachment that wasn't natural. I told her so.

'It would be better for you to weep and talk about him,' I said, 'it's the normal thing to do. Don't you think him worth your tears?'

'Don't try to goad me,' she was sharp, 'I'll grieve in my own way, Sarah.'

'What way is that? Where did you go the day his mother took him?'

She turned away, beckoning to Moll Hyland. The child was more than ever besotted with Allie and forever hanging about our nest.

'I went on a journey,' she said, 'that I needed to take.'

She'd been on a journey, right enough. She'd arrived back in the village worn and exhausted, carrying Daniel Casey's doctor's bag. She'd refused to answer questions then, just as she was refusing now. I had my suspicions about where she'd gone but if she didn't want to tell, then she didn't. She might, in time – or not, as the case might be. There are some things can never be told. Especially if they're between a man and a woman.

What she'd said was that she intended devoting herself to the medical care of the wrens. She wouldn't be leaving the village when I married. She would make Beezy well. She expected chest and other infections to be rampant through the winter. She would be on hand to care and do all that she could.

She was of the opinion that this sacrifice would be a tribute to Daniel Casey. When I told her he was most likely turning in his grave at the idea she walked away from me.

Just as she was doing now with Moll, going with the child to check on her mother. Clara Hyland was in a bad way with drink.

I had my own problems, but they were pleasant enough ones, in the circumstances. Two days after Daniel Casey's death Jimmy arrived with our marriage licence.

'We can be married in a week,' he said, 'the Catholic priest in the camp says he will do it for us in the chapel there—'

'So easy, in the end,' I interrupted, full of the joy of it and surprised too. 'After all the waiting it's to happen so quickly, and so simply.'

'The ceremony, yes.' Jimmy laid James, whom he'd been holding, on the ground. 'And giving James my name.'

There were just the three of us in the nest. Allie was with Beezy in Nance Reilly's nest.

'But it'll be another week or two before we get a place to live together.' He watched James's kicking legs. 'I'm asking you again, Sarah, to move out of this place and into a room.'

'Into the "she-barracks" is it?'

I wasn't as sharp with him as I'd been in the past. The cold and rain and constant patching and repairing of the nest had me demented with worry about James's health. Allie, thin as she'd been as a child of ten and pale, had had a fit of coughing in the night too. I couldn't leave her.

'It would be dry there,' Jimmy said.

'Drier than here anyway,' I conceded. 'But I'll stay here until we marry, since it's only to be a matter of days. Then, if there's any hold-up at all on our married quarters in the camp, I'll move as a temporary measure into the "she-barracks".' I knew I was choosing between Allie and James, that I was putting my son first, as I had to. I was hoping that she would have come to her senses in the week between me getting married and moving out of the village.

Jimmy Vance and I became man and wife on a bright, frosty Saturday in mid-November. I wore my blue cotton dress, transformed by Allie. Working through the night she'd sewn pale gold-coloured ribbons on to the bodice and neckline. On the end of the sleeves and around the hem she'd sewn a darker gold ribbon. My hair she bound and threaded through with more of the pale gold ribbon. As my bridesmaid she herself wore her lilac silk dress.

Clara Hyland was there with Moll and Ellen Neary came too. Both of the women looked respectable enough to be housemaids. Poor little Moll was so excited at the prospect of a wedding that she vomited early in the morning.

Beezy, too ill to do more than wish me well from her sick bed, wasn't there. It felt wrong to be married without her. I cried as she admired my dress and wished me good luck, feeble and hot-eyed from drink and fever, her rings rattling on her fingers when she lifted a hand to say goodbye.

It felt wrong to be married without my mother and father and grandmother too. I tried not to think about them, especially my mother, and to think instead how pleased they would be when they heard that Jimmy Vance had at last made an honest woman of me.

Captain Ainslie was there for Jimmy's side. There wasn't another army person present and I was glad. To have included Jimmy's soldier mates would have meant John Marsh being present. I didn't want that fiend next or near me on my wedding day.

Jimmy not being a Catholic meant we couldn't be married on the altar. This caused no great hardship since, by gathering around the Holy Water font in the porch and rechristening James as part of the ceremony, we managed two sacraments for the price of one.

Afterwards we filled two horsecars as we went to Newbridge and the Prince of Wales Hotel, all of us sitting down together to a meal. Marriage is a respectable business, and the meal had in any event been organised by Jimmy and Captain Ainslie, so we were attended to with decency and courtesy.

Allie and Captain Ainslie behaved in a polite, distant fashion towards one another. This was dictated by her. It was plain the captain would have liked to resume the easy friendship they'd had before Daniel's arrival, and death.

It was hard to see how she could do other than keep the captain at arm's length until her heart had mended. I wished all the same she would be less hard on herself. It wouldn't have killed her to allow him take her hand as she stepped down from the horsecar.

Or maybe it was that he'd already done more than hold her hand, so that she had other reasons for not touching or being close to him. There was something I didn't know about going on and I wished she would tell me. But I was too happy to be married to Jimmy to suffer much on account of it that day.

It was as well I enjoyed my happiness. It didn't last long.

'The captain's here. He came on his horse and he's in a great hurry to see the pair of you.'

Moll, breathless and only half dressed, came to the nest to Allie and myself early on the day after I was married. It was another bright, sharp morning.

'He's climbed down from the horse but he won't come into the village,' said Moll. 'I said I'd send you to him at once.' She held out her arms. 'Give me the child. I'll mind him while you talk with the captain.'

Captain Ainslie was stroking his horse and looking severe when I got to him. Allie came slowly after me.

'What's happened to Jimmy?'

I was sure Jimmy was hurt, or maybe even dead. I felt strangely calm and thought I was ready for news of any kind. I wasn't, though if Jimmy had been hurt or dead the news might have been easier to take.

Captain Ainslie handed me a letter. 'I can prepare you for the contents if you like.' He spoke quietly, his eyes on my face all the time. A tiny muscle flickered in the scar over his eye as Allie came up behind me. He didn't turn to her.

I noted these small things very clearly. It helped me avoid looking down at the letter in my hand.

'Tell her,' Allie put an arm round my waist. I allowed myself lean on her, a little.

'Private Vance left for India with his regiment early this morning. There's money in the envelope, as well as a letter. He wants you and the child to go to Dublin, Sarah, to take lodgings there and await his return. He's promised to send regular payments.' He stopped, then said the rest of what he had to say to Allie. 'I didn't know, yesterday, that he planned to do this today.'

'But you knew his regiment was going to India?' Allie was cold.

'Yes,' his lips tightened, 'but he told me he planned to feign illness and stay behind. He wanted to transfer to another regiment, one going back to Dublin.'

'He lied,' Allie said, 'to everyone.'

I looked down at the envelope. My name was there, written in Jimmy's own, careful, hand. The one I'd taught him.

'He lied right enough,' I said, 'but please don't be upset on my account, either of you.' I smiled at them. I really didn't want them to worry. There had been too much concern spent on me. This I would take on my own shoulders. 'At least James has his father's name,' I assured them, and myself. 'At least he's no bastard.'

Later, I told myself, I would face the loss of Jimmy. Later, when I'd had time to get used to it.

'Will you have tea?' I said to Captain Ainslie. He looked at Allie who said quickly, 'I think you had better read your letter, Sarah. First things first.'

She sounded so like our old schoolteacher that I nodded obediently, a habit from long ago, and turned away with my letter. I walked until I couldn't see the village any longer and then I stopped, in the flat open, and read what Jimmy had to say. His letter was no more than half a page in length. Even so, it must have taken him the night to write it. He'd laboured over it; the letters were well formed and there were no misspellings. But he was not a gifted writer and there was nothing in it of the Jimmy Vance I'd loved and now, it seemed, lost.

My dear Sarah, *he began*,

By the time you read this I will be on my way to India with the regiment. I will be gone no more than two years. When I come back I will have money and be in a position to discharge myself from the army.

I love you, Sarah, as much as I love life itself. I love my son. I do not want the life I see in the married quarters for us. Go to Dublin. I will come there for you to your parents' house. You will get money from me every month.

He signed it 'your ever loving, Jimmy Vance' and added a postscript telling me he'd deceived Captain Ainslie because he needed his help.

He'd deceived me too, and our son. He didn't seem to think this worth mentioning. Something in me died as I finished reading the letter. Died and then hardened into a knot of fury.

I'd believed so much in Jimmy Vance. For him, and love of him, I'd kept our son from the nuns and come to this hell-hole to find and live beside him. Allie had come with me, and Beezy Ryan who was now dying. All of us because of him. It was too much. Even the worm turned when he was trodden upon. If I could not have love then I would at least have back my dignity.

I counted his money. He'd given me thirty pounds. Thirty pieces of silver to buy me off. It wasn't a fortune but, together with the money Beezy Ryan owed me, it would open some door to a future.

I tore the letter into the smallest pieces, scattering them to the wind as I marched back to the village. By the time I got there I knew what I was going to do.

Allie, with Moll still holding James, was waiting for me

outside the nest. She'd built the fire bigger than we'd ever had it. I worried the nest would burn and told her so.

'The wind's in the other direction.' She frowned and took my arm. 'I've made tea. Sit and have it.'

To humour her I sat on an upturned pot. Moll, rocking James in her arms, stepped away a little and eyed me cautiously. That child was four hundred years old. I didn't take James from her. He was quiet and she liked nursing him. She wouldn't have many more opportunities to do so.

Allie put sugar in the tea and gave it to me. 'Some of Beezy's whiskey would do you more good,' she said.

'I'm going,' I said.

'To Dublin?'

'No . . .'

I saw Moll slide closer and lowered my voice. I wanted to be the one to tell Beezy that I was deserting her, just as I was about to tell Allie. I had James to think about, they only had themselves. This, cruelly and finally, was what Jimmy's letter had brought home to me.

'I'm going to America. I'll do what many before me have done and start a new life there. You can come with me, or not, as you choose.'

'You know that I've already made my choice.'

'You could become a proper doctor in America. You'll never become one here.'

'I'm a better healer as I am than many men who've spent years in universities,' Allie said and I knew she was thinking of Dr Maurice McDermott.

'You won't be healing here and you know it.' I poked at the fire. Her stubbornness had always irritated me. 'You'll be making things more comfortable for the dying and making the rest strong enough to go on drinking and killing themselves. The village will destroy you, Allie. You'll be finished by Christmas, diseased yourself and with no doctor to look after you.'

'You're wrong.' She was forbearing, treating me as if I was slightly gone in the head. 'I'm needed here. I *will* make the sick well.'

'You won't make Beezy Ryan well.' I stood. No one can make Beezy well. I'm going to her now. It's time she was persuaded to go to the hospital. She'll at least have the comfort there of dying in a warm bed.'

Allie followed me through the village to Nance Reilly's nest, two of her steps matching every one of my own furious strides. Moll, faithfully holding James, followed up in the rear.

The nest was full of a smell like rotting meat. Since it came from Beezy's wounds that, in a sense, was what it was. Beezy herself was a sight, weaker even than she'd been the night before. The drink was doing it, every bit as much as the poisoned and festering wounds on her back. Her hair had grown to below her ears and under it her face was a feverish mauve and thin as a knifeblade. The only resemblance to the old Beezy was in the length and boniness of the long body stretched across the nest.

'I'm leaving, Beezy.' I knelt and touched her burning forehead and put a damp cloth across it.

'You're right to go,' Beezy said, twisting restlessly on the straw pallet, 'but you'd be a fool to wait in Dublin for that bastard of a soldier you married. He's gone, Sarah. He gave the child his name and that's as much as you'll get from him.'

No point in asking where she'd heard about Jimmy Vance's departure. The village had a lightning-fast telegraph system.

'If you know so much then you know I got money from him too,' I said, 'not a lot but when I add it to what you owe me I'll have enough to get to America.'

She was silent for so long after this I thought for a while she hadn't heard me and then that she'd slipped into a waking coma of some sort. When she spoke at last her voice was flat.

'I always wanted to go to America,' she said.

'I know that, Beezy,' I said, 'but hospital's the place you should be right now. You'll get well there and when I'm set up in America you can come and join me.' This would never happen and both of us knew it.

'I know what I have to do,' Beezy said, 'and it might as well be now as in a week's time. I won't waste my money on any hospital. I'll go to the workhouse.'

'The workhouse!'

'Listen to me, Sarah.' Beezy, suddenly fierce and with a strength I'd never have thought left in her, sat and clutched my hand. 'I'll be damned if I'll waste any of the money I earned hard on a hospital and doctors that can't cure me,' she laughed, 'I'll be damned anyway so what's the odds . . .' She stopped, not because she expected an answer but to catch her breath. After a few gasping minutes she went on.

'I won't give it to any fat undertaker to bury me either. A pauper's grave will do me fine. I'll be past caring when the time comes to put me in the ground anyway. Don't interrupt me,' her hand tightened like a bolt on mine when I tried to stop her talking like this. 'I'll be dead in a week,' she went on, 'I'd planned to more than settle up with you when you left for your married life. Nance can drink some of it but the rest of what I have is yours, Sarah. There's more than enough to set you up in America. You and James and . . .' She stopped to take a couple of deep breaths. 'There's a condition. You're to take Allie Buckley with you. Not because I've any great *grá* for her but because she'll be useful if either yourself or James becomes ill.'

She released my hand and tried to find some comfort lying on her side. Nothing seemed to give her ease. The stench was almost unbearable. I wondered if she could smell it herself, or had become too used to it.

'You're not dying . . .'

'I'm dying, Sarah,' she closed her eyes, 'but that doesn't make me a fool so don't treat me like one. You know I'm finished and so does everyone else in the village. Dr Allie Buckley knows it better than anyone. All she can do for me now is give me the laudanum. My blood is poisoned through and through and there's no cure for that.' She opened her eyes and nodded to the whiskey bottle, standing in a hole in the ground. 'Pour me a drop of that into a cup. A good drop, mind. It's not doing me the good it used to.'

She watched and was silent while I poured. I couldn't speak myself. There was too much to say and no way of saying any of it.

'My mother died in the workhouse,' Beezy reminded me when I handed her the whiskey. 'She was the age I am now. Why should I think myself any luckier than she was?'

'We make our own luck,' I said. 'There's nothing says we have to repeat our mothers' lives.'

'Nothing,' Beezy agreed, 'but we do it anyway, too many of us. We make the same choices as our mothers and that's what does it. I knew I was making choices that would lead me down my mother's path but I made them anyway. I thought I was strong enough to rise above anything that God, or Fate, had in store for me. I was wrong.'

'You weren't wrong, Beezy, you could have been made well . . .'

'That Father Mangan is no better than a swine,' Beezy silenced me with a frown, 'but his was the hand of God all the same, striking me down.'

She wasn't raving. She believed all that she was saying.

'I knew it then and I know it now. Give me another drop of whiskey, there's a good girl. The pain is killing me.' She laughed. It was a sound like rattling bones.

'You made the choice to come here because of me, Beezy,' I said as I poured, 'and so did Allie. I'm the one should—'

'Lord, but you're an important person, Sarah Rooney!' Beezy, raising the cup at an angle, downed the whiskey in a gulp. She didn't spill a drop. 'So important that grown women with minds of their own follow you around the country. Or maybe it's that you've a magnet attached to your back.'

She held out the cup and I poured again, silently. The bottle was nearly empty. I'd no doubt there was another where it had come from.

'I was coming to the Curragh whether you came or not, Sarah,' Beezy went on, her voice hoarsening from all the talk, 'and Allie Buckley came because it suited her too.' She stopped, looking into the cup. 'We were support for one another, the three of us, and each was responsible for herself.'

She was right. Beezy had always had wisdom, a way of seeing things more clearly than most. Maybe she'd been right too in thinking that her time was up. My mother had always that said God's ways were strange ones

I couldn't believe it though. An evil priest had killed her before her time and that was it, pure and simple. It was my own belief that Father Mangan would burn in hell. But not Beezy. Beezy Ryan had had her hell on earth.

'The receiving officer will send a horsecar to take me to the workhouse,' Beezy said. 'It's time to get myself ready for the journey.' She slipped the rings from her fingers. They fell in a bright heap. 'The scavengers in the workhouse won't get any-thing off my body. I'll go to them in my shroud. I'll wear red. It was always a colour I favoured. Help me to sit,' she commanded, 'and then bring me my bag and the candle box.'

I did as she said.

'I'll have my own wake before I go. We'll finish the whiskey, and I'll divvy out my worldly goods. You and James first . . .' She took a fat candle from the box, turned it upside down and removed a circle of wax from its base. From the hollow inside she pulled a twist of notes.

'There's plenty there to get you started,' she stuffed it back into the candle and handed it to me, 'keep it in your bodice when you travel.' As I took it from her she lifted the green feather boa from the bag. 'Who should I give this to?' She put it round her neck.

'Don't, Beezy.' I stood, holding the candle. 'Allie won't come to America. You know as well as I do that she's all for making a martyr of herself.'

'She'll go with you, I'll see to it that she does,' Beezy said, 'send her to me with her laudanum. And send Ellen Neary for the receiving officer.'

Allie and I went with Beezy to the workhouse. She'd rouged her cheeks and put kohl about her eyes, giving her face the look of a painted death mask. She was so full of laudanum and whiskey that she was barely conscious for the journey. This was just as well since the springs on the car were far from good. It took us three hours to get to Naas.

In the workhouse she was examined by a young doctor and given a bed in a long, grey room. I stood holding her dry, wasted hand while Allie went outside and spoke with the doctor.

Because of the rouge and kohl it took me a few minutes to realise she'd stopped breathing.

'I never want to see this town or the county of Kildare as long as I live.' Allie, when she came to stand beside me at Beezy's deathbed, was bitter.

I knew then that Beezy had somehow persuaded her and that she would be going to America with myself and James.

CHAPTER THIRTY-SIX

Sarah

My mother cried for the three days I spent in Henrietta Street. If I'd stayed another three she'd probably have cried for them too.

'You might have been dead for all that we knew of you,' were the first words she said to me, 'we heard nothing except that you'd left the Magdalen with your child and gone God knows where your father was demented.'

We met in the street. I was walking slowly up the hill with James in my arms when she came out of the house and saw me. It was foggy, and late in the afternoon, and she stood for a while, unmoving as stone. She told me later it was because she couldn't believe her eyes.

When I waved to her she ran down the hill and gathered me into her arms. We stood for a long time holding on to one another, neither of us uttering a word. She felt like a bag of bones, she was that thin.

'You'd have heard if I was dead,' I said at last.

'There was no need for you to worry.'

'I knew you'd come back,' she contradicted herself, 'I prayed night and day and I'd no doubts but that God would listen to me.'

'This is James.'

She took him from me, and that was when she started the crying. 'I've never seen a more beautiful child.' The tears ran down her face as she touched his eyes and ears and then his mouth with her finger.

She was right about his beauty. At five months old James had the wide, dark grey eyes of his father and dark curls like my own.

'You'd no right to keep him away so long,' my mother said.

I didn't remind her of the reasons I'd gone in the first place. I couldn't find it in me either to tell her I'd be on my way again in days. She'd aged far more than was normal in the months I'd been away. Even her eyes had grown older.

'How's my father?' I said.

'The same your grandmother's gone she took sick in the night with ferocious pains in her stomach when she was no better by morning we sent for the doctor.' My mother took a breath. 'A new lad from the dispensary he took her to the Mater Hospital straight away.'

'And she died . . .'

It was very cold in the street. I wanted to move, go indoors. But not if my grandmother was dead. I wasn't ready yet to face the empty spaces.

'She died an hour after going into the hospital they did a post mortem and said it was a blockage in her insides killed her.' My mother turned her face from mine. 'Glory be to God but she had terrible pain.'

'When?'

'All the night and before she died.'

'When did she die, Mother, how long ago?'

'She's gone two-and-a-half months now I've a young woman from Donegal living in her room she pays me rent and she's clean she'll have to find somewhere else now you're home.'

'I'm married,' I said. I had to stop her building a life that had me and James in it.

'Thanks be to God and His Blessed Mother for that.' My mother made the sign of the cross. 'Your father'll be pleased.'

The rooms I'd grown up in were the same. My old bed still took up its corner and the bird sat inside the window chirping in his cage. Mary Ann's schoolbooks were on the floor by the wall where she'd always left them and my grandmother's shawl hung black on the back of the door.

But they were different too, quiet and still in a way they're never been. I didn't go into the bedroom my grandmother and Mary Ann had shared. I didn't want to see the lodger's belongings where theirs had been.

James began to cry.

'He's hungry,' said my father with authority, 'a growing lad needs feeding regular.'

My father looked younger, but less alive. My mother said he was spending a lot of his time sleeping and was drinking for most of his waking hours. His skin looked pale and smooth but he was like a man with no life inside him.

'I'm hungry myself,' I said.

My father held James while I got his food ready. He even helped me feed him when my mother made supper for the rest of us. It was going to be hard telling them about America.

I wondered how it was for Allie in Haddington Road. We'd shared a carriage from the railway station at Kingsbridge to Sackville Street and from there gone our separate ways home. We were to meet in two days to arrange the journey to America. Allie was the one rushing things now. She wanted to be gone and away from everything she'd ever known as quickly as possible.

Leaving the wrens had been difficult for her. The duty she still felt to them had pulled hard against the part of her bound by whatever Beezy Ryan had said on her deathbed.

Leaving Moll had been the hardest thing of all.

Moll had tried blackmail. 'My mother will die now you're going. She'll fall drunk into a ditch some night and without someone to make her well again she'll be finished.'

'You can come with me to Dublin,' Allie said, 'the nuns will take you in, or I'll find a family for you to live with.'

'I won't leave her,' Moll was stubborn, 'you'll have to stay.'

'I can't stay.' When Allie tried to put an arm around her Moll twisted away. 'You must look after your mother. Ellen will be staying and I'll leave you a letter to bring to Captain Ainslie in the camp if Clara gets very bad.'

'He doesn't want you to go either,' Moll said and she was

right. She stood three feet away from us, eyes brighter than the sparkling frost on the furze. 'Once you're gone he'll want nothing more to do with us.'

'I'll leave you the letter and you'll see that he's not like that,' Allie said. 'I'll leave you my lilac dress too, to wear when you grow a bit.'

Moll caught her breath. It was so easy to forget she was only nine years old and easily distracted. 'Your silk dress . . .' Her breath, when she let it out, made a cloud in the cold air.

Allie got the dress and went to Moll and held it against her. Allie was a small woman and Moll a big child. She wouldn't have to grow a great deal to fit it.

'How could I keep such a thing?' Moll took the dress and held it like it was a baby in her arms. 'What's the good of me owning it in a place like this?' She pressed it against her. 'I'll be killed for it. It'll be robbed from me.'

'Keep it secret then,' Allie said, 'until you've a life you can wear it in.'

'I won't even tell my mother,' Moll said.

Allie didn't say goodbye to Captain Ainslie. I don't even know that he knew she was leaving. He'd come to the village a few times on his horse but she would do no more than bid him good day and tell him to go. Her heart was locked on Daniel Casey and would be for a long time.

Time, now that we were going away, was sadly not on Captain Ainslie's side. He was a decent man and it was a pity but life doesn't run to order and wishing doesn't make it so.

Clara Hyland was drunk the morning we left. She was shouting that we'd be back, that we were wrens now and would be wrens forever, wherever we went. Moll stood beside her and said nothing. Ellen Neary wished us well. She fully believed, she said, that this would be her last winter in the village, that her soldier would be back before the spring. Nance Reilly let us go without a word or a wave and the other wrens didn't say much either.

I got into the horsecar with James. Allie, stiff as a marionette, followed me. She didn't look back once as we went across the Curragh. I kept looking myself until the village disappeared from view. Just before it did I waved and it seemed to me that several hands, lonely and small, waved back. Or it might have been the wind through the furze.

I told my mother about America on the morning of the second day.

'I knew you'd be going I thought about it in my bed in the night and I said to myself she's not home for good she's got plans,' she said as she took James on to her lap, 'why would she come back I said to myself when she's managed so much on her own there's no life for her in these lonely rooms she might as well strike out.' She looked at me over James's head. 'I never thought of America though it's a long ways away.'

'The further the better.' I thought of Jimmy Vance.

'Your husband won't be going with you?'

My mother, though she must have seen how things were, hadn't asked about Jimmy before. When my father had tried to question me she'd told him to be quiet and wasn't it enough for the time being to have me home? My father had agreed, saying that the fact I'd a ring on my finger was the most important thing.

'My husband's in India.'

'He won't be following you to America?' my mother asked.

'No.'

'He didn't leave you without money?'

'No. I have money.'

She poured me more tea. The bird began to sing in his cage and I brought James over to listen to him. I would get him a bird like it when we got to America. I said as much to my mother.

'Do that,' she said, 'a bird is a grand thing to have where there's children though I wonder will they have birds of his kind in America?'

I told my mother little about the Curragh and nothing about Beezy Ryan's money. I told her why Beezy had died and was glad when she condemned the priest. 'Some who are called by God are not as good as they might be,' she said. 'I'll pray for Beezy's immortal soul,' she paused, 'and for the priest.'

'If money should come for me from India I want you to have it.' I wanted nothing more from Jimmy Vance. I put James lying in a shaft of sunlight coming through the window. I doubted any money would ever arrive.

I went to the nuns in the Magdalen and told them about Beezy and how she'd died.

'It was God's will and we must accept it,' said Mother Stanislaus. 'When we choose a certain path in life there are consequences.'

I knew then the root of Beezy's fatalism.

I met Allie in the Bailey Tavern in Duke Street where, at her insistence, we had Red Bank Burren oysters. I didn't like them, and nor did she, but they were costly so we kept at them and ate the lot.

'Our lives have changed us,' Allie said, 'we must be adventuresome about food as well as everything else. There's no going back to tea rooms and politeness.'

Not knowing what she would find in Haddington Road, half fearful that whatever it was would change her mind about America, I hadn't told my mother and father Allie would be going with me.

I needn't have worried. There was nothing in Haddington Road to keep her here.

'My father spends his time making money and is rarely at home. He's agreed to give me what would have been my dowry to go to America.'

This didn't sound to me like the whole story. 'He wants you to go then?' I stared so hard she had to look at me. She was wearing one of her Paris creations, a costume of violet velvet and over it a loose, velvet paletot with revers of silk. Her bonnet had feathers at the back. She looked beautiful, even with her wind- and sun-darkened skin. Her hands, when she lifted a napkin to her mouth, were chapped and red.

'He wants me to stay. He wants me to be with my mother

when he's away. My mother and Mary Connor. He wants me to be a watchdog over her.'

'Is that what he said?'

Her eyes were hard and bright. 'He *says* he doesn't want me to go away. He *says* my place is here, enjoying the fruits of all he's labouring for. He *says* he's been praying to God for my return and that he had detectives in Dublin and Paris looking for me.'

'You don't believe him?'

'He must have hired very poor detectives.'

I had to agree with her about this. Any half-able detective would have found her. Then again, maybe not.

The wrens were outcast, in every sense. As far as the rest of society was concerned they didn't exist, had no names, were nothing but a collection of whores and drunkards and derelict women. When she became a wren Allie was as lost to the rest of the world as the other women. As I'd been myself.

'Maybe not,' I said, 'and you well know he missed you.'

'Not enough to put me before my mother,' Allie said.

This was true and was at the heart of the hurt her father had done to her. Allie, if she wasn't to be cherished for herself, preferred to make her way in life alone. She would have her dignity and, though she said in a thin-lipped way that she would never marry, could never love again, I doubted myself that she would be alone forever.

'My father has made enquiries about the best way for us to travel to America,' she said, leaning across the table to play with James, 'he says we should go to Londonderry and take a sailing ship from there. He's been told that the McCorkell company own the most reliable vessels crossing the Atlantic.' She paused then gave a shrug and half-smile. 'It seems the storms we had on the Curragh did us at least one favour. They delayed McCorkell's autumn sailings so that their ship, called the *Minnehaha* for some strange reason, will be sailing in eight days' time, to get to New York for Christmas. It's the biggest sailing ship in the Londonderry trade, he says, so we'll be sure of getting passenger packets. We'll be safer crossing the Atlantic on a bigger ship too.'

Her father gave her a thousand pounds which was more, he said, than he would have settled on her had she married. Allie called it conscience money and took it as her due.

'You've the price there of two houses in this city, three if you choose well,' he said, 'make sure you spend it as wisely in America as I would have here.'

In her room she packed two trunks with her Paris clothes and as many other bits of her life as she could. Into a separate bag she put Daniel Casey's doctor's bag, scented water, creams, soap and books. She would never again, she swore, be deprived of those things which refined life. 'Why should I?' she asked.

I could see no reason at all why she should live an inelegant or impoverished life. Why either of us should.

I was nearly as well off as her myself. Beezy Ryan's fortune and Jimmy Vance's thirty pounds gave me a total of six hundred and fifty pounds. Beezy had been an even better businesswoman than people suspected.

In Todd Burns & Co., a department store I'd never before been inside, I bought myself shoes and walking boots, a water-proof cloak, woollen stockings, two light wool dresses and three petticoats. I bought the softest of wool and cotton for James and a trunk into which I put the lot. When I'd paid for this, and given my mother fifty pounds, I still had almost five hundred and seventy left.

There was nothing to be done after that but get together the identification and other papers we needed for the journey.

That and say our goodbyes.

We left Dublin by train for Londonderry on the Friday of the week we'd arrived home. This time, once we were on the move, the both of us kept our eyes fixed forward. There was no point any more in looking back.

CHAPTER THIRTY-SEVEN

Allie

———◦◦◦◦———

Cold and bright; that was how Londonderry struck me as the train drew into the city. Cold and bright and, when we were inside its great walls, teeming with people and noisy.

As a city it was smaller than Dublin and nothing near as big as Paris. But it was governed by a wide river, just as those two cities were, and its citizens had the same indifference to people passing through as the Parisians.

For that is what Sarah, James and myself were to them: just three among thousands arriving to leave from Londonderry's quays for an Atlantic crossing. Nothing new, nothing strange, nothing interesting about us. People had been sailing in huge numbers from the city to the New World since the time of the Great Famine, more than twenty years before.

We were a part of the emigrant trade, and nothing more. But for me, after the accusing watchfulness of Kildare and Newbridge and the cloistered life of the wren village, to be anonymous and unnoticed had the freedom of shedding chains.

Sarah didn't like it as much as I did.

'We could be trampled in the street by animals,' she said as she gazed morosely through the window of the carriage taking us to our lodgings, 'or fall off the quays and drown. No one would notice. Or care.'

'We'll do our best to avoid animals and keep well back from the water's edge.' I took James from her lap on to my own. 'We can do what we like and be what we want, Sarah. Be glad that we're on our way to new lives.' I turned James so that he could see the waters of the river Foyle opening in front of us.

'I *am* glad.' Sarah closed her eyes and leaned her head against the back of the carriage seat. 'I'm very glad.' She clenched and unclenched her hands.

Her humour hadn't been great since leaving Dublin, but then it was harder for her to look forward than me. She was leaving a mother and father who loved her and whom she might never see again. She was taking her child, whose father had abandoned her, into the unknown.

As well as all this, she'd never been out of Ireland before and was full of foreboding about the sea crossing.

In my case my father was the only family I cared about leaving and he could follow me if he cared to. I doubted he would.

My fears were more about what we would find on the ship and, when we got there, in New York City. Daniel had told me how, because of the numbers who travelled and the condition of the ships during the Great Famine, typhus fever had for years raged unrestrained on sea and on land in New York. Hardly a ship had managed to cross the Atlantic without the fever breaking out during the passage. The mortality on land had been horrendous with many who survived the journey dying of the fever on the streets of New York.

Daniel. Things he'd said, the way he'd been, even his freckled face and serious smile — all sorts of things about him were never far from my mind. He was a part of me now and I would take that part to America and keep alive, in me, his belief in justice and rights for all. Because he'd helped me recognise those beliefs in myself I would live my life for both of us. It was the least I could do.

It was remembering what Daniel had said about the Famine ships made me check, before leaving Dublin, how much things had changed with emigrant sailings from Londonderry.

I went along to the newspaper officers of *The Freeman's Journal* and from their files discovered things were better, but not hugely so. Conditions were anything but ideal and the risks to health and personal safety still high.

Emigrants continued to leave the country in great numbers. The good news was that sailings which had once taken as long as 150 to 160 days now took an average of one month.

I found too that my father had been right to recommend McCorkell & Co. Their sailing ships were reported in the paper to be first class. To be sure of a reasonable trip, a report of only months before advised passengers to avoid travelling steerage, where there was overcrowding and the risk of disease, by paying the extra three guineas for a second-class cabin.

Passengers paying the additional fare didn't have to provide their own dishes and bedding – useful information since it meant travelling second class would have the extra benefit of allowing room in my trunks for my Paris clothes. I would be judged by my appearance in the New World, not my past; I would appear as a respectable young woman in Paris frocks. It would be as good a beginning as any.

What hadn't changed on the ships was the fact that many emigrants were poor and malnourished to begin with and brought fever and other diseases on board with them. Storms at sea still lengthened the travelling time and fights and bad feelings between passenger groups were notorious and common as they'd ever been.

Thanks to *The Freeman's Journal* I arrived in Londonderry fore-warned, and determined to book a second-class cabin. I was determined too to take fruit on the journey and to befriend and pay a seaman to bring us regular water for the duration. The signs of that city's prosperity from the trade in passengers to America were everywhere. Regulations and the regulated abounded.

We were met from the train by a barrage of porters with licence badges on their arms, all of them vying to carry our luggage to hackney carriages waiting outside. The carriage drivers were another surging barrage to be faced. The man we engaged in the end was a head taller than his companions and broader, his driver badge and licence hanging from under an inky-black, curling beard. When he waved to his carriage and shining black horse the gesture was as lofty as everything else about him.

'I'll charge only for the two of yourselves and let the child go free,' he said.

'The child travels free anyway,' Sarah nodded to the regulations pinned to a wall, 'since he won't be taking up a seat.'

'True enough,' the man grinned, 'but I'm still the best bargain you'll get from among this lot.' The horse gave a jerk and a snort when he slapped his hand roughly on its neck. 'You'll be looking to go to the north-west side of the bridge, no doubt? Wanting to buy passages to America for tomorrow's sailing?'

'What else on God's earth would bring us here?' Sarah glared from the driver to the stone buildings all around and back again. 'It's hardly to visit the city we came.'

'Taste is a queer thing,' the driver said, shaking a puzzled head, 'and there's no accounting for it. I went to Dublin once myself and could find very little to recommend it. Full of mean-eyed beggars it was, and sharp-tongued shawlies. The one good thing it had was beautiful women like yourself.' He put a hand on his tweedy coat where his heart might be. 'The most beautiful women in the land are to be found on the dirty streets of Dublin. Now there's a paradox for you, but that's the way life is. Full of paradoxes.' He saw the impatience building in Sarah's face and changed from philosophy to flattery. 'I'd swear I saw you in Sackville Street on a Monday morning two years ago. There's hardly two women with a face like yours in that—'

'I'd more to be doing than parading about the streets on a Monday morning,' Sarah cut him short, but she was hiding a smile.

'Now that you're in Londonderry it would be my privilege and pleasure to be your driver.' The driver gave a small bow. 'I'll get you to the public quays quicker and safer than any of the rest of them here.'

'Quicker and *safer*?' Sarah asked.

'There's a fierce amount of traffic going that way,' the man eyed our luggage, 'small accidents happen, sometimes. Trunks have a way of falling off the back of carriages and suchlike.' He lifted my trunk and a bag with ease. 'You'll want a place to stay until the ship sails. I can take ye to a clean boarding house too.'

He weighed our luggage and told us that, since it was more than fifty-six pounds, he'd have to charge us a shilling to take it.

'For another two shillings on top of that I'll take ye from the quays on to the boarding house. That's a better deal than ye'll get anywhere else in this city.'

He told us his name was Toby Magee and helped first Sarah and then me into the carriage.

He was charging us the fares displayed on the wall; there was no dealing to be done in Londonderry. It was a very honest place in some ways.

He brought us close as he could to McCorkell's offices. A wind gusted viciously off the water as we stood on the quays.

'Not a good sign,' said Toby Magee, 'they have to decide in the night whether to sail tomorrow or not.'

He was right. The ticket clerks in McCorkell's booking offices were spreading the word about a storm at sea.

'We'll be posting notices at first light in the morning,' said the worried, bespectacled young man who made out our passage, 'but it's not looking good, I can assure you of that much here and now.'

'How long might it be delayed?' I said.

'It is not this company's policy to sail in anything but the most clement conditions.' He wrote our details carefully before checking our papers. When he had that done he looked up and frowned and fixed his glasses more firmly on to the bridge of his nose. He had bitten fingernails.

'That'll be twenty guineas in all. Eight each for adults, four for the infant.'

Working on the principle that each should give according to her means, Sarah and I had agreed that I should pay our passage to America. She had already paid the train fares from Dublin; the wrens would have approved.

I gave the clerk the money and he counted it, twice. He nodded and handed us our papers and passage. 'The sailing's for midday, if the storm holds off,' he said, 'but I think myself she'll blow.'

'What *exactly* does a delay mean? Are you telling us it'll be days before we sail?' Sarah's look would have alarmed a more sensitive man. The clerk went on smiling and snapped his fingers for the next person to come forward.

'Could mean you won't sail for a week,' he said.

He was right; prophets of doom often are. The storm which rose in the night made me fear for the city walls. The boarding house groaned and its windows and doors rattled ceaselessly, some of them out of their fittings. Not, luckily, those in our room.

There was no chance we would be sailing in the morning.

'There's bad luck about,' Sarah paced the floor with a frightened James in her arms, 'staying in Londonderry is costing us money. I don't like this place. I've had a bad feeling ever since we got here.'

'We've been delayed by a storm.' I didn't want to hear any of this. 'It's the time of year for bad weather and has nothing to do with luck, good or bad. It seems to me you don't like any place outside of Dublin. You didn't like the Curragh either.'

'How could anyone have liked the Curragh?' She stood, from the safety of the middle of the room, looking through the window. The rain, driven by the wind, beat like gravel against the glass. 'I hope the storm isn't too hard on the wrens . . .'

'It's a sea storm,' I said, 'it won't travel inland as far as the Curragh.'

Wanting to believe this I lit a second candle. All its light did was bring to mind images of Moll, huddled and watching over her mother, and of Ellen Neary fiercely trying to hold her nest together.

'We're not meant to go to America,' said Sarah.

'You're the one wanted to go. All of this was your idea.'

'I know. But it seems to me now that we've ignored too many signs in the past. I should have known when my letters weren't answered that it was a sign to me not to go after James's father. You should have listened to Beezy and not gone there either.'

'Sit down, Sarah.'

I took James from her and laid him in his cot. He whimpered but lay quietly enough watching the candle. I sat beside Sarah and did what I could to put my arms about her; her being larger than me had always made this difficult.

'You're afraid and you're lonely about leaving everything you've known,' I said, 'but we *had* to go to the Curragh. If we hadn't gone there you would have had to give up James. I would have had to go away someplace on my own. I didn't want to. It suited me to continue the work I was doing in the dispensary on the Curragh.'

'Nothing you say will make me feel right about America.' Sarah was hunched and rigid.

'What do you want to do then?' I let her go.

'I don't know. I feel . . .'

'What?'

A long time went by before she said, 'Desolate. I feel desolate and that more desolation is coming.'

'You have your child to think of, you have the promise you made to Beezy Ryan when you took her money . . .'

'I'll give the money to the Magdalen.'

'That's not what Beezy wanted done with it. And what about me? Am I to travel on my own?' I lay on the bed. 'I don't want to talk about this any more, Sarah. I'm going to sleep.'

Only I didn't sleep. I lay remembering Beezy Ryan, sore and dying in Nance Reilly's nest, and the last time I'd spoken to her.

'Sarah's life and future are in your hands,' she'd said, 'I'll give her my money if you go with her. If you don't,' she glared at me with the last remnants of ferocity left in her, 'if you decide to make a martyr of yourself and stay here, then Nance can have and drink the lot. Sarah, without it, will go to Dublin and wait for a man who'll never come for her. She'll grow old and bitter in no time. You know she will, you know I'm right. It's a case of securing my investment. If the two of you go together the chances of Sarah and James making out in the New World are better than if they go alone. What do you say?' Her eyes had become pleading.

'I'll go,' I said. Beezy nodded. I don't think she ever doubted what I would say.

I spent a large part of the night in the Londonderry lodging house without sleeping. Sarah sat in the chair without sleeping. Sometime after midnight I slept, waking in a murky dawn to see her still awake in the chair. She looked infinitely sad. There was nothing I could do for her. Jimmy Vance was the only one could have made the world a bearable place for Sarah that night.

She came to bed as the dawn lightened, stretching herself carefully beside me.

'I'm awake,' I said.

'I'll go to America with you,' she said, 'I must do what's best for James from now on. There's nothing in Dublin for a boy without a father and a mother all the time stupidly hoping he'll come back. If there's an even half-decent shop in this place we'll go tomorrow and I'll buy ribbons for my hair for landing in New York. We should buy gloves too, the both of us. The furze and fire-making have made our hands redder and rougher than any scullery maid's.'

'You're right about the gloves,' I said, 'and I might see too what they have by way of point lace handkerchiefs. I left the one I had with Moll.'

I was thinking a lot about Moll.

The worst of the storm had died by midday. The shipping company, when we called, were hopeful that it would have died out at sea within three days and that we could leave Londonderry before the end of the week.

The Saturday and Sunday passed slowly. Our lodgings were clean, as Toby Magee had said they would be, and not far from the city's centre, which was known as the Diamond. Londonderry was full of narrow streets, lanes and alleyways and when it wasn't raining we walked along the wider thoroughfares and by the waterfront. On Sunday we went to mass in St Eugene's Cathedral, an outing James didn't enjoy. I thought it would do no harm to pray for a safe sailing, and maybe Sarah did too. In the event we left with the wailing James before any prayers were said.

What we did mostly after that was sit by the fire in our room, lit by the landlady at the cost of an extra sixpence per day and well worth it. There, with the rain against the window, the fire warm at our feet and James doing his funny, sideways crawl about the place, we wrote together into our journals. It was the first time we'd done this since childhood. Sharing the writing was like praying together, letting the final pieces of all that had happened go from us on to the pages. Some day, when we were older and had lives lived in another land behind us, we might read them together.

Then again we might not. The journals might, by then, belong better in the past. What we'd written would, at the very least, be faithful records of a time, place and people for those who came after us. They would explain too why we'd left it behind for a dream of something better.

On Monday the sun broke through the clouds.

'We'll buy the gloves and ribbons today,' Sarah announced, 'and I'll wash my hair in the evening. You should think about buying a proper bonnet, Allie. We'll leave Ireland in style, with our heads high and our hands covered. No one will ever know what's behind us.'

'I didn't fancy the look of any of the milliners we passed,' I sniffed, 'I've seen nothing in the window compares to the bonnets I have with me.'

'Maybe ribbons will do us both,' Sarah said. 'I've decided to get violet-coloured ribbon. Velvet, maybe. I'll tie my hair back in a bow and it'll match the shawl you brought me from Paris. Only I don't want to put my hands on the shawl again until I've got the gloves, so we'll buy the gloves first.'

Her hands were indeed a sight, red and chapped with old scratch marks showing white. My own were much the same but at least I had a pair of gloves already covering them. A second pair would be worth having.

'We'll get the gloves first,' I agreed.

The streets were thronged. Confined for days by the torrential rain, it looked as if the entire population had taken to the outdoors and fresh air. Not all that fresh either; the overriding smells were animal, not as bad as but not unlike Dublin. Impatience fouled the air as well; everyone was rushing and pushing and in the short ten minutes it took us to get to the glove shop we were twice forced off the footpath.

'They say New York's one of the busiest places on earth,' I warned Sarah after the second time.

'If busy means rude then we won't stay there,' she answered firmly, 'we'll move on.'

The glove shop was on the corner of Harvey Street. It was small and there were two women already inside, making a great fuss about buying a cheap pair of cotton gloves. Sarah, choosing from a tray of satin gloves, would take a while. I quickly decided I didn't like anything in the shop and that James and myself added nothing but congestion to the proceedings. I took him from Sarah.

'We'll wait outside,' I said.

There was a greengrocer's on the corner opposite. When a gap came in the carriages and carts turning in and out of the street I crossed over with James.

The greengrocer's was bigger than it looked from the outside and it took me a while to find the dried fruit. The cheerful owner had just finished weighing me a pound each of raisins and currants when I turned and saw Sarah come out of the glove shop.

'Wrap them for me,' I said, 'I must tell my friend where I am.'

I waved from the footpath. She saw me and waved back. She was wearing lilac-coloured gloves, close in shade to the Paris shawl. She was laughing.

She was still laughing when she stepped off the footpath and began running across the street to join me.

I saw the runaway horse and cart at once. Sarah never saw it at all. She heard the warning screams though, mine and others', and her face froze and her waving hand dropped just before the animal careered into her.

Long before I fought my way with James through the milling crowd, long before she was pulled from under the cart and laid on sacking and a long, long time before the police came and a doctor confirmed it, I knew that Sarah was dead.

CHAPTER THIRTY-EIGHT

Allie

The street fell silent. Death will do that. I knelt beside Sarah and held James so as he could have one, last look at her.

'Remember,' I whispered to him, 'remember always how beautiful your mother was.'

But he cried, so I turned his face away and held him against me while I smoothed a curl of hair from Sarah's forehead. There was no doubt that she was dead but I felt no loss yet, nothing but emptiness and chaos in the places inside me she had filled for all of my life. I couldn't conceive of a world without her. I'd never known a world without her.

Daniel's death had somehow seemed more possible. He'd carried a vulnerability about with him. Sarah had always seemed to me invincible, so full of life and of dreams. All ended now, her life and her dreams, all ended.

I knelt on, afraid to touch her, afraid to feel the cold coming into her skin. James's crying had become a whimper. People ebbed and flowed around us but no one tried to move her, yet. I wouldn't have allowed it. She had been my courage, she'd even been a part of whatever soul I had. All that I'd known and thought and felt, she'd had a share in. No one but me had a right to touch her.

I smoothed her skirts. I still couldn't bring myself to feel her face. I closed my eyes but even then I saw her. Images came to me, a lifetime of them, all of them to do with Sarah. I saw her in Henrietta Street, running to meet me as I came up the hill. Her face was laughing and her black hair loose and I wished, how I wished, that we were back there again, girls together and not women separated by death. I kept my eyes closed for a while, burrowing through the places and people we'd loved together. When Bess appeared and asked me what was wrong, asked why I was alone and where Sarah was, I opened them again.

I touched Sarah's face then, resting a finger first on one eye, then the other. She was warm, not going cold at all. I lifted her hand and held it against my heart. But there was no consolation, no matter how much I touched her, for either of us. I was alone now, alone with my life as Sarah was with death. The desolation of it took my breath away and began an ache in me that I knew would forever fill the places where she had been. I put her hand to my mouth to stop an anguished moan. Fear went through me like an ice storm. I began to shiver. I'd no idea how I would face life without her, how I would bear the ache.

James moved then in my arms, kicking with his legs. When I tightened my hold on him he began to cry again in earnest. I let Sarah's hand go. I had to. I laid it gently across her skirts and I touched her beautiful hair one last time. Then I abandoned her to death.

And faced the future. 'Goodbye, Sarah,' I said out loud, 'and don't worry about James.'

I would grieve for Sarah every day of the rest of my life. Grieve for a sight of her long black hair, the sound of her quick voice. I would carry her in my heart and mind and that would have to do. I would miss her, every long day, and I would curse, every one of those days, a fate so unjust as to have taken her.

Someone lifted me up, with James. I cradled his head and rocked him gently as they lifted Sarah into a horsecar. After they'd covered her they helped us in beside her. An old man who said he'd been a doctor came with us to the hospital.

I didn't plan. Everything I did afterwards I did because I knew it was what Sarah would have wanted me to. What Beezy Ryan, who had trusted me to look after Sarah, would have wanted me to do. Much, much later I would rage at life's injustice, cry for answers to a God I'd long ago believed in. He would give me no answers then, either.

In the hospital they said Sarah had died from severe contusions caused by the cart wheel catching her head when she fell.

'Her skull was shattered instantly.' A white-haired doctor tried to make me sit down. 'She wouldn't have known what hit her.' He cleared his throat, embarrassed that his remark might have seemed flippant. 'She didn't suffer,' he amended.

'She just died,' I said.

'Won't you sit down?' He was holding my arm, pointing to a bench by the wall.

'Things will have to be done,' I said.

'Is the child hers?' He touched James's black curls.

'He's mine,' I said, 'his name is James and he's my son. We sail on the *Minnehaha* for America the day after tomorrow. I must arrange my friend's burial before we go. Will you help me?'

He stepped back, looking at me as I imagined he would a patient, coolly assessing but not unkind. 'What do you want me to do?' he said finally.

'I would like my friend to be buried in Londonderry. She has no family to be buried with elsewhere. I'm expected in New York with James and would be glad not to be delayed by formalities,' I said.

'You were to sail together, you and your friend?'

'Yes.'

He touched James's curls again. 'Along with this little fellow . . .'

'Yes.'

'You can give me the details and I'll make out the death certificate straight away,' he became brisk, 'I'll bring a priest to you too, but you must sit down. You look ready to collapse and we've no beds here for any more patients.'

He made out the certificate for Alicia Buckley, the name I

gave him. When the priest came I gave the certificate to him along with two hundred pounds.

'It won't cost a quarter of this to bury her.' He was a young man and he kept looking at the money.

'I know that. But I don't know Londonderry. There's no one I can trust to bury her so I'll have to trust you.' I nodded to the notes in his hand. 'I want you to put up a headstone too, with her name, Alicia Buckley, her birth and death dates and the words ". . . and thence we issued out, again to see the stars". Whatever's left over can go to the church.'

'The words . . .' he hesitated, 'they're from the *Inferno* of Dante?'

'Yes. Will you need me to write them out for you?'

'I'm familiar with the work,' he was offended, 'you of course mean to say that your dead friend has left this hell for the beauteous things of heaven.'

'Yes,' I said again.

I meant the words to include me and James too, to have us together on her stone, at least. James and I were also issuing out, leaving everything we and Sarah had known to find our own stars. I said none of this to the priest.

He said he would do as I asked. He was no Father Mangan and I knew he wouldn't fund the church without doing the honourable thing and burying Sarah first. He would give her a decent burial too. He would pray for her; I was beyond prayer myself.

I went with him to see Sarah one last time. She looked beautiful, her face white as the sheet and her hair blacker than I'd ever known it. There was no outward sign of the injury which had killed her.

The young priest walked with me to the door. It was the last I ever saw of him too.

I told the police all that I'd seen and how the accident had happened. There would be a hearing in the new year, they said, for which I would be needed. I didn't tell them I would be long gone by then, nor that I was going to make sure they would never find me.

The *Minnehaha* sailed on Thursday morning.

I hired Toby Magee to take us to the quays; he said he was sorry to hear about my friend's accident and helped me get everything of Sarah's on to the ship. I gave him eighty pounds and asked him to care for her grave.

'There is no one who knew her here and no one else in Londonderry I can ask,' I said, 'you met her, at least. You seemed to admire her beauty . . .'

'She was a fine woman,' he said.

'Once a month is all I'm asking,' I said, 'once a month to ensure she doesn't lie under a wilderness of briar and grass. There's a lot of money here. Will you do it?'

'I'll do it,' he said.

I believed him. I'd no choice. The money I'd paid for Sarah's burial and for her grave to be looked after was exactly half that which Beezy had given her. The other half I would keep for James. Beezy, thus appeased, wouldn't haunt me.

I didn't stay on deck to watch and wail with the other passengers as the land slipped away. If I allowed tears to start they might never stop.

I went to the cabin with James and made us as comfortable as I could for the journey. I hadn't a single doubt but that I was doing the right thing. It would have been the act of a lunatic to go back to Dublin with James. Not only would he have no father there, he would have no mother either.

This way, since I firmly believe that truth is made and not born, he would at least have a mother. He would also have the new life Sarah had wanted for him. That Beezy Ryan had wanted for him.

There was nothing so very special about Allie Buckley that she should be kept alive. Dead she was at least serving some purpose.

We took thirty-five days to cross the Atlantic to New York.

I'd never been alone for so long a time in my life before and would never have borne it but for James.

I'd been made strong by the Curragh, by the months alone in Haddington Road with my mother and Mary Connor, by my work in the dispensary, by all that Daniel had shown me about life. But it was James needing me and having no one else which made me strongest of all.

We both knew I was his mother by the time we got to New York.

The weeks on the *Minnehaha* prepared me for life in America too. I kept myself and James apart from the other second-class passengers, partly because their notions of superiority reminded me of my parents' but mostly because I thought it best not to draw attention to us.

Our second-class tickets gave us privacy, but not immunity, from the life in steerage. The partition between us was so thin I could all the time hear the passengers being sick, their children's confused and terrified crying, the rattle of their dishes and spoons as they sat to eat.

When we ran into storms and were tossed about the fear and hysteria of people too closely packed oozed miasma-like through the partition. During my daily walks on deck with James the stench from steerage was even worse than the hot and putrid Dublin smells I'd arrived home to more than a year before. Steerage passengers, when I met them, had dried vomit in their hair and on their clothes.

It made me both glad and ashamed of my cabin and privacy. I never reconciled the two.

And still there was hope in steerage, and excitement and sometimes joy. Most evenings someone would play the fiddle and there would be singing. I listened to heated arguments about politics and stories which made New York seem both a heaven and a hell.

The hell had to do with the overcrowding in New York's tenement houses. This meant that fevers of a typhoid character were rampant, that people lived in waterfilled cellars, that small rooms were constantly divided into even smaller ones, that the air was damp and poisonous. The word in steerage too was that such houses were built with only the profit and economy of the owner in mind. The good news was that there were jobs, more for women than for men, and that the city was growing fast, and furiously.

I listened hard too to what the steerage passengers, and the second-class passengers walking on deck, had to say about other American cities.

By the time we were halfway across the Atlantic I knew that James and I would not be staying in New York. We would move on, cross the continent to a city where the sun was said to shine and where the life was bohemian and easier for women than in any other. We would go to San Francisco.

San Francisco also lay another three thousand miles from Londonderry and questions about the identity of a young Dublin woman buried in a grave outside that city's walls.

We sailed through Christmas and the New Year and were a part, but apart, from it all in our cabin. This suited us fine. I was in no mood for either seasonal celebrations or charitable thoughts and James wouldn't remember his first Christmas anyway.

We dropped anchor in North River, New York, just before noon on the third of January 1869. Never before, or since, have I seen it rain like it did that day. Steamers and barges brought us in to the emigrant landing depot at Castle Garden. There, I was able to change my and Beezy Ryan's money into American dollars.

In the same building, under the gaze of a blue-coated, brass-buttoned dignitary, I recorded the entry of Sarah and James Vance through what they called the Gate of the New World.

I also wrote that San Francisco would be our final destination and, under the same roof, bought tickets to cross America by train.

EPILOGUE

San Francisco, 1879

———◆◇◆———

I read about the wrens today.

A newspaper from Ireland called them an 'irrepressible evil' and said they were 'carriers of disease'. It held them responsible for the rampant immorality of 'half the country's married men and half its youths'. The writer went on to demand they be forced into the Magdalen asylums and kept there.

Plus ça change, as the French say.

I put the paper away as my daughter came into the room. But not quickly enough.

'What's that you're reading?' she said.

'Nothing of interest,' I said, 'just using the excuse to dawdle.'

'It interested you.' She held out a hand.

Clara never changes. Even in this wilful, half-grown city of gamblers, new rich and adventurers she is one of its sharpest, most acutely alert citizens. The lessons of her early life never desert her.

I handed her the newspaper and stood at the window while she read.

I liked the view. Our home on its hill, bought with my father's money, is high enough to watch the late afternoon sun burn itself out over the clippers and steamer ships in the bay. High enough to look down on the hilly streets between, all laid out in their parallel lines, and on the great stores, church spires and hotels. It gives views too of elegant wooden houses like this one, springing up every day next to wooden shanties. The great pot-pourri that is San Francisco suits me well.

Mostly I like to see how it's changing, every day. Where there's change there's a future.

'You're right.' Clara stood beside me with the newspaper. 'It's not interesting. It's pathetic. It's scandalous. It's disgusting.'

Only yesterday she told me she has decided to study medicine. She will make a better doctor than I ever would have. The heart for all that went out of me when Daniel Casey died. Clara is fearless and will not be side-tracked. She also remembers everything I taught her from Gray's *Anatomy* that summer on the Curragh.

'It's all of those things.' I took the newspaper, folding and refolding until the story about the wrens had disappeared. 'Your brother will be coming home from school soon.' I looked at her, tall and serious, with her birth-mother's dark hair and strong shoulders. 'You might go down the hill to meet him.'

She looked over my head to the street. 'He's coming,' she said. She pushed up the window and leaned out, waving and calling. Her quick-fire mood changes are another thing she's inherited from her birth-mother.

James, rounding the corner, waved back, impatiently pulling his father with him. His father's leg gave him trouble on the hills. San Francisco was about the worst city in the world for someone with a shattered leg to settle in.

Clara went to meet them. Side by side, with their dark hair and long limbs, she and James might have been a natural brother and sister. Their father is a good-looking man still, even if he has less hair than he used to. He's taken to wearing a top hat because of the hair loss and, because of the leg, to carrying a cane. It gives him a distinguished air.

There was nothing distinguished about him the first time he came climbing the hill. He was scarecrow-thin then, wearing a woollen suit far too hot for the day and the climb. I was standing at this very window and recognised him instantly, even with the limp and his hair long and bedraggled in a way it had never been previously. Even without his army uniform.

That was seven years ago. To give myself time to think, I moved back and out of sight when he stopped in front of the house. He stood there, in the middle of the wooden sidewalk, dangerously close to a couple of missing planks, and looked up at the windows.

There are no planks missing today. This neighbourhood has climbed the social ladder with a dizzy speed in the years since.

But that day, seven years ago, I let him stand awhile on the sidewalk. As well as thinking, my heart needed time to slow down.

He was the first to move, taking a step nearer the house. He wasn't going to go away, that was clear. I wasn't sure I wanted him to. I pushed up the window, exactly as Clara did just now.

'Be careful,' I called, 'if you disappear through the gaps in that sidewalk you might never be seen again.'

'You'd better let me come inside then.' He stared. It wasn't me he'd expected to see.

Standing beside me in the hallway he went on staring. Up close I could see the lines on his face and was glad that he'd suffered for what he'd done.

'Where's Sarah?' he asked.

'You know where Sarah is, Jimmy,' I said.

He sat on a step of the stairs and put his head into his hands. He sat for a long time without moving or saying a word. God knows how long he would have stayed there, or how I would have dealt with things, if it hadn't been for James. Left alone in the sitting room he called out to me.

'Mama!' He appeared in the doorway. 'Mama,' he said again, 'you didn't finish the story.'

'Hello, James,' his father said and the baby I'd made my own, the child I'd taught to walk and talk and for whom I'd lived every minute of the last three years, left my side and walked to his father.

'Hello.' He held out his hand as I'd taught him to. 'Who are you?'

'My name is James too. But people call me Jimmy.'

'Can I call you Jimmy?'

'You can.'

Later, when James was in bed, I told Jimmy Vance all that had happened. He'd put most of the pieces together in his head by then anyway.

'Sarah's was the grave I saw in Londonderry.' He said the words with difficulty.

I gave him a glass of whiskey and he drank it and turned away from me with tears in his eyes. He'd lost her, then thought he'd found her. Now he was having to accept that, finally and forever, he'd really lost her. I sat with him in this sitting room until long after it got dark. The light from the street lamps was making lonely shadows about us when he said, 'I didn't cross the Atlantic alone. I brought young Moll Hyland with me.'

'Moll.' I was glad of the dark. It hid tears I couldn't stop.

What had happened was simple enough. Jimmy had been less than two years in Kashima, India when a careless gunner had sent a bullet through his leg. Shipped home to England and discharged with a pension he'd gone immediately to Dublin and Henrietta Street. Bess Rooney had given him the letters and money he'd sent to Sarah and told him she didn't know where Sarah was, only that she'd gone to America.

Jimmy Vance had then gone to the Curragh, straight to the wren village. He'd hoped to find Beezy Ryan, or someone who could tell him about Sarah and James. He found only Moll to remember them, fending for herself since Clara's death three months before. Moll swore to him she knew where to find me and, as a consequence, Sarah. Jimmy, though certain she was lying, decided regardless to take her with him on his search for Sarah and his son.

'An atonement,' he said and I nodded, understanding.

In Londonderry Moll had been her resourceful self. With a

tearful story she'd persuaded a McCorkell clerk to allow them go through the passenger lists of two years before.

And so they'd discovered that Mrs Sarah Vance and her son had sailed on the *Minnehaha* but that Alicia Buckley had not. Another clerk remembered the sad story of the young woman killed by a runaway horse and cart.

'It was an easy matter to find someone to take me to the grave after that,' Jimmy said. 'It's well tended, not overgrown at all.' He paused. When I said nothing he went on. 'In New York I . . . persuaded an official to let me look through the destination lists. San Francisco is small enough. It's taken me only two days to find you.'

Moll moved in to live with me and James straight away. She would be a daughter to me, she said, as long as I let her keep her birth-mother's name. And so Moll became Clara Vance.

Taking Jimmy Vance in was a different matter. He lived for three years on the Barbary Coast, playing the gambling saloons and living God knows what kind of a life there. He made a lot of money and he came to see his son three times a week without fail.

Four years ago he asked me to marry him, for James's sake.

'James does not need us to marry,' I said.

'He's nearly seven years old. He needs a father, a family.'

'He has a family. He has me, and a sister in Clara.'

'A boy needs a father,' Jimmy said. 'Sarah knew that. It was why she followed me to the Curragh. It was why she married me.'

'She married you for love.'

'That too,' he said.

We were walking in the Golden Gate Park on a Sunday, James and Clara ahead of us, a family in all but the legalities.

'You already have my name,' Jimmy pointed out, 'and there are many kinds of love.'

This was true. I'd loved, in different ways, both Sarah and Daniel Casey. I always would.

I'd grown fond of Jimmy Vance. He was a decent man, quick and able for the ways of this city and the New World. We shared memories.

Surely, put together, all of these things amounted to a kind of love?

'We might as well make things legal and respectable,' I said.

We would grow together, the four of us, out of our shared memories. We would be a family, like any other.

Truth, after all, is made and not born.